Praise for Betty Webb

——— The Lost in Paris Mysteries ———

LOST IN PARIS

"A maelstrom of a mystery that combines grit, determination, and tragedy with social commentary."

—*Kirkus Reviews*

"The compelling story, filled with actual artists, models, and writers, will appeal to readers who enjoy fact-based mysteries involving history, racism, and conditions in postwar Paris."

—*Library Journal*

"If you're a fan of *The Da Vinci Code* and/or the Gilded Age, you'll love *Lost in Paris*. This book mixes cozy mystery and historical fiction with abandon, while leaving room for some romance and strong female friendships."

—Goodreads

——— The Lena Jones Mysteries ———

DESERT REDEMPTION
The Tenth Lena Jones Mystery

"In Jones's electrifying tenth...Scottsdale, Arizona, PI Lena is approached by Harold Slow Horse, one of Arizona's leading artists...[and] gets on a trail that leads her at long last to answers about her troubled past..."

—*shers Weekly*

"[A] satisfying conclusion to an underrated series."

—*Booklist*

DESERT VENGEANCE
The Ninth Lena Jones Mystery

"Former cop Lena has a fine sense of justice, which she achieves in this ninth entry of a series that features a vivid sense of place, an indomitable protagonist, and a sensitivity to painful social issues."

—*Booklist*

"Webb offers fans the profound pleasure of watching Lena mature as she comes one step closer to understanding and accepting her difficult past, while providing new readers with an introduction to this strong and genuinely likable character."

—*Publishers Weekly*

"Webb, no stranger to hot-button issues, takes on child molestation in a page-turner that presents both her flawed heroine and the reader with plenty of challenges to their moral codes."

—*Kirkus Reviews*

"Webb's pithy first-person narration cuts to the chase without a lot of filler, making *Desert Vengeance* a pleasure to read....Lena Jones is tough yet vulnerable, irreverent and sarcastic, yet dead serious at times...The Arizona desert and its touristy towns offer up a strange bonanza of desert tropes, and Webb mines them with enough restraint to strengthen, rather than overshoot, her themes of loss and retribution."

—*Shelf Awareness*

DESERT RAGE
The Eighth Lena Jones Mystery

"The Lena Jones series is notable for its persistent protagonist and vivid southwestern setting; this eighth entry, centered on a gruesome crime, also is particularly sensitive to the issues of foster children and what really makes a mother."

—*Booklist*

"Several red herrings arise along the road to a surprising and satisfying ending."

—*Publishers Weekly*

DESERT WIND
The Seventh Lena Jones Mystery

"Webb uses her expert journalistic skills to explore a shocking topic that private investigator Lena Jones uncovers with masterly resolve....a must-read."

—David Morrell, *New York Times* bestselling author of *The Protector*

★"Webb pulls no punches in exploring another human rights issue in her excellent seventh mystery starring Arizona PI Lena Jones."

—*Publishers Weekly*, Starred Review

"Webb's compelling exposé of the damage done to nuclear fallout victims (known as downwinders), accompanied by research notes and bibliography, makes for fascinating reading...Sue Grafton's alphabet series is a prime read-alike for this series; also consider Pari Noskin Taichert and Steven Havill for Tony Hillerman influences."

—*Library Journal*

DESERT LOST

The Sixth Lena Jones Mystery

"Richly researched and reeking with authenticity—a wicked exposé."

—Paul Giblin, winner of the 2009 Pulitzer Prize for Journalism

★ "Webb's Scottsdale PI Lena Jones continues to mix southwestern history with crime in her latest investigation...This is a complex, exciting entry in a first-class series, and it makes an excellent read-alike for Sue Grafton fans."

—*Booklist*, Starred Review

"Webb's sobering sixth mystery to feature PI Lena Jones further explores the abuses of polygamy first exposed in 2003's Desert Wives...Clear-cut characterizations help a complicated plot flow smoothly. As Webb points out in a note, polygamy still spawns many social ills, despite the recent, well-publicized conviction of Mormon fundamentalist prophet Warren Jeffs."

—*Publishers Weekly*

DESERT CUT

The Fifth Lena Jones Mystery

"Mysteries don't get more hard-hitting than this...Readers will be talking about Desert Cut for a long time to come."

—David Morrell, *New York Times* bestselling author

★ "A compelling story that will appeal to a broad range of mystery readers—and may bring increased attention to a too-little-known series."

—*Booklist*, Starred Review

"Webb's dark tale of a clash of cultures is emotionally draining and intellectually challenging."

—*Kirkus Reviews*

"This Southwestern series has a depth that enhances the reader's pleasure."

—*Library Journal*

"As in Webb's earlier adventures—particularly Desert Wives, with its critically praised exposé of contemporary polygamy—the longtime journalist manages to fuel her plot from the starkest of news stories without compromising the fast-paced action."

—*Publishers Weekly*

DESERT RUN
The Fourth Lena Jones Mystery

"This thought-provoking novel is a gem."

—*Denver Post*

"Webb bases her latest Lena Jones adventure on a real episode in Arizona history: the great escape of twenty-five Germans from Camp Papago, a POW camp located between Phoenix and Scottsdale...As in the preceding episodes in the series, Webb effectively evokes the beauty of the Arizona desert."

—*Booklist*

"Webb combines evocative descriptions of place with fine historical research in a plot packed with twists."

—*Publishers Weekly*

DESERT SHADOWS
The Third Lena Jones Mystery

"This third in Webb's series makes good use of both Tony Scottsdale and the small-press publishing scene. Lena makes a refreshing heroine; being raised by nine different foster families gives her unusual depth. Solid series fare."

—*Booklist*

"As the suspense builds, the author touches on such issues as consolidation in the book industry, the plight of foster children, mother-daughter relationships, animal rescue programs and more. The glorious Southwest landscape once again provides the perfect setting for Webb's courageous heroine."

—*Publishers Weekly*

DESERT WIVES
The Second Lena Jones Mystery

2004 WILLA Literary Award finalist

"Reading *Desert Wives* is like peering into a microscope at a seething culture of toxic microbes."

—Diana Gabaldon, author of the Outlander series

"If Betty Webb had gone undercover and written *Desert Wives* as a piece of investigative journalism, she'd probably be up for a Pulitzer..."

—*New York Times*

"Stark desert surroundings underscore the provocative subject matter, the outspoken protagonist, and the 'insider' look at polygamist life. Webb's second Lena Jones mystery, after *Desert Noir*, is recommended for most collections."

—*Library Journal*

"Dark humor and thrilling action inform Webb's second Lena Jones mystery...The beauty of the Southwestern backdrop belies the harshness of life, the corrupt officials, brutal men and frightened women depicted in this arresting novel brimming with moral outrage."

—*Publishers Weekly*

DESERT NOIR
The First Lena Jones Mystery

2002 Book Sense Top Ten 10 Mystery

"Another mystery strong on atmosphere and insight."

—*Booklist*

"A must read for any fan of the modern female PI novel."

—*Publishers Weekly*

—— The Gunn Zoo Mysteries ——

THE PANDA OF DEATH
The Sixth Gunn Zoo Mystery

"I became so fascinated by this righteous heroine and caught up in the tangle of improbable events that I whisked through the pages with a smile."

—*Bookreporter*

"Jealousy, crafty zoo critters, and unintended consequences wrapped in an often humorous mystery full of quirky characters."

—*Kirkus Reviews*

"There is one shock after another in Webb's sixth Gunn Zoo mystery, featuring zookeeper Theodora "Teddy" Bentley."

—*Booklist*

THE OTTER OF DEATH
The Fifth Gunn Zoo Mystery

"While examining some timely social issues, Webb also delivers lots of edifying information on the animal kingdom in an entry sure to please fans and newcomers alike."

—*Publishers Weekly*

"The best part here is watching Bentley's investigative juices start to flow (Webb's background as a reporter really comes to the fore here)...This one will satisfy multiple audiences."

—*Booklist*

THE PUFFIN OF DEATH
The Fourth Gunn Zoo Mystery

"Iceland's rugged and sometimes dangerous landscape provides atmosphere, while Magnus, the polar bear cub, appears just often enough to remind us why Teddy's in Iceland. Webb skillfully keeps the reader guessing right to the dramatic conclusion."

—*Publishers Weekly*

"The exotic locale, the animal lore, and a nice overlay of Icelandic culture and tradition provide an enticing frame story for this solid mystery."

—*Booklist*

"California zookeeper Theodora Bentley travels to Iceland to pick up animals for a new exhibit but must put her investigative skills to use when two American birdwatchers are killed. The fourth book in this charming series doesn't fail to please. Teddy is delightful as she copes with the Icelandic penchant for partying hard."

—*Library Journal*

"I finished *The Puffin of Death* with a feeling of regret that I have not been to Iceland...This book is the next best thing to a trip there. A good Christmas present for those friends who still suffer from itchy feet."

—*BookLoons*

THE LLAMA OF DEATH
The Third Gunn Zoo Mystery

"Animal lore and human foibles spiced with a hint of evil test Teddy's patience and crime solving in this appealing cozy."

—*Publishers Weekly*

"Webb's third zoo series entry winningly melds a strong animal story with an engaging cozy amateur sleuth tale. Set at a relaxed pace with abundant zoo filler, the title never strays into too-cute territory, instead presenting the real deal."

—*Library Journal*

"A Renaissance Faire provides both the setting and the weapon for a murder...Webb's zoo-based series is informative about the habits of the zoo denizens and often amusing."

—*Kirkus Reviews*

THE KOALA OF DEATH
The Second Gunn Zoo Mystery

"Teddy's second adventure will appeal to animal lovers who enjoy a bit of social satire with their mystery. Pair this series with Ann Littlewood's Iris Oakley novels, also starring a zookeeper."

—*Booklist*

"The author of the edgy Lena Jones mysteries softens her touch in this second zoo mystery featuring an amateur sleuth with a wealthy background and a great deal of zoological knowledge and brain power...Teddy's adventures will appeal to fans of animal-themed cozies."

—*Library Journal*

"Teddy's second case showcases an engaging array of quirky characters, human and animal."

—*Kirkus Reviews*

THE ANTEATER OF DEATH
The First Gunn Zoo Mystery

2009 Winner of the Arizona Book Award for Mystery/Suspense

"I've been impressed with Betty Webb's edgy mysteries about the Southwest, so I was surprised to find she has a softer side and a wicked sense of humor in a book that can only be described as

Also by Betty Webb

The Clock Struck Murder

THE
CLOCK
STRUCK
MURDER

A Lost in Paris Mystery

BETTY WEBB

Poisoned Pen
PRESS

Sourcebooks, Poisoned Pen Press, and the colophon are
registered trademarks of Sourcebooks.

Published by Poisoned Pen Press, an imprint of Sourcebooks
P.O. Box 4410, Naperville, Illinois 60567–4410
(630) 961-3900
sourcebooks.com

Cataloging-in-Publication Data is on file with the Library of Congress.

Printed and bound in the United States of America.
VP 10 9 8 7 6 5 4 3 2 1

For Paul, always

Chapter One

Zoe Barlow ordinarily loved Paris, but of late, she'd been loving it less now that the 1924 Summer Olympics were here. The previous Winter Sports Week had been bad enough, but at least the games had been based miles and miles from La Cité. Whereas now, for the better part of June and now July, Paris was awash with tourists babbling in a dozen different languages, getting lost, and wandering into busy intersections without bothering to look both ways. Taxis honked and screeched, and dray horses—never bred to suffer such crowds—neighed in distress. The air was redolent with human sweat, gasoline, and horse shit.

But even if the streets had been empty and the air pure, Zoe would have been unhappy anyway, now that her favorite clock lay in pieces. And it was her own, greedy fault.

Before the disaster, her regular Friday night poker game had been going well. Archie Stafford-Smythe, the disgraced son of the Earl of Whittenden, had unwisely tried to bluff his pair of jacks into something bigger. Seeing through his ruse, Zoe, secure with three eights, had raised another fifty francs, whereupon the wiser players dropped out.

But foolish Archie called, and as a result, Zoe raked in a two-hundred-franc pot, her biggest in months. He'd been gentlemanly about it—Archie was always gentlemanly—but since he'd been nipping on gin in between the many replenished servings of Château Margaux, he wasn't exactly shipshape when he rose from the card table. Once on his feet, he'd tipped backward.

Crash. Bang.

"*Oh, bloody hell!*" he'd muttered. "I'm sorry, Zoe."

Sighing at the memory, she made her way west along rue de Rennes. She'd loved that little porcelain clock. Only four inches high, its housing was a sweet-pea-green and rose art nouveau frothery of snake shapes curled around an opaline clockface. She'd fallen in love with the silly thing when she'd first spotted it at a Montparnasse flea market a year earlier, but *c'est la vie*.

Nothing lasted forever, did it? Best to be philosophical about it all. Besides, once Archie had been rendered perpendicular again, he'd promised to replace it, but knowing his taste—dark and Jacobian, just like his family—Zoe had told him to leave the clock-hunting to her. He'd still insisted on paying for the replacement, which she welcomed.

Zoe wasn't as rich as her friends thought she was. Despite her poker winnings, she was economically strapped. Of late, there was the rapidly dwindling stipend from Beech Glen, her family's Alabama cotton plantation. And then there were the checks she wired to the Pinkerton International Detective Agency to find her lost daughter. She would rather starve than discontinue their search.

As she walked along, she every now and then caught an admiring look from a male passerby, and rightly so. Since she planned on stopping off at La Rotonde for a celebratory glass of wine after her purchase, she'd taken pains with her toilette: Passion's Flame lipstick, rouged cheeks, kohl-rimmed blue eyes. Her hennaed bob contrasted wonderfully with her new ecru sheath, and she was especially proud of the bright blue sash that showed off her small waist. It perfectly matched her tiny clutch purse and T-strapped pumps. Like the dress, the shoes were handmade, the shoe on the left built up to accommodate her shorter leg. Wearing it, she hardly limped at all.

When Zoe was eight, she had so badly broken her leg in a fall that even a year spent in traction hadn't managed to correct its now-shorter length. But again, *c'est la vie*.

Ten sweltering minutes after leaving the house, Zoe reached the Vaugirard Passage, an alleyway crammed between rue Vaugirard and rue de Rennes. Once she entered the narrow alley, Montparnasse's tall limestone buildings receded, as did much of the street noise.

Thanks to the encompassing shadows, the alley was several degrees cooler, and the sparrows nesting in a low-branched chestnut tree trilled in gratitude. But Zoe's six years' residency in Paris had taught her a thing or two about its flirtatious weather. Those dark clouds looming in the south had a lot to do with the lowering temperature. They were far enough away, she hoped, not to necessitate a dowdy raincoat.

In contrast to larger flea markets, such as the monster by the Porte de Clignancourt, the market she headed toward was relatively small and run by two sisters, Veronique and Laurette Belcoeur. It had no protective roof, so even the smallest drizzle would drive the vendors away. When Zoe arrived, the desertion had already begun, with only five sales tables left. And no wonder. The market's location, in a narrow space between the shadows of two large apartment buildings, funneled a rising wind.

However, the remaining tables still displayed a treasure trove of

goods ranging all the way from rhinestone-studded cigarette holders to children's toys to hand-carved African masks. Once Zoe
squeezed past two long-skirted French women competing for the
same iron cookpot, she spotted blond Laurette, the sister who'd
sold her the now-ruined clock.

Laurette had changed dramatically since last summer. No
longer an ingenue, she'd entered the full bloom of womanhood.
Her wheat-colored hair, which last year had fallen past her shoulders, was now cut into a severe bob that accentuated her startling
beauty. And, as if to broadcast her sales savvy, instead of wearing
the drear clothes worn by the other saleswomen, she sported a
maroon-trimmed pink linen frock that wouldn't have seemed out
of place on a cinema star.

The dress's beauty was somewhat diminished by its short
sleeves, which revealed a series of bruises marching along its
wearer's arm. Zoe frowned. Those bruises hadn't been there the
last time she'd visited the flea market.

But the young woman was smiling—a sincere smile, too, not
the smile of a woman who'd been ill-used. Relieved, Zoe's eyes
lit on Laurette's sparkling amethyst earrings. Who would have
guessed that trading in used items could lead to such opulence?
The offerings on her table, however...

Some junk, certainly, but some treasures, too, especially among
the clocks. After a narrow-eyed study of the table's offerings, Zoe
spotted an art nouveau clock lurking behind an obviously fake
Louis XIV. No fragile porcelain on the art nouveau! The brass and
mahogany clock stood almost a foot high, its round clockface sup-
ported by two serpentine "legs." Between them dangled a long,
penis-shaped pendulum that made Zoe grin. *Très* naughty!

Hoping Laurette hadn't noted her delight, she asked, "How
much?"

"Ninety-six francs. As you can see, it even has the

original wind-up key." Apparently, Zoe hadn't stopped grinning soon enough.

Not that ninety-six franks was as much as it sounded. After the war, the French economy had collapsed, and now it took twelve francs to make up one American dollar.

Still, the price seemed high, so Zoe settled in for some serious haggling. "Looking at the clock more closely, I can see a scratch on the base and what looks like a paint blister on that suggestive pendulum. Why, it's in such poor shape that I doubt it can even keep time, so I'd say even half of what you're asking is too much."

For an answer, Laurette wound the clock, and it responded with a healthy *tick-tick-tick* while the minute hand started its slow tour around the pristine face.

"Okay, so it works," Zoe admitted. "But the price is still unreasonable. I can only afford sixty francs."

Overhead, a rumble of thunder seemed to punctuate her comment.

Laurette laughed. "You won't find another like this in Paris. But for you, Madame, I'll drop the price to eighty francs."

Progress. Maybe Zoe would be able to firm up a deal before the storm arrived. She flashed her ringless left hand. "I'm still Mademoiselle, Laurette, and I still can't pay more than sixty."

"Here's what I'm willing to do." The young beauty reached a slender hand under the table, rummaged through a box, and came up holding a set of dangling amber earrings. "I'll include these with the price. They will go beautifully with your hennaed hair."

Zoe's heart yearned for the earrings, but she didn't let it show. "I already have too many earrings." A lie there; a woman could never have too many earrings.

Laurette's lipsticked mouth drooped into a frown. "Still, eighty is as low as I can go. Let me see..." She paused and tapped her chin with a well-manicured finger; maroon nail polish, the same color as the trim on her dress. Then the hand disappeared into the box again, coming up with a lady's powder compact. Tortoiseshell, with pseudo-gold trim.

"That's not real gold," Zoe pointed out.

"Of course not, but it's pretty anyway, isn't it?"

Zoe agreed. "Eighty is still too high, I'm afraid."

Laurette chuckled. "*Ooh, la la,* you are a fierce bargainer! But eighty francs gives you the clock, the amber earrings, and this lovely compact. Oh, and I'll also throw in these nice salt and pepper shakers." She waved at a pair fashioned in cut glass, crowned by bronze caps. "A bargain in anyone's eyes."

"Seventy francs." Zoe would have paid eighty for the earrings alone.

A smirk. "Sorry, but eighty is the lowest I can go. Perhaps you should make room for the next customer. She seems willing enough."

Over her shoulder, Zoe spied a smartly dressed woman eyeing the clock. A shill? Some flea markets employed them to drive up prices, but when the woman made a comment to her companion, a plump man sweating fiercely, Zoe realized the woman was no French shill, just another American. One of the Olympics-goers with money to burn.

Turning back to Laurette, Zoe heaved a theatrical sigh. "If you insist, but oh, how cruel you are! So eighty it is. But, alas, we have a problem now. Thinking only to buy a clock, I now find myself with all these loose items. As you can see, my little clutch"—she held up the brown-and-ecru-patterned clutch bag "will barely manage the compact, so you'll have to help me out. A box, perhaps?"

Laurette frowned. "No boxes, just this big one, which I need. And I don't..." She stopped. "Oh! I know!" After rummaging through the box again, she unwrapped a porcelain depiction of a shepherdess and set it on the table. Then she took the paint-spattered piece of canvas the shepherdess had been wrapped in, laid it flat, and placed clock, earrings, salt and pepper shakers, and the compact in the middle. Before Zoe could get a good look at the messy shape on the canvas, Laurette brought the corners together and tied them tightly with a piece of string.

"*Voilà*, Mademoiselle! Now, that'll be eighty francs, please. Enjoy your new clock!" White teeth gleamed.

Zoe paid up, then started happily for home, leaving the Summer Olympics tourists to haggle over an ashtray in the shape of the Eiffel Tower.

··· ◊ ···

Upon reaching the little house she'd named Le Petit Bibelot—Little Trinket—she set the parcel on the long dining table and headed straight for her bath. Unlike most artists' flats, her home enjoyed both hot and cold running water, but now she ran straight cold after dumping a handful of Chanel bath salts into the water. When the desired height had been reached, she stripped off her sweaty clothes and stepped into the water. There she stayed until her housekeeper arrived.

"Someone's been shopping!" Madeline called from the sitting room, her light voice making her sound much younger than her fortysomething years. "May I see?"

"Help yourself," Zoe called back, rising from the soapy water and wrapping herself in a thick bath sheet. "Just a new clock to replace the one Archie broke, plus a couple other things."

Rustle, rustle from the sitting room. Then, "Yes, that I can see, but what's this they're wrapped in? Some child's work? Oh my, the lumps! Such a waste of good paint."

Curious, Zoe wrapped the bath sheet tighter and, not bothering to slip on her shoes, hobbled across the parquet to see what Madeline was going on about. At first, all she saw was a blaze of vibrant primary colors—blues, reds, yellows—but as she grew closer, she could make out the shape of a small village overshad-owed by an onion-domed church. On a nearby rooftop stood a violinist wearing a billed cap. Odd, yes, but even more amazingly, a red-and-dun cow floated across the night sky.

"No," Zoe whispered. "Not possible."

Hardly willing to believe the testimony of her eyes, she dropped her gaze to the painting's lower right corner and read the signature...

MARC CHAGALL

Chapter Two

If there was a leading artist in Paris today—besides Picasso, of course—it was Marc Chagall.

Russian by birth, Chagall had been working at La Ruche, a beehive-shaped collection of studios not far from Zoe's little house, when he'd decided to visit relatives in his former home of Vitebsk, Russia. Before leaving, he had locked around a hundred and fifty paintings into his studio, expecting to find them waiting when he returned.

His timing couldn't have been worse. While he was still in Russia, the Great War had begun, and in the middle of that, the bloody Bolshevik revolution erupted. When the chaos died down, Chagall had returned to Paris only to discover that his studio had been broken into, his hurriedly stored paintings vanished.

How had one of them wound up serving as wrapping paper at a Montparnasse flea market?

"Not a child's painting then?" Madeline, having worked for Zoe several years, recognized the wonder on her employer's face.

Zoe shook her head. "Does the name Marc Chagall mean anything to you?"

Madeline stretched out her mechanical arm and drew the painting closer. "Do you mean the Russian artist? You think he did this? Maybe it's just something done by a clever child."

"See those holes? That's where the canvas was attached to the stretchers. No child would know to do that."

She didn't bother to correct Madeline's assertion that the painting could have been done by a child, either, because there had always been a childlike quality to Chagall's creations. It was one of the main reasons his work had become so popular of late. Who didn't want to be transported back to childhood, when life seemed so simple yet so magical? A place where fiddlers perched on roofs and cows could fly!

"I need to get this back to Marc," Zoe said, carefully rolling up the canvas. "But first, I think we need to oil your arm. It's squeaking again."

Madeline had lost her right arm while nursing wounded soldiers in the Great War. A German mortar had landed in the hospital tent, killing eight men and wounding scores of others. With her arm blown off, Madeline would have bled out had it not been for the injured man she'd been attending to. As she'd lain unconscious on the ground, he used his belt for a tourniquet, then lugged her to another field hospital. Years later, when the prosthetic furnished by the French government developed problems, Zoe had convinced a sculptor friend to design a less trouble-prone prosthetic. The new arm worked perfectly. Its only drawback was its need for a weekly oiling.

"I want to find out how Laurette wound up with this painting," Zoe told Madeline, after returning the bottle of special oil to her studio. "She obviously didn't recognize the painting's value."

Madeline's wrinkled face creased into a worried frown. "Be careful. Remember what happened the last time you started asking about things going missing."

How could Zoe forget? The murder case had resulted in

numerous deaths and had almost burned down her studio. "Don't worry, I've learned my lesson." She flashed Madeline a reassuring look, then carefully rolled up the canvas.

On the way back to the flea market, Zoe was glad she'd finally had the sense to don her hooded raincoat. The day had turned dark, and serious clouds loomed to the south. Ignoring the ever-present ache of her problematic left leg, she picked up her pace, not that it helped. When she arrived back at the flea market, the first few drops of rain had begun to fall, and the last of the vendors were hurriedly packing up. Laurette and her wares had already vanished.

Stifling her disappointment, she saw a table she hadn't noticed earlier in her haste to buy the clock. It was presided over by a crabby-looking woman of about sixty who was busily folding brightly colored piecework shopping bags into a large box.

Shopping bags. If Zoe had visited that table earlier, Laurette wouldn't have had to cobble together a rough sack made out of a valuable Chagall.

What luck!

"Excuse me, Madame," Zoe said. "Do you know where I might find the young woman with the clocks? I bought one from her earlier, and I...." She brushed away a raindrop trickling down her cheek. "I was wondering if she perhaps had another of its size."

"You mean Laurette Belcoeur? If so, she's gone," the old woman snapped. "Are you blind? Everyone's done for the day." She glanced up at the angry sky. "Maybe even for the entire weekend."

Now Zoe remembered her. In the past, she'd attempted to buy a silver flask from the woman, but she'd been so difficult that the attempt had come to nothing. Zoe had walked away, inwardly dubbing the woman Madame Crab.

This time, Zoe pushed on with a lie. "Yes, but I've just remembered that my aunt's birthday is this coming Tuesday, and I thought a clock would make a lovely gift."

Alert to Zoe's American accent—all Americans were rich, right?—Madame Crab pasted an unconvincing smile on her weathered face. "You are here for those Olympics, eh? How about a pair of nice candlesticks to take back? Unlike temperamental clocks, candlesticks make fine gifts because they never break. For your aunt, I can offer one that was used by Louis the Fifteenth himself. Only fifty francs!"

Zoe's concern about the Chagall kept her from laughing. In these tourist-clogged days it was hard to find a flea market item that the guillotined king hadn't lain on, sat on, or shat on. Only last week Zoe had been offered a wooden toilet seat its seller claimed had been used by the similarly doomed Marie Antoinette.

Keeping a straight face, Zoe answered, "Sorry, but I really want another clock. Perhaps you could tell me where I could find Laurette?"

"You Americans and your clocks! You're as bad as the Germans."

Zoe winced, fearing that she was about to hear an anti-German tirade, because so many Parisians remained wounded in the heart as well as the body by the War to End All Wars.

"Well, I'm not German," she said, in an attempt to stave off the inevitable.

Then Madame Crab surprised her. "Some of my best friends— including my new son-in-law—are German."

"Really?"

"Really, Mademoiselle American. Unlike some people I know, I understand that while the Kaiser might be shit, it doesn't mean his people are."

"Why are you whispering?"

"Because you never know who's listening, do you?" Here the woman looked around to see which of the saleswomen remained. Seeing no one, she raised her voice again. "God forbid our pretty Mademoiselle Laurette would hear me talking like this. Talk about hating Germans! I remember the day she refused to sell a clock to a German girl, accusing the poor thing's brothers of bombing her family's château, killing her parents."

Zoe didn't know whether to believe her or not. For herself, she'd never heard Laurette say an unkind word about anyone. "Are you certain you're not confusing Laurette with someone else? Her sister, maybe?"

Madame Crab spat on the ground. "As if I can't tell one woman from another! I was standing right here when I heard her tell that German girl to go back to the pigsty she and her kin crawled out of."

"She said *that*?"

At a rumble of thunder from the darkening sky, the old woman scowled. "I said so, didn't I? At least today she didn't manage to steal away any of my customers!"

Zoe blinked in surprise. "Steal?"

A snort. "*Oui*. Whenever someone has a male customer who looks serious about buying, Laurette finds some way to lure him over to her table. It's a wonder that any of us can sell anything with the little minx around. But would Veronique do anything about it? No. In her eyes, her sweet little sister can do no wrong."

More thunder caused Madame Crab to cast a worrying look at the sky. "Well, we're about to drown, and here you are, going on and on about that bitch and her clocks. If you're that dedicated, Mademoiselle American, so be it. Either buy something or go away. I have to pack up."

Zoe bit back her temper. Dropping the subject of the German-hating, customer-poaching Laurette aside, she tried another tact. Money. "Ah, those colorful cloth bags you're about to put away. So pretty, yet so practical. I could have used one earlier to carry the clock and some other items I purchased from Laurette. How much for the red, gold, and violet one? It's large enough to hold a week's worth of groceries."

Madame Crab stopped packing. With a shrewd look, she said, "Twenty francs. The bags were made by nuns and prayed over during the sewing, so that anything carried in it would never rot."

A lie, of course, but the beautiful bag was worth the price. "Sold!" Zoe said.

After paying for the bag, Zoe dropped her tiny clutch into it—a bag to carry a bag!—then again asked for Laurette's whereabouts.

Mollified by the sale, Madame Crab gave Zoe directions to the nearby storage shed where the Belcoeur sisters kept their wares. "She's probably still putting her precious clocks away as we speak and gloating over how much she made you pay. No manners, that girl!"

··· ◇ ···

The storage shed was in a mechanic's scrapyard just off rue d'Odessa, so within minutes, Zoe was limping along a weedy footpath between two buildings: Napier's Garage, from which much banging and clanging emanated, and the quieter Heureur's Impressions, a photography studio. At the end of the footpath stood a tall wooden fence bearing a sign warning away trespassers. Since the gate was ajar and the threatened storm had yet to materialize beyond a mild drizzle, Zoe ignored it.

As she entered the scrapyard, she called out, "Laurette? Laurette Belcoeur?"

No answer. To Zoe's right she saw a pile of rubble made up of broken bricks, jagged splinters of wood, and uneven sheets of tin. Underneath the tin, rags waved in the rising wind.

"Laurette?" she called again.

Still no answer, just a rustling of tiny feet. Rats? But no. With relief, Zoe noticed a small wood-and-chicken-wire hutch at the back of the scrapyard, the ungainly structure inhabited by four plump rabbits. The hutch sat to the side of a large storage shed, where a protruding tin roof only partially protected the sales table she recognized from the flea market.

When she approached, she saw that the table remained scattered with porcelain figurines, miscellaneous jewelry, and clocks, clocks, clocks, many of which looked expensive. A Seth Thomas carved in oxblood mahogany. A flowered-porcelain Ansonia. A bronze Doré made saccharine with a host of simpering cherubs.

Why hadn't these treasures already been put away? If left to the mercies of the approaching storm, the inner workings of the clocks would be permanently ruined and the jewelry tarnished. Concerned for their sake, Zoe opened the unlocked shed door and stuck her head into the darkness. "Laurette? If you're in here, you need to come save your clocks!"

The only sound came from the low moan of the wind. Maybe Laurette had taken shelter at the garage next door.

Before leaving the scrapyard to check at the garage, Zoe made certain no other worthwhile merchandise would be ruined by the threatening downpour. She scooped up the clocks and rushed them into the protection of the shed. Then she followed with the jewelry.

Lastly, she turned back to the now-empty sales table.

Tucked underneath was the same wooden box from which Laurette had pulled out the Chagall "wrapping paper." A quick search disclosed several Chagall sketches on heavy canvas and yet another crumpled painting, this one a portrait of a dark-haired woman. His wife, Bella? Behind the woman, two calves danced in silvery moonlight.

Disregarding the tiny voice that whispered *Thou shalt not steal,* Zoe slid the Chagalls into her new piecework shopping bag.

Before leaving the scrapyard to hunt down Laurette, Zoe decided to commit one more crime. She knew the rabbits in the hutch weren't being kept for companionship; they were destined to become the main ingredient in *lapin à la cocotte*. Having had a pet rabbit during her childhood, a white angora she'd uncreatively named Mister Bunny, she couldn't help but feel sorrow over the rabbits' culinary future.

As she stooped down to open the hutch door, a flash of color overhead caught her eye. Looking up at the underside of the hutch's canvas roof, she froze.

It couldn't be.

But it was.

Vivid yellows. Sparkling blues. Proud reds.

Keeping the rain off the rabbits was yet another Chagall painting. From what Zoe could see, it was twice the size of the one already in her piecework bag. It showed a wedding party walking along the street of a small village, no fiddlers or cows. Having trouble believing what her eyes told her, she slipped her fingers through the top of the chicken wire fronting the hutch and brushed them along the painting's surface. Tiny ridges created from brushstrokes. Small hillocks built up by paint to intensify color.

Shock battled with fury to see such beauty treated so cavalierly, but common sense ultimately prevailed. Stifling a growl, Zoe picked up one of the clocks' wind-up keys. Using the key as a screwdriver, she began prying the canvas away from the nails that attached it to the hutch's wooden framework. She worked carefully, aware that if she rushed, she might chip the paint. But miracle of miracles, the oil paint that had created the artwork had also acted as a sealant, and the canvas withstood her efforts.

The nails were a different story. Most had rusted to the point where they were one with the canvas, and as she slid the key underneath their heads, several broke. Others bent. Fortunately, they were cheap penny nails, so those that did remain intact didn't take long to wiggle out of the framework.

The rabbits didn't mind. They'd been curious about her at

first, believing she might have brought food. When the food didn't appear, they went back to staring blankly through the chicken wire.

The hood on Zoe's raincoat couldn't keep the rain from dripping into her eyes, and once, when she tried to hurry, the key slipped on the drenched canvas. As her palm scraped across the wood, she picked up several splinters.

"*Shit!*" she yelped, jerking her hand back. She looked over her shoulder to see if anyone had been summoned by her cry. But no one came running, and she decided that the banging and cursing from the mechanic's garage next door covered her own oaths. Not that it made any difference. If Laurette suddenly appeared and tried to stop her, well, the sharp edge of the key would make a good weapon. Stab someone for Art's sake? Of course. After all, this was Paris.

Push, pry. Push, pry. Rain, rain, rain. When Zoe finally pried the last nail away from the wood, she took a relieved breath. Carefully lifting the painting away, she was pleased to discover that because of the weather, the canvas wasn't too stiff, so she rolled it up and placed it next to the other Chagalls already in her piecework bag.

One more thing to do, then she'd hunt down Laurette and find out where the young woman had found her "wrapping paper."

On the way to the scrapyard, Zoe had noticed a small park nearby, and if the rabbits could reach it, they'd grow even more rotund feasting on the park's lush flower garden.

Careful not to allow the chicken wire to snag on her raincoat, Zoe slowly tipped the now-roofless hutch over, spilling the rabbits out onto the ground. The little creatures wasted no time in hopping off as Zoe bid them goodbye.

"*Bonne chance, mes amis!*" Good luck, my friends!

As she turned to leave, a blast of wind slapped the rain into her face, making her turn aside.

She found herself facing the mountainous pile of rubble. That's when she noticed a flash of pink half-covered by a crumpled sheet of tin. Puzzled, she shielded her face with her sore right hand and moved closer. In her obsession to find more Chagalls, she hadn't paid much attention to the rest of the scrapyard. Now she did. That bit of pink cloth looked too new to have been lying in the weather for long. Maybe it was one of the Belcoeur sisters' errant treasures, blown there by the wind. A curtain, perhaps. Or a tablecloth. Wouldn't her scarred-up dining table look pretty covered in pink?

Curious, she walked closer. Yes, whatever it was hadn't been out long, so it might be salvageable. Delighted, Zoe bent over and slid the tin aside.

But what lay underneath was neither a tablecloth nor a curtain.

It was Laurette Belcoeur, her pink dress discolored by the blood that had already begun to dissipate in the rain. The left side of her beautiful face was caved in.

Chapter Three

Fortunately, Fabian Napier, the young mechanic whose garage abutted the scrapyard, had recently installed a telephone in his shop. After telling the two women already using the party line that he needed to reach the police, they kindly hung up and let him place his call. While he was speaking to the Sûreté, Zoe sat down on a rickety chair and tried to stop shaking.

Poor Laurette! Who could have...?

For what seemed like forever, Zoe just sat there, trying to organize her thoughts.

An inspector from Paris's Sûreté would arrive soon, and he'd ask what she'd been doing in the scrapyard. But how could she answer without mentioning the Chagalls tucked into her piece-work bag? He might even think the rabbit hutch had been knocked over during a struggle, and that would send the investigation off in the wrong direction.

From what she had seen after uncovering Laurette in an attempt to render aid, there were no defensive wounds on the young woman's hands—just that horrible indentation on the side of her face.

"Are you all right, Mademoiselle?" Fabian asked. His telephone conversation with the police finished, he leaned over her, his brow furrowed with concern. "Perhaps you would like a glass of water?" He was in his early twenties, with deep brown eyes and black hair; a fine-looking man.

"I'm okay," she answered. "Really. Just...just shocked."

When she'd first come running into the garage, he'd been listening to a heavyset customer explain the strange noises his Citroën was making. Unlike some men would have done, Fabian and his customer had taken Zoe seriously enough to follow her back to the scrapyard. At the sight of Laurette's lifeless eyes, both men had crossed themselves, and Fabian whispered a quick prayer. His face then froze into that glacial mask some men adopted when they didn't want to display strong emotion.

Since the men's distress appeared genuine, Zoe felt no fear waiting with them until the police arrived. The alternative wasn't attractive. Outside, the rain continued to fall, and every now and then a flash of lightning shredded the air. Then, as two police cars rumbled up, the rain stopped as suddenly as it had begun. Zoe's sigh of relief was cut short when she saw the tall man stepping out of the lead car.

"Ah, shit!" Zoe muttered to herself. Why did it have to be her temperamental, and very-much-married, lover? The same Detective Inspector Henri Challiot who had warned her many, many times to stay away from dodgy situations. What could she say now to avoid his almost certain wrath?

After making certain the top of her piecework shopping bag was closed tightly enough to hide its valuable contents, Zoe stood to greet him. As impeccably groomed as ever, Henri wore a dark green trench coat and a low-brimmed fedora, but the brim wasn't low enough to shadow his angry face.

"You? Again?" he huffed. They'd first met when she had inadvertently involved herself in a murder case that ended up with six people dead. Seven, if you included the now-guillotined killer.

She nodded weakly. "Yes, me."

Why did her head suddenly feel so heavy? And why were there dark spots dancing in front of her eyes? "But I didn't mean to... to..." She'd never fainted before, but as horrible as she felt, Zoe knew she was in danger of doing so right now.

Recognizing her distress, the anger drained from Henri's face, and he took her in his arms. He smelled of rain and expensive cologne. "Are you all right, *ma chérie*?"

It took a few seconds before she was able to stutter out an answer. "Yes. No. I mean I... I don't know. But I... I didn't do it!"

Henri kissed the top of her head, and his dark blue eyes seemed to echo her own sorrow. "Of course you didn't, Zoe. You would never harm any..." He stopped, possibly remembering a time when she not only did harm someone but had done it in a most horrific manner.

His eyes narrowed, he said, "Tell me what you're doing here and what happened."

She did.

Once she felt stronger, Zoe led Henri and the other officers up the muddy footpath to the scrapyard, explaining about her broken sitting-room clock and the desire to purchase another from the same vendor. Aware he would eventually find out that she'd made two separate trips to the flea market that day, she constructed a reasonable-enough story.

"When I got the new clock home, I decided it wouldn't hurt to have another one for my studio, so I came back. When I arrived, Laurette had already left."

"*Laurette*? You mean you know the victim?"

As Zoe had recovered her shock, his tone shifted back to investigative mode. "You went hunting for this Laurette even though a storm was about to break, and you weren't even carrying an umbrella?"

Moving her Chagall-stuffed bag out of his sightline, she

answered, "You haven't noticed the hood on my raincoat? Besides, the weather seemed fine enough at the time. Certainly not the downpour it turned out to be."

He leveled a knowing look at her. "What part of this latest adventure are you leaving out, Zoe?"

She turned her face away, hoping he wouldn't see her increasing discomfort at being further questioned. "I've told you everything I know."

A snort. "That would be a first! And don't think I haven't noticed your evasions. How well did you know Laurette? Was she one of your artist friends? Or was she one of your poker victims?"

The storm had blown the gate to the scrapyard shut, and the hinges complained loudly as the wind passed through. While Zoe had been falling apart in the garage, the storm had wrought more damage in the yard, but to her relief, one of Henri's men had placed a tattered pillow slip across Laurette's face.

"Not an artist friend. And she wasn't what you referred to as one of my 'poker victims.' I didn't know her from anywhere other than the flea market."

"Are you lying to me? If you are, I swear I'll arrest you!"

"I always tell you the truth, Henri," Zoe lied.

Henri bent down and pulled the pillow slip off Laurette's face. Some of the blood had washed away. "How long were you in the scrapyard?"

"Five minutes? Ten? Once I saw her, I immediately ran into the garage and..."

Henri touched his forefinger to Laurette's neck. "Still some warmth here. When you first arrived, did you see or hear anyone leaving?"

"If I had, I would have told you."

He straightened up. At more than six feet, he towered over her, but she was long past feeling intimidated by him. Like the proverbial dog, Henri was all bark and little bite. Except during love play, where he enjoyed a playful nip. As did she.

"I still think there's plenty you're not telling me, Zoe, so don't insult my intelligence with that ludicrous story about you wanting a clock for your studio. I know you better. When you're painting, you don't even care what year it is, let alone the minute."

"But it's true!"

Henri stepped back, allowing the two officers with him to roll Laurette's body onto a stretcher while others picked through the junk pile looking for clues. He watched their every movement, only stepping forward when it appeared they hadn't noticed a piece of Laurette's dress resting aside an old door. Once they'd corrected their lapse, Henri let his gaze fall on the upturned rabbit hutch. Frowning, he walked over to it.

"What's this?" he asked.

Oh, just a rabbit hutch formerly covered by a painting worth thousands of American dollars. "Looks like some sort of animal pen."

"You see any animals around?"

"No. But I'll bet there are rats nearby. You know Paris."

He grunted, then yanked enough of the chicken wire aside to allow his hand to rummage inside the hutch. When his hand came away, he stared with distaste at the small brown pellet in his palm. "Fresh rabbit turd. So I ask you again, when you first entered here, *did you see any animals?*"

Zoe shook her head. "I figure the wind must have knocked the hutch down and the rabbits got loose before I arrived."

"Strange hutch, not to have a roof."

"The wind probably blew the roof away, too. It was quite the storm, Henri." The humidity in the air made it feel like she was in one of those Finnish saunas she'd heard about.

"Why do you appear so uncomfortable, Zoe?"

"No one likes being questioned by the police."

"That's probably the only truthful thing you've told me."

When Zoe wiped a bead of sweat off her cheek, her hand came away streaked with rouge. Ugh. She must look terrible! But who cared how she looked? She had to get the hell out of here before Henri decided to search through her shopping bag.

"Look, Henri, I've told and retold you everything I know. But... But this heat is... Well, it's awful, and if I can't get something cold to drink, I might faint. Wouldn't that look nice on your report, that you interrogated a woman so cruelly you made her faint into the mud?"

Considering how she felt, that scenario wasn't much of an exaggeration. The scrapyard was a soggy mess, and she hoped the appeal to Henri's better instincts—he did have them—would work.

He didn't disappoint. "Go, then. If I need to question you further, I know where you live."

As she started to leave, he grabbed her arm. "Wait. Your leg. You're limping!"

"I always limp," she muttered.

"Not as badly as you are now. I'll have one of my men drive you home."

"No, I..."

"Hush!" Without further ado, he handed her over to a grizzled officer who didn't even try to look happy about his new assignment.

With a hurried *adieu,* she followed Henri's minion, her unsearched piecework bag clutched tightly to her chest.

· · · ◇ · · ·

Once back at Le Petit Bibelot, Zoe allowed herself to shed a few tears over Laurette. Who could have done such a horrible thing to a harmless young woman? A rejected lover? A friend turned enemy? Or had Laurette insulted the wrong German?

The War to End All Wars might be over, but the world remained a vicious place.

Finally drained of tears, Zoe comforted herself by rescuing the Chagalls from their hiding place in the bag. They were in varying stages of disrepair, but she knew Chagall could easily fix them. Before Henri showed up to interrogate her further, and he would, she needed to get them back to their rightful owner.

After fetching a leather portfolio from her studio, she smoothed out the sketches and paintings and slid them in. As she was tying it closed, she became aware that she didn't exactly smell like spring's fresh blossoms. She dashed into her boudoir to dab some Chanel onto her armpits, then put on a fresh cotton dress.

Forcing back the memory of Laurette's damaged face, she then set off again, limp and all.

Zoe had first met Marc Chagall when he returned from Russia after the end of the war and was going door-to-door to see if anyone knew anything about his vanished paintings. After hearing that she enjoyed a romantic relationship with a high-ranking Sûreté officer, he'd stopped by Zoe's studio. But that had been some time ago. She'd had nothing to tell him then. It was different now.

Chagall and his wife, Bella, and their eight-year-old daughter, Ida, had moved into a large studio and apartment at 110 avenue d'Orléans, not too far from Le Petit Bibelot. The storm clouds had cleared, so Zoe decided to walk it rather than take a chance on the Métro. Pickpockets were known to follow the Olympics-goers on their journeys to the various venues throughout the city, so for now, she was safer on the street. The portfolio wasn't heavy, and Zoe arrived at the studio in only a few minutes. Bella answered her knock and, upon spotting the portfolio, invited her in.

The family's sitting room was large, with Oriental-patterned throw pillows on the sofas. Paintings hung on every wall. Cheap but colorful carpets covered every inch of the wooden floor. Sketches for Chagall's present work-in-progress—illustrations for a new edition of *Dead Souls*, Gogol's masterpiece of Russian life—lay scattered across a long table at the side of the room. The room vibrated with life, as did its inhabitants. Bella was a dark-haired beauty, an aspiring actress with a lovely singing voice. Little Ida resembled her.

Chagall was shaggy-haired, and his dark eyes lit with delight when he saw who Bella had ushered in.

"Ah, Miss Zoe Barlow," he bellowed, in his barely there French, overlaid by a mixture of Yiddish and Russian. Spotting the portfolio, he added, "You have come to share with me your work, yes?"

Chagall had made that generous offer months earlier. Given his obvious distress—he had just returned from seeing an attorney—she hadn't taken him up on it.

"Not my work," she answered, taking out the paintings. "*Yours.*"

Upon seeing them, Bella screamed. So did Ida.

Chagall, however, went white as an untouched canvas and muttered something about angels bearing gifts.

"I'm no angel," Zoe corrected, handing over three paintings and six drawings.

Holding them to his chest as tenderly as if they were infants, Chagall said, "Where...? How...?" Then his voice broke and he began to sob. Bella wrapped her arms around him, her sobs matching his.

Ida, however, danced around in glee, yelling, "Daddy's paintings came home!"

In the face of such joy, Zoe didn't know what to do, so she just stood there feeling awkward.

The Chagalls finally calmed down, and while Bella rushed off to the kitchen to find their best bottle of wine, the artist begged Zoe to tell him everything she knew. Aware of the little girl hanging on her every word, she gave him a sanitized version of the paintings' recovery, leaving out Laurette's death. But Chagall, like most artists, noticed every sideways glance, every pause.

Turning to his daughter, he said, "Ida, why don't you go help your mother find the wine?"

Ida twisted her elfin face into a scowl. "Do I have to?"

Her father patted her on the cheek. "Not *have to*, but I wish it, my treasure."

As if giving her father's request serious thought, Ida ceased her chatter, nodded, then ran into the kitchen.

"Precocious," Zoe said admiringly. She tried not to think of her own child, who would be six now if she still lived.

Unaware of Zoe's heartache, Chagall leaned forward, his voice low. "Quickly! Now tell me what you have been keeping back."

Zoe did, finishing with, "Rest assured I looked all the way to the bottom of the box and found nothing else of yours. But that doesn't mean she didn't have more stashed someplace."

"You say she was using them for wrapping paper?" he repeated, for what had to be the tenth time.

"I'm afraid so."

"She thought they were the work of a child?"

"It certainly looks that way," Zoe replied.

"And now she is dead. Poor woman. You said she was young?" Unshed tears glistened in his eyes.

"About twenty."

"But who would commit such evil, Zoe?"

She shook her head. "A thief. An angry lover. Who knows?"

As they commiserated over the fate of Laurette Belcoeur, Chagall's face tensed. "Do you think the police are still there?"

"Inspector Henri Challiot is very professional, so they will be poking around the scrapyard until dark. Um, about your other missing paintings, Henri won't have time to talk to you now about any works of yours they may find, but if you wish, I can go with you to the Sûreté tomorrow and..."

Chagall shook his head so fiercely a dark curl flopped over his forehead. Brushing it aside, he said, "I don't want to get mixed up in police business."

Of course he didn't. The troubles Chagall had gone through during two regimes in Russia—the stuffy old Czarists and the crazy new Communists—and then the bureaucratic rigidity in Germany, where he'd also lost paintings, had made him distrustful of all authorities.

By now Bella and Ida had returned from the kitchen bearing a bottle of a delicate Languedoc. After opening it, Chagall gave a toast to "The Angel of the Arts," and as Zoe blushed fiercely, Bella hugged her again. Ida, having learned her manners from her warm and thoughtful parents, duplicated the hug. Embarrassed at such a fuss being made over her, Zoe switched the conversation to the ongoing Olympics. She hadn't fully followed them, but like most other Americans living in Paris, she'd been pleased at her native country's high medal count so far.

The Chagalls, however, were full of talk about Britain's Harold Abrahams, who had taken the Gold in the hundred-meter dash, matching the Olympics record of ten point six seconds.

"And they say Jews can't run!" Chagall crowed.

They all toasted the speedy Abrahams.

Zoe wasn't really interested in sports, although she did have a passing interest in the swim meets. She didn't know the difference between a butterfly and a crawl, but her friend Archie had managed to get tickets to the swim finals on the twentieth, and she'd promised to accompany him.

Eventually finding all this sports talk boring, she steered the conversation toward some of the milder Parisian scandals, such as the ever-squabbling Picassos. Artists loved scandal, and with each new story, the Chagalls laughed in delight. But since a child was present, Zoe paused before she shared the most delicious piece of gossip making its way across the city, in which a well-known actress had fallen pregnant while being unaware of the identity of the baby's father. Forgetting to insert her diaphragm, she'd attended a Right Bank opium orgy, and...

No, she couldn't share that one, not with a child in the room.

After they'd exhausted the more child-friendly stories, the Chagalls began praising Zoe again, and at that point, she decided to head back home. Ignoring their pleas to stay for dinner, she picked up her now-empty portfolio and limped toward the door, the painter close behind. As he opened the door for her, she asked, "Since you don't want to involve yourself with the police, what do you plan to do about the other paintings?"

Sad-eyed, he answered, "Accept their loss."

He gave her one final hug, then gently closed the door.

Chapter Four

—— Gabrielle ——

July 1924
Paris

Who am I and what am I doing here?

I must have asked that question aloud because someone whispers in my ear, "Your name is Gabrielle Challiot. Your hair is the color of flame and your lips are like roses. You are known for your beauty."

When I turn my head I find I cannot see the speaker, but something tickles my earlobe. "Speaker, who are you, and where are you?"

"My name is Odile, Madame, and if you look to the right, you will see me," she answers. "I am your best friend. The American woman considers herself your friend, too, but she lusts after your husband. Do you not remember what we discussed yesterday?"

I remember nothing about yesterday. In fact, the last thing I remember is walking through a flower-filled pasture, and I have the feeling that was long ago. But I follow the speaker's directions and turn my head. It is difficult, but after several false starts I manage it to see nothing but walls and plants.

"I still cannot see you," I tell her.

She laughs. "I assure you that I am here. Just look down at your pillow slip."

I do, but all I can see is a green thing the size of my smallest fingernail. It also appears to have too many legs. I only have two, and I, weak as I am, can tell that there is something wrong with both. Oh, la! I am sick. That must be why everything seems so strange. Also, why am I having trouble moving my limbs?

Ah, but look! I just wiggled my left toe. And my fingers, they are awake, too, tap-tap-tapping against my pillow slip, which is made of silk and has intricate embroidery.

Then I remember; the pillow slip was made by nuns. I may be ill, yet I do not lack for luxuries. Someone has taken excellent care of me.

Yes! My husband! This realization cheers my heart and makes me feel stronger.

Until I remember that, somewhere out there, is a woman who lusts after my Henri.

Chapter Five

— Zoe —

July 1924
Paris

Although still haunted by Laurette's dead face, Zoe showed up at La Rotonde the next morning for her usual breakfast of café au lait and a croissant but found all the outdoor tables occupied by tourists because of the cloudless sky. Her outfit—a mint-green chemise—earned looks of appreciation as she made her way through the din of people speaking in Greek, Russian, and other languages. Shoved against the back wall sat Zoe's good friends Kiki and Archie, who were fiercely defending an empty chair.

"A table by the kitchen, how the mighty have fallen," Archie mourned, pulling out the chair for Zoe.

"At least there aren't any damned Germans in here," Kiki muttered.

Kiki had lost a lover in a mustard gas attack during the Great War and had never forgiven the entire country of Germany or its inhabitants. But grief hadn't tarnished her beauty. The famed artists' model looked stunning in a short, pale-blue dress and matching cloche, although shadows underneath her eyes hinted at another night on the town. "After the hell those damned Germans put us through during the War, it's only right their athletes haven't been allowed to take part in the Olympics!"

Like Zoe, Archie was more forgiving, and he even counted a German or two among his many lovers. "Patience, dear Kiki," he said in his French vowel-heavy with an upper-crust British accent. "Only a few more weeks and we'll have Paris all to ourselves again. No more foreigners."

At that reminder of whom she was sitting with, Kiki had to laugh.

Then, as Archie addressed Zoe, the pleasant expression on his round face changed to one of concern. "But what's this I hear about you finding a dead woman in some scrapyard? What the hell were you doing in a scrapyard in the first place?"

Zoe almost asked him how he'd found out but then remembered that one of Archie's habits was to read the days' newspapers front to back, not skipping even the most trivial item. Sighing, she gave him her version of yesterday's events. The clock, the second trip to the flea market, the discovery of Laurette's body. She left out the part about the Chagalls.

"I've never been to that flea market," Kiki said, when Zoe was finished. "You say they have a nice collection of clocks?"

"Laurette did, yes. What's going to happen to them now, I don't know. Why would you need a clock in the first place? You always arrive hours late for everything."

A sly grin. "Maybe that's why I need a clock."

"She has a sister," Archie said, seemingly apropos of nothing.

"Who has a sister?" Kiki asked, batting her long eyelashes.

"Laurette Belcoeur, the dead woman. The sister's name is Veronique, and the article in *Le Figaro* said they ran the flea market together."

Zoe already knew this and would have commented, but the waiter arrived with her café au lait and a warm croissant, so she fell to it. Meanwhile, Kiki and Archie began a discussion about flea markets around the city, their good points and their bad.

"I almost bought a 'genuine' Picasso at the market over on rue Cochin the other day, but then I noticed he'd misspelled his own name," Archie said. "Yes, yes, you may laugh, Kiki, but odd things can happen to a painting on its way to fame."

Zoe couldn't agree more but stayed focused on her breakfast. The croissant was warm, just the way she liked it, and so perfectly baked that large flakes scattered onto the napkin in her lap. She was about to take another bite when a woman's voice rose at a nearby table.

"How dare you seat me near *that*!" Mississippi accent.

The room fell quiet.

Zoe looked around but could see nothing odd, just tables and chairs moved too close together to accommodate the overflow crowd. There was even a line out front of people waiting to be seated. While she wasn't crazy about sitting next to the kitchen, with its door swinging back and forth mere inches from her face, she considered herself fortunate to have gained a seat.

When the woman's voice rose again, this time into a near-scream, Zoe finally spotted her. She was somewhere in her forties, thin, with a pasty complexion, wearing an overly fussy green-and-white dress and a broadbrimmed straw hat festooned with fake flowers. She was pointing at a Negro man sitting at the next table. The white French couple with him looked appalled, but the resigned expression on the man's face hinted that this kind of situation was nothing new to him.

"I said, *how dare you!*" the woman screeched at her waiter again.

With that, the maître d' burst out from the kitchen and hurried over to the woman. Leaning over, he said something in a voice so low he couldn't be heard even in the brasserie's sudden silence. The woman stared up at him. Her mouth opened, but this time no words emerged.

The maître d' stepped back far enough to allow the woman to stand, and when she did, he pushed her chair back under the table.

"*Adieu, Madame.*"

The woman's pasty face turned scarlet. She grabbed her purse, bleated something unintelligible to the man she was with, and stalked out the door, her escort trailing behind. When the maître d' snapped his fingers and gestured to a couple waiting for a table, the newcomers almost knocked each other down in their rush to get to it.

Conversation rose again.

"As I was saying," Archie murmured, "one can't be too careful what one purchases at a flea market these days, can one?"

"One certainly can't, can one?" Zoe mimicked. "But I'm quite pleased with my new clock."

"Ah, yes. That new clock. How much did you pay for it? Remember, I said I'd reimburse you, since I was the one who broke the original."

Money changed hands. The younger son of the Earl of Whittenden, Archie was always flush. Generous, too, which helped cover up his many indiscretions. As he continued to chatter about other interesting articles he'd read in the morning paper—not all of them about Laurette's murder—Zoe worked on her croissant and café au lait. Every now and then Kiki interjected a salacious piece of gossip, the most delicious of rumors being the Russian nobleman who'd literally been caught with his pants down with the wife of an Austrian diplomat. The duel was scheduled for dawn tomorrow in the Bois de Boulogne.

Scandals duly tsked-tsked, Archie reminded Zoe about the Olympics swim finals they'd be attending.

"How could I possibly forget?" she said, hiding the fact that she wasn't looking forward to spending the day outdoors in the broiling sun. After adding a few more lies about how much she loved sports, she bade Archie and Kiki goodbye—Kiki was cursing the Germans again—and headed home.

· · · ◇ · · ·

For the first few months after Zoe's arrival in Paris in 1918, she'd lived in a hotel frequented by American expatriates. One day a friend had tipped her off to the sale of an unusual little house in the 14th arrondissement, the Montparnasse district. Formerly a stable, the house had been reconfigured by a wealthy parfumier for his mistress. It featured large sloping windows at the northern end, perfect for a studio, and at the south end, a boudoir with a mirrored ceiling. The sitting room was large enough to hold parties—always a plus—but the selling point for Zoe was the up-to-date plumbing. Free-flowing hot water in both the bathroom and kitchen! After a week of haggling, Le Petit Bibelot was Zoe's.

When Zoe let herself in the stout oak door, she heard the sound of conversation coming from the small kitchen. Madeline and a gruff-voiced man. Groaning inwardly, she fixed a welcoming smile on her face and strolled into the room. "Why, Inspector Henri Challiot, what a surprise!"

He stood up, bowed as low as his six-foot-plus height would allow him, and kissed her hand. *"Ma chérie."*

"Please tell me this is merely a social call, not a cross examination." But she knew better. She could still see the surprised expression on Laurette's dead face, and Henri was nothing if not faithful to his work.

His dark blue eyes were sad. "Unfortunately, Zoe..."

She cut him off. "I understand. You're here about that poor flea market girl."

Behind him, Madeline frowned a warning. Then, unless Zoe read her wrong, she mouthed the words *No Chagalls!*

Zoe led Henri to the sitting room and motioned for him to sit on the green horsehair sofa, while she took a seat in the matching chair. "It is never a misfortune to be with you, Henri," she said. Other than the steamy nights they shared in her mirrored boudoir, their relationship had become strained of late.

Mainly because of his wife.

"Don't play games with me, Zoe. I've been questioning another woman at the flea market—talk about a cranky old person!—and she didn't believe that the excitement you displayed during your return trip had anything to do with a clock. She said you questioned her about other things."

"Madame Crab must have a bad memory." Still smiling, Zoe fetched her new clock, and waved it under his nose. "You see? It keeps perfect time. So did the last one Laurette sold me, until someone broke it. After thinking the problem over, I decided it was only sensible to return to her for a replacement."

The morning sun streamed through the sitting room window, illuminating the clock's face as if to help support her story.

"And then you immediately take yet another trip? For another clock? That makes no sense." Henri also didn't seem amused by the clock's phallus-shaped pendulum. "You swear to me that your passion for knowing perfect time took you all the way back on the same day to the same flea market during threatening weather?" He motioned to her damaged left leg. "I notice you are limping even worse today. Apparently, your leg doesn't agree with all that unnecessary walking."

"Not even the most gifted cobbler can perform miracles, so the trouble comes and goes," Zoe sniffed. "When I first left the house, my leg was fine. Only when I was a block away from the flea market did it begin to ache, but there was no point in stopping then."

"Really? All this trouble and lameness by a woman who has always been so careless of time she doesn't even own a watch?"

"Ah, but now that my paintings are becoming known, I have so many appointments." Zoe paused a moment, wondering if she dared. Deciding that she did, she added, "On Tuesdays, especially, your ailing wife expects my visit exactly at one o'clock. Not a minute before, not a minute later."

His face darkened, as it always did when she mentioned his wife. Guilt, perhaps? Although God knew she felt enough guilt for the both of them.

Henri noticed Zoe's stricken face, and took advantage of it. "Gabrielle cannot tell day from night, let alone the hour."

Fighting back, she said, "You see her through fear. I don't. I see a woman who grows stronger every day."

"I know my own wife!"

"Said every husband, ever." Henri had his beliefs; Zoe had hers. "But back to the reason for my return trip to the flea market. As I've told you, when I discovered Laurette had already left, I hurried to her scrapyard to catch her there. That's when I discovered..." She let her voice fall away.

"How long do you think you were in the scrapyard before you discovered her body?"

He had asked that question before, and she had answered... what...five minutes? Ten? "It was mere minutes, no time at all, as I told you yesterday."

Henri leaned forward, his eyes narrowing. "Then you might find it interesting to note that Fabian Napier told me you'd been in the scrapyard for at least thirty minutes from the time he first heard you calling out Laurette's name, until you came screaming into his garage."

"He was busy working on a car, so I doubt he was paying much attention to the time."

"Yet his customer says you could have been there for as long as forty-five minutes. What were you *really* doing in that scrap-yard, Zoe?"

Truth, sometimes, but not always, appears to be the safest recourse. "If you must know, I was liberating some rabbits before they became someone's dinner."

He sat back. "Ah. You and your animals. Are you still feeding those wild cats?"

Finally, a question not relating to clocks and murder. "Those cats are not wild. They're just scared. Some of them are former pets who lost their homes in the war. And, yes, of course I'm still feeding them. I'm feeding homeless dogs, too. There's one who shows up at the same time every day, and I'm thinking of bringing him in. Long-haired, some kind of terrier mix. He'd look quite handsome cleaned up." She felt proud of herself for derailing Henri's suspicions.

"What covered the hutch roof? It was missing."

"Wha...what roof?"

"You've apparently forgotten that when we dined out together you once ordered the *Lapin en Croûte*."

"That rabbit was already dead."

"Again, what was on the hutch roof? It was bare when I inspected it, and no sensible Frenchwoman would have left the thing uncovered, because the animals could have died of exposure before they were fat enough to eat."

Zoe held out her palms, as if to show there was nothing she was hiding. Not even the scars from her old studio fire, which had almost burned a man to death. "Yes, there was a roof, just an old piece of tin and some rags. I tossed them aside, turned the hutch over, and it was bye-bye, Mister Bunny."

Henri's brow furrowed. "*Mister who?* This is the first I've heard about a man being with you."

Six years in Paris, and she still sometimes forgot the transatlantic cultural differences. "Sorry, I had a pet rabbit once, and that's what I named him. Mister Bunny. But I need to ask you something important. I've been wondering if I should send Laurette's sister a sympathy card. Do you know where she lives?"

In full inspector mode, he didn't answer right away, and when he finally spoke, he had a question of his own, and it seemingly had nothing to do with Laurette's murder.

"I hear that you breakfasted with a man this morning. Who was he?"

Zoe had always known that her lover had spies everywhere, and one of them must have been at La Rotonde this morning. She smiled at Henri's moment of jealousy.

"Ah, yes. Archie Stafford-Smythe. No one you need to worry about. I was at La Rotonde with the model Kiki and several dozen tourists."

"Oh. *Him*." Henri's immediate relaxation proved that he either knew about Archie or even personally knew him. An interesting thought, since it was well known that Archie preferred men for lovers.

"You know Archie?" Zoe asked innocently.

"Everyone knows Monsieur Stafford-Smythe. In case you're not aware—but I'm almost certain you are—he has a bad habit of showing up at certain places just before they're raided. Opium parties, for instance."

"Opium isn't illegal in Paris."

"Of course not. Unlike your prohibitionist America, the country of France doesn't play the game of Mommy-Said-No with its citizenry. But other behaviors take place at those opium parties that *are* illegal, such as robbing people while they're lost in their pretty dreams."

"Archie doesn't steal!" She yelled this so loudly that in the kitchen, Madeline stopped clanking around, a sure sign she was listening. "He doesn't have to steal, Henri. Archie has pots of money. And he's happily a very poor poker player."

"True. Your friend is always the one stolen *from*," Henri said, calming her. "Once I had to drive him home because the thief didn't even leave him enough to take the Métro."

"How kind of you."

"I'm not always an ogre, *chérie*." His voice was softer now, and Zoe guessed that if it hadn't been for Madeline working in the kitchen, he would have taken her in his arms and carried her off to her mirrored boudoir.

Titillated by that vision, Zoe slipped her foot from its shoe, stretched out her leg, and caressed Henri's thigh with her toes.

He sighed. "Unfortunately, I am on duty."

"Then the mirror in my ceiling will have nothing interesting to reflect, will it?" she purred. "*Très tragique!* But you were going to tell me where Laurette's sister lives so I can tender my condolences."

The leg massage had made Henri's eyes close. "Hmm? Oh. Yes. Poor Veronique. Well, you can send a note—flowers would also be nice—to her at 102 rue Lormel. Sixth floor." When he opened his eyes, they were warm. "You are kinder than I am, Zoe."

She was about to agree when two long and one short trills interrupted her. She'd had her new telephone for less than a week and was still having trouble getting used to it. "My ring is three short and one long, I think" she said to Henri. "Or was it two long and one short?"

"Pick up the phone and find out," Henri said dryly. As an important member of the Sûreté, he'd had his own phone for several years, but unlike her new instrument, his was a private line.

Zoe took her foot away from Henri's thigh and limped over to the small stand where her candlestick-shaped phone resided. "*Allô?*" she said, lifting the receiver off the hook, only to be answered by a staticky stream of French expletives from a woman telling her to hang up and mind her own business. In the background, Zoe thought she heard another woman crying but couldn't be certain. The line was never clear enough for her liking.

She replaced the receiver. To Henri, she said, "I was right the first time. My ring is three short, followed by one long. But she didn't have to be so rude."

Henri laughed. "Welcome to modern Paris."

Chapter Six

Zoe's new clock informed her that Henri had been gone less than a half hour before Bella Chagall and little Ida showed up at her front door. The weather gods being temporarily merciful, they arrived dry, with Bella carrying a loaf of freshly baked challah and a chocolate babka. But those delights were nothing compared to the gift little Ida handed over: a watercolor sketch her father had painted only hours earlier. It showed an angel hovering over an onion-domed church. The angel looked just like Zoe.

In her rough French, Bella said proudly, "He signed painting on the back, see?" Turning the painting over, she saw underneath today's date, the message *"To Angel Zoe, from Marc Chagall."*

The lump in Zoe's throat was so large it took her several seconds before she could vocalize her gratitude, but when she recovered, her words were fulsome. After she'd said *thank you* in every way possible, Bella smiled. "Yes, yes, I know you appreciate these little gifts, but they do come with one request. From me, not from husband."

"Anything." At this point, if Bella had asked her to take a swim in the Seine, Zoe would have grabbed her bathing costume.

But Bella's request was more sensible. "If you hear of other lost oil paintings out there, Marc wants to be...to be..." She searched for the word. "*Alerted.* Yes, he would like to be alerted."

"Alerted? Why, I'll tear them out of the thief's hands and bring them to you straight out!"

Bella frowned. "Violence not necessary. We do not wish trouble for you."

Zoe could have said that she and trouble were old friends, but she didn't. Instead, she gave Ida a small nod and a wink.

Bella wasn't finished. "I know of man you should talk with when he comes back to Paris?" She'd framed it as a question, as if suddenly unsure of herself, which Zoe found interesting since Chagall's wife was hardly a weak woman.

"Who would that be?" Zoe asked.

"Poet Blaise Cendrars."

Zoe had to force herself not to groan. During Chagall's early years in Paris, he'd lived and worked out of the beehive-shaped studio for artists and poets known as La Ruche, where he and Cendrars had first become friends. This was around 1912, six years before Zoe had been banished forever from her home in Alabama. The two men had become so close that Cendrars had even been allowed to watch Chagall paint. In 1913 those experiences moved the poet to write *Studio*, the last three lines of which were...

> *Chagall*
> *Chagall*
> *In rungs of light*

More poems about Chagall flowed from Cendrars's pen. Then, in May of 1914, Chagall locked up his studio and made a stop in Berlin to leave some paintings at the Sturm Gallery. After that business was accomplished and the required contracts signed, he set off for Russia to marry Bella, his longtime fiancée. But while he was still in Russia enjoying his new role as husband, the War to End All Wars erupted. During the European slaughter, the Bolsheviks assassinated Czar Nicolas and his entire family, and life in Russia turned upside down.

Although Chagall was sympathetic to the revolutionaries—minus the assassinations, because he was a peaceful man—political turmoil kept him stuck in Russia until he was able to return to Paris. That's when he discovered all his paintings in Berlin and Paris had been lost in the chaos of war. A dishonest dealer accounted for the Berlin disaster, but in Paris, the person responsible for the vanished paintings was his supposed friend, Blaise Cendrars.

When Chagall confronted Cendrars, the poet had refused to apologize, offering only the explanation, "We all thought you were dead, so I disposed of your work as I saw fit. You should thank me that your paintings were not burned as trash."

At that pronouncement, Chagall had ended their friendship.

None of the people who'd bought paintings and sketches from Cendrars were willing to give the paintings back or to reimburse the artist, which would have meant paying twice, so Chagall wound up not receiving one penny for many years' hard work. Apparently, not all of his paintings had been "sold" after his studio had been pillaged. As per Laurette Belcoeur's rabbit hutch, others had found different ways to disappear.

Cendrars was now in Brazil—he'd long been fascinated by the country—so for now, questioning him about the rest of Chagall's works was impossible.

"I wonder if the rest of Marc's paintings can be found?" Bella asked Zoe. "*The Procession? The Couple? Dedicated to My Fiancée*, which I have not seen, but Marc told me was his best yet."

"It had to be as beautiful as *Maman*," Ida piped up in her more fluent French. "Can I have some chocolate babka?"

··· ◊ ···

As soon as the pair left, Zoe treated herself to some babka, which was as delicious as it looked, then set off for Laurette and Veronique Belcoeur's flat. On the way she bought a mixed bouquet of summer flowers. Upon reaching the six-story building on rue Lormel, she discovered that the Belcoeur flat was on the sixth floor and that the building had no elevator. By now her bad leg was screaming, but she gritted her teeth and started the climb.

As she clunk-clopped up the last flight, she heard a woman's wails. The sister, probably. Feeling slightly guilty—Zoe had a sister, too, and knew how deep sisterly love could be—she rapped gently on the door.

More wails.

Deciding that this was a bad time, Zoe turned to leave, but as soon as she started down the stairs, the door opened and a man called out, "Yes, Mademoiselle? You are a friend bearing condolences?"

It was all Zoe could do not to gawk.

The man standing in the Belcoeurs' doorway made the statues of Apollo she'd seen at the Louvre look downright ugly. Tall, blond, with startlingly green eyes, he possessed not only the physique of that Greek god, but the timbre of his voice must have matched Apollo's, too. Deep. Colorful. An accent that spoke of aristocratic connections.

"Offering my, ah, condolences," Zoe blurted.

"And you brought flowers. How very kind."

"Flowers. Right."

His smile could have melted Satan's cold heart. "Since I haven't yet had the pleasure of meeting you before, may I ask which sister..."

"Laurette. We were, um, acquaintances."

Holding out a perfectly manicured hand, he stepped aside. "This door is always open to Laurette's friends. *Entrez.*"

Gulping out a clumsy *merci*, Zoe entered. As though to prove the man's god-like power, her bad leg stopped screaming.

Laurette's sister sat weeping on a long sofa that had seen better days. In contrast to the Apollo who had opened the door, Veronique was certainly no goddess, although she did bear a faint—very faint—resemblance to her beautiful sister. At least ten years older, with dark blond hair the same color as Laurette's, Veronique had a body that was too square to be considered feminine. She wore the same stylish bob as her sister, but on her it looked awkward. Her features were nearly identical to her sister's, but her nose was a millimeter too long, and her lips a millimeter too narrow. A matched set of crow's-feet made their appearance known at the corner of her too-small eyes. While Laurette had been beautiful, Veronique wasn't even attractive.

But perhaps Zoe was judging unfairly. After all, Veronique's face was distorted with grief, and her swollen eyes were so red it was a wonder she could see through them. And her poor cheek! A patchy burn scar ran from under her eyebrow all the way down to her chin. From the war?

As Zoe entered, the woman politely rose and thanked her for coming.

"How very kind," Veronique said, echoing the Apollo.

Zoe had never felt such a fraud. Here she was, intruding on two people's grief merely to satisfy her own curiosity. She decided to return home as quickly as possible and leave them to it. Then she saw the paintings on the wall and understood why Laurette had been ignorant enough to use Chagall's paintings for wrapping paper.

Five oil paintings were proudly displayed in expensive gold-leaf frames. One was an oil portrait of a young woman—Laurette?—holding a sunflower. Her face was almost as contorted as the women in Picasso's revolutionary *Les Demoiselles d'Avignon*, but her face was misaligned more out of ignorance of the human anatomy than playful experimentation. Like many amateur works, the woman's head was too big for her body. One eye sat higher than the other, and the jaw was so out of whack that if it had been on a living woman, she would have been unable to chew her food. And her poor sunflower appeared to be suffering from mold.

The other paintings were attempts at cityscapes and landscapes. Sick-looking trees on a pestilence-plagued field, a crooked Eiffel Tower about to topple onto a purple Fiat, a lumpy building perched on a hilltop that might—or might not—have been Sacré-Coeur. Worst of all was the picture of a sheepdog, which cruel Nature or an untrained artist had cursed with four legs of differing lengths. If the animal had lived, it would have been unable to stand up, let alone herd sheep.

No wonder neither Laurette nor Veronique had recognized the Chagalls for what they were; they had no taste.

Someone was talking to her. "Hmm?" she said, pulling her horrified eyes away from the misbegotten dog and back to the Apollo. "What was that you said?"

"I was apologizing for my rudeness in not introducing myself. I am Vicomte Gervais du Paget, but please call me Gervais. Laurette and I were to be married next month." A deep sigh.

God-like in visage, and a vicomte *to boot! Holy hell!*

The French were funny about their aristocrats. During the Revolution, they'd cheerfully lopped off the head of every aristocrat they could catch. Decades later, their victims' descendants' titles—and in some cases, certain portions of their properties— had been restored. In modern France, the average *égalité*-loving Frenchman looked upon aristocrats with an amused deference, but they were still thrilled whenever one married into the family.

"Please, I should be the one to apologize, intruding upon you like this," Zoe said. But she took the seat Paget—*Vicomte* Paget!— offered her, glad for the opportunity to study the room more closely.

The Belcoeur flat was wildly over-furnished, serving as yet another storage space for the sisters' flea market business. Enough chairs sat around to seat the Paris Philharmonic Orchestra. Several rolled-up Persian carpets leaned against one wall. At the other end of the room, numerous decorative end tables were stacked almost ceiling-high. One free-standing table held a candlestick-model telephone similar to Zoe's. Considering the business the sisters ran, the clutter was understandable—except for the dozens of clocks sitting upon a long table, some ticking annoyingly away. How could they bear the racket? After only moments in the flat, Zoe wanted to cover her ears.

Veronique stopped weeping long enough to offer Zoe a glass of wine, but she refused it. If the Belcoeurs' taste in wine was as poor as their taste in art, their wine might kill her. "I'm fine, but thank you," she said, disappointed by her own artistic snobbishness. To make up for it, she added, "I see those beautiful clocks I've enjoyed at your table."

"Laurette loved clocks," Veronique responded, sniffing back more mucus than was polite. "Always kept them wound. In the beginning, I found them irritating, but now every tick reminds me of her. What am I to do with them now? I can't tell one clock from the other!"

This led to a discussion of famous clocks Laurette had sold, Veronique claiming that her sister had even sold one to Rudolph Valentino. "He was very young then, not yet a movie star, and of course Laurette was too young to remember him, but the clock had a pair of kissing lovers on it. Rudy was a romantic even then."

Zoe knew that Valentino was Italian by birth but had spent some time in Paris, so the story might even have been true.

As if agreeing, the *vicomte* nodded his handsome head.

Veronique continued talking about sales to the great and near-great, but she never once mentioned art. Taking a chance, Zoe said, "I couldn't help but notice those beautiful paintings on your wall. Did you ever sell anything by an artist who later on turned out to be famous? An early sketch, perhaps?"

A frown. "I know nothing about art. Neither did Laurette."

Praying silently for forgiveness for the lie she was about to tell, Zoe said, "I find that hard to believe since you own such lovely artwork yourself."

The *vicomte* looked baffled, but Veronique smiled proudly. "They were done by our mother. You see her self-portrait there," she pointed at the horrifically mutilated face on the wall. "*Maman* painted that portrait just before she and our father died when our château was bombed. Laurette and I barely escaped both attacks and wound up living in the stables. As for the other paintings, they were of the places *Maman* visited and loved." Here she paused and shrugged. "The dog is Pepi. He died during the bombing, too. I never liked him much."

"Your mother had great talent," Zoe said, assuring herself of a one-way ticket to Hell.

"Yes, we...I am very proud of her."

"Since you are so sensitive to the qualities of real art, did you ever sell paintings? Even the kind that would be popular with tourists? Painting or drawings of the Eiffel Tower, perhaps."

As sad as she was, Veronique managed a small laugh. "Once in Paris, we met many artists. I suffered through all the interactions with so-called 'art' and artists that I ever intend to! The time was crazy, you see, and everyone—especially the artists—was starving, and those dabblers would steal the shirt off your back if you weren't careful."

Somehow Zoe managed to ignore this slander against her friends. "Moving from a château to a stable and then this apartment, did you..."

"You misunderstand me," Veronique said. "Our first Paris

apartment was nothing as fine as this. It was in La Villette, which as you must know, was a terrible place to live while the war was still going on."

Zoe winced. She'd been to La Villette, and the war had turned the neighborhood into a ruin.

Not noticing Zoe's discomfort, Veronique continued. "But you can't outrun bad luck, can you? After only a month in La Villette, the Germans went after it again. This time we moved down to Montparnasse, as far away as we could get from La Villette. After that, we didn't have to worry about the Germans—just artists and their messes."

An idea occurred to Zoe then, something that could account for the Chagalls' winding up at a flea market. "Did your new, ah, *flat* happen to look like a giant beehive?"

Veronique looked surprised. "No, but the building next to ours did. The woman who ran the place hired us to clean out the artists' abandoned studios. I'm sorry to tell you, but those people were pigs. Both with dirt and with images that should never have been painted at all! But Laurette and I—we were almost starving at that point— were given food by that kind woman, and she let us take whatever bits and pieces we could find. Tubes of paint and brushes and even an untouched roll of canvas, which we immediately cut up for coats. But we saw nothing worth selling."

It was all Zoe could do not to tear out her hair. After taking a calming breath, she asked, "Would that studio have been called La Ruche, by any chance?"

"Why, yes, it was," Veronique said, surprised. "How did you know?"

Not wanting to let Veronique discover that she herself was a "pig" of an artist, she said, "A friend of mine once had a studio there. What a coincidence."

"Life is like that, isn't it?" After another meandering account about selling items to stars of stage and film, Veronique finally returned to the subject of La Ruche. "But we were talking about those dirty studios. It took both of us over a week to clear them out. Laurette found a sketchbook that had never been used and paint jars that still had color in them. After we'd finished cleaning that pigsty, dear Laurette spent happy hours pretending to be an artist." There was a wealth of sadness in her smile. "But my poor sister did not have our mother's talent."

At this, the fancy Vicomte Gervais du Paget looked down at the floor.

Zoe framed her next question carefully. "Did you find any paintings, however badly done, among the debris they left behind? The Olympics crowd is hungry for souvenirs, so if you still have them..."

Veronique's lip curled. "Tourists! They're more interested in buying fancy ashtrays. But you are asking about something that happened years ago, when we found nothing at La Ruche that anyone with taste would wish on their walls. However, since we'd already started selling items at a flea markets, we did need wrapping paper, and you know what they say."

"What do they say?" Zoe asked.

"*Ne gaspillez pas, ne voulez pas.*" The French version of "Waste not, want not."

At that point, Gervais du Paget interjected, "This was all during the war, you understand, but I am happy to tell you that because of their hard work, Laurette, uh, *Veronique*, now runs three flea markets here in the city. Is that not admirable?"

At his mention of her sister's name, Veronique began to weep again. Within seconds, Paget was wiping away his own tears.

No further along in finding more missing Chagalls, Zoe left Veronique and the handsome *vicomte* to their grief.

Chapter Seven

—— Zoe ——

Summer 1917
Mercy, Alabama

Zoe knew grief, too.

It arrived in her life on a spring day in Mercy, Alabama, when she'd driven her new car, a speedy King Model EE, from her family's Beech Glen plantation to Birmingham to update her wardrobe. After she'd purchased a new dotted-Swiss dress at Miss Eleanor's Styles, her bad leg began throbbing. Not wanting to make a spectacle of herself, she took a shortcut through an unpaved alleyway to get back to her auto. She'd gone only a few steps before her ankle turned sideways on a rock, and—waving her arms to catch her balance—she dropped her package in the dirt. As she struggled to retrieve it, a Negro man, noticing her difficulty, rushed over to pick it up.

He carefully brushed the dirt off the package, soiling his immaculate white sleeve in the process. "I hope nothing was damaged," he said, with a slight Northern accent. "But first, are you hurt? Do you need me to call someone?"

"No, really, I'm fine. But thank you." She smiled in gratitude.

When he smiled back, she got a sense of familiarity, an almost certain belief that she'd met him before. But that was impossible. This was Alabama. Yet the young man's eyes were almost the same color as hers. Blue.

Then again, that in itself wasn't unusual. Alabama being Alabama, blue-eyed Negroes weren't all that rare, but the reason for them was more grounded in generations of cruelty than in the tenderness of love.

When she thanked him again, he said, "You are welcome, Miss Zoe."

He knew her name.

As she stared into those startling blue eyes, an old memory rose before her of a hot August day, when she'd been...what? Twelve years old? Thirteen? Truckloads of laborers had arrived at Beech Glen to harvest the plantation's five hundred acres of cotton. The plants' fluff-filled bolls waved in a light breeze as the pickers moved along the rows. Zoe had planned to draw their gnarled hands, their sun-burned skin, the women's flowery bonnets.

Her intended model was Dorothy Reed, a pretty blue-eyed Negro woman, her sepia-colored skin dark against her white pickers' gloves. Zoe didn't know her—the races didn't mix in Mercy—but she knew *of* her. Dorothy, a widow, taught at the Negro school. Trailing behind her was her son Peter, a good-looking young man who shared the same coloring as his mother. When Zoe had started to sketch the two, Peter had turned around and said, "Please go home, Miss Zoe, before your people see you with us and cause us trouble."

Disappointed, but well aware of the way things worked in Alabama, and knowing why Dorothy was a widow, Zoe had walked back to the end of the row and finished her sketch from memory.

Now, on this lovely spring day, here was Peter Reed, the

schoolteacher's son, all grown up. Through the plantation grapevine she'd heard about him receiving a music scholarship to some Yankee college. His years away from Mercy explained his unique speech pattern, a northern accent well into the process of shortening the slurred Alabama drawl.

But his years up North hadn't erased his sense of caution. When he handed her the rescued package, he said, "You are welcome, Miss Zoe," and quickly walked away.

Several weeks after that fateful Birmingham trip, as she'd been working on a watercolor of a brilliantly colored maple in the forest that bordered Beech Glen, she'd heard music floating through the trees. Curious, she'd followed the music, and when she emerged from a clearing, she saw Peter Reed again. He was leaning against a grandfather oak even larger than the one that had crippled her, and he was playing something sad on a gleaming trumpet. The music he made almost broke her heart.

Its memory still did.

Chapter Eight

July 1924
Paris

Deciding to make one more stop before returning to Le Petit Bibelot to paint, Zoe limped the few blocks to the Belcoeurs' scrapyard, intending to search for more Chagalls. It was possible that the other day, when she'd found Laurette's body, she'd been too upset to launch an adequate search. Given the Belcoeur sisters' ignorance of art, more treasures could easily be lying in wait under their piles of semi-treasures.

But when Zoe took her first step down that narrow lane between Napier's Garage and Heureur's Impressions, a man's voice yelled, *"Arrêtez!"* Stop!

When she turned around, she saw Fabian Napier approaching her with a large wrench in his hand. He looked angry.

"I just... I just..." she stammered, transfixed by that wrench. Was that oil on it, or blood?

As he recognized Zoe, the anger left Fabian's face and he lowered the wrench. But he still inserted himself between her and the scrapyard. "You're not allowed to go back there. No one is. The police locked the gate, and they've told me to keep an eye out."

She could hardly say she was searching for more Chagalls, because then she'd have to admit she'd already found some and, even worse, had illegally spirited them away. Thinking fast, she said, "I wanted to take another look at one of those clocks. I'd been discussing it with Laurette before, well, you know."

"Before she was killed," Fabian said grimly. "You need to talk to her sister about that, not go messing around here on your own."

Now that Zoe realized he wasn't going to bash her skull open with the wrench, she allowed some of her own anger to make itself known. "I wasn't going to steal anything."

"I'm certain you weren't, or you'd have been sneakier. You were clomping around like a hippo."

She felt her face flush. She'd tried to be quiet, but with her left leg hurting so much, her limp had indeed turned into a clomp. She looked down at it in disgust.

Fabian noticed. "Why don't you come into the garage where you can rest yourself for a moment? Maybe you'd like a glass of water, too."

Because of the day's heat, the garage door stood all the way open, but in the shade, it proved much cooler. Zoe appreciated the water and didn't mind the smell of gasoline and oil. It reminded her of her father's work shed at Beech Glen, where he'd liked to tinker with farm machinery. Although a general practitioner, he'd had the delicate hands of a surgeon.

But that was the past, a country Zoe preferred not to visit.

To steer her mind away from the heartaches of Beech Glen, she attempted a conversation with the mechanic, who was now frowning over a Renault's innards. "What with the Olympics, Paris is overcrowded, isn't it?" she asked, the Olympics having replaced the weather as a safe subject with people you'd just met.

"It's good for business," Fabian replied.

"I can't say I'm wild about it."

"Same with Laurette." He frowned at the Renault, apparently seeing something he didn't like. "She hated crowds."

That was surprising. "Did you know her well?"

Fabian hit something in the Renault's engine with the wrench, and the resulting clang reverberated around the garage walls. It was worse than the fleet of ticking clocks at the Belcoeurs' apartment.

"Know Laurette well? Ha!" Fabian answered. "You could say I knew her well enough, seeing as how I'm hers and Veronique's landlord. That storage shed is on my property."

Zoe was grateful that he was so intent on the Renault's motor he couldn't see the surprise on her face. Once she trusted herself to sound only mildly curious, she said, "I didn't know that."

Another clang, another echo. "My father left it to me. This garage and the scrapyard."

Although Zoe knew she shouldn't ask, she couldn't help herself. "The sisters paid you rent, then?"

He stepped back from the car and straightened up, irritation on his face. "No 'sisters' now, is there? But I expect Veronique will want to keep to our arrangement since she doesn't really have any choice. Want some more water?"

Zoe said yes, then drained the glass as Fabian turned his attention back to the Renault. "Laurette was beautiful, wasn't she?" she asked.

"One might say she was too beautiful." Another clang from the car.

"Oh? I would have thought..."

"Laurette's beauty made her overly pleased with herself," he said, stepping away from the car. "Now, as you can see, I'm busy, so..."

Taking this not-too-subtle hint, Zoe proffered her thanks for the water and bid him *adieu*.

As she limped back to Le Petit Bibelot, Zoe's thoughts raced. Fabian Napier had been helpful enough until she'd brought up Laurette, and then he'd turned surly. Had he shown interest in the girl, only to be rebuffed? He was good-looking, certainly, but no Apollo. And a mere garage mechanic would certainly come up short in competition with a *vicomte*.

Perhaps that bore looking into.

· · · ◇ · · ·

Madeline had already left for the day when Zoe arrived home, so she put together a dinner of chicken-and-onion sandwich, eased along by a crisp Sauvignon, and slices of Bella Chagall's challah.

Deciding not to further stress her sore leg by standing in front of the easel, she hobbled over to the sofa, picked up the collection of Colette stories she'd purchased at Shakespeare & Company, and began to read. Instead of being thrilled by *La Femme Cachée*— *The Other Woman*—she drifted off. After living in Montparnasse for six years, she didn't find a story about a man with two wives all that shocking.

· · · ◇ · · ·

Hours later, the waning of daylight woke Zoe from her nap. From the deepening of shadows outside the window, she figured it was almost eight, and a glance at her new clock—*thank you, Laurette*— proved her correct. Sometime during her nap, the Colette book had fallen to the floor, crumpling two of its pages. After smoothing them out, she placed it on the end table, then went to the big studio window. Soon the streetlights would fill the night with golden halos. She stood there as the day disappeared. Staying off her feet for a while had done her leg good, and now she didn't feel the slightest ache. Refreshed, she slipped into her smock and began to work.

Since her last big series of paintings—*Seven Godly Virtues, Seven Deadly Sins*—hadn't yet made her famous, this time around she vowed to stick to unthemed work. This new painting was a self-portrait, more in the style of the Surrealists than her earlier attempts at Expressionism. Rather than positioning her face in the center, she created a montage of Zoes. Zoe sketching her pony at Beech Glen. Zoe falling from the top of the massive oak in the horse pasture. Zoe watching her father's body swing back and forth from the barn rafter. No angels or violinists floated over the Mercy, Alabama, sky, but then, she'd never had Chagall's faith, had she?

She painted until two in the morning then went to bed, only to be thrown awake by a nightmare about a newborn baby abandoned in a dark forest.

Chapter Nine

It was overcast the next afternoon, but the clouds were too thin to hold any rain, so every event in the Olympics raced on. Boxing? Polo? Pelote basque (whatever the hell that was)? All too soon Zoe would find herself in the midst of that noisy throng, wishing she were anywhere else, even back in Mercy. But such was the price of friendship. She'd promised to accompany Archie to one of the swim meets to see some American swimmer named Johnny Weissmuller, who was expected to set a record or two. Not that she cared about any of that. Sports were boring.

In the meantime, Zoe enjoyed a shallot, thyme, and brie omelet and a glass of Château Margaux with Kiki at one of La Rotonde's outdoor tables. They'd been able to snatch the table after two Germans had abandoned it, although Kiki wasn't pleased to be sitting in the same chair that only seconds ago had been occupied by—as Kiki so succinctly put it—"a fat Hun ass."

Zoe shook her head, disapproving of Kiki's blind prejudice. The war may have been over, but some French hearts hadn't yet healed. Maybe someday that miracle would happen.

When Zoe had dressed for her outing, she'd thought her new

linen chemise—navy and lime green, tied at the hips by an orange bow matched to the color of her cloche—was *très* daring. Yet sitting next to Kiki made Zoe's dress appear staid. Kiki's ensemble included a calf-length purple skirt, a scarlet blouse, and a vest emblazoned in an eye-crossing pink-and-yellow pattern. Perhaps to tone down her rainbowed outfit, her neck was looped with several strands of jet beads.

Zoe didn't mind being shown up by Kiki, because no one in Paris knew such delicious gossip—not even Archie. After spending only a few minutes more bitching about the number of Germans in the city, the Château Margaux soothed her enough to begin recounting which of their acquaintances had recently made fools of themselves.

Kiki confirmed the rumor that Gertrude Stein and Alice Toklas, both probably atheists, really had been named godparents to Ernest and Hadley's son, John Hadley Nicanor Hemingway, better known as Bumby. In other news, she confided that Cocteau had allowed himself to get hooked on opium and was currently under a doctor's care. As for Picasso, his ballet-dancer wife, Olga, was threatening him with divorce if he didn't stop cavorting with his models.

Good luck with that, Zoe thought, not bothering to stifle her giggles.

Kiki wasn't finished. She'd heard that Morris Cavanaugh, of the snooty Boston Cavanaughs, got so drunk the night before, he'd fallen on his face and broken his nose. And that only last week, Coco Chanel was seen nuzzling the very-much-married Bendor, Duke of Westminster. Unlike Zoe, that woman loved aristocrats.

"You'll enjoy this next bit," Kiki continued. "Our friend Dominique Garron? She almost ran down some magistrate yesterday, claiming she couldn't see him because he entered the street from her blind side."

Zoe took time to swallow another bite of omelet before tsk-tsking. She adored Dominique, but the artist—who'd had one eye shot out during the war while she was heading to the Front to make sketches—really shouldn't be driving.

Zoe had just taken another sip of wine when Kiki added, almost as an afterthought, "And yesterday, when I was having a few drinks at the Jockey, I heard that awful Blaise Cendrars tell some American woman here for the Olympics that if it weren't for her extremely large nose, there was nothing memorable about her, especially not her mind, which was chock-full of clichés and prejudice. Then she..."

Zoe almost choked on her Château Margaux. "Cendrars? I thought he was in Brazil!"

Kiki lowered her voice. "Well, I hear there was a family emergency that required his presence. But he's heading back to Brazil tomorrow, and good riddance."

"Tomorrow?"

"Heavens, Zoe! What's your interest in that awful man? All the poets and half the artists are crazy about Cendrars, but for the life of me I can't see why you're interested in him. He's a nothing, and his poetry reads like a Cook's Tour travelogue." Then she gave Zoe a shrewd look. "Wait a minute. Could your curiosity about Cendrars have something to do with the murder of that flea market girl? I read in *Le Figaro* that you were the one who found her body, but now here you are, talking about that blasted poet. Does that mean you suspect him?"

"No, not at all. It's just that I heard someone mention him the other day, and I was surprised by the coincidence. By the way, where is Cendrars staying? At his flat?"

Kiki's hand made a waving motion, as if brushing away a mosquito. "He's not even in Paris." In the model's world, *La Cité* was the only respectable place to be. "He had to break off his trip because the crazy cousin in Reims, Edgard Sauser. tried to shoot one of the maids. *And* the butler! I hear Edgard is in a straitjacket now, locked away somewhere safe. Anyway, Cendrars had to help sort out the estate so the cousin's children—their mother died last year—can be properly taken care of."

"Where in Reims? Do you know?"

A shrug of those beautiful shoulders, whistled at appreciatively by a passing group of Americans. Kiki took a moment to wink at them, then answered, "Some big estate at the edge of town. They're filthy rich, I hear. Or were, before the cousin went running amok with his hunting rifle."

So Blaise Cendrars, the very man who'd played a major role in the loss of Chagall's paintings, was now back in France. And he'd be leaving tomorrow! If anyone knew where the rest of those paintings wound up, it would be him. Not wanting blabbermouth Kiki to notice her growing excitement, Zoe went back to eating. When she finished, she ordered another glass of wine, as if she had all the time in the world.

For the next few minutes, Kiki talked about Jean Renoir's upcoming movie, a story about a young woman who lived on a barge with her father and uncle. Renoir had promised her a starring role, and she was supposed to meet with him after her meal to discuss the contract she was going to refuse to sign.

When Zoe asked why, Kiki shook her glossy head. "Being an artist yourself, I'm sure you agree that contracts should never be part of the creative process."

Zoe, whose fervent wish was to sign a contract with a reputable art dealer, nodded. "No true artist would ever sign a contract."

In a satisfied voice, Kiki said, "That's exactly what I'm going to tell Jean."

As soon as Kiki finished her third glass of wine and Zoe her second, the two parted company—Kiki for Jean Renoir's office and

Zoe for Henri's flat. Regardless of her desire to speak to Cendrars, this was the day of the week she always read to Henri's wife, Gabrielle. For the last two years, Zoe had been reading to the bedridden Gabrielle. She saw it as homage to her own long-dead mother, who'd read to her daily when the eight-year-old Zoe had her broken leg up in traction. Sometimes she could still hear her Paris-born mother's exquisite French as she read the Babette series about a little French girl who lived near the Louvre. By the time Zoe's leg had healed, more or less, she spoke enough French to hold a conversation and had developed a passion for Art with a capital *A*.

But homages, even for dead mothers, weren't always pure. The main reason Zoe made her weekly pilgrimage to Gabrielle was guilt. Even in the *très* modern Paris of 1924, consciences couldn't help but nag when two women loved the same man.

Unlike Henri, Zoe believed Gabrielle was somehow conscious in that inert body. A week earlier, when Zoe read aloud the final sentence of Marcel Proust's *À la Recherche du Temps Perdu*, she'd seen a flicker of emotion on Gabrielle's face, followed by a single tear trailing down her cheek. But when she'd told Henri and Hélène Arceneau, Gabrielle's nurse, neither had believed her. They were convinced Gabrielle's mind had been wiped clean by the stroke.

••• ◇ •••

Today, with *À la Recherche du Temps Perdu* finally finished, Zoe was going to read from a modern novel by an American. Gabrielle, Henri had assured her, spoke fluent English.

Hélène, a tall woman of a certain age, caught sight of the book Zoe was carrying when she entered the apartment. "I see you have recovered from Monsieur Proust."

"After reading more than a million of his words—*aloud*—I'll never be the same again," Zoe responded. "At least I finally have my voice back."

Gabrielle Challiot was from an old, well-to-do French family, and the furniture in her large apartment reflected the family's ancient lineage. An eighteenth-century settee upholstered in yellow-on-yellow damask. A mahogany George III corner armchair fronted by a matching ottoman. A Louis XVI breakfront inset with Sèvres porcelain plaques. A Louis XIII glass-fronted armoire stuffed with books bound in leather and gilt. Such elegance would have been intimidating except for the fact that the colors were warm and the chairs soft. This was a home for living, not a museum.

"I'm brewing an herbal tea for you," Hélène said as she escorted Zoe to Gabrielle's room. "I'll bring it in as soon as it's ready. That should help lubricate your voice."

When Hélène opened the gilt-edged double doors, the green scent of a hundred plants rushed out to greet them. Before her stroke, Gabrielle had been a botanist, and Henri had done his best to furnish her sickroom with the plants she loved best. Lilies of the valley, daffodils, peonies, nasturtiums, irises, and dozens of non-blooming plants and grasses that Zoe, even with her plantation background, didn't recognize.

Only the street noise several stories below the open window reminded Zoe she wasn't in a garden. That, and the paintings. Not content with surrounding his wife with living things, Henri had lined the walls with Gabrielle's superb watercolors of sunflowers, pansies, and various grasses. So careful had been her attention to detail that in one painting of a spiky-leafed grass, she'd painted a tiny green spider. The spider was rendered so realistically that Zoe almost expected it to move.

But the true star in the room was Gabrielle herself. Alabaster skin, fire-colored hair splayed across a cream satin pillow. Despite her illness, a faint blush colored her cheeks. Zoe had been told Gaby had once been beautiful, but now her face reflected the ravages of years of illness. Yet Zoe remained convinced that the woman's mind was still there, trapped inside like a prisoner who yearned for escape.

As Zoe sat down in the chair next to the bed, she put aside her pity and forced cheer into her voice. "Good morning, Gabrielle! Today we start a new book from an American author, and I hope you enjoy it as much as I expect you will! It's *This Side of Paradise*, by F. Scott Fitzgerald."

She opened the book and began: "'Amory Blaine inherited from his mother every trait, except the stray inexpressible few that made him worthwhile. His father...'"

· · · ◇ · · ·

An hour later Zoe exited Henri's apartment and made her way to the taxi stand at the corner of boulevards Montparnasse and Raspail. She'd toyed with the idea of taking a train to Reims, but the idea of limping around a strange city asking strangers for directions didn't sound comfortable. For this trip, she needed a friend. And there was the proper friend, sitting in his vehicle just a few car lengths behind the official taxi stand.

"Avak!" she called. "Just the man I was looking for!"

Upon hearing his name, Avak turned around with a big smile. A big, handsome Armenian émigré with a magnificent moustache, he was an independent driver who ferried Parisians around in a black 1919 Avions Voisin motorcar nicknamed the Grim Reaper. The car did not always heed its driver's orders, and had survived several accidents its passengers almost didn't. But in a city long-practiced in the art of gouging naïve tourists, Avak's prices remained fair, and over the years, a warm friendship had developed between the two.

"Where I take you this beautiful day?" he said in his fractured French. A true man of the world, he spoke six different languages. He was fluent in Armenian, Turkish, Russian, and German, but the sentence structure of French and English still challenged him. Or so he wanted everyone to believe.

"Are you familiar with Reims?" Zoe asked, as he helped her into his temperamental car.

"No expert, but have driven many peoples in past. Very pretty church there, but bombed bad during war. You want see?"

"I've heard of that poor cathedral, but I have other business today. Do you, by any chance, know of the Sauser family, and the location of their château?"

The smile turned into a laugh. "Edgard Sauser! Yes, yes! He famous for being crazy, but not so much famous as his cousin. Cendrars's poetry your great love?"

Zoe's enjoyment of poetry tended toward the American Transcendentalists such as Ralph Waldo Emerson and Helen Hunt Jackson, but she murmured a vague assent. After learning about Cendrars's connection to the lost Chagall oil paintings, she'd tried reading his work—she'd found a copy of *Prose du Transsibérien et de la Petite Jeanne de France* on her bookshelves—but had developed no "great love" for any of it. As Kiki had stated, his work was too travelogue-ish.

"So now we are off to the wonderful Reims!" Avak cried. With a honk and a growl, the Grim Reaper pulled away from the curb and headed through *La Cité* until the buildings thinned and the countryside began.

Zoe didn't leave Paris often, the city's many pleasures being enough for her, but as they drove through green fields and lush forests, the aromas of fresh *everything* served as a time machine, sending her back to Beech Glen again. In late July, the cottonfields were alive with pale pink flowers, which would soon drop off, revealing the white cotton bolls waiting to be picked. As soon as that happened—usually in August—Silas Hansen, the plantation's overseer, would round up some field hands to fill the long cotton sacks dragging behind them. At this time, the lonely fields would swarm with human life.

The day before Zoe's eighth birthday, she had snuck into one of the fields to watch the picking. Ignoring the frowns of the field hands, she'd crept up to one plant that was almost as tall as she was, and pulled the white fluff out of its bolls. *Ouch!* Sharp-edged slivers of bolls and seeds marred the plants' cloud-like softness and pricked her palm. Belatedly, she realized why most field hands wore gloves.

One of the pickers, a dark-skinned girl about her own age, frowned at her. "Go home, White Girl, before Silas sees you and tells your Mam and Pop."

She'd scowled at the girl, not wanting to obey anyone, not even a busy field hand, but she knew she was right. Silas would tell on her and all hell would break lose—a white girl consorting with Negroes! And as it turned out, all hell did break loose.

But it would be ten more years before that happened.

··· ◇ ···

An hour after Zoe and Avak left Paris, the Grim Reaper attempted to investigate the base of a granite viaduct. Fortunately, no human was injured by the auto's curiosity, so they were able to continue on until they finally arrived at the cathedral city of Reims.

When Avak reached Edgard Sauser's château, Zoe was shocked to see how much it had suffered during the War to End All Wars. The west wing was little more than rubble, with most windows boarded up. What had likely been a gracious lawn was now a carpet of weeds.

In the distance, silhouetted against a fleecy cloud, Zoe saw what was left of the famed Reims Cathedral poking up over a stand of oaks. Workers were busy putting the walls together again, and even from this distance, she could hear the bangs and clangs in their attempts to bring the great cathedral back to life.

Nothing had been done to repair the château.

"That is man you wish see, Zoe?" Avak's voice pulled her out of contemplation of the war's destruction.

"I don't see any man."

"By big tree."

Tearing her eyes away from the woefully damaged cathedral, she spotted Cendrars smoking a cigarette under the broad limbs of an oak. He looked much like the portrait Modigliani had painted of him in 1917, just older. Long face. Long nose. The full, sensuous lips of a libertine. However, now he had only one arm. A German mortar had removed the other.

Zoe refused to feel pity. This was the man responsible for the loss of more than one hundred and fifty Chagalls, a man who'd been too haughty to apologize. Cendrars didn't approach the car, expecting its occupants to come to him. And why not? For years he'd been the toast of Paris. Celebrities on the level of Picasso, Leger, and Cocteau—not to mention composers Satie and Stravinsky—treated his words as if they'd fallen from God's own lips.

Avak opened the car door for Zoe. "Don't like looks of man. I go with you."

"No, you stay here, but if he touches me, you have my permission to shoot him."

"Left gun home, I did."

Startled, Zoe gasped, "I was joking! You have a gun?"

"If need gun in future, tell before leave town." No smile.

Jesus. You think you know someone, then suddenly you find out you don't know them at all. Throwing Avak a cautionary frown, she started the long walk across the ill-kempt lawn toward Cendrars. She cursed herself for not wearing her built-up shoes, because as she neared him, she noticed his merciless eyes.

Raising her voice, she asked, "You are Blaise Cendrars?"

"If I am not, you have hurt your leg for nothing, Mademoiselle." His voice was deep, his French melodious.

She refused to be intimidated. "My name is Zoe Barlow, and I have come all the way from Paris to find out what happened to Marc Chagall's paintings."

He didn't answer right away, just exhaled a smoke ring, which floated up into the oak's branches. After the ring dissipated, he said, "Gone to collectors. Hardly a secret."

Stung by his indifference, Zoe said, "Not true. I recently came into possession of several Chagalls, and I did not buy them from a collector or a gallery. I found them in a scrapyard."

"Then someone could not tell good art from bad. That is the way of the world and always will be."

"I don't care about the way of the world. If the paintings I found escaped your greedy hands, others might have, too."

"Then let us hope they found homes worthy of them. Does the mademoiselle wish a cigarette?"

"I don't smoke."

He blew another ring of smoke into the air, where it hung just below the oak's branches. "Smoking calms the nerves."

"I *am* calm."

A hint of a smile on those sensuous lips. "You are a liar. Good. I like liars. They are much more interesting than those who speak the boring truth. Tell me another lie, my pretty mademoiselle, such as why you walk with a limp. Were you, too, shot by the Germans? So many women were. And much worse."

Scowling, Zoe said, "I fell out of a tree when I was eight years old." *Why was she telling him this?*

The faint smile vanished. "Boring."

While a half mile crawl over rocks and horse shit while suffering from a compound fracture could hardly be described as "boring," Zoe let the comment go. Unlike most other poets, whose lives were dedicated to Truth, Cendrars feasted on lies. The biggest lies were those he spun about himself: that he'd studied medicine at Bern; that he'd stoked coals on the Trans-Siberian railroad; that he'd played piano in a Spanish brothel; that he'd mined for gold in California; that he'd traveled across Europe with Gypsies; that after a mortar strike during the war, he'd amputated what was left of his own arm.

No one would ever know if any of those things were true because as Cendrars himself once stated, "There is no truth. There is only action."

With such a man, Zoe decided it was best to stick to the topic at hand. "Forget about my boring leg. Chagall was your best friend. Why did you steal from him?"

"Do I own the words I produce? Does a painter own his brush-strokes?" He looked at her hands, where for the past two days she'd been trying to scrub away the Prussian blue that discolored a finger-nail. "Ah. I see I misspeak. Does a painter own *her* own brushstrokes?"

"Bolshevik, are you?" she asked.

"All property is theft."

"But Chagall trusted you!" she spat, aghast at his lack of conscience.

"War time is crazy time, Mademoiselle. Many people die, and I thought my friend was one of them. So did La Ruche's concierge, who in her goodness of heart allowed those who'd been displaced by the fighting to move into the vacant studios while their former residents fought off the Hun. Am I to be blamed if I believed it was better for Chagall's paintings to wind up safe in a collector's hands than to be shit on by war orphans?" His cigarette having burned to his fingers, he crushed its embers between thumb and forefinger, then tossed the butt to the ground. All without the slightest sign of discomfort.

Zoe wasn't impressed. "When you found out he was still alive, why didn't you help him reclaim them? At the very least, why won't you apologize for your error?"

So swiftly that it was hard for her to track, he reached into his pocket, took out another cigarette, and one-handedly lit it. After a deep inhale, another smoke ring flirted with the oak. "One does not apologize for deeds of charity."

"Charity is an odd synonym for theft."

Another deep inhale, another smoke ring. "Theft is an act of courage."

Zoe realized her trip to Reims had been a waste of time and money. Blaise Cendrars still felt no remorse, but at least she'd tried. Now she might as well admit defeat and go home. Not giving him the courtesy of an *adieu*, she turned away and limped across the ruined lawn toward the safety of Avak and the Grim Reaper.

Cendrars called after her, "Courage, Mademoiselle! In this lousy life you need nothing else!"

Without turning her head, she yelled back, "Bullshit, you phony!"

··· ◊ ···

It was dark when Avak delivered her back to Le Petit Bibelot, and Zoe was so tired and stiff she could barely walk. She'd planned on painting this evening, but as she collapsed into the welcoming arms of her horsehair sofa, she knew it was hopeless. Her mind was awhirl with things she should have said to Cendrars, regret for things she did say.

That night she dreamt of Henri, of his strong embrace, his body moving slowly in time with hers, the words of love whispering softly into her ear.

"I love you, too," she whispered back, feeling her fulfillment near. "Whatever happens."

She looked into his eyes, but instead of seeing Henri, she saw Blaise Cendrars.

Chapter Ten

—— Gabrielle ——

July 1924
Paris

Is a woman still a woman if she cannot move or speak or show love to her husband?

This is the question I have asked myself for—what?—five years now? Four? The first thing you learn when you are struck down is that time is not immutable; it shifts. Some days are longer than others, some days shorter. It is the same with the hours, the minutes, the seconds.

Am I still the Gabrielle who used to smile in the summer sun, who used to walk busily through forests and grass, who found joy in her plants and in her husband's arms?

I pray that may yet be true, and so every day I concentrate on moving a different part of my body. An arm. A hand. A finger.

Or a foot. A toe.

It is a painful business but one I must busy myself with if I want to rejoin my husband in life.

I am fortunate to have Henri. He has created this plant-filled bower for me, surrounded me with so many things I love. My plants. My paintings. My books. Although I cannot read the books themselves—how could I, when I can no longer hold them—he has brought a woman to read to me when he cannot. She is an American and is reading me a terrible book written by another American, Fitz-something. Her accent sometimes makes me want to laugh, but then how can I laugh when I cannot even speak?

God must love me, though, because He has sent me a true friend, one who does not lust after my husband like the American woman does. Instead, He has given me a tiny creature who brightens my day when I am alone.

And I am usually alone, except for my sweet, green Odile.

Chapter Eleven

── Zoe ──

Zoe was painting away her horror at dreaming of sex with the vile Cendrars when her phone rang. Three shorts, one long—her personal party line signal.

Setting down her brush, she ran to answer. She picked up before the fourth ring. "Zoe Barlow here."

"I know you're probably working," Hadley Hemingway said, "but I just wanted to remind you we're on for lunch today. Noon, Cloiserie des Lilas. I just finished having breakfast with Hem, and seeing how forgetful you've been lately, I took this chance to use Lilas's phone. You're okay with me bringing Bumby, aren't you?"

"Oh, of course, I..."

There was a noise, something like a click, then an imperious voice in French. "Who is this on my telephone? Is that Zoe Barlow, the American? Hang up this second, Mademoiselle, because I want to call my son. He's coming over tonight, and I need him to bring a bottle of Château Margaux. I'm completely out."

Madame Tailler again. No matter how often Zoe gently reminded her, the bossy old widow hadn't yet developed the laissez-faire attitude necessary for a peaceful party line. Not wanting to start off her day with an argument, Zoe quickly said to Hadley, "Noon. Lilas. Meet you there," and hung up. She almost wished the interruption had come from the mysterious woman who always seemed to be crying. Perhaps whatever incident had been bothering her was now fixed.

At noon Zoe sat on the private patio at La Cloiserie des Lilas, bouncing little Jack "Bumby" Hemingway on her knee, mimicking his giggles with her own. Through its usual magic, painting had dulled the revulsion she'd felt over her dream of Cendrars, and she was able to enjoy the delights of a clear, sunny day.

"So then, what did Hem say?" she asked Hadley, who was looking especially pretty in a navy suit and matching cloche.

"Why, then he told that silly Blaise Cendrars exactly how he felt."

"Such as? C'mon, Hadley, be more specific."

"Hem told him he wasn't only a thief but a bad poet, too."

Bumby giggled, as if he understood the insult.

As for Zoe, she'd never liked Hemingway, but she shrieked with delight. "And how did Monsieur Big Poet respond to that?"

"He just laughed and said no one ever died from a bad review."

Zoe was nodding her agreement at Cendrars's riposte, when Bumby grabbed a hank of her hair and put it into his mouth. *Was henna dye poisonous?* Not knowing for certain, Zoe carefully pulled her hair away from the exuberant boy.

"Cendrars was lucky Hem didn't throw his wine in his ugly face," Hadley said.

Zoe loved this. "Ah, well, gallons of wine get tossed in faces around Paris every day, but no one has died from that, either."

· · · ◇ · · ·

When one of the racier tabloids had dubbed Laurette Belcoeur "The Flea Market Beauty," the more conservative newspapers had leapt on it, and now Zoe's part in the investigation was fodder for them all. In its love for gossip, especially about beautiful women either alive or dead, Paris could be as shameless as Mercy, Alabama.

Just not as prissy.

Neither Hadley nor Zoe was immune to this schadenfreude. The two enjoyed eavesdropping on two upper-crust Brits professing outrage at Hemingway's "disrespectful" article about their team's less-than-stellar performance in the indoor bicycle races. One of the men resembled an overweight bulldog and was insisting that Ernest's press credentials be pulled.

Hadley was having a hard time not laughing at this. As for the French, they were too busy congratulating themselves over their fencing wins to worry about snippy newspaper articles.

Zoe aimed her ear toward a more generous American, who was talking about the upcoming swim finals and the physical beauty of its star swimmers, Duke Kahanamoku and Johnny Weissmuller. At the mention of Weissmuller, Zoe perked up. Wasn't he going to be competing the day Archie had tickets? For a moment her dread of sitting in the hot sun vanished as she envisioned a swimming pool filled with beautiful men. *Oh, wouldn't that be...*

"Stop daydreaming and pay attention!" Hadley's voice broke through Zoe's enjoyment of sleek male bodies clad in skimpy swimsuits.

"What?" she answered, still thinking about broad shoulders, tight bathing suits cradling firm male asses...

"I was saying you need to be more careful! Or have you already forgotten how you were nearly killed when..."

Zoe's chuckle interrupted her. "Oh, Hadley. That was two years ago! I've learned a few things since then." Such as to always keep her small Derringer close by. In fact, it was resting in her clutch bag right now.

Hadley showed no desire to stop giving unasked-for advice.

"From what I've heard, Chagall has accepted the fact that his paintings are gone for good, so why stir the waters?"

"I'm not stirring any waters. Anyway, let's forget about me. What's going on with you? Still working on your music?"

Before marrying Ernest, Hadley had planned on becoming a concert pianist, and Zoe, who'd heard her play on several occasions, admired her friend's concert-level talent. Even Ernest seemed supportive of his wife's ambitions. For once thinking of someone other than himself, he'd rented her a piano. Somehow, even with little Bumby tottering around and vying for her attention, Hadley managed to get in several hours' practice every day.

A woman must make her own life, Zoe mused, while listening to Hadley describe a particularly difficult Chopin étude. Husbands couldn't be counted on. Some committed suicide. Some died in wars. Some deserted their wives and children.

Problems occurred even in good marriages. Hadley should know, because her marriage hadn't been the same since she'd lost the only copy of a yet-unfinished novel Ernest had been working on. Although Zoe had found most of the manuscript, Ernest's resentment was eroding his marriage. Increasingly, he wanted to be the apple of every woman's eye.

Hadley might have been worried about Zoe, but Zoe was worried about Hadley.

· · · ◇ · · ·

Lunch had been pleasurable, but Zoe had an important business appointment, one she'd been dreading for some time.

She hadn't seen Hervé Raez, her supposed "guardian," in a year, and now, with her August birthday looming, it was time for the summing up. Next month she would turn twenty-four and come into the inheritance left by her French grandmother.

The monthly remittance she'd been receiving from Beech Glen had once seemed adequate, but no longer. Costs were rising in France, both for wine and for food. And then there was the money she cabled once a month to the Pinkerton Detective Agency. If it hadn't been for Zoe's poker winnings and the occasional sale of a painting, she wouldn't have been able to continue hosting what had become known as her weekly *Salon du Pitié*—Salon of Pity— where she fed her needy artist and poet friends. If the salons were to continue, she needed more money.

Theoretically, Zoe would come into several thousand American dollars on her birthday, but Brice, her unforgiving brother, had been determined to punish Zoe even further for sullying the family's honor. To ensure she suffered enough, he'd chosen one of the biggest scoundrels in Paris to manage her grandmother's bequest. God only knew how much of the original five figures remained. A hundred? Ten bucks? Loose change?

When Monsieur Raez's ancient secretary ushered Zoe into his office in the 12th arrondissement, the scoundrel was waiting. He was pushing seventy now, and because of a severe weight loss, his lined face had developed the drooping jowls of a basset hound. His office had aged along with him. Scarred wooden desk. Cracked leather chairs. Fly-speckled windows. A rug so thin she could see the floorboards beneath.

Judging from the rags Raez wore, Zoe figured she was the only client the old thief had left.

"*Bonjour,* my beautiful little Zoe," Raez said, kissing her hand.

"*Bonjour* back, my handsome guardian." She settled herself into the visitor's chair, having long since stopped resenting him. The man was what he was. Might as well expect a yak to turn into a racehorse. Prepared for bad news, she forced a smile. "I have a busy evening planned, so let's be quick about this."

His own smile revealed a mouthful of brown teeth. "Oh, yes. It's the day you hold your *Salon du Pitié,* when you feed all the starving artists of Paris."

"Someone has to do it or they might start holding up banks. Just tell me how broke I'm going to be." She bestowed a fond look on the old rascal. Not only did he look ancient, he looked sick. She hoped it was nothing serious, nothing a few stolen dollars couldn't fix.

Raez lifted a scraggly eyebrow. "Broke?"

"I'm a realist."

Those basset hound folds drooped into a frown. "Have you not been comfortable during your years in Paris? I mean, apart from your involvement in that unfortunate situation two years ago."

An unfortunate situation that had ended with ugly scars on Zoe's hands and a murderer's trip to the guillotine.

Loathe to dwell on past history, Zoe answered, "I've been comfortable enough to share my good fortune with others, and now I wish to know how long I can continue to do so. Can we get down to it, then? Just tell me what, if anything, is left of my grandmother's bequest."

He sucked his brown teeth and scrambled through some papers on his ancient desk. "You are much too young to have lost your faith in your fellow man."

She almost laughed. "Yeah, well..."

Raez finally found the papers he was looking for. With a sigh, he flipped through the pages, glanced quickly at the last one, then put them down. When Zoe didn't touch them, he said sorrowfully, "The remaining amount is on the bottom line of the last page. My heart is broken to tell you that the past few years have been poor, financially speaking, and for that I apologize. You being an American, I thought it best to invest in a few American companies when I visited my son in New York last year. And of course, I've put you into some French companies, such as Renault and Citroën, since you appear to have made Paris your permanent home.

"But America... Such a strange place in which to do business!" His jowls wobbled. "I was certain that little film company in Hollywood—Goldwyn Pictures—would do well, but they've shown little gain so far. Perhaps not all is lost. I've heard they've gotten together with those Mayer people and are planning to make bigger films. But you know these artist types." Here he shrugged. "No business sense whatsoever."

A movement out of the corner of her eye caught Zoe's attention. When she looked, she saw a fat-bellied mouse returning her stare.

"Shoo!" Zoe hissed.

The mouse didn't move.

"Pay no mind to Gigi," Raez said, waving away Zoe's concern. "She has a young family to feed, so I give her a morsel from time to time." After blowing a kiss at the mouse, he opened a desk drawer and pulled out a hunk of cheese an inch square. The mouse crept forward, then took it daintily from his fingers.

Zoe stared in stupefaction as the mouse squeaked a *Merci*, then pitter-pattered with the cheese into a barely hidden hole, where a chorus of squeaks welcomed her.

Raez cleared his throat. "You feed stray cats and dogs, I hear. Dirty creatures! Such generosity must cost you a pretty penny, so perhaps you could cut back there?" Finally noticing she hadn't bothered to look at the accounting figures, he inched the stack of legal-sized papers closer to her.

"I will continue to feed stray cats and dogs, as well as stray artists and poets." Zoe tried not to sound sarcastic, but it was difficult. She was going to be flat broke; she just knew it. Maybe *she* would turn bank robber!

Raez tsk-tsked. "A fool and her money, eh? My little joke. But to repeat, I fear for your future if you keep giving your money away. Paris is still recovering from the war, so the economy is not to be trusted. It will doubtless get worse. At least you'll still have that monthly remittance from your family. What's left of your grandmother's bequest isn't much, since her estate was pretty much decimated during the war. Château and all."

Sighing, Zoe picked up the stack of papers and flipped through them until she arrived at the last page: the Final Judgment. Steeling herself, she looked at the bottom line.

Blinked.

Looked again.

Blinked again.

Frowning, she looked up at Raez and said, "This can't be right."

He began apologizing again. "Not all car companies are created equal, it seems. Monsieur Ford has begun a very strange method of manufacturing, one that I find highly foolish, so you might wish to cash in those bonds and..."

She cut him off. "This figure doesn't support a word of what you've been saying."

The long face he pulled made him look more like a basset hound than ever. "You know how much I care for you, dear Zoe, and it grieves me not to be able to give you better news. But it was the best I could do, and for that I sincerely apologize."

"Stop apologizing."

"But I am so sorry that I could not..."

She leaned forward. *"Why do you keep apologizing when you've quadrupled my inheritance?"*

His long face grew longer. "But I would have done so much better if I hadn't indulged in my taste for long shots. And I have to confess that more than once I fell victim to my love for the racetrack and borrowed a few francs from your account. Oddly enough, those were the only times I actually won, so when I put the money back, I added a few more francs in appreciation for the loan. I shouldn't have borrowed the money in the first place, so if you want to report me to the Financial Crimes branch of the

Sûreté, I will not blame you. My life is in your hands, dear girl, along with my apologies. Oh, my! Now I find that I must apologize for apologizing, and for that I am very, very sorry."

With no words left, Zoe just sat there and stared at him.

··· ◇ ···

On the way home, Zoe picked up three bottles of Clos Haut-Peyraguey. Tonight, her friends would share in her good fortune. Tomorrow she'd send another cable to the Pinkerton Detective Agency. She could double their services now and speed up the search for her missing daughter.

Her baby *couldn't* be dead!

But then she started to remember that horrible night at Beech Glen—her wailing baby, her own sobs—when a screech of tires snapped her back to the present. She'd inadvertently stepped off the curb into the path of a Citroën.

"Watch where you're going, idiot!" the driver shouted at her in English. A tourist. Probably here to see the Olympics.

"Sorry," Zoe said, stepping back onto the sidewalk, vowing to be more careful.

When she finally arrived safely at Le Petit Bibelot, Madeline was still slaving away in the kitchen, creating a feast fit for the nobility, if not actual kings. Several choices of crudités, several pâtés, two cold chickens with herbs, baguettes, fruit tarts, and dozens of macarons purchased from the boulangerie on rue Odessa. Madeline greeted her good news with a hearty swig of an already-opened bottle of Pauillac.

"You will no longer have to buy your clocks at flea markets," Madeline said. "Now you can shop at Le Bon Marché and leave the criminal investigations to Henri and his bunch."

"Hmm." While Zoe appreciated Madeline's concern, she knew that solving the murder of a flea market vendor wasn't high on the

Sûreté's list as long as the Olympics were in town. Pickpocketing was way up, as were drunken brawls over which team should have won which match.

But not all drunken brawls were the same.

One brawl, this one between a German and an American at Au Lapin Agile, had resulted in the German's death. While the American's friends swore the victim had accidentally fallen onto the rock that had bashed in the German's brains, the investigating surgeon disagreed. The rock had been thrust, not fallen upon.

None of this would have mattered if there hadn't been political consequences attached to the rock. Germany was in the process of receiving a huge loan from the U.S. to be used to help settle Germany's thirty-three billion dollars in war reparations, à la the Treaty of Versailles. France, which would receive most of those reparations, desperately needed the money to rebuild its shattered infrastructure. Once it received the money, France had promised to withdraw their troops in the Ruhr region, and all would be peace and love throughout the world until the end of time.

Henri's superiors had strongly hinted that regardless of the surgeon's findings, they considered the rock—a neutral force—to be the killer, not the partisan American. Compared to this political snake nest, the murder of a flea market vendor counted for little.

This injustice made Zoe furious, but to placate her worried housekeeper, she said, "You don't have to worry about me, Madeline. I've learned my lesson. No more murder investigations."

Madeline was busy chopping and cooking, so she couldn't see Zoe's crossed fingers.

Chapter Twelve

Zoe was engrossed in adding a purple wash on a shadow when she heard footsteps behind her.

"You through cooking already, Madeline?" she said, not turning her face away from the canvas.

"I don't think your artist friends would appreciate Wiener schnitzel." A soft voice, not Madeline's.

With a shriek of joy, Zoe dropped her brush and turned around. "Lee-Lee!!!"

"Hi, Big Sis." Leeanne Margaret Barlow Carrolton stepped back before her dark gray dress got smeared with purple.

Zoe hastily wiped her hands on a paint rag. God forbid Lee-Lee's controlling husband, Jack, would spot any sign his wife had visited the Barlow family's infamous black sheep. Now more or less clean, Zoe threw her arms around her sister.

"It's been too long," she said, fighting back happy tears. "I take it I'm still *verboten*?"

"I'm afraid so."

This close to her younger sister, Zoe could see new worry lines at the edge of Lee-Lee's blue eyes, but even that couldn't detract from her sister's blond beauty. Marriage had been good to her, although she'd married a man who, because of his German heritage, still believed that Germany should have won the war. "But Lee-Lee, it's July, and here you are, covered up like a nun. High neck, long sleeves, hem all the way down to your ankles. Jack still telling you how to dress?"

Some of Lee-Lee's brightness dimmed. "Let's not talk about Jack. Let's just be sisters-too-long-apart."

Zoe felt a pang of guilt at her own insensitivity. "You're right. I won't mention him again. We'll just have happy talk. Why don't you tell me everything that's been happening at Beech Glen since I've been exiled. Now and then I received a letter from you that Aunt Verla was able to pass along, but not often enough. In your last letter, you told me Annabelle had a new suitor."

Zoe had hoped the story was true. Then her stepmother would marry away from Beech Glen and take up residence at a different plantation, leaving only one bridge to unburn: the estrangement from her brother Brice.

"Aunt Verla's rheumatism keeps her hands from writing too many letters or sending along mine to you, and as for Brice, well, Jack and I visited Beech Glen last winter, and he's pretty much the same as always. Drinks too much, carouses too much, and even with Prohibition, he has no difficulty getting whatever kind of liquor he wants. Lately it's been some foul-smelling whiskey smuggled all the way from Scotland. He gave me a sip and I almost puked.

"As for our beloved stepmother, Annabelle sent her suitor packing when she found out his Blue River plantation was about to be auctioned off by the taxman. You know what a mess that place has always been. Too many cotton crops over too many years, so the soil's pretty much done. Say what you will about Awful Annabelle, she at least knows better than to marry a bankrupt."

Zoe shook her head sadly. "You have time for coffee?"

"Nope, I'm jittery enough already. I was only able to sneak over here for a few minutes because Jack's meeting with some business associates, and I have to make sure I'm back at our hotel by the time he returns." To point this up, she pulled a tiny watch out of her purse, looked at it, and frowned. "We've only got about fifteen minutes left' then I have to run."

Zoe hoped her disappointment didn't show. "Well, what'll happen if Beech Glen goes under like Blue River did?"

"Then Brice would have to get a job. Not that he knows how to do anything. He always left the running of the place to Silas Hansen, and with Silas gone..."

At the name, Zoe stiffened.

Silas Hansen, Beech Glen's overseer. The man who'd caught Zoe's baby girl when Annabelle threw her across the room. For a moment, Zoe was almost choked by the memory of that freezing basement and her newborn daughter's cries.

"Get rid of it!" Annabelle had shouted to Silas.

Silas obeyed.

As soon as the baby had been taken away, Annabelle and Brice left Zoe alone, to bleed out or survive. When they exited the basement, Zoe heard Lee-Lee cry out, "Where's my Sissie! I want my Sissie! Why'd you lock Sissie in the basement?"

"She's not in the basement, you little fool," Brice growled. "She left for France to live with our Gram. Unlike you, Zoe's all grown up now."

"If she went to Gram's, why didn't she take me?" No more words, just sobs. Since that horrible night—six years and a million tears ago— thanks to Aunt Verla's machinations, they'd found each other again.

But Zoe's baby remained lost.

"If anyone knows what happened to my baby, Silas Hansen would," she said. "We have to find him."

Lee-Lee shook her head. "Some say he moved to Texas or California; nobody knows for sure. I thought that detective agency you hired would have found out by now. Not that it would make any difference. That poor baby is..."

"*Don't you dare say it!*"

Lee-Lee paled. "Oh, my God. I never meant to..."

Recovering herself, Zoe hugged her sister. "I know, sweetie, I know. I just..."

Wiping away a tear, Lee-Lee said, "There is one new thing I heard from one of the field hands. She said that right after Anabelle and Brice shanghaied you away, there was a cross-burning in front of Silas's cabin. Not being stupid, he skedaddled."

This came as a shock. "Why the cross-burning? Silas is White!"

"The field hand said there were whispers about him getting mixed up with some Negro woman in town." She flushed, then added, "You know how awful people can be about that kind of thing."

Zoe did. "Did anyone mention the woman's name? Or how Silas came to know her?"

"I'm not sure, but someone once said she was known as 'Dot.' Did you know a Negro woman by that name?"

The air disappeared from the room, and the earth slowed its spin. Speckles danced in front of Zoe's eyes. "Dot" had been Dorothy's nickname. Dorothy, Pete's mother. Dorothy, Zoe's mother-in-law. Dorothy, her lost baby's grandmother.

As soon as Zoe's vision cleared, she said, "If there was a Klan burning at Silas's house, did they do the same thing to Dot? Or worse?"

"They burned her house to the ground. The barn, too. You know the Klan never forgave her for setting up that school for the Negro children. But she was able to get out in time. At least that's what I heard, and I pray to God it's true."

Keep steady, Zoe. Inhale. Exhale. "Anybody know where Dot went?"

"Hopefully some place less hateful than Mercy, Alabama."

As soon as Lee-Lee left, Zoe headed for the telegraph office.

··· ◇ ···

By seven, when the guests began arriving for Zoe's Salon du Pitié, Zoe had gotten control of herself and was able to pay the proper attention to her friends. Despite her salon's name, not all of the attendees were poor. In fact, some had achieved a certain amount of success. Among them were several old friends who would use this evening for gossiping, not just feeding their plump bellies. These lucky few included Kiki, who never missed a chance to dig the dirt; Cubist painter Eloise Packard; sculptor Karen Wegner; one-eyed Dominique Garron; and portrait artist Archie Stafford-Smythe, who wanted everyone to know he'd spent the day rushing from one Olympic venue to another.

"Do not take the Métro!" he cautioned everyone. "It's hell down there, and you'll be lucky not to get pissed on!"

Tourists' bladders had developed into an unforeseen problem, chiefly where American women were concerned. Women were horrified by the public toilets at the Métro stations, which were not divided into male and female. It was all one big happy family down there, with women expected to piss in the same open room as men.

There had been accidents.

Not interested in hearing tales of tourists' fussy bladders, Zoe wandered over to a different group. They were buzzing about the latest Picasso scandal.

It seemed that a tourist—accounts differed whether the tourist was a Greek or a Scot—had bought a Picasso sketch at a flea market, then when he got it back to his hotel room, noticed something amiss. "Picasso" had been spelled "Piccaso." Since the seller at the flea market had already packed up and left, the

Greek-or-Scot then tracked Picasso to his studio and demanded the signature be "fixed." At this point, two different versions of the sorry tale diverged. In the first version, Picasso had scrolled FAKE in six-inch-high letters across the sketch. In the second version, he'd wadded up the drawing and stuffed it into the Greek's-or-Scot's mouth.

Knowing firsthand of Picasso's temper, Zoe was betting on the second.

After listening to more delicious tales of artists acting badly, Zoe decided that it was time to give the tarot readings her salon had become famous for.

The last time she'd been at Shakespeare & Company, she'd purchased a beautifully illustrated tarot card deck that was supposed to tell the future. The bookstore owner, Sylvia Beach, didn't normally stock such things, but this one—the Waite-Rider deck—had been illustrated by the half-Jamaican, half-British artist Pamela Colman Smith, who'd studied art in New York. Sylvia, a strong supporter of female artists and writers, had ordered several packs. Zoe bought one and now enjoyed a reputation as Paris's best tarot reader.

"Best," but not necessarily truthful, because every one of Zoe's readings promised fame, fortune, and the greatest of health. To make certain of happy outcomes, she'd stacked the deck.

Setting up at a small table near the kitchen, she began with Katrina Weisensel, a young painter she'd met at La Rotonde a week earlier. She liked the girl's style—or lack thereof. Although many of the artists at her salon were enjoying their best meal in days, most still looked chic. Paris being Paris, they wore their best, albeit patched, outfits, so unless you examined them carefully, they appeared little different than those of Montparnasse's fashion-conscious boulevardiers.

Not so Katrina.

Instead of dressing up for the occasion, Katrina wore rags. *Literal* rags. The hem on her black, calf-length skirt drooped, and her cheap print blouse was missing a button. Two pigeon feathers stuck in her red hair served as a hat. But Zoe, being from Alabama, had run across dire poverty before, and something about Katrina's get-up struck her as disingenuous, almost as if her dishabille had been carefully curated. Was she dressing down for Montparnasse? Or was she an unlucky woman like Zoe herself, thrown out of her family home? Judging from Katrina's slight accent—where she sometimes pronounced her *W*s like *V*s—that home would have been in Germany.

The tarot reading displayed the usual spread of wands, cups, pentacles, and swords, dotted with the Major Arcana cards dealt right side up, a spread the worst pessimist couldn't misinterpret. When Zoe turned over the final card, Katrina clapped her hands in delight. The card was The World, a naked dancer surrounded by a wreath made up of ribbons and vines. In the corners of the card were the emblems of Earth, Air, Fire, and Water.

"As you can see, Katrina, all your wishes will be granted," Zoe announced. "The world is yours!"

"It's about time my luck turned," Katrina said, laughing. "Ever since the war, Paris has been less than friendly to anyone vit a German accent. They have no way of knowing that my family arrived here three years before the war started. The Weisensels killed no one."

Katrina's escort, poet-photographer Yves Santigny, sounded less than happy. Zoe had been watching the two and wasn't sure she liked him.

Yves frowned at his girlfriend. "I wouldn't take that tarot reading seriously if I were you."

Katrina shrugged. "If the last card had been Death, or the Burning Tower, or the Nine of Swords, I certainly wouldn't! But since it was the World and everything in it? I *want* to believe that, and so I vill!"

With this, she crossed her surprisingly muscular arms over her chest.

Yves scowled. "I've heard that Zoe stacks the deck."

Zoe didn't respond, but Katrina told her, "However it happened, Zoe, thank you for cheering me up."

"There you go again," Yves grumped. "Believing what you want to believe, which is seldom the truth. Look at where you're living! In a basement apartment with no light to speak of. And you have rats."

Katrina laughed again. "No rats; my cat takes care of that. Anyway, my current address is all I can afford until my paintings start selling. But you're right in one respect. I'm so broke I'd even velcome a part-time job if I could find one."

Given Yves's dark hair and dark eyes, he would have been nice looking if not for his all-too-frequent frown. "Once this Olympic madness dies down, you may get lucky, but in my opinion, your paintings, although good, need more structure. And since you already do much of your painting in my flat, which enjoys north light, you should move in with me. Then I could teach you what poets and photographers know about structure. Come to think of it, you should stop..."

His nagging tone irked Zoe, so she put the tarot cards down and interrupted what threatened to become a lecture.

"Why are men are always telling women what they *should* do?" she asked, staring pointedly at Yves. "Even photographers like yourself, who *should* know better." Turning to a giggling Katrina, she continued, "But considering the wonderful future your reading forecasts, tell me more about your work. Do you follow any particular school? Cubism? Surrealism? Or..." Here Zoe took a breath. "Dada?"

Katrina wrinkled her nose at the word *Dada*, further endearing her to Dada-hating Zoe.

"I'm trying to do something original," Katrina said, "maybe even start my own school for other painters to copy. As a painter yourself, you know how things are. These days, few galleries vant to take a chance on work by someone with a German name. I have a double cross to bear, too. You know how galleries treat us females, right? They take it for granted women can paint nothing but sweet babies and kittens. Sometimes they're even more prejudiced against women than they are of Germans! Maybe I should disguise myself as a man, wear a stage beard, and lower my voice. Like this."

In a gravelly baritone, she recited a few lines from one of Yves's poems, something about a woman's breasts being twin Mount Everests waiting to be conquered.

Yves didn't appreciate his girlfriend's mockery. "Who are you to decide whether poems should rhyme or not? Keep on with that, and I'll bar you from my north light forever!"

When Katrina laughed again, Zoe realized Yves must have made that particular threat before but had never acted upon it.

Having faced down a similar problem, Zoe sympathized with Katrina. "Even in avant-garde Paris, art dealers consider women's work to be second-rate before seeing it," she said. "That's why we seldom see women's creations hanging on gallery walls."

Across the room, she saw several women nodding. Deciding this had been enough moaning about women's lot in life, Zoe changed the subject. "But back to francs, and the lack thereof, Katrina. You said you'd be amenable to a part-time job. Have you tried the shops? Surely with the Olympics crowd here the shops must be begging for extra help."

Katrina raised her hands so Zoe could see the paint embedded between several fingernails. "Not from artists, they're not. And before you suggest the art supply stores, which of course are more sympathetic to dirty fingernails, I've checked every one in the city, and they're all fully staffed. At least I managed to get some vork done before these Olympics started."

Given Katrina's unusual appearance and outgoing nature, Zoe decided to take a chance. "Do you, by any chance, know the difference between a Seth Thomas and an Ansonia?" she asked.

"You mean the clocks? *Mein Gott!* I'm too broke to own either!" At Zoe's nod, she continued. "My father, God rest his soul, owned a clock repair shop in Munich, and he vas always talking about this one and that one. But that vas years ago, and tastes are more modern now." With a sly grin, she waved toward Zoe's new clock. "However, if I vas able to find something like that naughty art nouveau phallus clock of yours, I'd rob a bank to buy it."

"You don't own a clock?" Yves didn't seem happy about being left out of the conversation. "That explains why you're always late for everything!"

Ignoring him, Zoe asked Katrina what arrondissement she lived in and was gratified to learn she lived in the same arrondissement as the bereaved Veronique Belcoeur. "I know someone in that area who needs sales help." She described the flea markets run by two sisters—one recently deceased—adding that the surviving sister needed someone who could knowledgably sell clocks. Zoe was careful not to mention how Laurette had died.

All mirth left Katrina's face. "Wait! If you are talking about that pretty blond saleswoman, she would never hire me. A few days ago I went to that flea market to buy some cheap paintings so I could paint over them—bad paintings cost less than untouched canvasses, you know—and all it got me vas insulted!"

Oh, hell. Katrina herself had been the cause of Laurette's anti-German tirade! But perhaps Veronique didn't share her sister's prejudice. It was worth taking the chance.

"Look," she said to Katrina, "the woman who insulted you, she, ah, she no longer works at the clocks table. Her older sister may not have the same feelings for, ah, Germans. At least you can try. And if it doesn't work out, then there are other markets all across Paris."

For a moment, Katrina's face was unreadable, but then a smile returned. "Since that day I've thought of all the words I should have shouted at that pretty bitch, so if her sister gives me trouble, I'll say them all to her!" Then she turned serious again and declared that if all went well, she'd be interested as long as the job didn't cut into her painting time. "I'm serious about my vork."

Zoe beamed. "As well you should be. Lack of discipline has sabotaged more artists than lack of talent." After telling Katrina she'd be just a minute, she headed for her telephone. When she picked it up, a woman was already on the party line, her voice ragged with tears.

"I can't take much more, I really can't," she was telling someone. "Please! You have to help me!"

The woman on the other end of the line said, "You made your bed, my little Better-Than-the-Rest-of-Us mademoiselle! Now go lie in it!"

A click, followed by sobs. Seconds later, there was another click, and the line came free again. Before Zoe could signal the operator to place her own call, someone else on the party line picked up. Frustrated, and more than a little upset, Zoe put the phone down. The sobbing woman's plight reminded her too much of her own, when at the age of eighteen she'd begged for mercy in that dank Beech Glen basement. Her pleas had been rewarded with the same heartless command: *"You made your bed, Zoe, and now you're going to lie in it. But somewhere other than here!"*

If her stepmother had had her way, Zoe would have died during the birth. But she'd lived. And she prayed that, God willing, so had her baby.

Setting aside the memory, she said to Katrina, "I'll call Veronique tomorrow. Give me your address, and I'll let you know as soon as I've talked to her. It might take a while, though. She's, ah, had a death in the family."

An odd look passed over Katrina's face. "Wait! You said '*Veronique*'? Would that be Veronique Belcoeur? The bitch's sister?"

Zoe was taken aback. "You know Veronique?"

"My flat's in the basement of her building, in what vas probably once a janitor's closet. But what's this about Veronique's nasty sister dying?"

At this, several heads turned. Artists loved nothing more than to wallow in someone else's tragedy. Even the poet-photographer deigned to be interested in this female conversation.

Lowering her voice, Zoe asked Katrina, "Living in the same building, how could you not know that the two women were sisters?"

"Because they live six floors away from me! I rarely go out, just stay inside and paint. That's all a painter *should* do." Despite her words, her voice trembled. "Poor Veronique! She is a nice woman. Unlike her sister."

Katrina's boyfriend took advantage of her moment of weakness. "You've always been oblivious to what's going on around you, which is yet another reason you should move in with me!" Yves tried putting his arm around her, but Katrina shrugged him off.

"I'll take Veronique some flowers," she said. "Daisies, because they are so resilient. They grow anywhere, even between cracks in the cobblestones."

After a moment of respect for such a tender observation, Zoe asked, "Did you ever hear if Veronique's sister was having problems with anyone?"

Katrina shook her head. "Not then, no. Over the year I've lived there, I came to know only Veronique. But a few months ago, we vere in the washroom und she told me she worried about her sister's boyfriend. At the time I didn't know she was related to Mademoiselle Bitch. Anyway, Veronique said he'd accused her sister—she didn't give her sister's name then—of cheating on him. I got the impression the man vas a brute."

Although Vicomte Gervais du Paget had been grieving, Zoe remembered the tenderness with which he'd treated Veronique. Then she reminded herself that fancy titles didn't necessarily ensure decent behavior.

"Did he manhandle her? Shove her around? Or worse? Gervais seemed quite gentlemanly when I met him."

"Who's Gervais?" Katrina asked.

Zoe frowned. "Laurette's boyfriend. Or, rather, fiancé."

Katrina shook her head. "No, no. I meant the other one."

"What other one?"

After a quick look at Yves, Katrina said, "Veronique was talking about a man named Fabian. He owns a garage not far from here."

My God, Zoe thought, *Paris really was a small town.* "You're telling me Laurette had *two* fiancés? At the same time?"

Katrina looked puzzled. "The only fiancé I know about vas that man Fabian. Veronique told me he was rough with her sister a couple of times."

Zoe thought about that for a moment. Upon first meeting Fabian Napier, she'd liked the young mechanic, but she considered woman-beating a sin unworthy of forgiveness. There was nothing she could do about that now, other than to ask Henri to look at Fabian's past more closely.

Impatient with all this female complaining, Yves inserted himself back into the conversation. "I met Laurette once as I was entering the building to see Katrina. She—I mean Laurette—was just leaving, but I noticed both her arms were covered in bruises. Poor woman!" Suddenly all concern, he said to Katrina, "Even if you don't want to move in with me, you should still find a new place.

Somewhere safe, in case her murderer is still hanging around. You could be next."

Katrina scowled. "I'm not moving, and that's that. All I need is a cot and an easel. If he tries anything with me, I'll stab him in the eye vit the pointed end of a brush."

When Yves responded with another argument, Zoe's attention wandered. Flashing back to the day she'd found Laurette's body, she remembered the auto mechanic's lack of tears and his calm demeanor while phoning the police. She contrasted that with Vicomte Gervais du Paget's red-rimmed eyes. If Laurette had been juggling two fiancés at the same time, it was clear which one actually loved her.

Then again, it wasn't unknown for a man to kill the woman he professed to love. Even aristocrats were known to commit murder. Zoe looked down at the burn scars on her hands. One had even tried to kill *her*.

Pulling her mind away from the horrific memory, she decided to pay another visit to Veronique Belcoeur. While recommending Katrina as a possible sales clerk, she'd see how much she could find out about Laurette's two "fiancés."

She told Katrina she'd be in touch, then left her and the boorish Yves to join the other guests. As she listened to the latest gossip, she wondered about this possible new angle on Laurette's murder. As motives went, jealousy was one of the most common.

Zoe wondered if the weeping woman on her telephone party line had been caught up in such a situation. In Paris, at least, lovers weren't always of the opposite sex. Perhaps the crying woman had once been the older woman's lover but had left her for a fling with a different woman. Now she regretted it and wanted to be taken back, but the older woman refused.

It made sense. Jealousy could so easily turn into hate.

In the past few weeks, while navigating the bureaucracy of

obtaining a telephone, Zoe had learned that party lines weren't like addresses; they weren't necessarily distributed next door to each other. The crying woman could be living in any apartment building near Le Petit Bibelot, so Zoe would start keeping an ear out when visiting nearby shops. One day she might put a face to the voice and offer her some comfort.

After all, love is love.

In the meantime, what should she call her, since "the crying woman" was an unsatisfactory label? Before giving Katrina's tarot reading, Zoe had surreptitiously removed four negative cards from the deck. Death. The Burning Tower. The Devil. The Nine of Swords. The painting for the Nine of Swords was especially striking. Inked mainly in black and deep blues, the card portrayed a woman sitting up in bed, weeping. Above her, nine swords hung suspended.

Some tarot readers called the Nine of Swords *Niobe*. In Greek myth, Niobe was a king's daughter, whom the gods had cursed to weep forever because of her arrogance. This could be the name Zoe would temporarily use for her weeping party line neighbor until she discovered her true identity.

But amid all this darkness and loss, there remained a few points of light. Chagall's newfound paintings. And Katrina, because if the art-astute girl went to work at Veronique's sales table, no more Chagalls would ever again be used as wrapping paper. Talent always recognized talent.

On that note of satisfaction, Zoe dedicated herself to the convivial joys of her salon.

In a huddle near her studio door, she learned that ballet impresario Sergei Diaghilev was running into trouble with the sets for *Le Train Bleu*, his latest project. And that there was a rumor that Suzanne Lenglen, one of the female tennis players vying at the Olympics, was threatening to wear a barely-butt-covering tennis dress.

This juicy rumor was followed by the good news that Bal Nègre, a club that had begun life as a dance hall for West Indians, had begun attracting business from all over Paris. Zoe made a mental note to check out the place, possibly with Archie. Due to her bum leg, she seldom went dancing, but maybe it was time she tried the dance floor again. It would make for a nice outing, and it didn't matter how clumsy her steps looked. Not that she planned several nights out on the town, of course. Painters derived their ideas from their social circles, but if they spent too much time drinking and dancing, they didn't have time to paint.

Katrina Weisensel had been certainly correct there.

Zoe was still musing on the contradictions of living the creative life when she heard a curse, then a slap, and the sound of breaking glass. Kiki and her sometimes-lover Man Ray were fighting again. Sighing, Zoe went to break it up.

That night, Zoe had no dreams of Blaise Cendrars, just dreamscapes of Alabama whippoorwills singing at dusk. Every now and then their songs were interrupted by the cries of an infant abandoned in the forest.

When the sun rose, Zoe did, too, and her eyes were almost dry.

Chapter Thirteen

After a quick breakfast at La Rotonde, Zoe returned to her studio and pulled out her long-neglected set of watercolors. She'd made a mistake the other day by merely describing Chagall's paintings to Veronique without showing them to her. Time to rectify that.

A half hour later, she'd completed two watercolor sketches using Chagall's favorite themes: fiddlers on roofs and fluttering angels—everything minus his genius. Once the watercolors were dry, she tucked them into her leather portfolio. Then she loaded up her new piecework shopping bag with treats left over from last night's feast: a round of brie, half of a pâté, and three juicy pears. She added an unopened bottle of Clos Haut-Peyraguey to round out the now-reduced feast. Hopefully, these gifts would serve as an entrée to the Belcoeurs flat.

Exiting Le Petit Bibelot, Zoe couldn't help but notice the humidity in the air. Combined with a blazing sun, the day felt uncomfortably sticky, and although she wasn't interested in sports, she hoped the Olympics athletes would be able to overcome it. Sweat trickled down her bare arms as she bought a bouquet at the flower shop at the end of the street. By the time she arrived at the Belcoeurs' apartment building, her light cotton sheath was stuck to her back. At least she'd had sense enough to wear a straw bonnet with a wide brim; God forbid she break out in freckles.

The steep stairs were a horror, of course, and when she reached the final landing, she had to take a moment to recover. Breath finally caught and the worst of the pain eased, she knocked on the door. It was immediately answered.

After thanking Zoe profusely for her gifts, Veronique invited her in. The woman's long hair spilled out of its pins. Completing her state of disarray, her unstylish dress was dappled with stains.

"So kind," Veronique murmured, setting Zoe's offerings on a table. Her eyes weren't quite as red as they'd been during Zoe's first visit.

"How are you holding up?" Zoe asked softly.

"I am heartbroken, of course," Veronique answered after first clearing her throat. "And I am failing in...in..." She took a deep breath. "I am failing in my responsibilities. I should have set up our sales table this morning, but I just couldn't bring myself to do it. I don't know when..." She trailed off.

"It's the shock."

A nod. "Yes. That."

"Sometimes it helps to talk about these things."

"I... I..."

Zoe gave her a sympathetic smile. "Maybe you could start by telling me what your sister was like."

Some of Veronique's grief left her haggard face, and it immediately made her look years younger. "Everyone loved Laurette."

Such a claim couldn't be true. No one on Earth was loved by *everyone*. Zoe herself knew of one woman who despised Laurette. But she didn't point that out. "Even the nicest people sometimes fall out with others. Was there anyone in particular she was having trouble with?"

"Laurette was too sweet to have trouble with a soul." When Veronique said this, Zoe noticed a shifting of her eyes, a stiffening of posture.

Zoe would never have described Laurette as *sweet*. The young woman had proved herself an excellent businessperson, a mighty opponent when arguing a price for her wares. She'd known what was what, and what it was worth. Nothing *sweet* about that.

"Sweetness can sometimes be misinterpreted," Zoe offered.

Veronique's eyes met hers again. "Perhaps you are right. Fabian once told me she had a temper. And I have to admit, that was true. Especially when it came to Germans."

The Belcoeur flat looked even more overcrowded than before, and given the soggy day, the open windows provided little relief. Zoe felt claustrophobic. Still, she soldiered on. Laurette's nasty tirade about Germans notwithstanding, what woman didn't feel irritable at times? Why, Lee-Lee, Zoe's younger sister, was among the most docile of women, but even she could resort to anger when docility didn't get her what she wanted.

Then again, woman-beaters always blamed their victims, didn't they? She remembered Yves Santigny's description of the bruises on Laurette's arms.

It was time to ask the question. "Veronique, did you ever notice any bruises on your sister?"

As an answer, Veronique stretched her own arms forward. Her skin was sallow, but it was still easy to see bruising on each arm. "You can't lug cartons around without hurting yourself from time to time. Laurette's skin was so pale the bruises showed more on her."

Katrina's boyfriend, Yves, hadn't mention seeing any marks on Laurette's face, so maybe those bruises meant nothing. Still, his accusation provided an interesting pathway to explore. "Do you know if Fabian meant something in particular when he complained about Laurette's temper?"

A fierce look. "It was something he said just before she broke off their engagement."

"Engagement?" Zoe tried to look shocked. "Laurette was *engaged* to Fabian?"

Veronique nodded. "For three or four months. But after several arguments—he wanted to rush the marriage, she didn't—she decided to break it off."

Zoe made her next question seem no more than natural curiosity. "Was this around the time she started seeing Gervais du Paget? The, um, *vicomte*?"

So Mademoiselle Sweet had exchanged a garage mechanic for a *vicomte*! Laurette being a young woman who knew what was what, and what it was worth, she would have found the title "Vicountess" more attractive than "Madame Mechanic." The only puzzle was why a young woman of such beauty had been engaged to Fabian in the first place.

"About that time, yes. Fabian told me she..." Veronique took a deep breath, then continued. "Fabian accused her of being sneaky."

"Laurette? Sneaky? Did Fabian say why?"

"He said he knew she was seeing someone else, but she kept swearing she wasn't."

"What made him suspect her?" Only when Zoe asked the question did she realize how far she'd allowed herself to wander from the two reasons she was really here: to find more Chagalls, and to recommend Katrina Weisensel for a job.

Before she managed to change the subject, Veronique leaned forward and hissed, "He said he smelled another man on her."

Zoe blinked. *Surely, she didn't mean...*

Unaware of Zoe's discomfiture, Veronique continued, "Gervais wears some expensive man's cologne—something by Creed, I believe—but of course Fabian smells like grease and sweat."

Zoe tried again. "Well, that's hardly surprising, given Fabian's profession. But, um, I wanted to ask you something." She reached down, opened her portfolio, and pulled out her watercolor copies of Chagall's paintings. "Have you ever seen any paintings that looks like these?"

Veronique gave the watercolors a quizzical look. "Children's work? Sweet, but there is no market for children's art. Why would some mother want to buy another woman's child's work, when her own child could furnish her with all she wanted?"

Disappointed, Zoe returned the watercolors to the portfolio. When she started to tie up the cords that held it shut, Veronique leaned forward and said, "Wait. Could I see the painting with the violinist again?"

Zoe pulled the watercolor back out and handed it to her.

This time Veronique looked at the watercolor more carefully, and as she did, her expression morphed from puzzlement to one of recognition. Then she smiled. "Now that I think about it, I did once see something like this, a violinist sitting on a roof. Oh, yes! Only the one I used was on canvas, which is much stiffer than paper. It was done in oil and was wonderfully waterproof, and..."

"You say 'the one I used.' What does that mean?"

"The roof to our rabbit hutch blew away in a storm, so I used the child's painting to make a better one, and I nailed it securely all around the edges. I was proven right, because it didn't blow away like the old roof did."

Zoe sighed inwardly, then asked politely, "Do you remember when this happened?"

Veronique shrugged. "Two or three years ago, I think. We've gone through a lot of rabbits in that time. Do you like *lapin en cocotte*?"

"Rabbit stew? It was once my favorite, but tastes change. Now, back to that 'child's' painting, the one you used to protect the hutch. Do you remember how you came by it?"

Veronique gave her an incredulous look. "Of course I don't.

Who remembers where they find rags?! Although I can tell you that during the war, even rags weren't easy to find, so whenever they showed up, we used them!" Her lip lifted in contempt. "Far different than these days, when rich American women flood the streets wearing their dresses once, then throw them away so they won't be seen in them twice!" Noting the expression on Zoe's face, she exchanged the sneer for a servile smile. "But of course, I don't mean you, Mademoiselle Barlow. You live here among us, and you are famous for your charity. You understand the value of things, which is why Laurette was so happy to sell you another fine clock. Your taste is almost as exquisite as a French woman's."

Zoe let the backhanded compliment pass. "I have another question. After losing your lovely sister, will you still be able to continue running all three of your flea markets?"

"I will continue on, of course. That's what we French people do."

"But how will you be able to handle all the work? Laurette was..." She paused. How best to say it without sounding offensive? Given Laurette's beauty and savvy bargaining, Laurette had been a great asset at the sales table. "Your sister was so much help to you. I can hardly imagine the burden you must be carrying now. You must find help."

Veronique's eyes teared up. "For an American, you are wonderfully compassionate. And yes, you are right; I need to find help before I...before I..." She swallowed. "Mademoiselle Zoe, do you by any chance happen to know anyone...?"

Zoe beamed. "What a coincidence you should ask!"

It was only later that she remembered Laurette wasn't the first woman she knew with a temper: Katrina had one, too. And she'd been deeply insulted by a Belcoeur. Even more troubling was the memory of Katrina's muscular arms.

Chapter Fourteen

—— Gabrielle ——

July 1924
Paris

At one time in that other life I painted a leaf of grass upon which sat a delicate green Huntsman spider. I thought little more about it at the time.

Then I fell ill, lay unmoving in this soft bed, in this indoor garden of a boudoir, hardly able to think or feel. Who was I? What am I doing here? Why am I so alone?

One day the little spider that had once graced my painting appeared on my pillow, and I gave her a name.

Odile.

She has proven herself a faithful friend, cheering me daily, telling me of her own sweet dreams, her dead husband, her many children, her loves, her hates.

And so inquisitive! Almost like a child.

"Why do you have so many paintings of plants, Madame?" the spider had once asked.

"Because I am—or was—a botanist," I answered. "Before this

terrible thing happened to me, I spent almost as much time out of doors as your kind do, and I know the names of thousands of plants, in both colloquial French and in Latin."

"You must be very wise then," she'd said to me.

"Was. Now I know nothing."

But since those early days with Odile, I have grown wise. My name is Gabrielle Beauvoir Challiot. I was born in the mountain village of Les Saisies, the only child of Claudine Lemarr and Louis Beauvoir. Both my parents were doctors, and they loved each other almost as much as I love my husband, Henri.

He loved me, too.

Until that American woman arrived.

Chapter Fifteen

—— Zoe ——

On the way back from the Belcoeurs' flat, Zoe was careless enough to look into the window of LeBron's Patisserie. Unable to ignore her taste buds, she found her eyes drawn to a pistachio-flavored *choux à la crème*.

She loved pistachios, especially when they were crumbled, inserted into dollops of whipped cream, and encased in a flaky pastry sprinkled with the chopped nuts.

Don't, Zoe! Your pink chemise is already too tight. Get any fatter and Henri might stop brightening your nights.

Zoe's feet, however, carried her into the shop, where she joined a line of women purchasing their evening dessert: frothy raspberry confections, large fruit tartes, small tins of crème brûlée. Ahead of her stood a dark-haired woman who would have been even prettier if her hazel eyes hadn't been rimmed in red.

When the brunette's turn came, she tapped the confectioner's glass case. "*Une, s'il vous plaît,*" she said.

The woman's voice sounded familiar to Zoe, but it took her a moment to remember why. The telephone. She sounded just like the weeping woman on her party line.

"*Voilà*, Isabeau," the counter woman replied, as she put the pastry into a small box.

Isabeau. That was the brunette's name. And she must live nearby.

When Zoe's turn came, she ordered quickly, and once the boxed *choux à la crème.* was in her hand, she hurried back onto the sidewalk, where she saw Isabeau turning onto rue Vavin.

Although her leg was screaming from climbing all those stairs to the Belcoeur residence, she increased her pace and followed until the woman entered the courtyard of a large apartment building. Not wanting her nosiness revealed, Zoe hung back and watched as Isabeau entered a first-floor flat. As soon as the door closed, Zoe checked the roster above the mailboxes. *Isabeau Gerrard—1-C.*

Now she knew the party line woman's name and where she lived. But was Isabeau's unhappiness any of her concern? What was the old Bible saying? *Sufficient unto the day is the evil thereof.*

Deep in thought, Zoe limped the remaining block to her little trinket of a house.

· · · ◇ · · ·

Madeline was long gone, and Zoe had been painting for hours when Henri stopped by.

"Good Lord, Zoe, what wretched soul is that?" he said, pointing to her canvas.

"You can tell it's a person?" Zoe was hardly a Realist, and only an astute observer could see a face emerging from seemingly haphazard streaks of Prussian blue and Payne gray. In a way she was disappointed that the form would be so obvious, but she also felt gratified that Henri understood her work. Few non-artists did.

"Oh, yes, and it is a female person, too," he added. "Not you, I hope. But if she is, I promise to leave you in a much happier frame of mind."

She tried to ignore the thrill that coursed through her body, but she failed. She knew what he was here for, and she wanted it as much as he did.

He moved close enough that she could smell his cologne. Houbigant's Fougère Royale, a blend of citrus, lavender, and Moroccan spices. At more than six feet, he towered over her, but she'd long gotten over feeling threatened by him. Instead, she leaned back. They stood that way for a while—he'd learned to let her pick the time—then she leaned forward again, her head touching his broad chest.

"*Yes*," she said.

Without another word, he swept her up into his arms and carried her into the boudoir. She smiled into the mirror on the ceiling as he unbuttoned her dress, whispering, "You are my sun and stars, my night, my day, my seasons, summer, winter, my sweet spring, my autumn song, the church in which I pray, my land and ocean, all that the earth can bring of glory and of sustenance, all that might be divine, my alpha and my omega, and all that was ever mine."

Stripped to her underclothes now, she whispered back, "Been reading Shakespeare, have we?"

His tongue found her ear. Probed. Then it moved to her neck. "I was going to tell you I wrote that for you, but sadly, your education has proved my lie. By the way, *ma petite*, you have paint on your neck."

Although she already knew, she asked, "What color?"

"Prussian blue. So wrong for this moment." His tongue moved lower.

Somehow, she managed to keep her breath steady. "You would have preferred cadmium red?"

Licking the sweat off her thighs, he murmured, "Oh, a much deeper red than cadmium."

"Alizarin crimson?" On fire, she could hardly get the words out. But she congratulated herself for teaching him well.

"Yes, alizarin. As deep as a cavern hiding a treasure. As deep as a woman's most secret place."

She raised her hips so that he could slide off her panties. "Be careful. The lace is delicate."

"Your panties are safe with me. As is the rest of you."

With that, he slid in, and the world disappeared.

· · · ◇ · · ·

Afterward, they lay side by side, looking up at the mirror. Zoe naked, Henri—except for his shoes—remained clothed, one of his many oddities. She couldn't make up her mind whether she liked that or not, but beggars couldn't be choosers, could they?

"My turn now " she said, finally recovered.

"If you insist."

She knelt over him, and after he'd helped her slip off his black suitcoat, she unknotted his burgundy-colored tie and pulled it off slowly.

"Be careful," he whispered, his throat hoarse. "That tie is silk. Made by nuns."

"As were my lace panties." She put the tie aside for later use, and then she unbuttoned his white linen shirt, revealing his hairy chest. "They say the swimmers in the Olympics shave their chests to make them go faster," she murmured.

"Speed is not something I am interested in, Zoe, for which you should thank *le bon Dieu*." He shivered, though, as she began to lick the rose-colored blossoms of shrapnel scars he'd accumulated in the Great War. His sweat tasted salty-sweet, like an expensive dessert. When she'd had her fill, she massaged the circular depression of a long-gone German bullet, a wound he swore never caused him pain. But she'd once seen him wince when her fingers pressed too strongly.

Wound gentled, she started on the rest of him. The Spanish leather belt was first. After she'd pulled it off, she cinched it around his right wrist, then twisted the end around one of the posts on her hand-carved headboard. His left wrist followed, wrapped in burgundy silk, secured to the other bedpost.

"And now for the business end," Zoe whispered, tugging off his trousers, then his underpants. "Oh, my. Look what we have here!"

For quite some time, Henri was content to lie there at Zoe's mercy. When she finally released him, he wrapped his freed arms around her while she cuddled against him.

"I think I love you, Zoe," he said, looking at himself in the overhead mirror.

"I think I love you, too." This was Zoe's standard response; a lie, like his. She would only truly love one man in her life, and he was buried under six feet of French soil. Besides, Henri had his own obligations, so for them both, the word "love" meant little. As she lay next to him, she thought how satisfactory their arrangement was, how safe. Some day in the future, when they would finally part, there would be few tears on either side. No broken hearts, no sleepless nights. Only fond memories of something that had been warm and comforting. She'd learned that caring too much for someone—truly *loving* them—was too dangerous.

A few minutes later, with both of them sated and giddy, Henri rose from the bed and walked naked into the *toilette*, Zoe trailing behind. They washed each other with lavender soap. Slowly. Tenderly. When he smiled down at her, Zoe wondered how, upon their first meeting two years earlier, she could ever have believed him cold. Now they rocked together, sighing, slippery with soap and sex. Once they were finished, they dried each other longer than was necessary, but the late hour—it was almost eight—brought an end to their pleasure.

"Madame Arceneau will have dinner waiting," Henri said as

Zoe knotted his tie. Since he never struggled against his bonds, the tie was only slightly wrinkled.

"I hope your dinner is delicious. You've certainly earned it."

He was still smiling as she ushered him to the door. Before opening it, she asked, "Have you made any headway on the Laurette Belcoeur killing?"

The smile vanished. "That is something you need not concern yourself with."

"She was my friend."

"No. She simply sold you a clock. Good night, Zoe."

He let himself out.

· · · ◇ · · ·

Once again, Zoe had trouble sleeping. She lay there in her mirrored bedroom, peace a stranger. She counted off the minutes, then the hours.

Giving up, she rose from the bed and made her way barefoot to the armoire where she kept Pete's letters. Untied the blue ribbon that held them together. Picked one. Took it back to her bed and lay down again, the letter clasped in her hand.

Oh, why couldn't the scent of the sender remain through the years?

· · · ◇ · · ·

1918
Mercy, Alabama

The spring of 1918 had been the happiest time of her life. She and Pete met at least once a week in the forest that separated the Beech Glen plantation from the small cabin where Pete had grown up.

They talked about everything. Music. Art. Books. Being the son of a school teacher, then the recipient of a scholarship to Oberlin Conservatory of Music in Ohio, his knowledge of all the arts surpassed even hers. And, of course, he'd play his trumpet for her; sometimes Jelly Roll Morton, sometimes Haydn.

They had so much in common, it reminded her of something her French grandmother had talked about during her last visit to the States. She'd said some cultures practiced a religion that believed in reincarnation, that we lived a series of multiple lives, not just one. At the time—she'd been only nine then—she'd been horrified to learn she could be reborn as a cockroach. Noting her alarm, Zoe's grandmother said, "But if you're good, you can be reborn as anything or anyone you want."

Now, lying here in the Paris night with Pete's letters in her hand, she wondered if she and Pete had once been songbirds.

It had never been hard to hide her assignations with Pete from her stepmother, Annabelle, or her brother, Brice, since neither of them cared much where she was, or with whom. They believed she was out somewhere drawing or painting, because whenever she left Beech Glen on one of those days, she made sure she always carried her sketch pad and drawing pencils.

The sketches she showed them when she returned had been drawn the night before. Some days, a feral pig. Other days, a deer. No one bothered to tell her to be careful, that feral pigs could bite, stags could gore.

Zoe already knew that.

She also knew that if any dangerous wildlife ever attacked, Pete would lay down his life to protect her.

Despite the dangers of their love, she always felt safe in his arms, so when one day, after making love on the blanket he always brought from Dorothy's cabin, Pete asked her to be his wife, she whispered, "Yes."

But times being what they were in Mercy, Alabama, a proper

church wedding was impossible, so they were married in the same way his people had married for centuries.

They Jumped the Broom, with only Dorothy; Dorothy's cousin Rafael, a preacher; and Henry, Pete's younger brother, present as they promised to love each other through sickness and health, through life *and*—not *until*—death.

Forever.

The next week Pete and his trumpet left for New York to find a job and an apartment for the two of them in a city where love between a Black man and a White woman didn't result in a visit from the Ku Klux Klan.

$$\cdots \diamond \cdots$$

1924
Paris

Zoe began to read...

April 1918: New York City

Dearest Zoe,

My love, my light, my wife, my darling. How I miss you!

I miss your laughter, your love, your warmth! You are my island of calm in this crazy world.

New York is stormy this week. I have never felt such a punishing wind, and yet it's supposedly spring! But enough of my complaints. Thanks to my music studies at Oberlin, I've found steady work. Upon hearing me play at a small club down the street, the famous bandleader, James Reese Europe, hired me on the spot to play second trumpet in his Clef Club Society band.

This is a great thing, my darling, because I will soon be making enough money to afford a place for us. Then I will send for you and we will never be parted again.

Oh, Zoe, keep yourself safe until that happy day!

All my love,

Your heart-husband Pete

· · · ◇ · · ·

1924
Paris

Zoe pressed the letter to her lips, cried for a while, then fell asleep.

Chapter Sixteen

After breakfasting at La Rotonde, Zoe decided to visit Fabian Napier again. Maybe the mechanic hadn't actually lied to her, but he certainly hadn't told the entire story about his relationship with Laurette Belcoeur. If anyone had a reason enough to kill her, it was a fiancé who'd been left in the lurch.

Fabian's garage wasn't far away, and her stroll down boulevard de Montparnasse would be pleasant under a sun that, for once, didn't feel too warm.

Slipping through the Olympics crowds headed in the opposite direction, she reached Napier & Son in only minutes, where she found Fabian standing outside the garage, smoking a cigarette.

"No broken-down Citroëns this morning?" she asked, noting his clean hands.

Fabian took another puff, exhaled, and answered, "One is on the way as we speak. I'm merely waiting for it."

Zoe squared her shoulders, summoning the strength to ask the question she'd rehearsed. "Monsieur Napier, the last time we talked, you didn't tell me you'd once been affianced to Laurette Belcoeur."

A Gallic shrug. "You didn't ask. Yes, she traded me for a *vicomte*. She was already well practiced in that kind of thing." He pretended fascination with a cricket hopping on a crack along the sidewalk.

Zoe didn't trust men who wouldn't, or couldn't, meet her eyes, and the cricket wasn't really all that interesting. "But the day I found Laurette dead you didn't seem in the least upset." If the street hadn't been swarming with tourists, she would have been wary of questioning such a rough man, but many of them—the women, least—gave him more than a once-over as they passed by. Witnesses assured, she forged on. "Even now Laurette's death seems not to bother you."

Fabian took the cigarette out of his mouth and, almost as an afterthought, stomped on the cricket. "You know we had a war, correct, Mademoiselle?"

"Don't be ridiculous. Of course I know."

A smile, but not a pleasant one. "When the Germans started killing Frenchmen, I went to the front with my brother, Antoine, who was two years older than me. During our first battle—it was at the Marne, you understand—I took a bullet in the arm, but I didn't cry about it, even though I was only thirteen."

"What has that got..."

Fabian cut her off. "I also didn't cry when Antoine was machine-gunned and got caught up in the barbed wire, and I couldn't get to him. But he had plenty of company. Other boys— some even younger than me—were hung up in the wire, too, and some of them cried and screamed for their mothers all night. I couldn't tell if the last scream I heard was Antoine's, but I like to believe he bled out before he had to listen to that chorus of pain." Another Gallic shrug. "So I ask you, Mademoiselle, why should I cry over the death of a soulless bitch who died more mercifully?"

How did one answer such a heartless question? Unnerved, Zoe managed to say, "My God, what kind of man are you?"

"A man who knows there are other apples on the tree." He returned the cigarette to his mouth and took a deep inhale. He choked, though, when she asked her next question.

"Did you ever beat her?"

When he finished coughing—it took a while—he stuttered out, "Are... Are you insane? Do I look like the kind of man who beats women?"

"Laurette had bruises all up and down her arms. Someone put them there." She didn't bother giving him Veronique's explanation.

His eyes narrowed. "Bruises? Better ask her fancy new fiancé about them. Or do you believe that just because someone has a fancy title, they can't be violent? Monsieur Vicomte has a long history of knocking people around, sometimes even killing them."

Before Zoe could ask for clarification, a black and yellow Citroën came gasping down the street toward them. Without another word, Fabian threw his cigarette into the gutter and walked into the garage, leaving Zoe standing on the sidewalk, her mouth open.

· · · ◇ · · ·

While walking away from the garage, it occurred to Zoe that since she was already in the neighborhood, it might be wise to stop by the flea market and see if any of the saleswomen could tell her anything about Laurette she didn't already know. The tables were only a few blocks' walk away, and so far her bad leg was behaving itself. What was that old country saying? *Make hay while the sun shines.* After all, in Paris, the sun often didn't.

She was just passing the Metro stop at rue Vavin and Montparnasse when she spotted a familiar face emerging from the Metro's stairway. Of all people, it was Vicomte Gervais du Paget, and he was carrying a large package. From the sweat on his brow, she could tell it was heavy.

When he spotted her, a big smile made his handsome face look even more so. "*Bonjour*, Mademoiselle Barlow! You look so beautiful today even the sun dims in comparison."

Zoe didn't bother dithering a gratitude. The memory of the bruises on Laurette's arms—much larger and more numerous than Veronique's—put a halt to such fakery. Gesturing to the heavy-looking package, which was wrapped in a blanket, she asked, "Have you been shopping?"

"Merely fulfilling a promise to Laurette," he replied, falling into step with her. "I promised to donate this to the sales table."

Then they were both headed to the same place. Nothing to worry about there, since it was full daylight, and hundreds of tourists and Olympics-goers crowded the streets. She smiled back at him, determined to maintain a civil conversation. Who knew what he might let slip.

"So what is 'this'?" Zoe pointed to the package.

"A wall clock I no longer have any use for. Laurette admired it when she was last at my flat, and when I told her I'd recently discovered it was merely a copy of the Boulle original—he was the acclaimed cabinetmaker to Louis Fourteenth, you understand—I'd decided to get rid of it. When she asked if she could feature it at her sales table, of course I said yes." Sadness shadowed his eyes. "I could deny that woman nothing."

"Then you're still giving the clock to her sister?"

"Of course. Like Laurette, Veronique is an honest woman and would never tell one of her customers the clock was an original Boulle."

Blind trust of others hardly being an aristocratic trait, this raised Zoe's suspicions. "How did you come by the clock in the first place?"

"I didn't. My father did. Toward the end of his life, Papa's vision grew dim, and when he was offered the clock in payment of a debt, he was delighted to accept. If the clock had been genuine, it would have repaid the man's debt many times over, but alas..." He mimicked a fake frown at the package.

"Did he die recently, your father?"

"In June."

Only a month earlier. Zoe couldn't help feeling sorry for him, losing a father and a fiancée in such a short span of time. She remembered how she'd felt upon discovering her father's body swinging from a barn rafter. She hadn't been able to speak for days. Yet although Gervais had suffered a double blow, he seemed to be doing fine, and suspicion blunted her sympathy.

Steeling herself for a probable mind-your-own-business, she said, "I was wondering about those bruises on Laurette's arms. Do you know what happened?"

His voice revealed not a shred of discomfort at the question. "Only what she told me, that carrying around boxes of sales items was rough work. Of course, when we married, such toil would no longer have been necessary. Servants would do the carrying. The same for her sister. I'd see to that. Neither of them would have to work at a sales table again."

Before Zoe had time to ask another question, they arrived at the flea market, where she found Katrina Weisensel working at Laurette's old table, although closely supervised by Veronique. To Zoe's delight, the artist looked rosy-cheeked and happy. Being out of that dreary basement apartment agreed with her.

Katrina greeted Zoe with a grin. "I sold two clocks today!"

It looked like she was about to say more, but upon spotting Gervais, Veronique cut her off. "Oh, Gervais! What a pleasant surprise!" Her flushed cheeks made her look almost pretty.

Paget started to set the package down, grunting a bit under its weight, but Katrina reached forward and took it into her muscular arms with ease. When she did, Zoe couldn't help remembering Laurette's caved-in face.

Could a woman have done such damage?

Ignorant of Zoe's thoughts, the *vicomte* took Veronique's rough hand and kissed it. "I bring you a beautiful clock, although its beauty is greatly surpassed by your own."

Zoe fought back the urge to gag.

Veronique, however, accepted the *vicomte's* florid compliment as truth. Smiling, she said, "You always know the perfect thing to say, Gervais! But, yes, I admit I took extra care with my toilette today, even put on my best earrings. Do you recognize them?" She touched a trembling hand to her ears, each adorned with a gold-rimmed opal.

"How could I not, *chérie*? I once gave them to you. Beauty for a beauty."

Veronique giggled like a schoolgirl. Then she calmed herself by unwrapping the clock. "Oh, how glorious!"

"Perhaps," Katrina said, frowning. "But not an original Boulle, correct?"

The *vicomte* smiled at the new saleswoman. "You know your timepieces, Mademoiselle."

Zoe found the faux-Boulle a baroque mess. Gilt cherubs, birds, and butterflies crawled up its side, and near the top, an armored knight hoisted a pennant. Was the knight celebrating lopping off an opponent's head? The gaudy thing was almost four feet high, and so heavy that its buyer would need to triple-bolt the monstrosity to a supporting wall. Otherwise, it would fall, killing whatever poor wretch who happened to be walking by. Gervais's father must have been blind, indeed, to have thought it an original Boulle.

Putting the clock's fakery aside, Zoe said to Katrina, "What a delight to see you working here!"

Katrina started to respond, but Veronique broke in. "The

girl is a natural. I have to thank you, Zoe, for letting me know about her, even though she is German." Then, catching herself sounding condescending in front of the handsome *vicomte*, she quickly added, "Germans, ah, understand clocks since they make so many of them."

"As do the Swiss," Katrina said. "But I am fond of clocks, whether they're originals or not, as long as they keep good time. Time being so fleeting."

A hint of sadness there, Zoe thought. It couldn't be easy being German in Paris these days. Like Laurette, many Parisians still mourned the lives lost in the Great War and were quick to fling insults at anyone with a German accent.

Veronique was obviously a more forgiving soul than her sister and had not been crippled by the need for revenge. Zoe was also encouraged by the light in Veronique's eyes. Her plain face glowed under the *vicomte*'s chivalric flattery. But Zoe—who'd been on intimate terms with grief for the past six years—knew sorrow would return when Veronique went home. It would come fiercest in the night, when the woman was alone in her bed with no one to comfort her and...

Don't think about Pete.

Shaking away her own sorrows, Zoe said, "It's a lovely day to be outdoors, isn't it? Not too hot, and no rain."

Gervais, Veronique, and Katrina all agreed and chatted happily about the weather for a while. When the chance of a new shower had been summarily dismissed, Zoe bid farewell to the three and moved along to another sales table, this one tended by a sweet-faced elderly woman whose table was covered with a mixture of items, some pristine, some battered. She wore a patched but once-elegant dress, its long skirt covering her ankles. Her deeply creased face was thin, and one of her eyes was filmed by a cataract. Both hands were heavily scarred. Burns. Had she reached into flames to rescue her wares? Or to save someone she loved?

Touched, Zoe greeted the woman with more than usual respect and scanned her offerings: various circlets and barrettes, along with several pocket flasks.

After a brief chat about the fine weather, Zoe took a moment to closer inspect the items on the table. She was drawn to a bejeweled circlet studded with pearls and peridots. Although she hadn't planned on buying anything, she soon found herself involved in a bidding war against another American. The woman was telling the saleswoman in atrocious French that she'd been invited to a party at the American Embassy and thought the circlet would "spiff up" her green shantung dress, as long as the price was right. To lower the price, the American made the mistake of saying the circlet looked a bit shabby. The saleswoman, although not understanding much of what the American had said—especially not the word "spiff"—took offense at the insult and pursed her lips into a thin line.

Seizing her chance, Zoe said in her fluent French, "Madame, you are to be congratulated on the excellence of your wares. The circlet is exquisite, fit for a queen. I will throw myself on your mercy and pay whatever you ask."

The sweet-faced old woman returned Zoe's good deed by quoting a reasonable figure that made the other American walk off in a self-righteous huff.

"Madame is both kind and generous," Zoe said, opening her purse.

A smile lit the old saleswoman's face. "The circlet will look beautiful on the lovely mademoiselle." She wrapped it in an old newspaper—no ill-used Chagalls here!—and handed it to Zoe, adding a question. "Wait! Aren't you the American who bought that clock from Laurette the day before she died?"

Zoe nodded.

"*Tragique*, was it not? So young, and with such a shining future ahead of her. Then some crazy man comes along and bashes in her lovely face."

Zoe didn't feel comfortable discussing Laurette's death since Veronique and Gervais appeared to be watching her closely. "*Tragique*, yes," Zoe said, placing her new treasure into her ever-present string bag. "Well, thank you for the lovely circlet. I'll wear it tonight."

After stopping briefly at Madame Crab's table and noting the shopping bags, she bought one for Madeline. She then moved on to the next table, which specialized in student-level watercolors. A rendering of Notre Dame's gargoyles showed promise, and since it was cheaper than it needed to be, she bought it. The color scheme, gray gargoyles silhouetted against a pink-and-yellow sky, was perfect for her *toilette*. She already owned the perfect frame; one she'd purchased at a different flea market.

Glancing back at Veronique's table, Zoe noticed that she was still engrossed in deep conversation with the *vicomte*. Disappointed, she turned to go and, in doing so, saw an odd expression flicker across Katrina's face. Anger, yes. But it was followed immediately by the blankness of befuddlement. What had the young artist heard or seen to bring on such a clash of emotions?

Before Zoe could ask her, the table was engulfed by a crowd of tourists, all bidding on the hideous faux Boulle, and Katrina's expression resumed a saleslady smile.

Unsettled, Zoe went home.

Back at Le Petit Bibelot, Madeline had finished putting everything together for Poker Night. She accepted the piecework bag with delight.

"This will make shopping so much easier," Madeline exclaimed. "And with that, I am off to ready my own flat for guests. My sister and her husband are up from Provence, and I want to surprise them with a Parisian feast."

Zoe bade her housekeeper goodbye, then realizing she still had plenty of time before her gambling friends arrived, donned her painting smock, and headed into her studio. She hoped painting would take her mind to places other than murder.

··· ◇ ···

Two hours and a canvas later, Zoe finally washed away the acrid smell of oil paint and turps. Her old friend Archie Stafford-Smythe had promised to bring a new player to Poker Night, and Zoe was eager to meet him. Or her. After all, women loved gambling as much as men did. Thanks to the good news delivered by her surprisingly honest guardian, she'd purchased a new mint-green-and-cream raw silk dress. It hung loosely until it reached her knee, then swung out in a great "mermaid" flare. Over her bobbed and hennaed hair, she slipped her new circlet of pearls and peridots.

Dressed to the nines, Zoe walked into the sitting room, where Madeline had already covered the long dining table in green felt. The new deck of cards on the table had not been opened; Zoe was known as much for her honesty as her skill.

As her new phallus clock struck the hour eight, the regulars began to arrive.

The first to enter was Kiki, dragging along Grant Jackson Knickerbocker, her wealthy new boyfriend, having left Man Ray for good. At least that's what she claimed.

Right behind came Dominique Garron, wearing a black eyepatch studded with rhinestones. Next to arrive was Louise Packard, the American cubist, followed by Archie Stafford-Smythe, arm-in-arm with a thin gray-haired woman who looked as wealthy as she did elderly. Some poker-playing widow he'd picked up at another game?

The minute the old woman opened her mouth, Zoe knew different.

"I am so happy to finally meet you, Zoe," said Guinevere "Gwennie" Stafford-Smythe, the Countess of Whittenden. "My son has told me so much about you."

"All good, I hope," Zoe responded.

The countess, although blessed with centuries of good breeding, winked. "Of course not. Otherwise I wouldn't have bothered to come."

Archie snickered. "Don't say you haven't been warned, Zoe. Mater's a better hand at poker than I am."

Gwennie patted her son on his cheek. "Almost everyone is, dear."

Thoroughly delighted, Zoe led the old woman to the table, where the others had already settled themselves. After handing the package of cards to Gwennie to open, Zoe dealt, and play began.

Archie's warning proved prescient. The Countess of Whittenden won four out of eight hands, once with a straight flush, another with a full house, and once with three treys. The most galling win, however, came as the result of Gwennie's stone-faced bluff when she held nothing other than the nine of hearts as a high card. This risky bluff delivered Zoe one of her only losing nights, but she took it in stride. Only innocents and fools expected to win all the time.

As Gwennie raked in the large pot, Archie reminded everyone that next week he, Zoe, and Gwennie would attend some Olympics swimming contests at the Piscine des Tourelles. He looked disappointed when his announcement didn't garner the enthusiasm he'd expected.

Kiki gave a playful snort. "I don't know about the countess, but Zoe and Archie only want to see nearly naked men frolicking in a swimming pool."

"Don't leave me out, dear," Gwennie remarked, stuffing her

pearl-encrusted purse with a mixture of American dollars and French francs. "I also like watching nearly naked young men, whatever they may be doing."

Dominique and Louise Packard guffawed. So did Archie, who knew his mother well. He'd once confided to Zoe that the countess had enjoyed a fling with the same stableboy, which led to Archie's banishment from England.

Zoe looked benignly at Kiki. "Well, you're not totally wrong. Personally, I'm not one for watching other people swim, but everyone is talking about how good-looking some guy named Weissmuller is. They say he's certain to break records, so the day shouldn't be too awful."

"Oh. Weissmuller." The look on Kiki's face underwent an immediate change, perhaps because a picture of the handsome Weissmuller in his skin-tight bathing suit had appeared in the newspapers.

"Yeah," Zoe grinned. "Him."

Louise grumped, "I'm sure the boy looked lovely, but would someone please deal? I'm here to play poker, not talk about pretty men!" In her late sixties, and half-crippled by arthritis, the Cubist no longer cared about pretty men. Or so she claimed.

Kiki's greed proving superior to her lust for scantily clad men, she began dealing.

··· ◇ ···

After the last poker hand had been lost to the countess, and everyone had tottered home, Zoe stayed up late finishing the leftover bottle of Champagne, thinking about Laurette Belcoeur's bruised arms, and Katrina's more muscular ones. Then there was Laurette's plan to marry into the old aristocracy. Fabian Napier had been right; just because your blood was blue didn't mean you couldn't be violent. There was a reason the citizens of

France had lopped off the heads of so many aristocrats during the Revolution; the aristocracy's crimes against the peasantry had been considerable.

Still...

She'd pay a visit to the *vicomte* and do her best to get the details of his—in Fabian Napier's words—"long history of knocking people around." And hadn't he also said something about "killing"?

But first, she had to find out where the *vicomte* lived.

Chapter Seventeen

Librarians know everything, so in the morning Zoe took the Metro over to the Right Bank and 10 rue de l'Élysée. The former residence of the Papal Nuncio, the building now housed the American Library, which Zoe had frequented since moving to Paris. This time she was looking for a person, not a book.

The library had been founded in 1920 by the American Library Association and the Library of Congress, which gave it the motto *Atrum post bellum, ex libris lux*: After the darkness of war, the light of books.

Upon arriving, Zoe found library volunteer Grace Atkins on a tall ladder in the History section. Despite being an American, Grace probably had the information Zoe needed. If not, she'd know who did.

The two were close friends. Grace was one of those adventurous women who'd arrived in France from Georgia during the Great War to help nurse the wounded and, like so many American citizens, hadn't returned to the States after the Armistice. In her late thirties, Grace had never been pretty, and the horrors she'd seen during the war showed clearly on her face. The scar across her forehead wasn't completely disfigured, but the permanent crease between her eyebrows did tend to keep others at a distance.

Not Zoe. When they'd first met at the library in 1922, they'd bonded over a yellowing copy of Madame de Staël's treatise on Napoleon—de Staël hadn't cared for him—and since then, at least half of what Zoe knew about French history came from conversations with Grace.

Spotting Zoe, the librarian hurried down the ladder, then shook dust off the front of her dress. It was a simple gray chemise, as plain and straightforward as she was.

"Oh, Zoe, you arrived at just the right time," she said in her warm Georgia drawl. "Nancy Carstairs, over in Fiction, told me she'd just received Agatha Christie's new *The Murder on the Links*, and an only slightly used copy of Conan Doyle's *His Last Bow*. Our remaining copy disappeared last year, but such is life, eh? The Doyle is short stories, of course, but they're all quite brilliant." She pointed at her desk, where the two books sat.

Not being one of the many fans of Sherlock Holmes, Zoe waved away the offer of *His Last Bow* but gratefully accepted *The Murder on the Links*. Tucking the volume under her arm, she said, "Actually, I didn't come here for a book. I'm looking for information."

"And what better person to ask than a librarian, right?" Grace said, grinning. "What do you need to know?"

"Are you familiar with the Paget family, the *vicomtes* of Paget?"

The librarian winced. "A sad family. So many died on the guillotine."

"Correct. But some escaped, I hear."

"Yes, some set sail for Canada, where they were received warmly in Quebec, but others fled to England and stayed until the Revolutionaries died off and it was safe to return to France. Since then, the remaining Pagets reestablished themselves in their old holdings near Amiens. A few even moved back into the family château. It's not the treasure house it used to be, what with being damaged so badly and looted, first during the Terror, then during the war. Château Paget was in such disrepair that old Geraint, the ninth *vicomte*, took up quarters in Paris. He lived here until he died last year, but he was entombed in a crypt on the country estate. Is that what you wanted to know?"

Zoe shook her head. "Actually, I'm more interested in the new *vicomte*. What do you know about him?"

Grace looked up at the ceiling. There was a frieze up there showing cherubs and a grumpy-looking old man lolling about on clouds. She appeared to study it for a moment, but when she looked back at Zoe, her sunny expression had vanished. "If Gervais Paget has asked you to dinner, don't go. Not unless you bring along that pet cop of yours."

Zoe sighed; there were no secrets in Paris. "Then he has a bad reputation?"

A mirthless laugh. "The man is *infamous*. But I'll admit, the handsome *vicomte* seems to have behaved himself after all that trouble last year."

"Oh?"

Just as Grace was about to answer, a well-dressed Englishwoman of at least seventy entered the History section and asked her for a French account, translated into English, of the Battle of Hastings. She was looking for the list of Norman knights who'd invaded England with William the Conqueror. She explained that she'd always been told her family was descended from one of those knights and wanted proof for her grandson, who thought the entire story was "a bunch of malarkey."

"Ah, yes," Grace said, cheerfully. "Ten-sixty-six. The Battle of Hastings shelves are right over here." After telling Zoe she'd be back in a minute, Grace ushered the woman to a nearby reader's niche, which held a small table and chair.

"These six shelves are all our reference books on the battle," the librarian told her. "Most of them, but not all, are in English. You can copy from them if you wish, but I'm afraid we can't lend them out. Do you have pen and paper?"

When the woman replied in the affirmative, Grace left her to it and rejoined Zoe, where in a voice barely above a whisper, she said, "As I was saying, Gervais Paget is a man you don't want to be mixed up with. Bad, bad reputation."

Zoe did her best to mimic a Gallic shrug. "The word 'bad' means different things to different people, so exactly what kind of 'bad' are we talking about here?"

Darting a quick glance behind her, and seeing that the Englishwoman was pouring over a book, Grace took Zoe's arm and led her toward two comfortable-looking chairs. Once they sat down, Grace began, "First, the fisticuffs. This was a couple of years ago. Paget was in a brasserie with a woman when some man said something rude to her, and he—Paget, I mean—punched the guy in the face. Broke his nose and knocked out a tooth. The second time, pretty much the same thing. In a café with a woman, a guy said something rude, and Paget hauled off and slugged him. That time there was no broken nose—just a bloody one. No lost teeth, either."

Zoe took a moment to think about this, then said, "So both times he felt he was protecting a woman." She wondered if the woman in question had been Laurette. But two years ago? Probably not. Laurette would have been around sixteen then, too young to be hanging out in brasseries with high-and-mighty *vicomtes*.

"You say *protective*, but I say *vicious*," Grace argued. "I've learned that when a man is in the habit of knocking other men around, he tends to do the same thing with women. However, a man like the fancy *vicomte* would probably hit her somewhere other than the face. Wouldn't want to spoil that beauty, would he?

Our pretty *vicomte* is a great fan of beautiful women. And then of course, there've been the duels."

Zoe frowned. "Tell me about them."

A nod. "Looking back, I think there were three, and all took place in the Bois de Boulogne. Paget's family are aristocrats living in a republic, so the whole passel of them get challenged to duels from time to time. His father fought several, but no one ever got killed. You know how it goes. The duelists say harsh words to each other, go out to the park, and fire their guns in the air. Honor satisfied; no harm done. It was the same thing in Paget's case during his first duel. No blood, just some idiotic shooting at the sky. But in the third duel, he killed his opponent."

Zoe couldn't shrug that away. "If someone died, why wasn't he arrested? Dueling's a crime in France, whether someone gets hurt or not."

"You'd have to ask your pet cop that. Hardly a month passes in Paris without dueling fools disturbing the peace of the Boulogne."

"But Paget actually *killed* someone!"

"They say the other man shot at him first, not at the sky. And that he did hit Paget, although it was just a flesh wound."

"Still..." Zoe murmured.

"Yeah. *Still.*"

They sat in silence for a moment, thinking about all the crimes society's higher-ups could get away with. Before Zoe could ask Grace another question, the elderly Englishwoman emerged from the stacks, her face a mask of disappointment.

"I didn't see my ancestor's name on the list of the Conqueror's knights," she told Grace.

The librarian gave her a warm smile. "Don't take it too hard, ma'am. The fact that his name wasn't on the roster of knights doesn't mean he wasn't there. He might not have been an actual knight, just a member of the Norman army not high enough in rank to make the list. There's another possibility, too.

"He may not have been a Norman at all. He could have been from some other part of France and joined the invasion to get his share of the spoils. There were hundreds, possibly thousands of men like that. Historians realize that not everyone who was at the Battle of Hastings made the rolls. Only the higher-ups."

At this, the Englishwoman looked less depressed. "That must be it." Her step firmer, she walked away.

"That was kind of you," Zoe said.

Grace looked resigned. "We get them all the time. It never ceases to amaze me how many English people want to believe an ancestor was part of an invading army. You'd think they'd prefer having their ancestors numbered among the defending Saxons."

"Well, the Saxons lost that battle," Zoe said. "And then they lost the rest of England, too, if I remember correctly."

"True. People don't like to identify with losers. Now, tell me why you are so curious about Vicomte du Paget? In all the time I've known you, you've never struck me as interested in *aristocrats*." While uttering the word, Grace's face assumed the expression one would use after finding half a worm in the apple one happened to be eating.

"I need to find out where he lives."

Grace gave her a hard look. "Does this have anything to do with that young woman's murder the other day? The salesgirl? Laurette-something-or-other? Word's going around that she was engaged to him. But really, a *vicomte* marrying a *salesgirl*? Bed her maybe, but marry her? Never!"

"Yes, that does seem odd. But she was extraordinarily beautiful, and surprisingly refined. It's possible that before the war her people were something of importance, if not quite on Paget's level."

"Beauty can make up for a lot."

"It always has. Besides her being beautiful, I found Laurette to be an honest person. Unlike some salespeople, she never misrepresented her merchandise."

For the first time during their conversation, the librarian looked worried. "I see. But Zoe, surely your friend at the Sûreté is capable of finding out who killed her."

"Capable, yes. But with the Olympics here, the police, including Henri, are too busy investigating hundreds of reports of hotel theft, pickpocketing, and drunken brawls. Since I knew both sisters, even if only slightly, I thought I'd look into it enough to offer Henri some leads. Don't worry. I won't take any chances. Once I find out where the *vicomte* lives, and I'm certain you can help me with that. I'll make a point of *accidentally* running into him. In public. With witnesses. Maybe there's a nearby business I can pretend to be visiting?" Zoe made it sound like a question, which it actually was.

Grace made a mournful sound. "I wouldn't tell you, except that his residence is hardly a state secret, and you'd probably wind up finding out from someone else anyway, so here goes, and please don't make me regret it. Your *vicomte*'s city apartment is in the same fancy Haussmann building near the Opéra where so many other blue bloods reside. But for God's sake, whatever you do, don't accept any invitations to see his etchings. I'm not saying he'd murder you or anything like that, but bad things do tend to happen to the people around him."

Zoe assured her friend she'd be careful; then she checked out the Agatha Christie and left.

· · · ◇ · · ·

Zoe was familiar with the *vicomte*'s building, although she'd never entered any of its rooms. It had been designed by Baron Georges-Eugène Haussmann himself and was elegance personified. The structure was also living proof that when the memory of the

Revolution faded, most of the French had adopted a laissez-faire attitude toward the very class their forefathers had once dragged to the guillotine.

Zoe took the Metro to the Opéra station. Once back at street level, she found the formerly sunny day had clouded over, threatening rain. And here she was, toting Agatha Christie's new novel with nothing to protect it.

Irritated at her lack of foresight, Zoe scanned the rest of the street. To her relief, she spotted a café on the corner and, next to that, a stationer. Wine and fine stationery, two items aristocrats always needed. Stopping off at the stationer's first, she bought a leather journal priced twice its worth. Before the stationer wrapped the journal in an old newspaper, Zoe asked if he'd also include her library book, pointing to the looming clouds outside.

The stationer, a young man who pronounced himself a Hercule Poirot aficionado—"But, of course he is Belgian, not French, alas"—obliged, and Zoe left the store minus a few francs but with the Christie well protected. Her luck held. A light rain began to fall as she approached the café, so she hurried inside, only to see Vicomte Gervais du Paget sitting alone at a table next to the window, an Apollo studying lesser mortals as they splashed along in the rain.

She steeled her nerves and started toward him. "Vicomte Paget! What a lovely surprise to find you here."

Noting the stationer's rain-speckled package in her hand, he smiled. "Gervais, please. Let there be no formality between us. We seem to use the same stationer. Now, don't keep standing there, Zoe. You must join me." He rose and gallantly pulled back a chair. As she sat down, he said, "I see you are taking some time away from your easel. Are you painting anything of interest?"

"How would I know what interests you when I hardly know you at all?" To ease the statement, Zoe batted her eyelashes coquettishly.

"Well played, Mademoiselle! But perhaps you are not aware that I am one of your collectors. When we met at the Belcoeurs' flat, I wasn't certain you were the same Barlow who'd painted the Expressionist piece that is now hanging on my salon wall. When I double-checked your signature—Z. Barlow—I found the proof."

This was working out even better than she'd hoped. "Which painting was that?" she asked.

"It was titled *Lust*."

Of course. The god Apollo had been known for his sexual conquests. "Liked all those reds, did you?"

"Oh, it was more than that. I found myself entranced by the way you took the same red—Alizarin crimson, I believe—in which you'd painted the cojoined man and woman, and juxtaposed them with a man dying of his wounds on a battlefield. A reminder that life is precarious, whether or not we want to believe otherwise."

His last words were somber, reminding her that he had just lost his fiancée. But Zoe knew that many murderers rued their deeds, especially when the victim was someone they'd loved.

"You talk of battlefields. Were you in the war?"

"Everyone was in that war, even you Yanks."

Had he seen action with Pete? "Where were you, ah, stationed?"

"Here and there." His eyes didn't leave her face as he sipped his wine. Chablis?

Knowing from past experience that veterans seldom liked to talk about the war, she bit back her disappointment. "You don't want to talk about it?"

A shrug that on him looked elegant, not careless. "There is little to tell. Wars are all pretty much the same. People die." He called to a passing waiter and ordered a glass of Chablis for Zoe.

Zoe remembered Fabian's story about the barbed wire, about his brother screaming all night until he died. So she tried again. "Were you badly hurt? So many of my friends were." For the first time she noticed the stiffness of his right arm and that he held his wineglass with his left.

As she sipped her just-delivered glass of Chablis, he said, "The Devil protects his own."

Zoe didn't know what to say to that, so she feigned interest in the scene outdoors, where the rain was now falling steadily. As a result, a group of expensively dressed men and women hurried into the café. Within minutes, few empty tables were left, and the air in the café became musty with the odor of wet clothes and cigarettes.

"I hope the rain doesn't last long, or it'll curtail some of the Olympics activities," Gervais said, changing the subject. "But it looks like you Yanks are performing brilliantly."

Zoe hadn't been keeping up with who'd won what; she'd long lost her enthusiasm for men's games. Javelin throw, shot put, discus throw. What did such ancient sports have to do with modern life? The only events she was interested in were the equestrian events— horses had not yet been entirely replaced by automobiles—but even Archie hadn't been able to get tickets to any of them. As for the swim finals, she wasn't looking forward to them. The vision of pretty men in tight swimsuits notwithstanding, the day was certain to be boring.

Ignoring Zoe's lack of enthusiasm, Gervais continued. "For instance, Harold Osborn, one of your countrymen, won the high jump and set an Olympics record. Remarkable, when you realize the poor man is almost blind and has terrible depth perception."

Gervais's last sentence aroused Zoe's interest. "Blind, did you say?"

"Not completely. He has a little vision left, I hear, but needs very thick glasses to get around due to an accident when he was a child."

Zoe knew all about childhood accidents since her fall from a tall oak had left her with one leg shorter than the other, but Gervais's story about Osborn intrigued her, so she reminded herself to pick up a newspaper on her way home. She wanted to know more about the "almost blind" jumper.

Come to think of it, hadn't she heard that swimmer Johnny Weissmuller had contracted polio and taken up swimming to get his strength back? But for now, her interest in childhood injuries had to take a back seat, because she needed to know more about Gervais. Since he'd rebuffed her question about the Great War, she tried a different approach.

"Have you seen Veronique lately? I wonder how she's doing." She had to raise her voice over the noise in the café, where several American voices could be heard above the clatter of French and God-knows-what-all.

"Veronique is still grieving," Paget answered. "She was always the more sensitive of the sisters."

"*Always*, you say? You've been acquainted with them for a long while?"

"I've known them both since childhood."

Zoe raised her eyebrows. A *vicomte* and two flea market saleswomen? Maybe the Belcoeur sisters had worked for the family in some capacity. Maids? Cooks? But how to ask such a delicate question? Gervais probably wouldn't enjoy being reminded that his fiancée had "commoner" origins, so she summoned up a neutral "Oh?"

He appeared to understand her confusion. "The Belcoeurs didn't always run flea markets, you understand. In fact, they are descended from an ancient family, one which has been connected to mine since even before the Revolution. Auguste Belcoeur, their progenitor, was a distant cousin of Louis Fourteenth, the..."

"The Sun King," Zoe interjected.

A smile. "I see you've been studying French history."

"To a certain extent. But what happened? How did...?" She trailed off, not knowing how best to frame the question: how did an "ancient" family wind up selling secondhand clocks? Her librarian friend hadn't explained that.

"The Revolution happened. Great houses fell, as did theirs, as did mine, and certain families were lucky to escape with their heads. Same with the Belcoeurs, although they weren't quite as lucky. They lost everything but their nobility."

Nobility. In these modern times, the concept was almost a joke, as long as you forgot about the guillotine and severed heads rolling along the cobblestones. However, it did explain certain things, such as how a *vicomte* would deign to marry a salesgirl. Laurette's wasn't a Cinderella story at all. It was a reunification of ancient families.

"Your families kept in touch?" she asked. "All these years?"

"Not really. Life after the Revolution was too..."

"Complicated?" Zoe offered.

"*Exactement!* But one day, when I was on my way to a gallery showing just off the Vaugirard Passage, I happened to spy Veronique at one of the sales tables. She looked just like one of the portraits that had escaped the destruction at our château, so I stopped to speak to her. During the following conversation, I realized who she was and the long history our families shared. After that, we began seeing each other—a dinner here and there, that sort of thing, and we became more or less—what is the English word—*affianced.*"

Zoe blinked in surprise. "Are you saying you were once engaged to *Veronique?*"

"Given who we were, it was only natural. Veronique is a lovely person. Kind. Intelligent. And wonderfully self-reliant, a trait I have always admired in a woman. For a while I thought we would be happy together."

He fell silent, looking out the window again and at the people rushing through the rain. The sun peeked out through a gap in the clouds, painting a rainbow across the sky.

When he turned back to Zoe, he had tears in his eyes. "But then I ran into Laurette. When I'd known her before, she'd been only a child but had blossomed into a woman—a *beautiful* woman."

Zoe was just about to bring up the bruises on Laurette's arms when the café door opened and Henri strode in. She'd been so eager to talk to Gervais that she'd forgotten her lover lived nearby. Not wanting to be seen, she twisted in her seat, turning her back to him. Fortunately, he didn't glance around, just made a beeline for the kitchen. Police business? A stolen recipe?

Not police business at all, because in answer to his shout of "Emile!" their waiter emerged from the kitchen with a big smile. The waiter said something they couldn't hear over the din, whereupon Henri slapped him on his back and handed him a large cigar with a blue bow tied around it. The people near the two erupted into applause, chanting congratulations.

"Happy news for *le garçon*, no?" Gervais said.

Zoe forced a smile. "Yes."

He leaned toward her. "Are you all right, Zoe? Your pretty face, it's..."

"I'm fine," she whispered, trying to keep her voice from carrying, "but please don't say my name so loudly. I don't want that tall man over there to see me."

Too late. At the sound of Gervais's voice, Henri had turned, and although Zoe ducked her head, he spotted her anyway. Henri gave the waiter a final pat, then approached her, his face thunderous. Upon reaching them, he snapped, "Zoe, what are you doing here? With this... this *person*?"

She could hardly tell Henri the truth, or at least the whole truth, so faking a calm she didn't feel, she said, "I needed some notecards, nice ones, and I'd heard that the stationers down the street had the best selection, so I made the trip. Then it began to rain, and I ran into Gervais, who, like me, was sheltering in here."

"Do you take me for a fool?" Henri barked.

At that, the noise in the café lessened as both Americans and the French—united in their nosiness—paused their conversations to listen.

"Shhhh!" Zoe hissed. "Jesus, Henri, you're making a scene!"

"Then try telling the truth for a change. What are you doing with this murderer?"

A collected gasp from their audience. *Murderer?* Oh, how *delicious!*

His face contorted with rage, Gervais started to rise from his chair. "Take that insult back, Monsieur!"

Was Gervais about to challenge Henri to a duel? Reaching out her hand, Zoe attempted to coax the irate *vicomte* back into his seat. "Please, Gervais. He is not a *Monsieur*, he's *Detective Inspector Challiot of the Sûreté*, and he imagines he has business here, *but he doesn't.*"

To Henri, she cautioned, "Gervais and I are simply having a friendly conversation while we wait out the rain." By way of illustration, she waved her rain-spattered package at him.

Henri was taller than Gervais by at least two inches, but that didn't seem to bother the *vicomte*. "I am no murderer, Inspector. My solicitors successfully answered that accusation in court, and the matter was found in my favor."

"Yet the other man remains dead."

"True. As I almost was, because he fired first. It was only by the grace of *le bon Dieu* that his bullet lodged in my shoulder instead of my heart."

"Duels are illegal in France," Henri snapped.

"So is disturbing the peace in cafés."

The two glared at each other for a few more seconds. Then, almost as if he were backing down, Henri turned to Zoe and hissed, "I'll talk to you later, Mademoiselle."

With that, he stalked out of the café.

Chapter Eighteen

After Henri's unfortunate intrusion, Zoe's conversation with Gervais devolved into bland remarks about Paris's unpredictable weather. As soon as the rain stopped, the two said their *adieus* and went their separate ways. Gervais, to do who-knew-what (fight another duel, probably), and Zoe, to...

To what?

Maybe the men's behavior had rattled her, but the clouds were rushing northward, and the sun was out again. She decided that it might be a good idea to spend time in a more peaceful setting.

The Jardin du Luxembourg, so close to her own little house, fit the bill perfectly. The three-hundred-year-old park was a delight, strewn with flowers, statuary, and comfy benches to sit upon. When she'd first arrived in Paris, she avoided it because the park was a major draw for the city's children.

She'd been weaker then, and the sight of so many children had crushed what was left of her heart. Over the years, her initial despair had softened, and thanks to Gabrielle and her plant-filled room, Zoe had learned that Nature could blunt the sharp edges of pain.

Two Metro stops later, Zoe was walking through the park's entrance on rue Auguste-Comte, enveloped by the scents of thousands of flowers and the rustling of a million leaves. Ready to test herself, she headed straight for the park's Grand Basin, knowing what she would see there.

Children. Masses of children. Some of them the same age her own child would be.

Yet with all that had happened to Zoe in the past few years, she still felt hope. Hope that the Pinkerton Detective Agency would find her daughter, hope that she would someday see her face, and she would hold her, hold her, hold her....

If only she'd been stronger right after her birth! Strong enough to prevent her stepmother from *throwing* her newborn across the room, only to land in the outstretched arms of Beech Glen's awful overseer.

Zoe had lost so much blood, enough that they all—including herself—believed she might die. And to be truthful, would death have been so bad? Her heart was broken, her body was broken, and she'd been ready to follow Pete's ghost wherever he led, be it Heaven or Hell.

But in extremis she'd still known she must turn away from Pete's memory and instead live for the squalling infant Silas carried out of the basement and into the night. Had he killed her? Buried her somewhere out in the woods, her tiny body condemned to rot in Beach Glen's rich soil?

Could even Silas have been so cruel?

As Zoe took a seat on a bench facing the Luxembourg's Great Basin, she remembered the day she'd fallen from the oak at the back of Beech Glen's immense horse pasture. The pain from her shattered leg notwithstanding, she'd somehow managed to crawl over a quarter mile to the gate to get help. And what had Silas said to her when he found her? He'd called her a "dumb little shit."

But when it counted, Silas had stretched out his sinewy arms and caught her baby in the air instead of letting her drop to the basement's brick floor.

Today, sitting on a bench in the Jardin du Luxembourg, Zoe was finally strong enough not to suffer at the sight of other mothers' laughing children. Back straight, she turned her attention to three small boys floating their little sailboats in the garden's Great Basin. One of the boats, commandeered by a dark-haired boy, was wobbling over, a fate that the other boys—both towheads, both bigger—found entertaining.

Unkindness was part of childhood, too, wasn't it, because the world wasn't overrun with saints. Especially not in Paris. When the dark-haired boy waded into the basin to rescue his craft, he took time to slap his bullying friends' boats on their sides, briefly sinking them.

A scuffle ensued. Once they all were runny-nosed and crying, their mothers dragged them apart. One of the mothers turned to Zoe and said, *"Les enfants sont impossibles."* Children are impossible.

Zoe nodded, although she disagreed. *Not having your child with you is impossible.*

The heat of the day had gentled in the shade of ancient oaks and maples. A soft breeze tickled Zoe's cheek while she watched the other mothers depart with their weeping boys.

A girl would be gentler, she thought. *Not as selfish.*

Then, despite herself, she chuckled. She remembered Lee-Lee, her younger sister, tearing the hair out of Zoe's favorite doll because Zoe wouldn't share.

We were both monsters!

She wouldn't expect perfection when she and her daughter were reunited. She'd know better.

This moment of realism roused Zoe out of her reunion fantasy. Her child—if she still lived—would be no saint. But, oh, how she would delight in her daughter's imperfections!

Zoe sat there for almost an hour, smelling roses and leaves, hearing laughter and tears, until she finally calmed. Then she stood up and brushed away a shell-pink petal the breeze had carried into her lap. It looked so fragile, so helpless.

Fragility.

Katrina certainly wasn't fragile. The spirited young artist, who was now working for Veronique's flea market, hadn't seemed bothered when her boyfriend acted the bully; she'd sassed back. And when Yves had pushed her to move in with him, she'd simply laughed and walked away, swinging those almost masculine arms.

Zoe looked through the limbs of a garish maple, where a bird's nest nestled near the narrowing trunk. Now that the children were gone and the park was quieter, she could hear strained peeps emanating from their little abode. They were hungry, calling for their mama. She smiled up at them.

Once, while visiting the flea market, she'd seen a lovely bronze birdcage and had been tempted to buy it. It was only upon reflection she realized she'd have to buy a bird to keep in that beautiful prison. She couldn't do that, but she came close.

Beauty could be so seductive that it overwhelmed conscience.

Is that what had killed Laurette? Her beauty? It was possible, so it might be wiser to consider Fabian, the man Laurette had wronged. He was strong enough to kill, and certainly no saint. A tough man who could easily have put those bruises on Laurette's arms. As for motive, hadn't Laurette exchanged him for a high-and-mighty *vicomte*?

Men killed because of hurt pride every day.

Then again, so could a woman. As Zoe left the Luxembourg's grounds and headed home, she cautioned herself not to blindly accept the obvious. This reminded her of Madame Crab, the flea market saleswoman, who'd claimed that Laurette hated all Germans.

Had that actually been true?

Advanced age—Madame Crab had to be at least sixty—did not necessarily confer peacefulness or sanity upon its sufferer. Zoe knew this from experience.

While she was still living at Beech Glen, Jolie Mae, her aged aunt, had dropped by for visit, whereupon it became apparent that the old woman's mind was failing. During a fraught conversation, she had taken issue with Zoe's comment that the June afternoon was a fine one. For some reason known only to Aunt Jolie Mae, that innocent statement had angered her so much that she'd slapped Zoe across the face. Only the swift intervention by a passing maid had kept the old woman from delivering another blow.

Given Madame Crab's age, her mind might have been as damaged as Aunt Jolie Mae's. So it wasn't beyond belief that she would take revenge on the customer-poaching Laurette.

Not beyond belief, maybe, but certainly not likely. Especially since there was someone else who might have had a different grudge against Laurette.

Katrina.

If Laurette had insulted the German girl, as Madame Crab had claimed, the insult could easily have led to an act of vengeance.

"*Merde!*" Zoe grumbled.

Unfortunately, a stylishly dressed woman walking toward Zoe heard, and hissed, "*Ne m'insulte pas, salope américaine!*" Do not insult me, American slut.

After squeaking out an apology, Zoe ducked her head and picked up her pace.

$$\cdots \diamond \cdots$$

Before she'd left the house that morning, Madeline had been putting the finishing touches on a big pot of coq au vin. Her housekeeper's niece was due to go into labor any day now, and she didn't want Zoe to starve while she was attending the delivery.

Thinking that a pastry would make a nice complement to the chicken's wine-fueled tartness, Zoe stopped off at LeBron's Patisserie, since that last pistachio cream puff had been so heavenly. Today, she might try one of those fruit tartes.

As she raised her hand to push open the bakery's door, it swung toward her, and Isabeau Joubert rushed out, crashing into her. The impact made the fresh baguette tucked under the girl's arm fall to the ground, along with Zoe's library book and expensive stationery. They all landed in a dirt-colored rain puddle.

"So sorry!" Isabeau cried. Her eyes were no longer red, and with her creamy complexion and black hair, she no longer looked pretty; she looked beautiful. As the two scrambled to retrieve their soggy treasures, Isabeau kept repeating, "My fault! All my fault!"

"No, it wasn't," Zoe responded. "I should have paid more attention and seen you coming out. Here, let me buy you another loaf."

"Oh, that's not necessary. This one's still edible."

"Nonsense," Zoe said, tossing the ruined baguette into a nearby waste receptacle. "We don't know what else was in that puddle. People walk their dogs along this street." With her free hand, she took Isabeau by the arm and led her back into the bakery, where she ordered a replacement baguette for her and a fresh fruit tarte for herself.

Once outside again, Zoe used the chance encounter to find out what she could. Life in Paris could be difficult for a woman alone, especially if that woman was given to apologizing for something that wasn't her fault. Smiling, she said, "I think I've seen you here before. Do you live in the neighborhood?"

Isabeau motioned toward the tall apartment building down the street.

"Then we're almost neighbors!" Zoe exulted. "Now that the rain's stopped, let's walk home together."

Paris was especially lovely after a rain. The clearing sky reflected onto the wet streets, turning them blue. The gray buildings' reflections rippled in the puddles, almost as if they were waving at them. The air was a warm bouquet of cement and greenery, redolent with the yeasty smells of baking bread. To hurry along during such a sensory feast would be a crime, so the two ambled slowly, sharing stories about their lives in *La Cité*.

Zoe gave Isabeau a heavily edited version of her life, that she'd come to Paris to study art, which was only partially true. She left out the part where she'd been banished from her Alabama home for loving the "wrong" man and having his baby. Instead, she talked about the art school she'd attended, her first gallery showing, the painting she was working on now, and how much she enjoyed the pastries at LeBron's Patisserie.

By the time they reached Isabeau's building, Zoe had learned Isabeau was nineteen and that she'd moved to the city only a year earlier from a small farm northeast of Avignon. Both her parents were dead, one killed by a German gun, the other by grief. The only member of her family remaining alive was her father's sister, with whom she didn't get along.

"Aunt Delphine is living in our old farmhouse now," Isabeau continued, "and manages as best she can. She wanted me to stay and help, but there was nothing left for me there. Most of the men in the area either died in the war or moved away, so farmhands are hard to come by. Same with possible husbands." After a pause, she added, "Lately I have been thinking I made a mistake, that I should never have come to Paris, that I should have remained on the farm and died a virgin."

"*La Cité* not to your liking?" The very thought someone could dislike Paris seemed shocking, but Zoe appreciated the young woman's candor.

Instead of answering, Isabeau silently watched a dray horse pulling a cart heaped with scrap metal. As it passed, the horse deposited a load of road apples on the cobblestones. Then, meeting Zoe's eyes, Isabeau said, "My job isn't everything I wished for."

"Oh? What is your job?"

A weak smile. "I was hired to do accounting work. My mother taught me the skills before she died. You'd be surprised at the amount of figuring that needs to be done on a farm. I think that's why my aunt is so angry with me now. It's not that she misses me; she misses her accountant!"

At that, Zoe told Isabeau that keeping the accounts on the family plantation back in Mercy, Alabama, had been a demanding job, too. It often kept her brother, Brice, cursing far into the night, only to begin cursing again the next morning.

"Then you understand! To do a good job of accounting, you must be able to concentrate, and given, um, given my current situation, that's nearly impossible." Her smile faded and she looked back out at the street. The horse and cart had disappeared into an alleyway.

"Current situation?"

A strained laugh. "Oh, nothing. I guess every job has its drawbacks. I began by working on the Île de la Cité, which as you know is lovely. However, I was recently transferred to St. Jean de Riis, which is *not* so lovely."

"You work at the church, then?"

"Not at the church per se, but at one of the buildings nearby owned by the Diocese."

"I would have thought nuns did all that work."

Isabeau shook her head. "Most of the time that's what happens. But the nun who earlier had my job was transferred to a different diocese, which left an emergency at St. Jean, so they brought me on as a temporary replacement. I'd been attending Mass there for almost a year and they were acquainted with my accounting skills. But I guess you could say my placement there has become untenable, because...because..." she took a deep breath and looked up at the sky. "Oh, my! Isn't that sky beautiful?"

The sky was streaked with pink and orange. Deep purple clouds scuttled behind Isabeau's building, hinting that the rain might be over for the day. Before Zoe could agree that it was indeed beautiful, Isabeau slipped past her and vanished into the building's courtyard, leaving Zoe frowning on the sidewalk.

Her frown deepened when she turned the corner and spied Henri lurking at her front door. Madeline must have already left for the day.

"What took you so long?" he grumped, entering the house behind her. "I've been waiting out here in the rain!"

"Well, it's not raining now. And I don't remember inviting you here."

"What were you doing, sitting in a café with the most notorious man in Paris?"

Fumbling through her clutch for her key, she answered, "What I do when I'm not with you is none of your business. You don't own me." She had yet to look up, purposely keeping her face hidden. Otherwise, he would see her smirk of satisfaction at his jealousy. Despite their frequent arguments—almost always about her disinclination to obey his orders—Henri still wanted her, and she gloried in that.

"It *is* my business, Zoe. Death follows Vicomte Paget around like a faithful hound."

"So? Some people are just unlucky." She unlocked the door, and when she entered, he followed hard on her heels.

"Go ahead, ignore me!"

She set her packages on the table. Then he paused, took a deep sniff, and added, "What's Madeline made for you?"

"Coq au vin. Sorry, but there's not enough for two."

When she unwrapped her packages, she was delighted to find that neither the library book or her new stationery had been ruined by their fall into the rain puddle. The tarte looked as fresh as it had been back at the patisserie.

She would write a couple of notes this evening, then start reading the Christie. She'd always loved a good mystery when it was only fictional.

Finally facing Henri, she said, "Gervais was hardly going to bash me on the head in the middle of a crowded café."

"*Gervais?* You are on a first-name basis with that villain? You keep on putting yourself in danger, Zoe! I... I don't know what I'd do if you...if you..."

"If I what?"

When he put his hand on hers, she jerked it away. Boundaries firmly established, she took pity on him. "Perhaps you would like a glass of wine. It's good for the nerves. I have some excellent Château d'Yquem left over from the poker game last night." But she wasn't about to share her fruit tarte.

A heavy sigh. "I'm on duty."

She smiled. "Like you were on duty when you gave a cigar to that waiter?" At his chuckle, Zoe began to relax. Henri had been in the wrong. He knew it, and he knew she knew it. "Then how about a nice glass of water?"

He thought about that for a moment, then said, "Come to think of it, I've always enjoyed a good Sauterne."

Ten minutes later he was tied to the bedpost.

Chapter Nineteen

After Henri left, Zoe had her dinner—the tarte was as good as it looked—then painted past midnight. She fell into bed, exhausted. Tired though she was, she couldn't sleep. She just stared up at the mirrored ceiling as the hours ticked past. Around two, she finally drifted off, only to find herself in a mishmash world that somehow tied Beech Glen to the Parisian women's prison. In the dream's mixed-up geography and chronology, she'd escaped from the prison to hide in a basement, leaving her baby behind in the prison.

She woke up crying.

Realizing more sleep was impossible, she dried her eyes, threw on a smock, and ran into her studio. She spent the next few hours painting a gouache portrait of her daughter, who would be six years old now. Big enough to ride horses. Big enough to ask questions. Big enough to...

To *what*? To realize someone was missing from her life?

At birth, the little girl's curly hair had been almost the same color as her skin, a glowing amber; her eyes, the same startling blue as Pete's. Zoe painted and wept, wept and painted, until the portrait was finished. Then she stood back.

Yes, her daughter would look something like that—a symphony of amber and blue. That first year in Paris, Zoe had started calling her *Amber*, after her lost child's beautiful coloring.

· · · ◇ · · ·

When the sun finally rose, she put the painting aside and drew a hot bath. Her toilette complete, she donned a jaunty lavender chemise and headed to La Rotonde for breakfast. This morning she allowed herself an herb-and-cheese omelet, a fruit plate, and a croissant, washed down with several cups of café au lait.

At least she didn't have to eat alone. The day was mostly clear, and the humidity wasn't too awful, so she was eventually joined by a couple of friends eager to discuss Paris's latest scandals. What artist was having sex with another artist's model. Which writer was having sex with a poet's wife. What musician nearly died post-coitus at an after-hours opium party.

"And then, of course, there's *your* affair with the handsome police inspector," noted Archie Stafford-Smythe, stealing a slice of pear from Zoe's fruit plate. "He visited you yesterday, didn't he?"

"Does it show?" Zoe asked, flushing.

"Oh, please," grouched Louise Packard, crankier than usual because her arthritis was acting up. Her eyesight wasn't what it used to be, either, and she was squinting. "We've talked that one to death, Archie. Let's hear something fresh for a change."

"Well, there's Mater," Archie ventured.

Louise arched her eyebrows. "What is the randy Countess of Whittenden up to now?"

"She's fallen in love with one of the American swimmers. Johnny What's-His-Name. *Le Figaro* ran a photograph of him in his swim costume, and she's decided she *must* have him."

Louise frowned. "That would be Johnny Weissmuller, probably, and fat lot of good her crush will do her. She's what? Sixty-three to his just-turned twenty? To further the impossibility, I hear the American team's coach is keeping all his boys confined to their quarters in Olympic Village. He believes sex drains an athlete's energy."

Derisive laughter all around.

By the time Zoe finished her breakfast, she not only knew who was having sex with whom, but also who *wanted* to have sex with whom. It being Paris, the list was long.

Gossip session finally ended, Zoe said a quick *adieu* to her friends and headed for the flea market. The gouache portrait was already dry, and she needed a frame for it. But when she arrived, she didn't see Katrina. Instead, the Belcoeurs' table was being manned by a furious Veronique.

"Do you know how many sales I've already lost this morning because that girl didn't show up?" Veronique complained when Zoe approached. "Almost ninety francs' worth!"

Zoe turned her hands over in a display of helplessness. "I don't know what to say."

"Maybe my sister was right, that we can't trust Germans!"

Zoe was about to point out that she'd personally known several Germans, and they were—the Great War aside—nice people. But seeing futility in that, she let Veronique vent her fury. During that time, several possible customers approached the sales table, then, recognizing trouble, beat a hasty retreat.

Despite the loss of even more business, Veronique only settled down when Zoe finally said, "Katrina doesn't live far from here, so I'll go over there and see what's up. Maybe she's sick."

"I doubt that," the angry woman said. "Those damn Germans are healthy as horses."

Zoe didn't bother reminding Veronique that horses weren't really all that healthy, often suffering one life-threatening colic attack after another, nearly bankrupting their owners with ever-climbing vet fees.

Her need for a picture frame forgotten, she headed for Katrina's apartment. Halfway there, she spotted Yves, Katrina's photographer boyfriend, hurrying along the other side of the wide boulevard. When she called over to him, he didn't turn, just sped up as if the Devil himself was nipping at his heels. Maybe he'd run out of photograph paper.

The rest of her walk proved uneventful, and as she approached the six-story building on rue Lormel, the sky was a vast dome of blue. Given the refreshing breeze, she wondered if more records would be made today at the Olympics, not that she actually cared. In fact, the closer the day drew when she'd be joining Archie and his mother at the swim meets, the more she dreaded it. Zoe hated crowds. Sports weren't for everyone, especially not a woman whose left leg was shorter than the right. At least Katrina lived in a basement apartment, so today there would be no miserable six flights to climb.

Upon arrival, Zoe pushed open the building's main door. Like last time, it was unlocked. She entered the courtyard just in time to see a squirrel climbing up the small garden's chestnut tree. The surrounding plantings, mostly flowers mixed with a few herbs, were too meager for the tree to be the squirrel's home, so something was up. As she studied the tree closer, she saw a small birdfeeder hanging from a low branch. Aha! Mr. Squirrel was a thief! She watched in delight as he scampered across the limb to the feeder, hung upside down to reach it, then stuffed his cheeks with birdseed. When his cheeks could hold no more, he clambered back down, scolding Zoe as if he suspected her to indulge in thievery, too. Zoe liked squirrels. So did some Parisians, especially when the animals were served in a nice Burgundy sauce.

Bidding Mr. Squirrel *bonne chance* in his future endeavors, she headed for the short flight of stairs that led down to the basement apartments.

Katrina lived in B-4, well along a dark corridor bereft of

sunlight. For a painter, such a location had to be hell, but at least
the girl's boyfriend allowed her to paint in his atelier on the building's top floor. Zoe guessed the favor came with strings attached,
including having to put up with Yves's list of "shoulds." Maybe, if
Katrina didn't lose her job today for being late, she would eventually be able to afford a flat with a window that bathed the room in
the steady northern light so prized by painters.

Zoe rapped on Katrina's black-lacquered door and waited.

No sound of rushing feet. Maybe, like Zoe, Katrina had
painted into the wee hours. If so, it was time the woman hauled
herself out of bed and did what she could to soothe Veronique's
righteous indignation.

Zoe knocked again, louder. Still nothing. Irritated, Zoe hardened her fist and banged on the door with all her might. This time
the racket roused someone: a cat. It sounded hungry.

After spending a few moments cursing under her breath, she
decided that Katrina might be upstairs in Yves's flat, painting away,
oblivious to the time. As Zoe steeled herself for the dreaded seven-
flight climb to Yves's atelier, she gave the door a final hearty kick
with her good leg.

Surprisingly, the door flew open and the still yowling cat rushed
out and ran outside.

Merde! Now Katrina might not be only minus a job but minus
her pet cat, too. Why in the world did the foolish woman leave her
door unlocked? This was Paris, not some placid country village
where everyone knew everyone else and crime was rare. But now,
given the monied, sports-obsessed Olympics crowds, Paris was a
mecca for thieves.

Zoe stuck her head into the apartment and yelled, "Katrina!
Get out here! Your cat got out!"

A door opened down the dark hall, and a bearded man in an
undershirt yelled for Zoe to shut up, that he'd had to work all night

and deserved at least a few hours' sleep without some stinking American making a racket. Ignoring him, Zoe decided to rouse the painter from whatever sweet dream she was enjoying and, if necessary, frog-march her over to Veronique's flea market.

None of that proved necessary.

Katrina's body lay just beyond the doorway, her face beaten so badly that if it hadn't been for the Prussian blue paint under her fingernails, Zoe wouldn't have recognized her.

She heard someone screaming. Only after listening to the shrill lamentations for several seconds did she realize the screams were hers. She couldn't stop herself until the suddenly kind neighbor pulled her away from Katrina's body.

He was still standing with his arms around her, still murmuring comforting words when the police finally arrived.

Chapter Twenty

"What in God's name are you doing here, Zoe?" Henri's face was white as a bone.

"I... I..."

The man in the undershirt tightened his arm around her and whispered, "Tell him, *ma petite*. I promise it will be all right."

But it wasn't all right. When Zoe stumbled through her explanation, it made no difference. Katrina was still dead.

"I'm having one of my men drive you home, Zoe."

What? What was Henri saying? Something about *home*? Did he mean Beech Glen?

No. Beech Glen wasn't home anymore. Le Petit Bibelot was.

"Y...Yes. Home," she stuttered. "*Home.*"

· · · ◇ · · ·

The rest of the morning was a blur, and when she finally came back to herself, she was lying fully dressed on her bed, staring up at the mirrored ceiling.

"Drink this," someone said.

Madeline. Touching a liqueur glass to her lips. It was filled with something clear, but from its scent, it wasn't water.

"What...?"

"Drink, *ma petite*. Then we can talk."

Zoe drank. Whatever it was tasted horrible, but it helped ease the burden of grief. Some of it, anyway.

"Katrina's dead, Madeline, and I'm afraid it might be because of the job I got for her."

The housekeeper shook her head. "The only person responsible for that girl's death was her killer."

Zoe shook her head. "Death seems to follow me." Her mother. Her father. Her best friend. Laurette. Now Katrina.

She forced herself to sit up. "What time is it?"

"Just after one. I couldn't leave you alone, now, could I?" For some reason, the smile made her housekeeper's face look older. Maybe even fifty.

Zoe took another sip of the fiery liquid. Gagged. Swallowed. "I'm fine now."

"Inspector Challiot ordered you to stay in bed."

"He was here?"

"No, he sent word with the policeman who drove you home. Your friend is probably still at the crime scene but said he'll be along as soon as he's finished."

Now that Zoe's head was clearer, she knew she couldn't handle being questioned again, which Henri was certain to do. "I have to get out of here," she told Madeline.

"But where will you go?"

Zoe knew exactly where she'd go. To the most peaceful place in all Paris.

With Madeline's presence no longer needed, she sent her home, then washed her face, put on an unwrinkled dress, and headed out again.

Upon arriving in Gabrielle's vibrant room, Zoe greeted her as if nothing was wrong. She sat down in the bedside chair, picked up *This Side of Paradise* from the table where she'd left it several days before, and took a deep breath. The window was open, and she could hear the din of passing traffic, both mechanical and horse. A heady blend of gasoline and newly laid asphalt floated in, almost overwhelming the scent of the room's lush greenery. But from where Zoe sat surrounded by potted grasses, a pocket of peace remained.

Not in Fitzgerald's book, though. At this point in the novel, the Rosalind character had just broken up with Amory. No surprise there, Zoe thought. Amory's family had lost their money, and greedy little Rosalind had always had an eye to the main chance. With a toss of her pretty head and a less-than-sweet goodbye, she quickly fell *out* of love with the woe-begotten protagonist.

Now Zoe began to wonder if she'd made a mistake in choosing the Fitzgerald. How could poor Gabrielle relate to the behavior of such shallow Americans? Gabrielle, with her degree from the Sorbonne. Gabrielle, who before her brain drowned in an orgy of burst blood vessels, had plumbed the universe of plant life.

If only Fitzgerald's words would stop blurring. And if only the sight of Katrina's battered face would go away. Zoe soldiered on to the end of the chapter, vowing never to start another. Yes, Fitzgerald had been a bad choice. Poetry would have been more appropriate. Something uplifting by Wordsworth, or something French like the naughty Rimbaud. Or Verlaine, perhaps. Or Apollinaire. Or even the nonsensical Cendrars.

But could Gabrielle's injured brain, no matter how superb it had once been, grasp the convolutions of poetry? Sighing, Zoe closed the book. "I'm sorry," she told the unresponsive woman. "I think we'll switch to something by Colette. I'll bring my copy of *Claudine in Paris* next week."

With that, Zoe left the apartment.

Chapter Twenty-One

—— Gabrielle ——

The night is clear, the moon full. Venus has risen above the gray-blue rooftops, but the street below remains alive with lovers cooing to each other while they stagger home from the brasseries. I cannot sleep, but Odile understands. She remains on my pillow, stroking my cheek with one of her eight delicate legs.

"Do the lovers disturb you, Madame?" the little spider asks. She is smaller than a woman's fingernail and as bright green as a new-mowed lawn.

"Not really. But as I grow stronger, I am finding it more and more difficult to stay asleep."

"Bad dreams, Madame?"

"Lonely dreams."

"Surely you cannot be missing your husband." A Huntsman spider, a genus infamous for eating their mates, Odile has difficulty understanding my love for unfaithful Henri.

"Yes, Odile. I miss him."

"But he visits with you every day, so what is there to miss?"

"His embrace. The very same embrace he now shares with the American woman."

How long has it been since I have felt Henri's love? Four years? Six? I do not know. When I was at the height of my illness, I could remember nothing. Not the taste of a good meal, not walks in the forest, not making love with Henri…

But as I grew stronger, so did my memory. With it came an almost intolerable loneliness until the day this tiny green spider crawled up on my pillow and began to speak. In an even bigger miracle, I—who had been rendered silent for so long—was able to answer her!

"It is a warm evening, Madame," Odile says.

"Evenings are usually warm in July."

"There are so many people outside. Where did they all come from?" Odile asks.

"A few days ago I heard Nurse Arceneau talking with my husband about the Olympics, so I imagine they have come here from all over the world. When I was a girl, I swam daily in the lake near our château, dreaming that one day I would swim competitively, too. But dreams change, and when I became a woman, I dreamt of becoming the first female botanist to discover a new leaf."

"What do you mean, 'new leaf'?"

"It's a plant no botanist has yet to discover and classify."

Another stroke from a tiny leg. "A leaf is a good place to hide."

"Only because you are green yourself. A plant would have to be as large as a full-grown rhododendron bush to hide me." I try to smile, but the weak muscles in my mouth make it difficult. The hurtful brainstorm that felled me remains stronger than I am.

But Odile knows a joke when she hears one. "Madame is most amusing today."

"No one loves a sourpuss."

The spider chuckles.

We are silent for a while, each of us thinking our own thoughts, listening to the chatter of the crowds outside. I hear Spanish. Russian. Mandarin. Swahili. And so much English! English consonants are almost as aggressive as German, so I must thank le bon Dieu that Zoe's French is softened by a Southern drawl. Her accent renders some of the passages she reads aloud to me unintentionally humorous. When she first began that huge novel—or was it a memoir?—by Monsieur Proust, her long vowels poked through her French, making me laugh, but the sound came out "Ack-ack-ack."

Zoe thought I was choking and ran to fetch Nurse Arceneau.

I am now careful not to scare or humiliate her, because next to Henri and Odile and Arceneau, Zoe is the person I need most in this world.

How unfortunate that I have to kill her.

Chapter Twenty-Two

—— Zoe ——

Having stewed indoors for several days, Zoe finally felt able to leave the house. Through mostly sleepless nights she'd come to believe that Madeline had been right: the only person responsible for Katrina's death was her killer. She emerged from her dark place with a purpose: finding the killer, no matter how much it cost her. But first she needed to just get out of the house.

Once bathed and dressed, she hobbled her way through throngs of Olympics-goers toward breakfast at La Rotonde. The unused muscles on her left leg ached so that she had to stop one block short of the café. This displeased the man and woman following too close behind her, and the man, an American, snapped, "Quit blocking the sidewalk!"

Zoe shuffled to the side and leaned against the building. The sign on its window proclaimed in delicate script, *Hervé Pompanon, Les Meilleurs Vêtements*.

A new dress! Maybe that would chase away whatever remnants of misery she still carried. Something startling and outrageous, perhaps, a frock that celebrated the vivid colors of life, not the darkness! She entered the store and was immediately seen by a salesgirl who couldn't have been more than eighteen.

"With her lovely, hennaed hair, mademoiselle would look charming in topaz."

It was almost the same color as *Amber*. The name she'd chosen for her lost daughter.

"Blue, I think," Zoe responded, leaving the past behind for now. "Or green. No. What do you have in yellow, and I really mean bright screaming yellow, not gold?"

Bafflement scampered across the girl's face, stopping only to change into a half-hearted attempt at admiration. "Mademoiselle is bold!" She disappeared into the back room and, before Zoe could change her mind, returned with three yellow dresses, holding them up for inspection. The first was too frilly, something that would have better suited a child. The second was too plain. But the third...

The color of sunrise announcing a perfect day.

"It just so happens to be in mademoiselle's size!" the girl exulted.

Zoe needed another dress like she needed more grief, but she found herself being led into a small fitting room. The girl helped her disrobe, and within seconds, she was attired in a bright yellow sheath. It fit perfectly, hugging her hips like a lover. It was too long, though.

"Mademoiselle will be thrilled to know that we have a cunning cloche the same color as the dress."

By now, Zoe had made her decision. Although the dress hung inches longer than she would like, she had an idea. This was the dress she'd wear to the Olympics swim finals, and since she'd be sitting outside in the merciless July sun, a straw boater would offer more protection than a cloche. "I'll need the hem taken up," she told the girl. "A full three inches."

The girl's eyes widened and her cheeks flamed. Now she looked more like fifteen. "*Three*, did mademoiselle say?"

"Yes, three. I also want you to take the fabric you cut away from the hem and use it to make a hatband for that wide-brimmed boater over there." She pointed to a brown straw hat on a fabric dummy. "Adorn the band with a yellow bow the same color as the dress." Zoe made a circle with her hands to illustrate the size she wanted. "You can have that done, correct?"

"It... It would be a large bow. And such handwork would be expensive."

"Cost doesn't matter," Zoe answered, momentarily thrilled at being able to make such a statement. "I will arrive at the Olympics wearing a piece of the sun."

• • • ◇ • • •

A happy surprise awaited Zoe when, after breakfast, she returned to her little house. Parked in front was a large green truck. She recognized the vehicle as one of the Berliet CBAs left over from the Great War. On its sides were the words TRANSPORT DE MASQUE DE PORTRAIT. Portrait Mask Transportation. Below those blood-red letters was a hand-painted copy of two lifelike masks used to cover the disfiguring facial wounds suffered by so many of the war's soldiers. The truck had been purchased after the war by her friend Reynard Dibasse for his haulage business.

When she entered Le Petit Bibelot, she found Reynard sitting at the long banquet table, conversing with another man. Both wore portrait masks over what was left of their faces.

"Madeline let us in," Reynard said. The smile in his voice matched the gentle smile on his mask, which had been painted by Zoe herself.

"And that good woman fed us!" said his friend. "She didn't even flinch when we took our masks off to eat."

Of course Madeline hadn't flinched. A former battlefield nurse, the housekeeper had seen worse.

Now that Zoe had returned, Madeline began gathering up her

things. On her way out the door, she called over her shoulder, "Oh, by the way, you received a letter, and I left it on the sideboard. It's from the States."

Zoe tensed. Her brother, Brice, had been sending a series of angry letters demanding that as soon as she came into her inheritance, she begin paying her share of Beech Glen's expenses. The house needed a new roof. The double doors on the stock barn were coming apart. Their best bull had died. The tax man was making threats.

Zoe hadn't answered any of his letters, and she wouldn't answer this one, either.

Forcing a smile, she said to Reynard, "It's nice to see you again, although I must say your mask's looking a big battered."

Reynard laughed, then introduced the other man as Antoine Tremblay, a member of the same battalion during the war and who'd suffered similar facial wounds. He explained that Antoine had been an arts critic before the war, and still practiced his profession by freelancing articles about painting, theater, and dance for *Le Figaro.*

"Not that anyone cares what we critics look like; they already hate us for much less," Antoine cracked. "You can guess why we're here, no?"

"You need touch-ups," she said, leading them into her studio. Both men's masks were dinged and scraped, much like a fender on a Peugeot after a run-in with a Renault.

Reynard nodded. "*Exactement!* Karen hammered out the dents, but as you can see, she could do nothing with the paint."

Karen Wegner, sculptor friend and a regular at Zoe's Poker Fridays, had fashioned the masks out of copper while she and Zoe were volunteers at the Studio for Portrait Masks, a charity for wounded veterans funded by American sculptor Anna Coleman Ladd. Ordinarily, the studio's work would last a lifetime, but as the condition of the men's masks testified, haulage was a rough business. Reynard had been one of Zoe's early clients, but Antoine's mask had been made by Ladd herself before she'd returned to America.

"It'll take the paint time to dry," Zoe warned. "Will that create a problem?"

In answer, Reynard slipped a piece of linen out of his pockets. It had two holes cut out for eyes. He'd worn a similar cloth over his damaged face before receiving his lifelike mask.

"We don't have any work to do for the rest of today or all day tomorrow, so we'll be fine. Might scare the cat, though," Reynard chuckled. He'd been a recipient of a gift cat, one of the kittens Zoe had rescued from the feral litters prowling the neighborhood.

She had seen what was left of Reynard's face and was no longer shocked at his true appearance. A German gun had torn away part of his lower jaw, his nose, and an eye, but in a severe mercy, the same gun had spared both his ears. He was a mess, but wearing his mask, he cut a dapper figure.

"How's Karen these days?" Zoe asked him, leading the two men into her studio. "The last time I saw her she looked ill."

Since he hadn't yet put on his linen mask, Zoe could see a grin on what was left of his mouth. "Karen's pregnant, thank *le bon Dieu*! But the poor woman's sick every morning and curses the day she met me."

Zoe was delighted by this news. The couple had desperately wanted to grow a family, and now they'd begun just that. "When is the baby due?" she asked, clapping him on the back.

"We figure she'll arrive around *La Toussaint*." All Saints' Day.

"Or *he*," Zoe corrected.

Reynard waved his hand in dismissal. "I want a girl who looks like her beautiful mother, but she wants a boy who looks like the very handsome me before I formed a close relationship with a German gun."

"Then one of you will be disappointed," Antoine said. "Maybe even the Germans, who might even now be plotting another invasion of France."

They all laughed at such an impossibility.

Preparing flesh-colored paint for Reynard's mask was easy, his skin tone being similar to Zoe's own. A mixture of titanium white, yellow ochre, umber, and a touch of vermillion. Since he was a natural redhead, she also mixed colors to match the worn-away freckles across his mask's nose and cheeks.

She was in the process of adding a new freckle when Antoine spoke up again. He'd taken off his own copper mask but hadn't covered his face with a linen square. His wounds were terrible, but not as terrible as Reynard's, and most of his mouth remained intact.

"I read in *Le Figaro*," he began, "that you knew those flea market women who got themselves murdered and that you are the actual person who found them."

Zoe stiffened. After days of being wracked by guilt, she'd vowed to banish the two women's dead faces from her memory, but now they'd returned, delivered by a so-called "journalist." In a frigid tone meant to staunch more comments, she said, "You've expanded your literary beat by writing about crime?"

Antoine was either unaware of her changed mood, or he just didn't care, so he plowed ahead. "I'm thinking about it. Do the police have any suspects?"

Zoe composed herself before saying, "Not really. Are you asking for yourself, or for some other news rag?"

A flutter of fingers. "Just curious."

"Then I must disappoint you. There are no suspects yet. The police are still investigating."

Zoe made a big business of handing Reynard's mask back to him and watched as he carefully set it down on a side table so as not to smear the fresh paint. He kept his gauze mask on out of courtesy, and his eyes—visible from the two holes cut into the fabric—looked at his friend with irritation.

Antoine ignored him. As Zoe started repainting his mask—a deep olive, perhaps a throwback to some Algerian forebearer—he said, "I have found that when someone says 'not really,' they often mean 'yes.'"

Zoe somehow managed not to tell him to shut up.

"Mademoiselle Barlow, I promise not to put your name into print if you tell me your suspicions. I can work with that."

"A promise of secrecy from a journalist?" She managed a laugh. "Will wonders ever cease?"

For a brief moment, Antoine had the decency to look abashed, but his discomfiture wasn't great enough for him to drop the subject.

"Yes, you have my word. As you have probably heard, there's been interest shown in a certain notorious *vicomte*, whom I believe you know."

"He's merely a passing acquaintance."

Aghast at his friend's lack of sensitivity, Reynard made a noise that sounded like *pfft*.

Antoine ignored that, too. "Whenever there's a murder, there's always interest in the Vicomte du Paget. Wasn't his fiancée—Laurette, I believe her name was—once engaged to the man who runs the garage next to the Belcoeurs' scrapyard? What about him? Men do not always take lightly to being cast aside for another."

"You mean Fabian Napier?"

A twisted smile. "I always say what I mean."

"That's probably your biggest lie yet, Monsieur Journalist."

"Perhaps it is. But jealousy, especially when accompanied by damaged pride, is a common enough motive for murder, don't you agree?"

At this point, Reynard cut in. "Shut up, Antoine. If every man who got his pride hurt murdered the woman who wronged him, there wouldn't be enough prisons in all of France to hold them all."

"That does not disguise the fact that they frequently do!" But after that, Antoine shut up.

In the ensuing silence, Zoe worked quickly, and within minutes she handed the repaired mask back to him, saying, "I'd keep my curiosity in check, Monsieur, or you might attract the wrong kind of attention."

As soon as the two men left, Zoe went into the kitchen to see what kind of lunch Madeline had left for her. Warming in the oven was a large bowl of onion soup, topped with bread and cheese. Next to it, a puffy chocolate soufflé. She lingered for a while over her meal—especially the soufflé, which was so delicious it could have come from the patisserie down the street. Once finished eating, she put the dirty dishes in the sink, then poured herself a glass of merlot.

Carrying her glass, she walked back into the large sitting room and picked up her copy of *Le Figaro* only to discover it was yesterday's edition, not today's. She had already read every page.

"Oh, hell!" She tossed the newspaper to the floor.

Frustrated, she wandered over to the sideboard, where she'd left her copy of Colette's *Claudine in Paris*. As she reached for it, she saw the letter Madeline had told her about. It bore U.S. stamps. Another dunning notice from her brother, Brice. Well, he could go take a flying leap off...

Wait. The address wasn't in Brice's awkward scrawl; it was typed like a business letter. Had Brice taken his grievance against her to an attorney? Well, good luck with that, because no attorney would ever...

Then she noticed that the envelope was postmarked New York City, not Mercy, Alabama. And the name typed in the upper left corner didn't say Brice Barlow.

It said *Pinkerton International Detective Agency.*
Hands trembling, she opened the envelope.

••• ◇ •••

July 1, 1924

From: Albert Grimes MacGregor, New York City, USA

To: Miss Zoe Barlow, Paris, France

Dear Miss Barlow,

We at the Pinkerton Detective Agency have put out feelers for Silas Hansen's possible residence in either California or Texas. But so far, we have come up with little. Our search for the overseer who was the last person to see your child alive will continue as long as you wish.

In better news, we have found a probable lead on the whereabouts of Mrs. Dorothy Reed, Peter Reed's widowed mother.

A reliable source in Mercy, Alabama, one who wishes not to be named, informed our agent that after the Reeds' house was burned by the Ku Klux Klan, Mrs. Reed and her youngest son took refuge with a neighbor. According to the same source, several days later Mrs. Reed and her son left for New York City, where they intended to join her two daughters already in residence.

Before their escape from Mercy, Mrs. Reed had been seen with a healthy female infant who appeared to be part White. It is possible the infant was your daughter.

So far, our agents' efforts to locate Mrs. Reed in the Harlem neighborhood of New York have come up short. We believe that the Reed family, fearing further action by the Klan, are now living under assumed names. Unfortunately, many Harlem residents are wary of anyone who appears to be any sort of government official, especially when that person is of the White race.

Yet there is some good news. Next month, John Scobell III, the grandson of Pinkerton's first Negro agent, will be transferred to the New York office from Chicago, and we trust that Agent Scobell will be more successful in questioning the residents of Harlem.

Yours truly,

Albert Grimes MacGregor, Head Agent

Pinkerton Detective Agency, New York office

As Zoe held the letter, the past descended on her with the ferocity of an invading army.

Falling in love with Pete. The "Jump the Broom" ceremony that married them because interracial marriage was illegal in Alabama. Planning their lives together in New York, far away from the small minds of Mercy. Pete's trip north to find a job and an apartment for them. His sudden decision to put their plans on hold to join the U.S. Army alongside other members of the Harlem Hellfighters.

The day his mother, Dorothy, flagged Zoe down as she was driving past her mother-in-law's small cabin. Somehow, she'd known Dorothy had received a letter, which began...

"We regret to inform you..."

Chapter Twenty-Three

August 1918
Mercy, Alabama

Pete was dead. In France, killed by a German bullet in the War to End All Wars.

Zoe had to do her grieving in secret, in the thickest part of the woods so that no one at Beech Glen could hear her sobs.

That first terrible night, when questioned by her stepmother about her wan coloring and red eyes, Zoe had answered that she'd come down with a summer cold. The lie served her well enough until she learned how to silence her emotions. Pete's mother had taught her how.

"Never let them see you cry," Dorothy had counseled Zoe. "Tears give them power over you."

Zoe had never seen her mother-in-law cry. Not when the cross had been burned in front of her cabin for setting up the Negro school. Not when her husband had been lynched. Dorothy hadn't even cried when she'd handed over the letter announcing Pete's death.

Instead of weeping, Dorothy made plans.

"You can't give birth here," she said as the two sat by Beech Creek, hidden from the big plantation house by a hundred acres of trees. "If your people learn you're having a Negro man's baby, God only knows what they'll do to you. And the baby."

Zoe agreed. Brice, her hard-drinking brother, belonged to the local Klan. Isabelle, her stepmother, although beautiful on the outside, enjoyed watching livestock slaughtered.

"It's too bad your family sold your car," Dorothy added.

For a moment Zoe had been puzzled. Yes, her family had sold her King Model EE after she'd foolishly run it into a big oak, but what did her poor driving habits have to do with her pregnancy?

Dorothy enlightened her. "We still need to get you to New York somehow. The apartment Pete rented for you has been released to another couple, but you can stay with my daughters. They've rented a flat in Harlem, and there's plenty of room for you and the baby."

After weeks of grief and fear, a strong feeling of gratitude almost brought Zoe to her knees. Then guilt that she'd wrecked her only means of escape. Why had she driven so fast?

But Dorothy wasn't finished. "I've been trying to reach them, but my letters haven't been answered." She looked down at the ground, where a small lizard awaited a fly. When she looked back up, she said, "You know how it is for us."

Yes, Zoe knew how it was. Few telegraph offices in Mercy County would do business with a Negro. Handwritten letters sent by Negroes often got "lost in the mail." The only communication that was almost certain to arrive would be anything sent by the U.S. Government.

"Don't worry," Dorothy continued. "I have some other ideas on how to reach them. It might take some time, friends traveling back and forth, for instance. Even if the mail can't be counted on, my friends can. In the meantime, I'll show you how to hide your pregnancy until we can get you out of here."

Dorothy fell silent for a moment, then added, "If I can't help my child, I can at least help yours. And I think I'll go with you. I'm tired of listening for hoofbeats in the night."

It had been a good plan, but in the end, it hadn't worked.

Dorothy hadn't been able to communicate with her daughters until December. By then it was too late.

The next few weeks were a horror.

That cold night in the woods, when premature labor had begun as Zoe limped through the trees toward Dorothy's house. Falling, then being dragged back to Beech Glen by her enraged brother. The agonizing birth. Her baby being torn from her arms. Being forced onto the ocean liner, her breasts still swollen with milk. The rough crossing to France. Learning that the family château was no more, leveled by a German bomb, her French grandmother and aunt killed, the staff dispersed.

But then there was the gentle stranger who'd rescued Zoe as she stood sobbing in front of the bank in Paris where her brother had deserted her, as if the bank account set up in her name would make everything all right...

Zoe remembered everything she'd vowed to forget, but she'd be damned if she would ever forget Amber.

Now, sitting in the buttery glow of a Paris afternoon, Zoe composed a telegraphed response to the Pinkerton detective's letter.

PUT AGENT SCOBELL ON CASE UPON ARRIVAL IN NY-STOP-

DOROTHY REED ALABAMA TEACHER NEGRO SCHOOL-STOP-

CHECK HARLEM SCHOOLS-STOP-MONEY NO OBJECT-STOP-

SEND WEEKLY UPDATES-STOP

Chapter Twenty-Four

The next morning, not feeling up to indulging in Parisian gossip, Zoe skipped her usual breakfast at La Rotonde and foraged through the kitchen cabinets for whatever she could find. She was rewarded with a stale baguette and coffee left over from yesterday. There would be no culinary rescue today from Madeline, who was now attending her niece's labor some ten miles south of Versailles.

It had not escaped the family's notice that midwives' and nurses' patients survived the birth process more frequently than those attended by doctors. Perhaps because midwives washed their hands more often.

After forcing down part of the stale baguette, Zoe busied herself sending cancellation notes to her usual *Salon du Pitié* attendees, adding that she would more than make up for it next time. Then she went into her studio and painted feverishly for the next three hours, stopping only when she heard a knock at the door. To her delight, it was Bella Chagall and eight-year-old Ida, bearing gifts in a piecework bag similar to Zoe's.

Bella frequented the flea markets, too!

Bella opened her pretty blue-themed bag to reveal a still-warm challah loaf and a large sampling of spiced cookies.

"Talk about angels!" Zoe exulted, leading them straight to the long table. "How did you know I was starving?"

"A violinist sitting on a roof sang the news to us," little Ida answered, grinning.

It occurred to Zoe that Ida was only two years older than her own little girl would be, and for a moment the realization cast a shadow over her delight. She recovered quickly and after a short trip to the kitchen, served her visitors freshly made tea. Then she slid the baked goods out of the piecework bag and attacked the warm challah. Mother and child both claimed they'd already eaten, but Ida did accept one cookie.

"I'm surprised Chagall didn't come with you," Zoe said, although she could guess the reason.

"Marc planned to—you know how much he adores you—but as we were gathering our things to leave, a dealer dropped by to see his current canvas, and…" Bella shrugged. "Being an artist yourself, I'm sure you understand."

"All too well." With much of the challah already resting in her stomach, Zoe moved on to the cookies. They were seasoned with honey and anise and so delicious that she had to force herself to stop before she ate herself sick.

For the next few minutes, the two women discussed art and artists and the eternal struggle between the two.

"When Marc's not painting, he feels guilty, and when Marc's painting, he feels guilty he's not with us," Bella said. "You are fortunate to have no one to tempt you away from your easel."

Bella didn't know Zoe's history and therefore had no idea of the pain she had just inflicted, but Zoe took care not to let it show. "Solitude can be a gift to an artist."

"Or a poet!" sang Ida. "Or a philosopher!"

Surprised, Zoe asked the child, "They are teaching those subjects to eight-year-olds these days?"

"You can blame Marc for that," Bella explained. "You know what an inquisitive mind he has. He was reading aloud something by Jean de la Fontaine the other day, and Ida memorized one line."

Thus cued, the little girl recited, "*La patience et le temps accomplissent plus que la force ou la passion.*" Patience and time accomplish more than strength or passion.

Zoe clapped her hands in delight. Well, of course Chagall would have been drawn to that particular quote. He'd waited several lonely years before he could bring his wife and child from Russia to France, and he did it without losing his famously sweet temperament. For a moment, Zoe felt a rare despair. Would Dorothy—if she was, indeed, raising her little girl—read French poetry to her? Or would Dorothy, a teacher, maintain the standard American curriculum for six-year-olds?

And did any of that matter, as long as her child was still alive?

To escape from these thoughts, Zoe clapped her hands and said, "I have an idea! Why don't I use the tarot cards to tell Ida's fortune? I can't wait to see what her future holds. Something wonderful, no doubt."

Ida, for once losing her sophistication, cheered, but Bella appeared less happy. For a moment, Zoe feared she might have made a religious faux pas. The Chagalls were Jewish, and from everything Zoe had heard, the Jewish faith maintained even more Thou-Shalt-Nots than did the Baptists in Mercy, Alabama. Uncertain, Zoe said to the child, "If that is, ah, if fortune-telling is all right with your mother."

Now Bella gave Zoe a cautious smile. "Telling Ida's fortune is fine." But she leaned forward to whisper, "Just as long as her future is a happy one, which I trust it will be."

"I'm certain your darling Ida has a splendid life in front of her,"

Zoe whispered back, knowing that her tarot deck was minus its scariest cards.

Zoe's card-culling paid off. After a good shuffling, she laid them out in a Tree of Life spread and began her reading. By the time she was finished, Ida had been promised a long life involved in the arts, an exciting move to another country, a handsome and successful husband who was crazy about her, and several well-behaved children. The final card, which signified the querent's Highest Ideal, was The World.

"*Et voilà, Ida!* The World means you will have everything you wish for!" Zoe said as Ida began to clap again. "Art! Love! Money! Children! Who could ask for more?"

"A kitten?" Ida turned a pleading face to her mother.

"We'll have to see about that," Bella said, throwing the girl a mock frown. Lowering her voice again, she whispered to Zoe, "I'm curious about the card that shows so many men fighting with long staffs. You glossed over that one."

Zoe reminded herself to pull the Five of Wands before giving another reading. Bella had been right: there was no optimistic reading of that particular card. Waving away Bella's worries, she answered, "The card forecasts children's squabbles, nothing more."

This explanation was only partially true. Zoe knew that the Five of Wands signified a more serious quarrel than children's squabbles. In some readings, depending on the card's placement and the cards surrounding it, the Five of Wands forecast war. But of course, after witnessing the horrors of the War to End All Wars, the world would never again be so foolish.

Besides, Lee-Lee would be safe in today's Germany because the Germans had learned their lesson. And maybe one day, her sister would find the courage to leave her awful husband and come live with her in Paris. Along with Amber, of course.

A family reunited.

When she tasted the tea she'd made for her guests, she found it slightly bitter, but she solved that by adding a spoon of sugar—three for Ida. Now it was fine, especially when the remaining bitterness was contrasted by the spiced sweetness of the cookies. With the tarot cards safely tucked away, the conversation segued from happy futures to the problematic present. Bored with this, Ida busied herself on the floor, playing a game of jacks. Judging from her skill in picking up the jacks during one bounce of a red ball, the girl's fingers proved as nimble as her mind.

Meanwhile, Zoe and Bella chatted about the crowded streets, for which they shared a mutual loathing. "The sidewalks were so crowded we could hardly make our way here." Bella grumped.

"And it gets worse every day," Zoe agreed. "But we only have a few weeks more to bear it; then everyone will go home."

An expression of sympathy crept across Bella's face. "I read in *Le Figaro* that you found both those murdered flea market women. That must have been so painful for you. Is it true that no one has found the killer yet?"

"Unfortunately, yes." Zoe looked over at Ida, who was now picking up three jacks at the same time.

Bella shook her head. "Terrible! Someone told me, I forget who, that you are friends with the detective heading up the investigation. Are the police getting close to an arrest?"

Zoe sighed. "My friend—his name is Henri—never tells me anything about his cases. Whenever I ask, he tells me to mind my own business."

Disappointment clouded Bella's lovely face. "So you know nothing?"

"Nothing."

Bella frowned. "If someone important had been murdered, the case would have been solved the next day. But mere flea market salesgirls..." She cleared her throat, which had grown raspy. Then, holding up her piecework bag, she added, "I bought this at the same flea market you must have. The saleswoman was rather crabby and pretended not to understand me, so I wound up paying more for this than I should have. The girl at one of the other tables was very pleasant, though, and seemed to have no trouble under-standing my Russian-accented French. So I bought a clock from her. A small one, of course."

Zoe blinked. "You bought a clock from Laurette?"

"A German with a French name?"

"Did you say *German*?"

A nod. "Oh, yes. I understand the hatred so many people feel toward that country because of the war, but I have found that not all Germans are awful. Katrina was a delightful person. What? That look on your face, Zoe. Is something wrong?"

"I... I was the one who put her in harm's way by recommend-ing her for a job at that flea market. She'd only worked there for a couple of days before..." Zoe's voice lowered so Ida couldn't hear "...before she was killed."

After a moment's silence, Bella responded, "I read in the news-paper that the second victim was found dead in her apartment, not in the scrapyard like the first."

"Yes." Zoe's own name had been mentioned in the article, something Bella couldn't have missed. "You didn't drop by just to chat, did you?"

Caught, Bella said in a rush, "I must confess that when I saw your name in the article I said to Marc, 'Look, this is the angel who saved your paintings!' He began to worry that you might be in danger yourself, and then he asked me to come over here and see if you were all right, and he would have come himself but the dealer was there looking at his new work and since I'd been baking all morning I thought that..."

Zoe held up a restraining hand. "So you thought you'd bring me challah and cookies and have a nice little chat. Ah, Bella, you know my weaknesses! But now it's my turn to ask a question. When you were chatting with Katrina, ah, the German, did she say anything that might be of interest to the authorities? If so, I beg you to share your information with them."

Bella shook her head so fiercely that a tendril of her glossy black hair came unpinned. Hurriedly pinning it back up, she said, "Nothing good happens when Jews talk to the authorities. If you know anything about the Dreyfus affair..."

Thanks to the time Zoe had spent in libraries, she did know, although the scandal had happened decades earlier. French Army Captain Alfred Dreyfus, a Jew, had been found guilty of treason for sending classified documents to the German military. On the basis of extremely flimsy evidence, Dreyfus had been sentenced to life imprisonment at the notorious Devil's Island. Two years after his imprisonment, proof arose that the real traitor was Major Ferdinand Esterhazy—who was not Jewish. Yet the military court refused to admit its error.

In the end, it took a presidential pardon and a not-guilty ruling by the Supreme Court to get Dreyfus released from Devil's Island and given, as an unofficial apology, the rank of major. Later, during the war, this innocent man, whose only "crime" was in being Jewish, bravely served the country that had treated him so unfairly.

France's Jews hadn't forgotten the lessons of the Dreyfus affair, so of course Bella preferred not to contact any government official about anything.

"I understand," Zoe said. "I originally became interested in the subject when I first overheard my French grandmother talking about Dreyfus when she came to visit us in Alabama. She didn't know I was listening." Zoe shot a quick look at Ida. Otherwise, the descriptions her grandmother had given of France had made the country sound like the Garden of Eden. But Zoe was now old enough to know that every Eden has its snake.

"Marc told me everything he knew about the Dreyfus affair," Bella went on. "He was told by an elderly friend who lived in Paris during that terrible time. But here is what I personally know about the flea market's German salesgirl. She was sweet to me and Ida, too, although I could tell something was bothering her. As we made our transaction for the clock, she kept looking around, as if she was afraid of something. Or someone."

"Do you remember when this was?" Zoe asked.

Bella shook her head. "Saturday, I believe. I'm not certain of the time, but I think it was before noon. Or maybe after. I do remember that Marc was busy painting when Ida and I went out."

It took Zoe a moment to digest this. "You say she appeared fearful?"

A shrug of those delicate shoulders. "Maybe I'm imagining, but..."

Bella was interrupted by Ida's voice. "Mama, that German woman was scared as she could be. *Anyone* could tell that!"

The little girl had been so quiet while playing jacks that Zoe had almost forgotten she was there. "How, Ida? What do you mean when you say, 'Anyone could tell'?"

"Because she kept looking at those other two women as if she was scared to death of them."

"What other two women?" Bella asked her daughter. "You and I were the only customers."

Ida's face grew cross, as if her mother had just said something foolish. "But we weren't the only ones there!"

"Well, there were the other two saleswomen..."

"Yes, Mama! Those other saleswomen! And they were both giving her dirty looks. Like maybe they wanted to kill her."

Zoe listened to the two argue—precious little Ida and shocked

Bella—until she stopped them with a question. "Ida, do you *really* think they looked like they actually wanted to kill Katrina? Really?"

A pout. "Isn't that what I said?"

Bella threw Zoe an exasperated look. "I wouldn't put too much stock in what Ida says. She tends to exaggerate."

Thoroughly disgusted now, Ida glowered. "I do not!"

"Sweetheart..."

"I'm not talking anymore! Not for the rest of my life!" With that, Ida put her jacks away and crossed her arms in defiance.

Chapter Twenty-Five

When the Chagalls left, Zoe picked up the phone to give Henri the information she'd just learned. Unfortunately, her party line was already in use. On it, young Isabeau Joubert was pleading to be allowed to return home.

"I can't bear it anymore," Isabeau said, her voice hoarse.

"Can't bear much, can you?" the older woman muttered, her provincial French sounding rough. "Guess you forget about the time you said you couldn't bear living with me!"

"Please," Isabeau pleaded. "Please, Aunt Delphine, I..."

"The welcome mat has been removed." The woman slammed down the receiver, forestalling more pleas for mercy.

Appalled, Zoe decided to call Henri later. For now, she needed to find out what made Isabeau sound so desperate.

$$\cdots \diamond \cdots$$

By the time Zoe arrived at Isabeau's small apartment, the young woman's eyes were blurred with tears, which she hastily wiped away with the back of her hand. "What a nice surprise," she said, accepting Zoe's gift of a small platter of Bella's cookies. "Sorry, but I seem to have contracted one of those awful summer colds."

Zoe didn't respond to the lie. "A friend made these cookies for me, and I can't eat them all. Then I remembered that you, too, have a sweet tooth and might enjoy them."

Isabeau tried to smile, but the attempt was wobbly. "That was kind of you."

Although Isabeau's apartment was a mere one-room studio, it had been furnished with love and flair. The settee, little larger than a child's cot, was actually a daybed draped with a bright red-and-yellow paisley-patterned coverlet. Several cushions served as backrests, each echoing one of the coverlet's colors. There was only one chair in the tiny room, a deep maroon horsehair thing that had probably been around since Paris fought off Viking raiders, but when Isabeau bade her to sit down, Zoe found it surprisingly comfortable.

A scarlet rug that lay over the dark parquet flooring added to the room's warmth, while the white walls played host to framed covers from *Le Petit Écho de la Mode*, the women's fashion magazine. A surprise there, because each time Zoe had seen Isabeau, she had been wearing a black ankle-length skirt and a black blouse that, despite the July heat, had long sleeves and was buttoned up almost to her chin. It was obvious Isabeau took work home, too, because the small desk facing the opposite wall was heaped with accounting ledgers. A candlestick phone identical to Zoe's held down a large stack of papers; the girl must have an important job to qualify for that phone.

Maybe overwork was Isabeau's problem. Still, would overwork account for the level of anguish in her face?

When Isabeau offered tea to go with the cookies, Zoe shook her head. "No, no, I don't want you to go to any trouble. Besides, there's an important matter I'd like to discuss with you."

Bewilderment clouded Isabeau's face. "Something important? With me? I... I don't know about anything *important*."

This was where it could all go wrong, that Zoe's concern for the girl's travails could be put down to mere nosiness. But she had no choice. Continuing to listen to those painful phone calls wasn't to be borne.

"You may not realize this," she began, "but you and I share a party line."

"Oh." Isabeau looked down at her scarlet rug.

"Yes. And I'm sorry to say I've heard you beg your Aunt Delphine to allow you to return home, and I've heard her refuse. So I ask you this. Are you behind in your rent? If that's the problem, I am willing to help."

After a few half-hearted attempts to speak, Isabeau finally managed, "That is very generous of you, but...but I'm all right in that way. At least for now."

"For now?"

"I may have to quit my job, but I do have a little put aside, enough to keep me going. For a while." When she looked up at Zoe, a single tear tracked down her cheek. "Maybe I can bear what's going on, I mean, just put up with it, because... Well, because. It's probably all my fault, anyway. I just wish..."

Without planning to, Zoe crossed the room and put her arm around Isabeau. "Tell me."

So Isabeau did.

$$\cdots \diamond \cdots$$

When Zoe arrived home from Isabeau's, her bra, panties, and slip were drenched in sweat, and her once-pristine dress was now wrinkled. After patting some Chanel-scented powder over herself, she changed into fresh clothes, then headed back out. Next stop: the flea market.

The temperature had risen from hot to scorching, and by the time Zoe arrived limping on her bad leg, the sales tables had diminished from dozens to a mere six, and only two of the vendors were familiar. Veronique with her clocks, and Madame Crab with a new collection of piecework shopping bags. The sweet old woman with the circlets wasn't there today, but some of her items had made their way to Madame Crab's table.

Zoe once again paid her condolences to Veronique, who looked like she'd aged ten years in the space of a week. The shadows under her eyes were darker, and her lips had compressed into such a tight line they'd almost disappeared. Her table, though, was as organized as ever. Sensitive to her grief, Zoe pretended to be merely shopping, not gathering information, so she moved over to Madame Crab's table and pretended to examine her new wares.

"Why, I see you are offering flasks today," she said to Madame Crab. "Some of them even look familiar to me."

"My sister is ill, so I am doing her a favor. That's what sisters do. But she's a worthless woman, makes mistakes all the time, doubling my work!"

Zoe bit back a laugh at learning Madame Crab and the sweet Justine were sisters. Then again, sister duos weren't unheard of at flea markets, were they? Madame Crab and Madame Sweet. Veronique and Laurette. Sharing the work, sharing the profits.

For a moment Zoe's memory drifted back to Beech Glen and her own sister, Lee-Lee. They had been so close, but after that night in the freezing basement...

She wrenched the memory away and rejoined the present, where she saw an array of colorful piecework bags and other goods. Junk and treasures.

Ignoring a sudden breeze that made the piecework bags flutter, she picked up a semi-silver flask etched with a curlicued art nouveau design. "How exquisite!" she said. "Too bad I don't drink whiskey."

"Whiskey is good for the health," Madame Crab replied. "It heals the lame." With that rather insensitive remark, she gestured at Zoe's leg. "Or if perchance it doesn't heal, it serves as a palliative to make the pain go away."

Palliative be damned, Zoe thought. Whiskey could also make the wise foolish, as it had done so often with her brother, Brice, whose overindulgence in drink was bringing hard times to Beech Glen.

Besides, Zoe already had a flask.

Seeing that her sales pitch was going nowhere, Madame Crab tried something else. "Mademoiselle must have a friend who would enjoy a flask."

"Hmm."

Glancing at Zoe's hands and seeing the paint under Zoe's nails, she added, "You're an artist, correct? Well, most artists drink all the time and often find themselves in need of a good flask, no?" Making the pitch more personal, she picked up the silver flask and waggled it in front of Zoe. "This one's so small you can keep it on your taboret next to your palette. Or in your pretty clutch bag."

The breeze, hastening through the gap between the surrounding apartment buildings, intensified. Somewhere a street singer was singing about unending love.

Pulling herself together, Zoe asked the price of the flask. Her friend Louise Packard might enjoy it, and maybe whiskey would tone down the Cubist's arthritis pain.

"Only thirty-five francs, even though it's real silver."

Like hell it was. "Too much."

"Thirty, then."

"I'll think about it. By the way, I hear that Katrina looked upset the day before she was killed. Do you know anything about that?"

"If you don't have a string bag tucked into that cunning little purse of yours, I can wrap it in newspaper for you."

"Don't bother. I plan on buying another of those beautiful piecework bags of yours. But you didn't answer my question about Katrina." Zoe felt sweat trickling down between her breasts. Sneaking a quick look, she noticed a ring of sweat under both arms. Damn! This was the coolest dress she owned, which meant she'd probably have to launder everything she wore today.

Madame Crab frowned. "Katrina? She was a puzzle, that girl. Nice one day, short-tempered the next. And that last day she worked here, she looked upset about something. But being a German in Paris, who can tell what names she'd been called."

"Do you know what Katrina was upset about that day?"

"Just the usual, I expect. Tourists. Traffic. The heat. And like I said, maybe someone had called her a dirty Hun."

Looking around, Zoe noticed that in just those few minutes since she'd arrived, several tourists were scouting the tables' wares. All were drenched in sweat. One middle-aged woman, a Mississippian, Zoe guessed by her accent, was holding one of Veronique's clocks and squabbling about the price. Meanwhile, the young man with her—a son?—was checking out a pretty girl who seemed entranced by a sequined headband at a different table.

Zoe leaned closer to Madame Crab. "Do you know if Katrina had a falling-out with anyone here at the tables?"

When Madame Crab didn't answer right away, Zoe wondered if the old woman had become annoyed with all the questioning.

The Crab's sour face grew even more sour. "A falling-out? Ha! Mademoiselle Artist, let me tell you how it is. No matter how we feel, we have to smile and smile and pretend we are happy and gay, even when the heat is killing us, our feet hurt, our customers complain about our prices, and complain about how cheap our wares look. Then they whine, especially you Americans, that we can't give them free string bags to tote their little purchases back to their hotel rooms and then they..." She went on like that for several minutes, until Zoe couldn't stand it anymore.

"Yes, yes, but you've been doing this for years, am I right? Given your joviality and ease of manner, you've obviously learned how to deal with rude customers. But unless I'm mistaken, this was the first time Katrina had to interact with the public—you are so right, there!—and given the expense of many of the clocks, she was probably deluged with indignation from people who didn't know value when they saw it. Just like your beautiful flasks. And your lovely piecework bags."

Madame Crab grunted assent. "Ignorant, that's what they are. But not Katrina."

"You are an astute observer, Madame! Perhaps you noticed a particularly difficult exchange between Katrina and a customer?" After another short pause, she added, "Or even hard words with another saleslady?"

"I've told you everything I know. Now are you going to buy that flask or not?"

Recognizing there was little more to glean from talking to Madame Crab, Zoe hurriedly paid for the flask, then wandered over to a table manned by a round-faced girl with hennaed hair. She was selling a wild mixture of objects: circlets, cigarette cases, cigarette holders, ashtrays, and postcards—none of them racy. As it turned out, the girl's innocent face hid a clever mind.

"Did you..." Zoe began.

The girl—she announced her name as Mimi—cut Zoe off. "I heard you talking to that old crab, and there's nothing I can add. I know little about Katrina, other than her being new at the sales game. I have my own table to worry about and don't have time to snoop around."

Zoe didn't quite believe her but decided to play along. "My, what a lovely headband that is!"

"You bought a similar circlet from Madame Justine the other day. It had pearls and peridots."

"Justine?"

"That nice old lady with the table next to the bitch's. She told me all about it, the artist who made a purchase just so she wouldn't feel guilty about wasting a saleswoman's time. Maybe you want the circlet with rhinestones? They look just like diamonds."

No, they didn't, but Zoe could take a hint. "A woman can't have too many circlets, can she?"

"No, she cannot. And for you, Mademoiselle, I only charge thirty francs."

"Thirty?" Zoe raised her voice in horror. "Why that's..."

"Unfortunately for you, I am a better businesswoman than sweet Madame Justine. But some information is included in that price, so I should actually charge you more."

Outfoxed, Zoe pulled the francs from her clutch bag before the price of the circlet went up. "Your information better be worth it."

Mimi's face split into a grin. "If it isn't, you will still have a lovely circlet." Lowering her voice, she leaned over the sales table. "I can tell you that Katrina wasn't an easy person to work with, but maybe that was because she lived in a basement. That would make anyone irritable, *non*? She complained all day. About the weather. About the crowds. About her pushy boyfriend. About something being very wrong."

"What do you mean, 'something being very wrong'?"

A shrug. "Who knows? She might have been referring to the clocks, that they weren't what they were supposed to be. But just the other day I heard Veronique tell a customer that the clock she was interested in was not a true Ansonia, only a copy, so I might have been mistaken. Veronique is honest, perhaps even too honest, because she could be making more money than she does. She would have demanded the same honesty from Katrina, so there'd be no playing around there. And yet, I remember that when Katrina said something was wrong, she'd been looking at a handful of American dollars a customer had handed her."

"You think there was a problem with the money? Like it was counterfeit?"

Although the wind had gentled some, it was still strong enough to muss Mimi's hennaed hair, but she didn't seem to mind. "Such a thing wouldn't be unheard of at a flea market, especially when we accept American dollars. Some people think we salesgirls have no brains and that it's easy to get rid of their bad money with us. A German who didn't know much about dollars would probably have been the perfect person to try it on."

Having known sharp-eyed Katrina, Zoe knew better. Plus, there was something about the girl's story that didn't make sense. "But you just said that Katrina knew something was wrong when she looked at the money. Then why did she take it?"

The girl shrugged again. "Maybe she was very busy at the time and didn't look at it again until the end of the day, when we were all counting out our proceeds. By then, that customer was long gone. Now, which circlet do you want? The diamond or the emerald? They're still thirty francs."

More questioning proved Mimi had nothing more to say, so Zoe scooped up the rhinestone circlet and passed over the money. Maybe she'd overpaid, but what she'd learned was probably worth it.

She learned little more at the next two tables, even though she made certain to purchase items at each. By now she truly needed a roomy shopping bag, so without further ado, she retraced her steps to Madame Crab's table and looked over her remaining wares. Several piecework bags had been sold while she'd been talking to the other vendors, but a pretty shades-of-turquoise bag remained.

"Oh, these bags are so exquisite!" she told Madame Crab. "You say they were made by nuns?"

Madame Crab's face creased into a bit of a smile. "Actually, I made them. But my sister, Justine, who'd once been a nun before she came to her senses, does pray over them."

Zoe was long past being surprised that crabby people could create beauty; after all, she was well acquainted with the temperamental Pablo Picasso. "Well, Madame, you are to be congratulated. Your color combinations are exquisite."

"Of course they are." Then the crab's frown returned. "Now you need to either buy another bag at the same price as before or leave my table. This is a flea market, not a museum."

After buying another piecework bag, Zoe stuffed her other purchases into it and headed toward Katrina's building. The short walk was made more complicated because she had to stop often to give directions to American tourists who had become confused trying to navigate Paris's centuries-old streets. She finally made it to the Belcoeurs' building but had to rest her leg several times as she hobbled up the long climb to Yves's atelier. By the time she arrived at the photographer's apartment, she was limping badly. Ignoring the pain, she knocked politely on the oak door.

"What are you doing here?" Yves snapped, upon opening it.

Although his rudeness would normally have irritated her, it brought only pity now. The man was a mess. His eyes were swollen, and his beard, so striking when she'd first met him, had degenerated into scraggly wisps. His clothes looked like they'd been slept in. He reeked. So did his atelier.

"I need a favor from you," Zoe said. "And I'd rather not talk about it in the hallway."

"Why should I do you a favor?" he sneered. "You made it obvious you didn't think I was good enough for her."

While that might have been true, this wasn't the time to admit it. "But you loved her, and in the end, that's the only thing that counts, isn't it?"

To her horror, Yves began to cry in great, gulping sobs. Although disgusted by the stench of alcohol and unwashed male, Zoe stepped forward and put her arms around him, which made him cry even harder. Speaking in the soothing voice she used while feeding the feral cats around her little house, she led him back into his filthy atelier and over to a sofa that was losing its stuffing. She sat him down and let him cry, and when his sobs finally shuddered to a halt, she asked when he'd last eaten. He told her he couldn't remember.

She patted him on the shoulder and limped across a debris-filled room to the corner that passed for a kitchen. After hunting around, the only things she could find were a couple of rotting apples, and a baguette so stale it could have been used as a club.

Sighing at the thought of the building's long staircase, she said, "I'll be back in a few minutes."

··· ◇ ···

Thirty minutes later Zoe returned, her new piecework bag stuffed with pears, slices of smoked ham, and a loaf of still-warm bread. No wine, though. He'd already had enough alcohol, so she'd purchased a large bottle of iced lemon drink. After she set down the groceries on his small dining table, she made him a primitive sandwich. He chewed on the sandwich until it was down to a crust but stopped when she shoved a pear at him.

"You need something fresh, too," she ordered.

"I detest pears." His chin quivered. "And I don't want to live."

"Eat the pear and live anyway."

Weak from weeping, Yves obediently ate the detested pear and washed it down with lemon drink while Zoe decided to do something to make his atelier less germ-friendly. Dying for love was one thing, but dying from filth was ridiculous. For the next hour she moved around the flat, gathering empty wine bottles and picking up all sorts of debris from the floor: orange peels, moldy bread, cigarette butts, crumpled sheets of photographic paper, yellowing copies of *Le Figaro*. One of his cameras—it was the kind that took moving pictures—had been thrown against the wall, chipping the plaster. She returned the camera to the dining table to join some others, then swept up the fallen plaster, hoping his landlord wouldn't notice the damage.

Finally, with the atelier returned to some semblance of order, she limped back over to the sofa to rest her bad leg.

"That was nice of you," Yves said, taking another sip of lemon drink. No more chin-trembling, no more tears. He wiped away some bread crumbs that had been caught up in his raggedy beard. "Now, what was that you said about needing a favor?"

Chapter Twenty-Six

Still sore from yesterday's stair-climbing, Zoe was daubing a touch of chrome yellow onto her work-in-progress when her phone rang. After the fourth repeat of three shorts and one long, she picked it up.

"Zoe, you have to come over immediately." Henri, a rare note of panic in his voice.

"What's wrong?"

"It's Gabrielle! She's having some sort of fit!"

"But isn't Hélène Arceneau a nurse? And she's already there, right?"

Henri's voice rose even higher. "Hélène's tried, and it didn't help. But Gaby's always so calm when you read to her that I believe she'll...she'll..." A deep-throated sound, like a sob.

Jesus. Another weeping man. Zoe set down her brush without cleaning it. "I'll be right there."

Twenty minutes later, after two Metro transfers and a hobbling run along three blocks, Zoe was holding Gabrielle's paralyzed left hand as the woman's right hand struck at Henri. Her eyes were wild, and a froth had developed at one corner of her mouth, from which emerged animal-like grunts.

"Calm down, Gaby!" Henri commanded, apparently unaware that yelling at a disturbed woman was pointless. The proof was already scratched onto his face.

When Zoe motioned for him and Hélène to leave, they were only too happy to oblige.

Murmuring to the still-flailing Gabrielle, she cooed, "Did you have a bad dream, dear one? Goulies and ghosties and awful things like that? As I promised, we're dropping the Fitzgerald book, and see? I brought *Claudine in Paris!*"

As she began to read, Gabrielle's thrashing slowed, and those horrible grunts faded. By the end of the chapter, she was asleep.

Zoe rose quietly and tiptoed out of the room. "What started that?" she whispered to Henri and Hélène, who had been lingering just outside the door. "I haven't seen Gaby that disturbed in ages."

"I may have made a mistake," Henri said, wiping blood from the corner of his mouth. "I tried reading to her like you do, but the more I read, the more disturbed she became, until she... she started doing *that.*" He winced at the word. "I tried to calm her, and it didn't work, so I called for Hélène, and she came immediately, but she wasn't any help, either."

How odd, Zoe thought, that the husband couldn't calm the wife, but the husband's mistress could. "She just likes the sound of my voice."

They were now far enough away from the bedroom that whispering was no longer necessary, so the rest of the conversation continued at the usual level. "But I was reading the same Fitzgerald story as you were," Henri argued.

Zoe shook her head. "Part of the problem might be that she doesn't like Fitzgerald all that much, so we've switched to *Claudine in Paris.*"

Henri looked stricken, so as soon as Hélène disappeared into the kitchen, Zoe gave him a comforting hug. "How were you to know?"

"I'm beginning to think I know nothing."

She kissed his hand. "Which is exactly where wisdom starts. To know that we don't know, correct?"

"Perhaps. But sometimes we are better off *not* knowing." When he glanced back at the double doors leading to his wife's room, Zoe understood.

Regardless of Henri's love-words while enjoying sex, she had always known the depth of his love for his wife. He might now be physically unfaithful to Gabrielle, but that would end the day Gabrielle was well enough to become a complete wife again.

No blame there. Wasn't Zoe herself still in love with a memory?

Unaware of her thoughts, Henri sighed. "Oh, Zoe, I don't know what to do anymore."

"Love her. That's all you can do."

"Sometimes she looks at me like she hates me!"

She had never seen him look so bereft. A man of action, Henri's energy sparked the air whenever he entered a room. Crowds parted for him when he strode down the boulevards. Even tourists could sense he was a man of authority, but now he looked deflated, a man old before his time.

She covered his hand with hers. "Gaby still loves you. I can see it in her eyes."

"I see nothing like that. Just emptiness."

Gabrielle had been bedridden since the stroke felled her, and to Henri, her progress seemed minimal. When you saw someone every day, their path on the slow road back wasn't as noticeable as to someone who saw them only once a week. During the last two years since she'd been reading to Gaby, Zoe had seen blank eyes brighten and those once-flaccid hands move. Slow progress, yes. But Gaby was still young and was so well cared for by her husband and Madame Arceneau that recovery was almost certain. Zoe had steeled herself against the time when Henri returned to his wife's bed.

"Henri, you can't possibly..." she began, and then Hélène exited the kitchen, bearing a carafe of coffee and slices of a lemon gâteau.

"We're so glad you came," Hélène said. "You are such a calming influence for Gaby."

Zoe gave her a weak smile. The idea that she could be a calming influence on anyone seemed strange.

As soon as Hélène returned to the kitchen, Zoe asked Henri, "Do you have any suspect yet in Laurette's murder? Or Katrina's?"

The sorrow vanished from Henri's eyes, leaving them cold. "I'll tell you as soon as there's an arrest. In the meantime, I'd better not hear you've been talking to any of the suspects."

"So you're saying you have suspects?"

"If I do, that's none of your business!"

"There's no need to be rude, Henri. I was just making conversation."

"We've talked about this before, Zoe. Meddling in police business can get you killed. Once it almost did. I... I couldn't bear to lose you, too."

"That was years ago. Things are different now."

"*Things*, as you put it, have become more dangerous. Especially for civilians. Only yesterday an American was found beaten in Pigalle. He almost died!" Without warning, Henri put a gentle hand to her face. "If anything were to happen to you..."

"Nothing's going to happen to me."

"If it did, I... I'd be all alone."

She shook her head. "You'd still have Gabrielle."

It took him a moment to reply, and when he did, pain shivered across his face. "Yes. I would still have Gabrielle. Sometimes I feel so guilty about..." He couldn't say it.

But she could. "About us."

A silent nod.

She touched his hand. "You're not a monk, Henri. And I'm no nun."

Chapter Twenty-Seven

—— Gabrielle ——

When the American bitch leaves, I allow myself a deep inhale. Thus alerted, Odile emerges from her hiding place behind the frame of a watercolor and scurries across the room and onto my pillow.

"You did not enjoy Mademoiselle Zoe's visit today?" the little spider asks me.

"No. I'm still angry about that Fitzgerald novel. Why would she read such tripe to me?"

"Ah, but it was a sad story, and I felt so sorry for the man. He didn't deserve the way he was treated."

Although the stroke has weakened my face muscles, I manage to twitch my mouth into a half-smile. "I am surprised that a Huntsman spider who has killed and eaten her mate can feel sympathy for any male, especially a fictional human male."

Odile allows herself a chuckle. "My husband was only a spider, and once we mated, his duties on this earth were finished. Besides, after the mating, I was very hungry, and there he was, so delicious!" Another chuckle. "But this sort of thing isn't true of human males, who must not only fulfill the requirements of impregnation and must remain alive in order to provide shelter and food for their mates and children. The humans the American reads about are much more complicated than spiders."

I will not let this pass. "But that's no excuse, is it? When men such as my husband are fools about women, they deserve what they get. Both in fiction and real life."

Odile sighs. "Madame has become harsh of late."

"Not harsh. Stronger! I can make a fist now." With this, I curl the fingers of my right hand so that my fingernails touch my palm. "I am working on my left hand, too, and when it is as strong as the right, I will strangle the whore!"

Odile is silent for a moment, then says, "But who will read to you then?"

"I will teach you how to read, dear friend. And together we will read all of Colette's stories!"

A spider's smile is a wondrous thing to see.

Chapter Twenty-Eight

—— Zoe ——

The night was a bad one, with demons of guilt galloping through her head. *You are an adulteress,* they claimed. *Used by all, loved by no one.*

Zoe didn't bother arguing. She let the demons clamor on, and by the time they vanished, the sun was up.

Although she normally spent much of Friday mornings helping Madeline prepare for Poker Night, her housekeeper was still at her niece's birthing bed and would probably stay a couple more days. Zoe was on her own. Before Madeline had left, she'd made two quick pâtés for the poker players and stored them in the icebox. Now it was up to her to do something about the wine and crudités.

Tired though she was, Zoe's shopping trip took less than an hour. As she carried her purchases back to Le Petit Bibelot, a rough plan formed in her head. While she could do nothing about her own exhaustion, she could help someone else with hers. Namely, Isabeau Joubert. To put her plan into motion, she'd need a witness with steady nerves and good eyesight. Such a person also needed to have an unsullied reputation, which ruled out just about everyone Zoe knew. Including herself.

Both Hemingways were out of the running, mainly because of Ernest's increasingly bad behavior. War artist Dominique Garron only had one eye. Hervé Raez, her former "guardian," had endured several brushes with the law. Karen Wegner was too arthritic. Henri was out, for obvious reasons (he'd probably have her locked up in an asylum if he found out her plan). Avak Grigoryan, her trusty taxi driver, was miles away in the little village of Mesnil-Théribus, romancing a barmaid. Gervais, the Vicomte du Paget, was out, too. Due to the *vicomte's* participation in illegal duels, he'd narrowly escaped prison himself. Not that he'd care one whit about what was happening to a young woman he didn't even know.

Who, then?

The answer came to Zoe while she was slicing the vegetables for the crudités.

Reynard!

A bona fide war hero of the French Republic, Reynard had achest full of medals that proved his courage, and his mutilated face would remind the authorities of what he'd endured to earn them. To flesh out his qualifications, he was a faithful communicant at St-Germain-des-Prés, one of the city's oldest churches. On this occasion, that might count for more than medals.

A half-hour later, with the crudités safely stored in the icebox, Zoe hurried to the telephone.

Due to Reynard's thriving haulage business, he had a phone, and as soon as she rang him and described her plan, he agreed. In fact, he agreed so heartily that she had to warn him against any act of vengeance he might attempt.

"Don't make us look like thugs," she said.

"But..."

"I know what you want to do, but you can't. Promise me."

A few fierce grumbles, then an assent of sorts. "I promise not to kill him. Satisfied?"

Knowing that was as good as she was going to get, Zoe agreed. They would put their plan into action first thing tomorrow morning, but first, the still-sleepless Zoe had to endure Poker Night.

··· ◊ ···

Zoe hadn't paid much attention the other day when Gwennie, Archie Stafford-Smythe's countess mother, had asked if it would be all right if she brought along a new friend.

"He's such a charming boy, and has pots of money, so I am confident you two will hit it right off," the old woman had chirped over the telephone. "And from what he's told me, I don't think he's played a lot of poker. Isn't that delightful?"

Without thinking it through, Zoe had said yes, so now here she was, facing Gervais, the loathsome Vicomte du Paget, over the table. The fact that he could hardly tell a jack from a king didn't make her feel any better. She didn't like the way he kept staring at her, either.

Fortunately, both Archie and Gwennie kept talking about the Olympics swim meets that had occurred earlier in the day. They enthused about it so often, the *vicomte* couldn't get in a word edgewise.

"As a Yank, you should feel proud that the Weissmuller boy is doing so well," Gwennie told Zoe. "We might see him win a medal when you accompany us to the finals on Sunday. Wouldn't that be lovely? Right, Archie?"

Busy fussing with his cards, Archie managed a grunt of assent.

Gervais started to say something, but the countess cut him off.

"They say he swims something called 'the American Crawl,' a stroke he designed himself. He's supposed to be the fastest swimmer on the planet. But, of course, that friend of his they call 'Duke' is almost as fast. He's Polynesian, I believe. From some little island in the Pacific. Hawaii? Tahiti? You must be so excited, Zoe, about coming with us."

Zoe agreed, although she didn't really care. All she wanted right now was the poker game to be over before she bankrupted herself. She was so tired she was playing like a complete amateur. Maybe she'd get a good night's sleep, but she doubted it. Tomorrow was going to be hell.

Poker Night dragged on. Gervais du Paget proved to be a fast learner and managed a comeback during the sixth round, which he won with a straight flush. While he was collecting the pot, he said, "I'm beginning to like this game!"

He liked it all the way to the second-to-last hand, when a red-eyed Zoe managed to beat his full house with her four queens. He rebounded in the last hand, though, by beating her pair of tens with three sevens.

When the interminable evening finally ended and everyone was either cheering their wins or mourning their losses, Zoe waved her goodbyes as they vanished into the night. Only Gervais seemed reluctant to leave. Surely, he didn't want to crow about his good luck some more!

"You wanted to say something?" Zoe asked, yearning for her soft bed, her downy pillow.

He took her hand and kissed it before she could snatch it away. "I just want to tell you that I had a lovely time tonight, Mademoiselle Barlow."

As she started to close the door on him, he stuck his foot forward so that she had to choose between squashing it or...

He gave her a blinding smile. "I was wondering if you would do me the honor of accompanying me to dinner at the Café de la Paix. Your choice of evenings, of course."

"What?!" Zoe was so astounded she could manage nothing else.

"The chef is a genius."

Getting her breath back, she said, "Me? Go to dinner with *you*?"

"My good friends the Duke of Uzès and the Prince of Orleans dine there frequently, and I would love to introduce you to them. They are great collectors of modern art, and perhaps..."

"*Merde*." she muttered under her breath. Recovering from her shock, she said, "Yes, I've heard of them. But you know nothing of my work."

His smile grew broader. "Ah, but remember, I own one of your paintings, and I'm thinking about buying another from that little gallery on rue Friant. You need a higher level of exposure for your reputation to rise to the level of—who knows?—even Modigliani's, and..."

Zoe knew a quid pro quo when she heard one. The *vicomte* probably expected to be paid in bed for his introduction to those high-and-mighties. Oh, the gall! But she kept her outrage tamped down enough to say mildly, "These days I'm too busy for dinner with anyone." Then she kicked his foot away from the door and slammed it before he could say another word.

For a moment Zoe just stood there, stewing about the morally corrupt *vicomte*, but her brief moment of self-righteousness faded as she remembered her own failings. After all, wasn't she bedding a married man?

Longing for a more innocent time, she walked over to her desk and took out her husband's letters. Although her eyes were bleary from exhaustion, she began to read.

May 1918. New York

My darling Zoe,

Less than a week has gone by since my last visit to you, but it seems like forever. How can I live without my Zoe? I can still taste your lips and feel the embrace of your arms. Oh, how I wish I could have stayed with you longer, but I must continue to play lead trumpet with the Clef Club Society. Rest assured that every song I play, I play for you.

And now I must confess that I have done something which might make you unhappy. Mr. Europe, our bandleader, has proposed we take our music to our brave American soldiers fighting in France. To do this, we must join a new army regiment, which I have done. We will soon be headed for basic training.

The next time you hear from me, I will be wearing the olive drab uniform of the U.S. Army, but my weapon will be a trumpet, not a gun.

Do not cry, Zoe. I will be safe. When this war is over—and it will be soon, I promise—I will send for you and we will begin our life together in New York City as husband and wife.

Your heart-husband

Pete

Unable to help herself, she opened another letter, the one letter he would ever send her.

August 1918. Somewhere in France

My dearest Zoe,

So now we will be three!

You have made me so proud, my darling! I've been awake all night thinking of names. Jennifer? Harold? Samuel? Elizabeth? Moira? Perhaps I should leave the naming to you, my precious one!

Now, I know this may worry you, but today we heard the sounds of German gunfire—and we returned it! Yes, the days of playing music at rear bivouacs are over, and we have joined our French brothers in the trenches.

Do not be afraid for me, my darling. Instead, be proud of the history I will make with the Harlem Hellfighters. Be proud of your husband, who will prove today that he is a man equal to all other men.

Oh, Zoe, how much I love you! I pray for the swift end of this war so I can meet our child and hold you in my arms once more.

I must hurry now. Our lieutenant is calling out our orders.

Your heart-husband,

Pete

Zoe's eyes were dry when she returned the letters to their drawer, so she thought she'd be able to sleep through the night without dreaming.

She was wrong.

In the first dream, she was eight years old and lying at the foot of Beech Glen's massive oak, her leg broken in several places. In the next, she was standing in the barn, watching her father's body swing back and forth from a noose.

She was reading the letter announcing Pete's death in the slaughterhouse of the Great War. She was back in the damp basement, watching her stepmother throw away her baby. She was drugged and locked in the "stateroom" of a bare-bones ship carrying her from Mobile Bay to France. She was standing on a cold Paris boulevard, weeping and alone.

In the worst dream of all, she was reading a telegram from the Pinkerton Agency announcing they had found her baby's grave.

Chapter Twenty-Nine

At ten Saturday morning, Yves, Reynard, and a bleary-eyed Zoe set off for St. Jean de Riis in Reynard's *TRANSPORT DE MASQUE DE PORTRAIT* moving van. The sky was a clear blue, and the temperature was bearable. Unfortunately, this mildness had encouraged more tourists to leave their hotels, and several times Reynard had to brake sharply to avoid hitting fools who crossed the boulevards without looking for traffic.

As per Isabeau's instructions, they were all wearing black, the better to hide in the shadows. Yves kept fussing with his camera, double-checking and triple-checking, while Reynard started shaking his head. He worried aloud that "the girl" possibly had an overactive imagination, that nothing was really wrong—just mistaken. Zoe allowed him his concern; it would make him an even more valuable witness if things played out the way she believed they would.

Men thought one way about these kinds of situations; women thought differently. Most importantly of all, men never feared— never even *thought* about—the one thing that terrified all women all the time. Which was why Isabeau needed a woman present.

To keep herself from worrying about what lay ahead, Zoe allowed her thoughts to drift back to Gervais's invitation. *Have dinner with me*—and something else, no doubt—*and I'll introduce you to powerful men who can further your career.* That from a man who had just lost his fiancée to murder! Where was the grief? Where was the thirst for justice?

Damned aristocrats. The guillotine-happy French Revolution notwithstanding, aristocrats continued to believe that their supposedly elevated station made them immune to the decency they demanded from the "lower classes." As they drove toward the St. Jean de Riis complex, she fed her rage until she was almost trembling with it.

Good. She'd always preferred anger to fear.

The drive was not uneventful. Tourists of every size, shape, sex, and nationality thronged along the boulevards, some happy (their team had won!), some not so happy (their team had lost!). Near Gare de Lyon, two women—one waving a tiny Dutch flag, the other waving a Canadian flag—screamed insults at each other. A block farther on, a man dressed in last night's white-tie-and-tails vomited in the gutter.

Probably an American, since with the advent of Prohibition, Americans had forgotten how to drink.

Zoe and her friends arrived at St. Jean de Riis without personal mishap. The church's imposing stone edifice dwarfed the buildings surrounding it, but their target wasn't the church; it was the shabby-looking building behind it.

As promised, Isabeau was waiting for them at the rear door. Dressed plainly in her usual high-necked blouse and long skirt, the contrast between her clothes and her pale skin made her look sickly. So much so that for a moment, Zoe worried that Isabeau might be on the verge of backing out.

"Three of you?" Isabeau's voice shook. "I don't think..."

"*Mais oui*," Zoe said, in an attempt to surmount the woman's growing reluctance. "From what you've told me about the size of those cupboards, there'll be more than enough room. And as you can see, we're wearing enough black to staff a dozen funerals! We'll blend in with the shadows."

"But..."

Zoe didn't let her finish. "Which is better, Isabeau? What we've planned, or continuing to live in fear?"

"I... I..."

Before Zoe could interrupt her again, Yves stepped forward. The tenderness in his voice almost, but not quite, hid the fact that he was still grieving Katrina. "Courage, Mademoiselle. It will only take a minute or two; then you will be safe again."

"One way or another," Reynard grumbled behind his portrait mask.

"You don't believe me?" Isabeau asked him, but her voice was respectful. From the way she studied Reynard's mask, she was aware of the horror behind it.

"I am trying to, Mademoiselle, but what I believe won't count without proof, which is why Zoe asked me along to bear witness. So let's get this unhappy situation over with."

Encouraged, Isabeau inserted a large key into the lock. It took several tries before the lock clunked open. "He'll be here at ten thirty, and he's always punctual, so we must hurry."

Zoe checked her watch: ten fifteen. "Ready?" she asked the others. At their nods, Isabeau ushered them into the church's office.

Weak morning light shone through a high, narrow window, revealing stuffed bookcases. More books lay stacked on the tiled floor. Joining the books were scatterings of papers that no longer fit into a file cabinet so overfilled that its drawers couldn't close. A stack of account ledgers leaned against the side of a battered oak desk at the far end of the room. In opposition to all this clutter, a handsome blond Gramophone 450 Lumiere rested on a mahogany corner table, several carefully sleeved records lay next to it.

"He loves music," Isabeau explained. "I did too, once."

Zoe gave the Lumiere a brief glance—it was similar to her own phonograph, which had cost a pretty penny—then turned her attention to the cabinet in the opposite corner. Tall, but only a yard wide, the top of the cabinet's door had a mesh screen, which made it resemble part of a junked confessional. She watched as Yves opened the structure's narrow door and looked in.

"I'll have to stand on my toes to see out. You sure this is where you want me?" he asked Isabeau, his eyebrows lifted almost to his hairline.

She nodded. "It's the only way."

With an unhappy grunt, Yves squeezed his slender body inside. After a few moments of fussing around, he positioned his camera's lens against the screen.

"Do you think that'll work?" Zoe asked.

"It's actually not too bad," Yves said, his voice muffled. "I'll focus on the desk, but the camera will capture blurs of the mesh on the edges. That won't matter because I can edit them out during printing. My biggest problem is that it's so musty in here I can hardly breathe, and I'm all hunched over, probably ruining my back for life."

"That's where we normally keep donated clothes to give to the parish's poor," Isabeau explained. "but I took the clothes out and shoved them under my desk so he..." She swallowed. "Well, so he wouldn't see what I'd done."

The massive maple wardrobe standing next to the cabinet looked ancient enough to have been old long before Notre Dame rose above the Paris skyline. At some point in its rough life, the wardrobe must have served as a home for woodpeckers, because its double doors were marred by holes. Some were shallow, but others passed completely through the wood and into the darkness beyond. The doors were so badly sprung that one hung askew. When Isabeau opened it with a shaky hand, the hinges shrieked.

"This is where you and Reynard can hide, Zoe," Isabeau said, pointing to it. "Sorry."

Zoe was sorry, too. The open door revealed not only more piles of clothing but dozens of pairs of shoes. Some of the better-quality men's coats and women's dresses dangled from hooks at the wardrobe's back, while lesser items lay on the floor, topped with shoes still good enough to walk in.

"Oh, Isabeau, Reynard and I can't possibly fit in there!" Zoe said, her concerns building. Would they have to rethink their strategy, or cancel their plan entirely?

It was Isabeau's turn to reassure them. "There's still room under my desk." She began grabbing up the clothing and shoes, transferring them to join the others. True enough, once she'd cleared out the wardrobe, enough space was left for two slender people to stand together if they were on friendly terms. Even better, one of the holes in the armoire's crooked door was at eye level, giving Reynard a good view of the room.

"All that clothing under your desk is visible now," Zoe said, gesturing at the pile.

Isabeau shook her head. "I'll be sitting at the desk, blocking his view, and..." She paused and took a quick breath. "...and besides, it won't be the desk he'll be looking at. Or the cabinets."

Without a word, Zoe stepped inside the wardrobe, pushing herself as far back as possible. Reynard followed. Muttering bleakly, he turned this way and that in a failed attempt to get comfortable. "This is the most ridiculous thing I've ever done," he grumped. "Uh, Zoe? Could you please remove your elbow from my side?" His portrait mask had slipped enough that she could see the remains of his shattered jaw.

"I can't," she said, turning her head to sneeze. "Not enough room." The air in the wardrobe smelled of dust and old sweat.

Reynard groaned. "If either of us sneezes, we'll wind up in prison."

"Trust me."

A bitter laugh. "That's what our lieutenant said as he ordered us to go over the top, and you've seen the result." When he tapped his copper mask back into place, it made a hollow *ding*. "*Merde*, Zoe! Stop moving around! And that elbow's still in my side."

"Sorry, sorry," Zoe said. "I'll try my darndest not to poke you."

"Better do more than *try*."

Fortunately, they didn't have to wait long. As punctual as Isabeau had promised, her tormenter entered the room only seconds after the church bell finished tolling the half-hour.

"*Bonjour*, my precious mademoiselle," Father Arnaud said, his voice as creaky as the wardrobe's hinges. "Are you looking forward to our time together today?"

Zoe could hardly make out Isabeau's soft reply, although it didn't matter. They weren't here to eavesdrop, and the only word that mattered would be a shouted "Help!"

A deep cough. A few rustlings. A click, then a hum, and the music of Richard Strauss's *Salome* began to play loudly, but not from the opera's rather staid opening act. The Gramophone's shrewd operator had skipped directly to one of the most erotic pieces ever written: *Danse des Sept Voiles*. Dance of the Seven Veils.

"You see, *ma chérie*, what we are about to do will bring you closer to Christ than you already are," the priest cooed.

The sound of scuffling almost drew Zoe out of the wardrobe, but Reynard whispered, "Not yet."

"No, I...*please*." Now an edge of panic marred Isabeau's lovely voice.

The priest's horrible rasp continued, underlining Isabeau's

whimpering. "What we are about to do is not a sin, my dear. It is a blessing, a sacred act created by our Father Himself."

At this, Zoe felt, rather than heard, Reynard's intake of breath. His entire body had gone rigid. She mentally cursed at not being able to see, but it was more important that Reynard witness what was happening and that Yves document it.

Isabeau pleaded again, but from the shuffling sounds Zoe could hear, Father Arnaud was paying no attention to the girl's protests.

A clattering of something being knocked over. A chair?

"No!" Isabeau cried.

Even though Strauss's melody soared toward crescendo, it couldn't climb above the sounds of Isabeau pleading, or a man calling upon God and His angels to witness the holy event that was about to take place.

Then the sound of fabric ripping. A sob from Isabeau. "Please, I don't..."

"Hush!"

"But it's a sin..."

The sound of a slap. "Foolish girl, to think a priest could ever sin. Now you must pray to our Holy Father for forgiveness, to make you worthy of the honor I'm about to bestow upon you."

Another sound of ripping. Then the word Zoe had been waiting for.

"*Help!*"

Reynard burst out of the wardrobe with Zoe right behind. Across the room, Yves emerged from his own hiding place, his camera still snapping away at the man bending Isabeau backward across her desk.

Snap, snap, snap. Lightning-quick film windups.

Time seemed to stop for all of them. Zoe. Yves. Isabeau in her torn blouse. Even for the priest.

The world moved again as Reynard's fists made bloody contact with the priest's hawk-like nose. "Heretic! Father of all lies!" he hissed, as the priest crumpled to the ground.

"*Jesus*," Zoe whispered.

"No, this isn't Him," Reynard growled, ripping the cross off the cringing man's neck.

Chapter Thirty

While they waited for Yves to emerge from his darkroom with the proof of the priest's assault, Zoe found herself relaxing. Taking advantage of this brief respite, she leaned her head back against Yves's ragged sofa. It was ugly, as was pretty much everything in his atelier, but it was comfortable. She closed her eyes, contentedly listening to Isabeau and Reynard go over the details of their new friendship. Yes, life could be fair *and* good...

When it wasn't being horrible.

She was just about to drift off when she heard, "Zoe?"

Isabeau's voice.

Zoe opened her eyes to see Isabeau leaning over her, concern on her face.

"Are you all right?" the girl asked.

Zoe had to smile. What a genuinely good person Isabeau was. Here the girl had just escaped from a horrific situation, but she wasn't worried about herself. She worried about Zoe.

"I'm perfectly fine," she answered. "Just tired. I just didn't get a lot of sleep last night." *And no sleep the night before.*

Isabeau's face relaxed. "Neither did I."

"Of course you didn't. Anyway, that's all behind you now, and it's time to start thinking about your future. You'll need a new job, and..."

"I already have a new job. I guess you weren't listening. Reynard has hired me to do the books for his haulage company. I'll be making more than I was getting at the...at the..."

"At the church," Zoe finished for her. "Good! I knew his haulage company was getting busy, but I never figured it was getting *that* busy."

Reynard said, "*Mais oui.* We were all so busy earlier that I didn't have time to tell you I've had to hire two more men—both portrait mask veterans like myself—and I bought another truck to handle the increase. Seems that everyone in Paris is on the move these days."

Either that, or the people of Paris wanted to reward their veterans for their lost faces. Zoe's heart warmed again at the generosity of her adopted home. She started to say something when the door to the darkroom opened and Yves emerged carrying two perfectly focused prints.

"*Voilà,*" he crowed. "We have proof!"

They gathered around him, looking at the photographs. Here was Father Arnaud ripping Isabeau's blouse. Here was Father Arnaud grabbing her crotch. All they needed to do now was present their proof to the bishop, and the priest would certainly be defrocked, maybe even arrested.

His reign of terror was over.

As Zoe studied this proof of the man's wickedness, something someone had said began to nag at her again. What was it? Something about Laurette's broken engagement? Yes! That was it! Laurette had broken with mechanic Fabian Napier to marry a *vicomte.* What had Fabian exactly said? Something like *By then she was well practiced at that kind of thing.*

Had those words been a meaningless phrase used by an embittered ex-fiancé? The more she thought about the conversation, the more it worried her. Maybe she should see Fabian again to get things straightened out. Immediately following that thought came the realization that no matter how angry Henri became at her snooping, it was time to tell him what she'd discovered so far. After all, her relationship with him had shown her that officers of the Sûreté often wasted so much time looking for proof they could be slow to act.

Sometimes fatally so.

When the celebration over the damning photographs finally died down, Zoe asked Reynard to drop her off at Fabian's garage.

$\cdots \diamond \cdots$

After a short drive, she was staring into the garage's open double doors. The blazing sunlight revealed three men—one of them bleeding—hovered around an almost new Citroën Roadster. With its bright red chassis, removable black leather top, its dazzling chrome grill, and daring black bumpers, the automobile would have looked the epitome of French engineering except for the badly mangled driver's side door. Hovering over this tragedy was the handsome Fabian Napier, slowly shaking his head.

"You will have to order a new door from the factory, Monsieur Blanc," he told the bleeding man.

Monsieur Blanc, his face a map of insurmountable grief, wailed, "But that will take weeks, maybe months, and I promised to take Simone to the opera *tonight!*"

"Not in this thing, you won't." Fabian straightened up and lit a cigarette. After taking a deep draw, then exhaling, he said, "Again, there is nothing I can do for your Roadster. However, I will loan you my own auto so that your friend Stefan here can drive you to the hospital. Your head is bleeding quite badly."

"Who cares about my...my..." Blanc whimpered as he slowly crumpled to the concrete. "...head," he finished, closing his eyes.

The man's friend tied a clean handkerchief around Blanc's bleeding head as Fabian backed a wooden-sided Ravel out of the garage, then gentled him into the car. While Stefan climbed into the driver's seat, Fabian told him how to get to the hospital, adding, "Please bring my automobile back unharmed. Her name is Lili, and she is greatly loved."

Nodding, Stefan drove off.

Once the Ravel turned out of sight, Fabian growled, "What the hell do you want this time, Mademoiselle Barlow? Can't you see I'm busy?"

"I need information," she answered, unsettled by his swift transition from compassion to annoyance.

"You want information, go read a newspaper." He turned his back on her and reentered the garage.

Before Fabian could close the double doors behind him, Zoe slipped around the crumpled Roadster and followed him inside. There she saw the ruins of an elderly Citroën, its innards spread across the floor. After the freshness of the air outside, the rank odors of grease, petrol, and tobacco almost overwhelmed her, and she had to pull a handkerchief out of her purse to serve as an emergency gas mask. It didn't help much, and she began to cough. Ignoring her distress, Fabian leaned over the Citroën's open hood and began banging around.

Zoe raised her voice. "What did you mean when you said Laurette was 'well practiced at that sort of thing'?" Merely asking the question made her cough again. But if necessary, she would stand here, inhaling the stench, then cough and cough and cough until the garage closed for the day. Then she'd stand outside on the sidewalk and cough some more.

"I don't know what you're talking about." *Bang.*

"You said it the last time we spoke, when we were talking about Laurette leaving you for the *vicomte*."

"Why should you care what bad habits a dead woman had?" *Bang. Bang. Bang.*

"Because, as you inferred—which I didn't realize at the time— was that leaving fiancés was one of those bad habits. So I was wondering if that was true."

Another cough. The handkerchief wasn't helping, but Fabian appeared to be immune to the fumes.

Cough.

The banging stopped as the mechanic turned around, revealing fresh grease smears on his face. The grime should have made him look thuggish, but it didn't. "We all have to die sometime."

Under ordinary circumstances, Zoe would think this comment heartless, but Fabian's woebegone expression betrayed his sorrow.

"True," she agreed, "but most of us don't leave this earth through murder. There's another woman dead now. Her name is Katrina. She's the girl who took Laurette's place at the sales table."

A sigh. "If I explain, will you go away?"

"I promise." *Cough.*

Fabian's scowl wiped away this brief moment of vulnerability. "I am well acquainted with women's promises. They mean nothing."

She scowled back. "That's a matter of opinion."

Apparently reading the stubbornness on her face, he took another deep drag on his cigarette and said, "All right, American. You win. I wasn't the first man Laurette left to climb a higher rung on the social ladder. In fact, I was once that highest rung."

He vented a bitter laugh. "This was...what? Three years ago? Yes, about then. It was when Laurette and Veronique had only been in Paris a few months. Laurette had been engaged to some pig farmer from Picardy, a lout with shit on his boots. Then she met me and apparently decided a sophisticated Parisian who owned an auto repair business was better than some country oaf. So the pig farmer was out, and I was in. Temporarily, anyway."

During this long-for-him speech, Zoe lost all desire to cough, perhaps because her lungs had accustomed themselves to the rank air. "Do you think he...uh...the lout with shit on his boots could have come up here and tried to change her mind?"

"And leave his darling pigs to starve? I doubt it. Besides, a little while later, it was my turn to be thrown out with the garbage."

Zoe plastered an unfelt expression of sympathy on her face and said, "Well, I'm certain you'll find someone more, ah, more suited to you. As pretty as Laurette was, it sounds like she wasn't a very nice person."

"Veronique warned me about her, but I was too blinded by that pretty face."

"You knew them both, then? Laurette and Veronique?"

Fabian gave Zoe an odd look. "I thought you knew."

"Knew what?"

"That Veronique and I were once engaged to be married. In fact, I first became aware of Laurette's charms when I was helping select the furniture Veronique would bring when we married and she, of course, would move into my place. A sofa, four chairs, a small dining table, a nice rug, some lamps. My father had never been much on decorating, you see, and even though our flat was roomy enough, he had no time or inclination to run around look-ing for the proper furnishings."

He paused to take another drag on his cigarette. "Anyway, during our conversation that day, Veronique decided that Laurette would continue living at their flat, taking care of their larger sales pieces. Despite our upcoming wedding, Veronique had every intent of continuing to manage her flea markets."

This surprised Zoe. "You didn't mind?"

Fabian managed a faint smile. "Of course not. I have no

problem with a woman making her own place in the world. My own mother, God rest her soul, was a violin teacher. She was so gifted that she taught three violinists who were eventually hired by the Paris Conservatory Orchestra. She taught me, too. Ah, from the expression on your face, you find it surprising that this greasy brute of a mechanic plays the violin? So did my father!" He laughed.

Caught in her moment of snobbery, Zoe blushed. "I didn't..."

"Oh, yes you did! But some evening when you have nothing else to do, drop by the Salle Gaveau when there is a performance by the Debussy String Quartet. I'll be the violinist with axle grease under his fingernails."

"Uh, I..."

Fabian's smile vanished. "Now get the hell out of my garage." With that, he turned his back on her and banged away at the Citroën again.

Chapter Thirty-One

After the conversation with Fabian, Zoe felt so rattled she broke her own rule: she'd visit Gabrielle without being expected. Reading to her friend always proved a calming experience.

A few Metro stops later, Zoe was walking into the Challiots' flat.

"Are you all right?" Hélène Arceneau asked, an expression of concern on her face. "You look..."

"Oh, I'm fine," Zoe lied. "Since I was already in the neighborhood, I decided to read to Gaby again. Is she in a better frame of mind today?"

"She's been more peaceful, yes."

"Good. I thought we might double up on the Colette novel."

The nurse arched her eyebrows. "*Chacun à son goût.*" To each his own taste. But she was smiling as she escorted Zoe to Gabrielle's room.

As Zoe walked into the vibrant room, long fronds of grasses bent in her wake, and her tension began to slip away. The air, moved along by the addition of a large fan, carried the scent of green fields and luxuriant gardens.

"*Bonjour,* Gaby," she said, noticing that the woman's eyes tracked her as she took her seat by the bed. "I hope you are as happy to see me as I am to be here. Especially so we can enjoy the brave Claudine's adventures in Paris together!"

Did that grunt mean agreement?

Zoe opened the book and began to read.

A few minutes later, Gabrielle's eyes closed, and she drifted away. Disappointed, Zoe closed the book and tiptoed out of the room.

"Finished so soon?" Hélène asked, worry lines creasing her face. "You usually stay for at least an hour. Is she unwell again?"

Zoe made herself smile. "No, I think she's improved even more."

Instead of being pleased with this information, Hélène looked at Zoe strangely. "Are *you* all right, Zoe? You look pale. Let me make you some tea."

"No tea, but thank you for the offer."

"Then how about a nice glass of sauvignon blanc, perhaps? I was just about to pour myself some."

"Again, many thanks, but no." Zoe forced another smile; she was getting good at such fakery. "I may have been doing too much lately and probably need to do less."

Hélène looked at Zoe's hands. "Not less painting, I hope."

"Never. Just business matters, that's all. You know how they can sap the energy right out of you."

"Ah." An understanding smile.

"So I guess I'd better go."

Hélène walked her to the door, but before Zoe could leave, the nurse took her hand and pressed it warmly. "You understand that no matter what happens with Madame Gabrielle, you and I will remain friends, correct?"

Zoe felt color flood her cheeks. "Correct. No matter what happens."

With that, she left.

Chapter Thirty-Two

—— Gabrielle ——

"I must hurry my recovery so I can kill her," I say to Odile, my spider friend. "I cannot bear her presence much longer. And that silly Colette novel! I didn't mind Monsieur Proust. Although he spent much too much time on small things, he was at least literate."

Odile strokes my cheek with a little green leg. "I seem to remember that while she was reading Proust to you, you did not always care for him, either."

"I was wrong. Now I would like to hear more of his work."

"You must not expect new works from Monsieur Proust, Madame. The man is dead. But, alas, that Fitzgerald writer you dislike so much, he is still alive. And young. He will last many more years."

"And will probably write many more books, but I don't have to listen to them. Perhaps you are right, though, Odile. I should be less critical of that Colette person. When Zoe was telling me about her, she said Colette was an actress as well as a writer, so I imagine she has many adventures to share. Humiliations, too. Zoe told me there's an incident in the novel where Claudine wants to go to a concert, but her Papa berates her, saying that 'women are on a level with the least intelligent of she-asses.' Isn't that a hurtful thing to say to a daughter?"

Odile shakes her head sorrowfully. "Claudine's mother should have killed and eaten him after they were through mating."

"It would have served him right!"

A tiny chuckle. "You are beginning to sound like me, Madame. And while it is appropriate for spiders to kill and eat those closest to them, such behavior is forbidden to humans. Spiders follow spider rules. Humans are supposed to follow human rules. Your god, your Great Rule Giver, would call such behavior sinful."

I snort. "Ha! What does a spider know of God? Or sin?"

"More than you would expect, Madame. Before I came to you, I lived in a church named St. Jean de Riis, where I learned about sin from the rules written down in that big black book. I also learned that the words in the book had little effect on the church's priest. Apparently telling humans to behave is one thing, but making them actually do it is another."

"Do not preach to me, spider!"

"Now I have made Madame angry. Do you want me to go away? There is a park nearby with beautiful flowers, and flowers attract aphids, which are very y-y-yummy." At this, her voice broke.

"Oh, Odile! I didn't know spiders could cry."

"They do when their hearts are b-b-broken, Madame."

With great effort I raise my right hand—it was getting stronger every day—and gently caress my friend. "Then you must unbreak your heart immediately, Odile, because you are the only friend I have."

"But Madame, you have another friend—Mademoiselle Zoe."

I begin to laugh. "Ah, such a life, when a spider's heart is more loving than a human's!"

Chapter Thirty-Three

—— Zoe ——

As Zoe stood in front of a prepared canvas, she realized that what little optimism she'd started the day with had evaporated. Gabrielle remained bedridden, still mute. Lee-Lee's husband would take her back to Germany any day now, determined to stamp out her sister's spirit.

Laurette's and Katrina's killer was still free, possibly to strike again. And despite the Pinkerton Detective Agency's best efforts, Zoe's little Amber girl remained lost.

Maybe it was time to recognize the fact that it was hopeless. Why, she couldn't even help herself, let alone others. Her entire twenty-four-year-old life had been a failure and would continue to be.

She was useless.

Just as that grim thought started to bore its way into her soul, she felt a touch on the shoulder. "Madame Zoe?"

Startled, Zoe whirled around to see Madeline looking at her with a worried face. She had returned from the country with the news that she was now great-aunt to a healthy boy, so why did she look so worried?

"Are you all right?" the housekeeper asked.

"I'm fine." *Why were people always asking her that question?*

"But you look so pale."

"Like I said, I'm fine!"

Madeline's worried expression vanished, replaced by one of exasperation. "Then you must leave your studio now, because you have visitors."

"I didn't hear a knock at the door."

"Only because you weren't listening."

That much was true. Whenever Zoe's art failed her, so did her senses. Turning away from the canvas as if it were covered by a writhing pile of snakes, she followed her housekeeper into the sitting room, where Marc Chagall, Bella, and little Ida waited with expectant faces. The scent of warm challah filled the air, dispersing the acrid smell of fresh gesso.

"What a lovely surprise!" Zoe said.

Chagall grinned, even though he was standing in an awkward position, his legs spread, his arms behind his back. "Such a sad face! You must be having trouble painting."

Zoe started to lie that she never had trouble working, but she knew she'd never fool a man whose eyes saw so much. "Well, a little trouble, but it'll pass. It always does."

"Helped along by *this*, I hope." He thrust forward an object approximately three feet by two feet, wrapped in old newspapers.

With a gasp, Zoe grabbed the package and ripped away the paper, revealing a mad rush of color: aggressive reds, luscious blues, yellows so strong they chased away her earlier sense of failure. A barn. A synagogue. A crescent moon. A flying cow. And at the center, a winged, henna-haired woman sat on a roof, painting a canvas that mimicked her surreal surroundings.

"Its title is *The Angel Paints Paradise*. And it is for you, dear Zoe."

"I... I..." She couldn't speak.

Like her husband, Bella Chagall noticed everything. "Have some challah," she said. "It'll clear your throat."

An hour later, their magnificent deed accomplished, the Chagalls went home. In their wake, they left a renewed Zoe. A Zoe who no longer felt desolate. A Zoe surrounded by bright colors, flying cows, and angels. A Zoe who had almost forgotten that Art exists to give hope to the hopeless.

· · · ◇ · · ·

The renewed Zoe put on a sun hat and struck out for the nearby taxi stand, because she now knew what needed to be done.

Despite the increasing herds of Olympics-goers, Zoe found Avak, her taxi-driving friend, still waiting for a fare at his regular station near boulevard Montparnasse. When she told him what she needed, he immediately agreed.

"I not been to Amiens since war," he said, as the traffic rumbled by. "Is pretty drive across Picardy. Wonder if cathedral still there? Could be big mess, thanks to damn Germans."

Zoe looked at her watch. It was already past one. "More of a little mess because they propped up the walls with sandbags. We'll be back before dark, right? I have a busy day planned for tomorrow. I've promised some friends I'll accompany them to the Olympics swim meets, and afterward to see the show at the Moulin Rouge. I don't want to start the day already tired."

"Two hours there, same back. If all good there, we back Paris before sundown. Who we look for in Amiens?"

Smiling—she liked the "we"—Zoe answered, "A pig farmer."

Avak turned out to be right about the beauty of the drive. Once they'd escaped from the bustling boulevards of Paris, a series of green-swathed hills unfolded before them. Even the growls and hiccups of the Grim Reaper's motor couldn't drown out the music of the French countryside. Birds singing, cows lowing, sheep bleating, and every now and then children calling to one another as they played in farmyards. The lushness of the landscape soothed Zoe's frazzled nerves until the road cut through a section of forest that held an uncanny resemblance to the dark woods surrounding Beech Glen.

Beech Glen. Where her newborn Amber had been ripped from her arms.

Zoe squeezed her eyes shut against the memory and didn't open them again until the birdsong disappeared. The lush countryside they'd driven through earlier had vanished, leaving only the charred and skeletal remains of trees that had once borne witness to the madness of the War to End All Wars. Dead oaks clawed at the sky, and pastures once green were now barren.

"Battlefield," Avak said. "Can still see trenches. Sometimes bones."

They drove on in silence for a while, until Zoe couldn't take it anymore. "How much farther?" she called to Avak, once she was certain her voice wouldn't tremble.

"This be Picardy. Big fighting here. Many dead, but blood makes for good soil, they say."

There was no decent response to that, so Zoe kept silent as they passed one ruined château after another. Some had been so demolished it was difficult to tell the house from the stone fence that marked its territory.

But parts of the countryside had been miraculously spared the war's wrath, and within a few miles, they emerged from the fields of death to enter more innocent terrain. Here the oaks had kept their leaves, and the fields once again blossomed with crops. At the edge of the road, a big yellow dog exited a sheep-filled pasture and began chasing after them. Yipping with excitement, it kept alongside the Grim Reaper until they crested a hill and the dog veered off into a farmyard.

"Fast dog," Avak said.

Slow car, Zoe thought.

A few miles farther, they began to see ruins again. Whatever battle had raged here hadn't spared the barns and other outbuildings, let alone the houses. A church had collapsed in on itself, but someone had taken the trouble to righten all the crosses in the church's small graveyard. Many appeared ancient, but at least half the crosses looked fairly recent. Victims of the Battle of the Somme, no doubt. She'd read somewhere that during almost five months of blood-letting, the death toll had risen to more than three hundred thousand, and of that number, many were civilians.

"Where go now, Zoe?" Avak asked as they neared another half-ruined village.

She forced herself to look away from the graves. "To the first brasserie or café we see. If any are left standing."

"Then you are hungry like me."

"We can have something to eat while I ask around and see who knows where that pig farm is."

They soon found themselves in Le Chat Noir, where they received an excellent onion soup and a fine merlot. The kindly waitress, whose accent was Alsatian, directed them to *Ferme Porcine*, a local pig farm. Once there, they learned that the young widow who ran the farm had never heard of a woman named Laurette Belcoeur. However, she did inform them there was another piggery in the vicinity, although she was quick to explain that the swine there couldn't match the quality of hers, and did they want to purchase a pig?

"*Merci*, but no thanks." Zoe gave her a pained smile.

"Very tasty!" The widow wasn't ready to give up. "Tender, too. If you want, I can kill it and wrap it so it won't bleed all over that fine automobile of yours."

Avak, who Zoe knew was a vegetarian, yelped, "*Non porc!*"

But the trip to *Ferme Porcine* wasn't wasted, because as they started back to the Grim Reaper, the widow gave them directions to the next pig farm. For this parting gift, Zoe slipped her a few American dollars.

Ten minutes and two dirt roads later, Zoe and Avak arrived at Etienne Mercier's farm—sixty perfectly groomed acres and buildings—where they discovered that the garrulous, redheaded Mercier wasn't the man they were looking for, either. After a few minutes of bragging about his pigs, he announced that, yes, he was acquainted with a farmer named Quintrell Sault, who had been jilted by a woman who had been too good for him in the first place.

"She was hardly a beauty, though, and she and her sister had lost their house—a fine one, too—along with all the paintings their ancestors had collected over the centuries. And..."

Paintings? This surprised Zoe, since she'd seen the abysmally bad art hanging on the Belcoeurs' walls. "What do you mean, 'paintings'?"

Being more interested in pigs than art, Mercier ignored the question. "As I was saying, Sault was an up-and-coming man back then, but those pigs of his..."

"Forget his damned pigs, Etienne," said the farmer's buxom wife, who had stopped to listen while herding two identical red-headed toddlers toward a blue-shuttered stone cottage. "Tell them about the paintings."

"So you're telling me how to talk now, Ilianne?" Mercier returned. Despite his words, he was grinning.

"Someone has to, you old goat." She gave him a friendly swat across his bottom. The twins giggled.

"You see?" Mercier said to Avak. "This is what happens when you let a woman get an education. Okay, just to shut up my bossy wife, here's what I know about those paintings. The talk around here is that the Belcoeurs' great-grandfather was an art collector—this was back in the day the Belcoeur family had substance, you understand—and he'd purchased a Rubens and two Caravaggios, which were lost in the war. Although maybe I'm wrong."

"You usually are," his wife said. The twins giggled again.

Although Mercier tried to stop grinning, it didn't work. Pointing to his wife, he said, "Pay no attention to this hussy. She reads too many books." That earned him another swat across the behind, but he continued bravely on. "Now, about Veronique. There was a fine woman! But as I said, no beauty. She would never have become engaged to Sault if her and her sister's straits hadn't been so dire. And Sault himself was no beauty, neither were his wire-haired pigs—ill-tempered Gascons, almost inedible. But their engagement didn't last. The younger sister, I think her name was Laurette, soon caught his eye. Next thing you know, Veronique was out, and Laurette was in. Two high-born sisters lowering themselves for the chance of marrying a pig farmer!"

At that, his wife, said, "Well, I married a pig farmer, didn't I?"

"More fool you!" Most of his face was taken up by another big grin.

The woman laughed, making her great bosom heave. "Yes, I tell myself that every day. More fool me for marrying you, you rogue."

In a mock whisper, Mercier said to Avak, "You see? There's no pleasing a woman." Raising his voice again, he said, "Anyway, if the Belcoeur sisters had been able to save their paintings, neither of them would have paid any attention to Sault, so the whole thing finally fell through. After the fiasco with the Belcoeurs, Sault never married, which is just as well. Unlike my own little beauties." Here he gestured toward the little redheads gazing up at him in adoration, "Sault's children were certain to be monsters. But at least if they were boys, they would be strong, and that's what a farmer needs, *non*? Muscles and endurance! Sault certainly has those. Say, let me show you my prize Landrace sow. Fourteen piglets she's already given me, and this is her first breeding season!"

After Zoe declined Mercier's kind offer to view this rising star of swinish fecundity, he gave them directions to Sault's pig farm.

Ten minutes later, Avak steered the Grim Reaper up the lane to a farmhouse that had seen better days. Built of local stone, its south wall was badly damaged, and its occupant hadn't bothered to fix it. Shutters hung crookedly from the windows. Piles of rock and crumbling mortar dotted the yard, among which scrawny chickens pecked up bugs. Drawing closer, Zoe spied a stoop-shouldered man in ragged overalls carrying a pitchfork.

Quintrell Sault looked as ill-used as his domicile. His sweat-dampened hair had been bleached almost white by ceaseless toil in the sun, and his dirty clothes hung loosely on his thin frame. He had the red face of a drinker, and as they approached him, his expression promised an uncomfortable interview. His callused hands were the size of dinner plates.

"What the hell do you two want?" he asked in a whiskey-nourished rasp.

From somewhere behind several ramshackle outbuildings, Zoe heard a chorus of porcine squeals. They were out of sight, but their odor announced their presence.

After introducing herself, she said, "Just a few words, if you would be so kind, Monsieur Sault. I'm trying to find out what I can about Laurette Belcoeur."

An expression that could have been a sneer disappeared so quickly it might have been a grimace. When he wiped away the sweat on his brow, she saw he was missing three fingers. From wartime service or a bite from an ill-tempered pig?

"That Belcoeur *putain* has nothing to do with me," he grumbled. "Now go back where you came from, Mademoiselle Fancy, and take your Turk with you." He spit something nasty on the ground.

"Avak's not a Turk; he's Armenian," Zoe said, stung on her friend's behalf.

"He could be the Devil for all I care." Sault started to turn away but stopped when Zoe's shout made him face her again.

"Laurette was murdered!"

A slow, malicious smile. "Give my best wishes to her killer."

"Did you kill her?"

For a moment, Sault's cruel smile wavered, then steadied. "Unfortunately, I did not. I would have, but I didn't have the time. Too busy with my pigs."

"You were once engaged to her," Zoe said, limping closer to him over the rocky ground.

Behind her, Avak grunted a warning, which she ignored, and she kept walking until she was close enough to smell Sault's *Eau de Pig*. She stopped then, realizing for the first time what a big man he was, well over six feet tall and heavily muscled.

He looked down at her. "So what if I was engaged to her? In wartime, men do stupid things." There was no trace of sadness in his cold blue eyes.

Zoe swallowed. "Laurette and I were on friendly terms, so I'm trying to find out what I can to help the police."

"You? A cripple? Helping the police?" A bitter laugh. "But let's say you're telling the truth—which I doubt, Mademoiselle Liar— why do you think I care what happened to a faithless woman who moved to the City of Lies? I should have gone ahead and married Veronique, like I'd originally planned before my cock outvoted my brain."

Then the harsh expression on his face softened. "Ah. Veronique. Now there was a woman who knew how to work! She is all right, I hope?"

Zoe nodded. "She's doing well, but you left Veronique for Laurette. You don't argue the fact that Laurette jilted you?"

A laugh that held no humor in it. "*Jilt*? I guess you could call it that. I showed up at the church and Laurette didn't. Next thing I knew, I was the laughing stock of Picardy, and Laurette and her sister had moved to Paris. Never heard from either of them again."

Zoe thought about that for a moment. Like Fabian, Sault remained embittered by Laurette's callous treatment, but was he bitter enough to commit murder? Then she looked at his large hands again. He wouldn't need a rock; his fists would suffice.

She gestured toward the remnants of the crumbling house, the leaning outbuildings, the battered tractor, the scrawny chickens. "Did you find a new woman to help you with all this?"

Sault snorted. "No, I didn't. I'm finished with women. That includes you, Mademoiselle Liar. Now get off my property before I take this to you both." He leveled the pitchfork in front of him as if it were a rifle.

At that, Avak jumped out of the Grim Reaper, grabbed Zoe by the arm and half-dragged her back to the auto. He didn't speak to her again until the pig farms of Picardy lay far behind them.

··· ◇ ···

As promised, Avak delivered Zoe back to her little house while the sun still hung in the sky. Although the light remained good enough—chiaroscuro, the artist's dream—she was too tired to paint. Instead, she took a quick bath to divest herself of any remaining traces of *Eau de Pig*. Once smelling like Chanel instead, she brewed herself some black tea and took it to her favorite reading chair. As she sipped the too-strong tea, she tried to lose herself in another Colette novel, but her brain kept skittering around the different things she'd learned today.

Given Quintrell Sault's continued bitterness toward Laurette, he could easily have killed her. But what reason would Sault have for killing Katrina? Had the artist witnessed something? Or could he have killed Katrina simply because she was German, and a German had shot off his fingers during the war?

She'd also learned that Le Château de Belcoeur, the women's destroyed home, had once contained priceless paintings. Everyone she'd talked to believed they'd gone up in flames with the château. Well, maybe they had, but maybe they hadn't. But if the paintings had survived, why had Veronique, and then Laurette, allowed herself to become engaged to a surly pig farmer?

Zoe put her book down and returned her empty cup to the kitchen. She tried once more to immerse herself in the Colette novel, but her brain continued spinning, so she wandered off to bed.

Later that night, her restlessness made itself known in a dream where she was back at Beech Glen, saddling up one of the horses, only to have it turn into a monstrous wire-haired pig.

And the pig was hungry.

Chapter Thirty-Four

The sun had barely peeked over the horizon when Zoe heard pounding at the door.

Archie, perhaps? Had he decided that seeing Johnny Weissmuller in a form-fitting bathing suit was worth getting up for at this ungodly hour? He'd promised her they'd only be attending the afternoon's one-hundred-meter freestyle finals.

Whatever a "finals" was.

So the pounding at the door couldn't be Archie. And none of her other close friends were early risers. Especially not Archie. Whenever they'd met for breakfast at La Rotonde, it was because he was still up from the night before!

For a few moments she just lay there, cataloging a list of people who might show up at such a ridiculous hour, and all she could come up with was firemen, tax officials, and the police. Which included, of course, Henri.

But what the hell would Henri be doing here so early in the morning? He knew better than that! Unless...

Unless something awful had happened to Gabrielle.

Zoe shrugged herself out of her stupor and into a robe. Then she ran barefoot to the door and flung it open.

Lee-Lee. She'd been crying.

"What's happened?" Zoe threw her arms around her sister, then led her into the house. "Did someone die?"

"No, it's... It's just that Jack has decided to go back to Germany tomorrow, and I just can't bear being away from you again! I thought that, now, with Germany's inflation easing up and people starting to get enough to eat, he wouldn't feel the need to keep helping out. But that hasn't happened, at all. Even worse, he's decided to rent us a house in Munich."

Zoe hadn't heard her sister sound this upset since the night Amber was born.

··· ◊ ···

November 1918
Mercy, Alabama

The labor had ended hours ago, but the basement was still dark. Someone was crying. Herself, surely, grieving over the loss of her baby, tossed away like garbage. But someone else was crying up in the kitchen.

"I want my Sissie!" Lee-Lee screamed.

"We told you! She's gone to France and won't be back, so shut up." Anabelle.

"But...but I know she'd have taken me with her!"

"Keep on crying like that and I'll slap your face off!"

"You're lying! My Sissie wouldn't leave me!"

The sound of a slap.

Lee-Lee's cries grew louder. "My Sissie told me we'd always be together, that even if she got married, I could come and live with her."

Another slap.

"Sissie! Sissie!" Screaming louder now. The slaps continued, but the cries of "Sissie! Sissie!" continued too, until Brice, sounding drunk, yelled, "Hit her one more time, and I'll kill you, you bitch!"

The slaps stopped.

But Lee-Lee didn't.

· · · ◇ · · ·

1924
Paris

Zoe pointed to the sofa. "Sit. I'll make us some coffee."

Lee-Lee shook her head, but she sat down. "I don't have time for coffee, Sissie. Jack's out signing some papers, something about aid to Germany, but it probably won't take long. And if he gets back before I do, I'll just tell him that the weather was so nice and cool that I went for a walk."

"Cool?" Zoe almost laughed. Instead, she said, "But anyway, you wrote me once that Jack hated Munich."

"Oh, he does. But he wants to be within driving distance of Landsberg Prison so he can help a prisoner there write a book about his experiences. They've become pretty close, belonging to the same political party and all. You know how political he's always been."

Jack was helping someone write a book? Zoe couldn't remember her brother-in-law being literary-minded. "From what you've been writing me, it seems Jack has a lot of friends these days, while you, well, you don't seem to have any at all. That can't be healthy."

Lee-Lee shrugged. "I've tried to learn German, but when we were staying at his grandparents' farm, nobody was willing to help me; they just kept jabbering away in German. How can you make friends when everyone speaks a different language than you?"

Although Zoe had arrived in Paris without a friend in the world, she'd quickly made friends, and in doing so, the support they'd given her had changed her life—and had possibly saved it. Then again, she'd already spoken fluent French. She heaved a sigh and asked again, "Which one of Jack's buddies are you talking about now? And why is he in prison?"

"Oh, that awful Adolph person. I think I wrote you about him. The guy with the ridiculous moustache? Jack thinks he's the bee's knees and says his book will fix everything that went wrong in Germany."

Zoe frowned. "What 'went wrong' is that Germany started a war they wound up losing. Now they're paying for it."

"I know." Lee-Lee's voice was weak. "But Jack won't listen."

"You could always leave him and stay with me."

Lee-Lee looked at her sister in shock. "Leave Jack? Oh, I can't do that. Not now."

"But you've been unhappy since you married him. And now it sounds like he's choosing another person's welfare over yours."

The expression on Lee-Lee's face was almost painful to look at. "I'm pregnant."

It took a moment for Zoe to digest this, but once she did, she said, "All the more reason to stay with someone who loves *you*, who will take care of *you*, not some jailbird."

Lee-Lee stood up and started walking toward the door. "That's really why I snuck out again, to tell you I'm pregnant. Now I have to get back to the hotel before he does or he'll have a fit."

Zoe trailed after her. "But he..."

"No more 'buts,' Zoe. I still love him."

··· ◇ ···

Several hours later, Archie Stafford-Smythe and his mother picked up Zoe in the Countess's chauffeured Rolls-Royce Silver Ghost, then struck out toward the Piscine des Tourelles. Zoe had been tempted to beg off but, fearful that she might start crying over Lee-Lee again, she didn't.

Soon they were in the thick of an already-steaming crowd swarming into the stadium. It had to be one of the ugliest buildings in Paris, an immense roofless structure with fat cement columns guarding the entrance. Once the trio made it inside, she noticed that the interior wasn't any prettier, nor more comfortable. Rows and rows of seats were exposed to the blazing sun, making Zoe relieved she'd eschewed a chic cloche for her new straw boater, as had Archie and Gwennie. For a brief moment, Zoe thought they resembled risqué triplets.

Near the bar, everyone was talking about that morning's eight-hundred-meter freestyle relay, during which Weissmuller had swum the last two hundred meters, winning the gold by setting a new world record of 9 minutes and 53.4 seconds.

In a way, Zoe felt disappointed at his success. She would dearly have loved seeing the American win a gold, but now he'd be too exhausted for his three o'clock meet to do much. Oh, well, at least she'd see his handsomeness for herself.

Once they were past the bar area and into the stadium proper, it didn't take them long to find their seats in the middle of Section Four, at the far end of the fifty-meter pool. Not the best in the house, but at least they were situated toward the end of the row, which made for easy access. They only had to crawl over four people before sitting down.

"Isn't this lovely?" Gwennie remarked, smoothing her white linen skirt.

"Oh, yes. Lovely." Zoe was simply being polite.

Archie, however, never thought before he spoke. "What's that god-awful smell?" he complained, once he'd settled himself on a seat that was almost too small for his brawny frame.

"Chemicals in the water," Gwennie answered. "I read an article about it. Not pleasant, certainly, but the scientists behind it said the chemicals kill germs. Can't have all those fine young men getting sick, can we?"

"Then let's drink to their continued health!" With that, Archie pulled a silver flask out of his pocket and handed it around.

Gwennie turned it down, saying she'd stick to the Cointreau in her own flask, but Zoe—who'd forgotten to bring her new flask—took a nip. Some form of Scots whiskey. It burned going down but had a pleasant woodsy flavor, so she took another sip. And then another. She normally hated crowds, but the fiery liquid helped blur the noise and soften the sun-searing heat.

As she handed the flask back to Archie, the loudspeaker announced in several languages that the next contest, the hundred-meter finals, was about to begin. Vying for the gold were Johnny Weissmuller, United States; Duke Kahanamoku and his brother Samuel, United States; Arne Bord, Sweden; and Katsuo Takaishi, Japan. No Frenchmen, Zoe noted, although the mostly French crowd roared its approval at the mention of Weissmuller's name. After his morning's triumph, the French had decided to love him.

Weissmuller's good looks didn't hurt. At a height of six feet three inches, he towered over his opponents, and with his flawless physique—revealed by his form-fitting swimsuit—his golden tan and light brown hair, he looked every bit the "American Adonis" the French press had dubbed him. The press had also been quick to point out that neither Weissmuller nor Duke and Samuel Kahanamoku were native-born Americans. Johnny had been born in Romania and the Kahanamoku brothers in the U.S. Territory of Hawaii. But only die-hard legalists cared, and even they knew enough to stay silent in the face of such international acclaim.

Zoe was still marveling at Weissmuller's beauty when the starter gun fired and the swimmers hurled themselves into the water. No fancy dives, just a whitewater rush to get to the other end of the fifty-meter pool and back. Weissmuller immediately took the lead, but with all the screaming from the crowd and the furious water churned up by the swimmers, Zoe could hardly tell the difference between Weissmuller's famous "American Crawl" and the other swimmers' more traditional strokes.

To her, they all looked like bullets in the water.

Fifty-nine seconds later—an Olympic world record, she later learned—the race was over when Johnny Weissmuller slapped the wall three meters ahead of Duke, sending the crowd into a frenzy. The Americans had swept the race, Johnny winning the gold, Duke the silver, and Samuel the bronze. Despite their valiant efforts, Arne Borg and Katsuo Takaishi were also-rans.

His chest still heaving from the exertion, the grinning Weissmuller mounted the winners' blocks, trailed by his also-grinning teammates. Overwhelmed with joy, the Americans in the crowd threw their hats into the air, screaming "Johnny! Johnny! Johnny!" Three American flags were hoisted up the flagpoles of honor, and when a scratchy recording of "The Star-Spangled Banner" screeched out of the speakers, Zoe found herself crying. She cried even harder when a race official placed the medals around the American swimmers' necks.

"Oh, look at that beautiful boy," Gwennie said, her voice thick with emotion.

"Smashing, absolutely smashing," Archie agreed.

"The Kahanamoku brothers are pretty good-looking, too," Zoe pointed out.

Archie grinned at her. "See, I didn't lie, did I, Zoe? A swimming pool filled with handsome, barely clad men!"

As Zoe wiped away her tears, she noticed the race official attempting to lead Weissmuller and the other medal-winners away, but the fans increased their cheers. They weren't ready for him to leave.

"Johnny! Johnny! Johnny!"

Recognizing that the crowd wasn't about to let their hero go so soon, the smiling official stopped, shouldered a shrug, and just stood there, letting the Americans glory in their well-earned tribute.

And "The Star-Spangled Banner" played on.

Chapter Thirty-Five

"Weissmuller is swimming again today? What is he, super-human?" Zoe asked Archie as they watched Gwennie replenish her flask at one of the temporary bars. Despite the heat, the old countess looked fresh and frisky.

Zoe didn't. As the temperatures rose throughout the afternoon, made even more insufferable by the poolside humidity, she worried she might not be able to handle the sun much longer. Her lace handkerchief was sopped with sweat, and she felt lightheaded. The small bottle of Perrier she'd purchased from a vendor was long gone.

"Ladies will be swimming in the next two meets," Archie explained. "And we won't see Weissmuller again until after that, when he'll be one of the teammates in the water polo contest. People are saying it should be quite amusing, because a man on one of the opposing teams has only one leg and is known for his dirty tricks."

The countess, having refilled her flask, said, "I don't care about the man with one leg. And water polo? Ugh! The only polo I'm interested in is the kind with horses."

Archie knew which side his bread was buttered on. "If you're not interested, Mater, then we won't bother with it."

Zoe's spirits rose. "We won't?"

Winnie patted her on the arm. "No, we won't. We've seen what we wanted to see. Besides, it's terribly warm, and I'm looking forward to a nice cool bath. My hotel has a lovely one." She handed Zoe a fresh bottle of Perrier. "Drink this, dear. You're looking rather red."

Zoe accepted with gratitude, but Gwennie wasn't finished issuing commands. "We'll drop you off at that sweet little house of yours so you can clean up, maybe even take a nap. I've made us reservations for eight o'clock at the Moulin Rouge. I heard that their dancers wear, ah, *revealing* underwear, and I want to see if that's true."

Zoe wasn't looking forward to venturing out again, not even to the Moulin Rouge. But she'd do it for her friend, Archie, if for no reason other than to protect him from his dictatorial "Mater."

"I can hardly wait," she lied.

··· ◇ ···

Zoe's cold bath helped. As she lay in her big porcelain tub, surrounded by Chanel-scented bubbles, she was able to relax enough to almost fall asleep. But the moment she closed her eyes, the memory of the previous day's drive through Picardy stirred her back to wakefulness. Those skeletal trees. Those ruined fields. And Quintrell Sault, Laurette's former fiancé, as ruined as the landscape.

Had Sault driven all the way to Paris to take his revenge on Laurette? But if so, why kill Katrina? Simply because she was German? That made no sense. Well, maybe if the two women had been killed on the same day, but they hadn't been. This meant that Sault would have taken yet another long journey from Amiens to kill some random German in Paris when there were other Germans closer to hand. Another point: did the man even have an auto able to make two trips?

What about Fabian? The mechanic had much the same reason to kill Laurette, and possibly Katrina, if she'd seen something she shouldn't have. There would have been no long trip from Amiens, just a short walk over to Katrina's basement flat.

Then there was Gervais, Vicomte du Paget. While he didn't appear to have a motive for killing Laurette, or even poor Katrina, there was no way of knowing what had gone on between him and his fiancée. Laurette had been a flighty woman, breaking engagements right and left. Could she have been about to leave Gervais for seemingly greener pastures? But after a *vicomte*, what else was there? Some deposed European king?

The more Zoe thought about it, the more her head hurt. Frustrated, she shook off the scented bubbles clinging to her and climbed out of the tub.

She needed to get good and drunk tonight.

Chapter Thirty-Six

Given the Olympics crowds, the Moulin Rouge was even busier than usual, but thanks to the insistence of Gwennie, the imperial Countess of Whittenden, a tuxedoed maître d' was leading them to a table near the stage. Although Zoe had been there numerous times, she was still amazed at its extraordinary size. Redesigned after a ruinous fire, it could now seat up to seventeen hundred patrons per show. In addition to the huge main floor, a balcony and several loges snaked around the hall, each filled to capacity. But the Moulin Rouge's great size wasn't the only thing extraordinary about the famed music hall; it was the color. Red walls, red carpet, red lights, red draperies, and a huge red curtain accented with gold art nouveau scrollwork spread across the large stage. Red, red, red. Sodom and Gomorrah would have approved.

The floor level teemed with life. More than a hundred waiters scurried back and forth between the linen-covered tables, while smoke from French cigarettes drifted above each table. Fire danger or not, Parisians loved their tobacco.

"Loud, isn't it?" Archie yelled over the din of a thousand conversations. Not being titillated by the female form, he habitually ignored the Moulin Rouge, taking his pleasures elsewhere. "How are we supposed to enjoy the show?"

"They'll shut up when the curtain rises," Zoe told him, nearly tripping over a waiter as he thundered by with a tray full of drinks.

After battling his way through a fog of tobacco smoke and expensive perfume, the maître d' finally seated them at a long table so close to the stage Zoe could see a pink feather from one of the dancers' costumes lying on the boards. She was sharing this observation with Archie when her words suddenly fell away. Sitting next to them were Johnny Weissmuller and Duke and Samuel Kahanamoku.

The three Olympians were almost unrecognizable in street clothes, but Gwennie's sharp eyes missed nothing. Less awed— possibly believing that placement near greatness was only her due—Gwennie leaned over the table and congratulated the three, Johnny for his golds and the Kahanamoku brothers for their silver and bronze.

The medalists looked magnificent, but the room's reddish light glowed more brightly on Weissmuller, lending him an almost saintly presence. Up this close, Zoe could see that his features were perfect, from his firm chin to his sculpted nose. His shoulders were broad, and even his ill-fitting suit couldn't disguise those powerful arms. He reigned over the table without saying a word until Gwennie began to discuss his record-breaking win.

At that point, the Olympian held up a warning hand, cutting her effusions short. "Shh, ma'am," he stage-whispered. "Pretend you never saw us. If Coach Bachrach finds out we snuck away from Olympic Village, he'll blow his stack."

"Forget the 'ma'am' business, my dear boy. I'm Gwennie!" Whereupon the countess—probably for the first time in her life— followed someone's order. Placing a manicured forefinger against her lips, she pledged her silence. Then she giggled like a young girl. "But you snuck away? Oh, you naughty, naughty boys!"

Zoe would have giggled, too, but the man sitting next to Weissmuller was none other than the poet Blaise Cendrars. Cigarette dangling from his thick lips, and louche as ever, he snatched up Zoe's hand and kissed it before she could jerk it back. "Ah, the beautiful mademoiselle who, in her wisdom, does not always adhere to the truth. What a pleasure to see you again, my dear Zoe! And you, of course, Countess. You both look lovely."

Weissmuller widened his eyes. *"Gwennie" was a countess?*

Like most other well-bred girls, Zoe responded automatically to Cendrars's shallow effusions. "Charmed." But she jerked her hand away and wiped it against her skirt. "I thought you'd be half-way back to Brazil by now."

"Since I am not the swimmer these heroic gentlemen are," he gestured toward the three Olympians, "I must wait until my ship leaves. But there is delight mixed with that unfortunate fact, because now we can renew our too-brief acquaintance. I think of you often, Mademoiselle. And I've had some very sweet dreams about you." He batted his eyes like a flirtatious coquette.

Gwennie, who'd been fawning over the now-awed Johnny Weissmuller with undisguised adoration, finally remembered her own manners. "How wonderful that you two know each other!"

Zoe decided to put the countess right. "We only met the once," to which Cendrars immediately said, "And during that brief meeting Mademoiselle Barlow proved herself to be one of the most charming women I know."

Forcing a civility she didn't feel, Zoe said, "Monsieur Cendrars is renowned for his tendency to exaggerate." Then she leaned across the table and hissed, "Steal any more Chagalls lately?"

Unoffended by the insult, Cendrars replied, "Those paintings were headed for the trash heap. You should be thankful I saved them for posterity."

"But you lost your best friend over it. Chagall won't speak to you now!"

A self-satisfied smirk. "No, Mademoiselle, it is *Chagall's* loss."

"Why, you arrogant son of a..."

Gwennie took a pause from her adoration of Weissmuller to snap, "Children! Behave yourselves!"

The poet gave the countess a courtly nod. Zoe just seethed. There was so much more she'd wanted to say.

Archie, who knew Zoe better than did his mother, hurriedly changed the subject. Addressing Weissmuller, he said, "You must give us the details of how you escaped your coach's clutches. Although, I must say, your performance during the Olympics rather proves Mister Bachrach's wisdom, doesn't it? No drink, no late nights, no leaving the compound. The French newspapers are giving their own countrymen a rough time for not being as abstentious."

Thus encouraged, Weissmuller launched into a tale that made the swimmers' escape sound like soldiers fleeing an enemy prison camp. "Monsieur Cendrars here went up to the guard and shared a whole lot of drinks from his flask—it was solid silver, Count...uh, *Gwennie*— and told them some, uh, French *jokes*. So when they were having their, uh, *fun*, we crept away to a small café he'd told us about. Sure as shootin', a few minutes later, he joined us..." Here he gave Cendrars a dazzling smile "After ordering us some bubbly stuff which made us dizzy, he said he'd treat us to a night on the town. So that's how we got from the Olympic Village to the world-famous Moulin Rouge!"

Zoe fumed. How like Cendrars, the attempt to soil the three innocents.

Archie seemed not to share Zoe's outrage. "What a marvelous story!"

Gwennie patted her hands together in polite applause. To Cendrars, she asked, "What in the world was a poet doing at the Olympics?"

"Writing a poem about it, dear Countess." He produced a note-book from his pocket and waved it at them. "Here you see the first draft of 'A Human Poseidon.'"

The handwriting was illegible, but Zoe could recognize verses, so for once, the man wasn't lying. Eager to get the topic back to the true hero of the day, she said to Weissmuller, "We saw you win the one-hundred-meter today, setting yet another record. What does it feel like, knowing you'll go down in the history books?"

Johnny's blush made him appear much younger than his twenty years. "History books? Oh, I don't know about that. I just went for a swim. Nothing special."

Everyone at the table, including his teammates, hurried to dis-agree, which made Johnny's blush deepen. "Okay, okay. How did it feel? It felt *swell!*"

Laughter all around.

When two bottles of chilled Champagne arrived, conversa-tion dimmed a bit while they refreshed themselves. In seconds, Archie killed his entire glass and poured himself another, while the swimmers merely sipped at theirs. Nighttime escape or not, Coach Bachrach's warnings still carried weight.

Zoe sipped at her Champagne, too, mainly because she didn't want to lose her temper any more than she already had. While Johnny and Gwennie chatted, she looked around and saw that every table in the enormous room was filled to capacity. Every now and then, over the clamor of the crowd, she could hear a tootle from a clarinet or the sigh of a violin as the orchestra tuned up.

The show would be a relief from the sorrows of the preceding week. Laurette. Katrina. Isabeau. Well, at least Isabeau was alive, Zoe reminded herself, despite the shameful treatment she'd suf-fered at the hands of a hypocrite.

Shortly, the orchestra eased into a musical rendition of Verdi's aria "The Willow Song."

Oh, not "The Willow Song"!

She shut her eyes, as if by closing them her ears would shut down, too. Her stepmother had played that damned aria time and time again on Beech Glen's Victrola until the sound of even one oft-repeated measure drove Zoe from the big house. Not that music had been the worst of her unhappiness.

The hidden pregnancy. The death of the man she'd been forbidden to love. The agonizing birth in Beech Glen's dank basement. The exile to Paris without her baby, without Pete, without hope.

"Why does the lovely mademoiselle look so sad tonight?" Cendrars asked.

She pulled herself together. "Sad? I am merely tired."

"Mademoiselle continues to be a great fabricator."

"Nice word, that. *Fabricator.*"

He smirked. "We poets are good with words."

Zoe noticed Johnny Weissmuller staring at her. "Is there something in your eye, Miss Barlow?" he asked kindly. "The light's pretty dim in here, but my eyesight's good, and I might be able to fish it out." He flourished his linen table napkin.

"Call me Zoe. And thank you for your kind offer, but I believe whatever's in there has watered out. Must be the smoke." She narrowed her eyes at Cendrars' cigarette, his fourth of the evening. Yes, she'd been counting.

Cendrars tilted his head back and blew a smoke ring into the air. It drifted slowly upward until it blended with the sweeter aroma of expensive perfumes.

"You Frenchmen certainly like your cigarettes," Gwennie said.

"Yes, we do." Another annoying smirk.

With relief, Zoe felt annoyance eclipsing her sad memories, but before she could manage a retort, the orchestra rose into a spirited version of "Dardanella."

"I do believe that's an American song!" Archie exclaimed over a trumpet blast.

"Probably in honor of the Americans present," Gwennie said. "Especially these Americans." She waved an elegant hand toward the three Olympians.

Gwennie was right, Zoe decided, and it was probably time to avoid old memories, none of which she could do anything about tonight. Instead, she should enjoy the beauties the present afforded her. Lifting her glass, she smiled across at Weissmuller. "To the American Swim Team!"

The two Hawaiians took the toast in stride, but Johnny blushed again. "Aw, gee."

After a set of songs delivered by a feather-bedecked Mistinguett, the red curtain lowered, announcing Intermission, and there was a mad rush toward the bars. Gwennie's party remained seated, since she'd already ordered three more bottles of Dom. When the Champagne arrived, the Olympians barely touched their glasses— they were getting dizzy, they explained—but Archie more than made up for it. In fact, he sounded well and truly soused as he asked Weissmuller, "So whass your shhecret, eh?"

Johnny looked puzzled. "Secret?"

"Yass. How'd you get so...so fash?"

Yet another blush.

Although surrounded by hundreds of half-drunk patrons who sounded almost orgiastic in their libations, Johnny stood out like a blond angel. But his seeming innocence was probably thanks to his coach, because Weissmuller was still a man, thus prey to a man's usual vices. After all, he was here in this famed den of iniquity, wasn't he?

"I don't have any secret," Johnny answered Archie. "I just swim."

"Now, now," Gwennie gently rebuked. "We've seen you swim. The minute you leapt into the pool, there was something...something *intangible* in your movements through the water, something that made you different from all the rest. Now be a good boy and tell us what that is."

Johnny gave her the sweetest smile Zoe had ever seen, possibly his reaction to that *good boy*, which made her sound like a mother speaking to an especially cherished son. Or dog.

"All right, Countess..."

"*Gwennie!*" she insisted again.

"Sorry, ah, Gwennie." More blushes. "But here's the thing. It's bound to disappoint you because it's really very simple. People are always asking me, is it my kick, is it my stroke, is it my breathing technique? What special thing do I do that makes me different from anyone else. I never have an answer because I'm *not* different from everyone else.

"I'm plain old Janos Weissmuller, born in Freidorf, Romania, to Peter and Elizabeth Weissmuller, all of us now citizens of the beautiful United States. I'm just another immigrant, no better or worse than any of the others. But tonight, after we snuck away and were walking toward that café, I started thinking about all the interviews I've done in these past few days. After all the questions the reporters were asking—the very same questions you ask—I came up with a better answer. Not that it makes me special, you understand."

"I refuse to believe that, young man!"

"Well, like I say, I was thinking about how people are always complicating stuff, and how everyone gets all caught up in this stuff about my kicks and my strokes and my breathing. Geez! People are always complicating things, but it really isn't complicated at all. I just dive in and swim toward the wall as fast as I can."

Gwennie blinked. "That's it?"

"Yep, that's it."

"Bu... But..." Archie began.

"No buts," Johnny said, shifting his attention from Gwennie to her son. "All that fancy thinking can drown you. Just like too many glasses of Champagne!" He pointed to his still-full Champagne flute.

Before anyone could ask another question, the lights dimmed, the curtain rose, and a bevy of feathered dancers flitted like bejeweled moths across the stage while Mistinguett sang of *amour*.

Zoe heard none of it. She was too busy thinking. Yes, Johnny Weissmuller was right.

People are always complicating things, but it really isn't complicated at all.

Later, when someone asked her if the dancers had performed their famous cancan at the end of the show, her answer was "I wasn't paying attention."

Because thanks to Johnny Weissmuller's naïve wisdom, she finally understood. She knew who had killed Laurette and Katrina.

And why.

As Weissmuller said, it really wasn't complicated at all.

Chapter Thirty-Seven

—— Gabrielle ——

"They're fools, all of them," I tell Odile. "They can't see what's in front of their eyes, that I am almost back to normal!"

The little green spider strokes my cheek with a spindly leg. "That is not true, my friend. Only your right side works well. Your left is not…"

"I twitched a finger on my left hand this morning!"

Odile ignores this. "As I have pointed out, even your right side remains weak. One working side of your body is not enough to consider yourself healed."

I attempt to push out my lower lip in a play-pout, but only the right side of my mouth responds. I can tell from Odile's expression that this off-kilter result mars my beauty. "It's getting stronger."

"But not strong enough for your plan."

Odile does not realize my determination. "I was thinking what I could do to kill her. You see that beautiful flower over there? That's foxglove—digitalis lutea—and just a crumbled leaf, ingested, can kill a woman."

Still argumentative, Odile points out the obvious. "If it is bitter, and most poisons are, no woman would be foolish enough to eat it."

"Ah, but some teas are bitter, too. You must have noticed that every time the American arrives to read to me, Nurse Arceneau brings her tea or coffee, whichever suits her mood. All I need is to get strong enough to rise from this bed, pluck a leaf, shred it, put it into her drink, and voilà! No more limping whore to tempt my weak Henri."

"The foxglove is on the other side of the room, Madame."

"You think I haven't noticed that? I am no fool, so every night, when they are all in bed, I exercise my legs to build up the muscles. I..."

"But still your left leg hardly moves," Odile reminds me, as if I didn't know.

"I will drag it if necessary!"

"Then you must hop on your other leg, and hopping makes noise. They will come and see what you are doing—or at least attempting to do—and they will take you to some sanitarium where you will waste away. Then she will be free to do whatever she wishes to do with your Henri. I warn you again, Madame, your plans are as dangerous to you as they are to her."

"Pah!"

Tired of the little spider's arguments—those, from a creature who has killed and eaten her own husband!—I turn my face away from her and enter my dream.

Henri and I, walking through a magical field populated with plants no one sees anymore: fiabellidiam moss clinging to rocks; slender columns of bromus bromoideus providing a vibrant sea of grass; shrubs of heliotropium pannifolium prickling our bare legs; soft fronds of sphenophyllum, gone for millions of years, all alive and fluttering.

Oh, miracle!

In my dream, I turn to an astounded Henri. "You see," I tell him, "I brought them back from death just for you."

Chapter Thirty-Eight

Since Zoe hadn't made it home until two in the morning, she woke later than usual with a head so groggy she could barely think. After she made herself some bad coffee—today was no day for having chatty breakfasts with friends at La Rotonde—she knew what she needed to do: call Henri. Once in the past she'd sat too long on her suspicions and had almost been killed for her bad judgment.

Not this time.

When her head finally cleared, she picked up the phone and asked the operator to connect her with Inspector Henri Challiot, at the Sûreté.

"*Allô?*" someone answered. Not Henri. Older. Gruffer. Chewing something, maybe an apple.

"I need to speak with Inspector Henri Challiot, please."

"Not here."

"I have some very important information for him. When will he be back?"

"Who knows? I am not his mother." More chewing, then a gulp. "Give *me* this very important information of yours."

Irritated by the man's rudeness, Zoe snapped, "And you are?"

"Inspector Challiot's superior officer, and I'm not in the mood for women's games. Tell me why you called before I hang up."

"I know who killed Laurette Belcoeur! And Katrina Weisensel!"

A cynical snort. "Of course you do, as does half of Paris this morning. You are all using your sweet little telephones to waste police time. Let me guess. The killer is German, correct?"

"If you'll just lis..."

"What is your proof? Some German gave you a nasty look on the Metro? Some German shortchanged you at the stationery store? And you, with your excellent detective skills, learned from that detective novel about the Belgian detective Madame Christie has inflicted upon us, used your own little gray cells to put two and two together?"

"No! *Please* listen, it's really easy, because..."

Click. He had cut her off.

Breaking into the silence, the operator asked, "Would you like me to reconnect you, Mademoiselle?"

"Never mind." Zoe replaced the receiver.

She sat there for a long while, watching through the big studio windows while the shadows grew increasingly shorter as the sun rose over Paris. On the street outside, a child laughed and a woman laughed back. Less peacefully, a frightened horse whinnied in alarm when an automobile with something wrong with it clanked by.

Although Henri's boss had been unnecessarily rude, he'd had a point. Without proof, no one would listen to her, maybe not even Henri. But the annoying man had made Zoe realize something else, so she rose from her chair and headed for the boudoir's wardrobe. A long walk lay in wait, and for that, she needed her most comfortable pair of shoes. And a loose skirt.

Fashion be damned.

A few minutes later, a barely limping Zoe arrived at Fabian Napier's garage, but to her dismay, the place was shuttered. Tacked to the big double doors was a sign that read PICKING UP HEADLIGHT LENS—WILL RETURN BY NOON. She checked her watch: not quite ten. Refusing to allow her long walk to be wasted, she decided to do more snooping, just to make sure. If she was still at it when the mechanic came back, well, too bad. She would solve that problem if and when it arose. Steeling her resolve, she started up the narrow dirt path that led to the scrapyard. No caged rabbits would welcome her today, just a stiffening breeze that carried the sharp perfume of the Seine.

When she reached the end of the weedy path alongside the garage, she discovered that the ancient wooden gate sported a new lock, one sturdy enough to discourage breaking. The gaps between the gate's horizontal planks were too narrow for her to slip through, and there assuredly wasn't enough room to squeeze by the gateposts attached to the garage and the building next door. She could give it all up as a bad idea and go home, or wait until Fabian returned and try to talk him into unlocking the gate. Or maybe…

Congratulating herself on her wise fashion choices, she pulled her loose skirt up over her knees and began to climb.

At first it didn't go well. A rising wind blew her bobbed hair into her face, half-blinding her. Her thick-soled shoes, although sensible, kept slipping off the wooden planks, upsetting her balance. Once, both feet slipped off together, leaving her dangling, held up only by her splinter-damaged hands. As her feet searched for a more secure toehold, she remembered climbing Beech Glen's big oak and the twenty-foot fall that had permanently lamed her. But she had survived, hadn't she?

So she hung on.

Ignoring the pain in her hands, she raised herself up until her scrabbling feet found a toehold and she was able to boost herself onto the next plank. After that, the climb grew easier, and soon she found herself teetering at the top of the gate. She paused for a few seconds, gauging the safety of the drop. What good would it do if she further crippled herself by falling on a broken piece of machinery or a rain-rotted piece of wood? But the ground below turned out to be clear.

Zoe swung her other leg across and let go.

She landed on her derrière, and although the welcoming earth hadn't quite given her a love pat, it hadn't damaged her either, so she rose to her feet and hobbled toward the scrapyard's collection of junk.

Where to start? Under those fluttering strips of oilcloth? Behind the stacks of rotting planks? The piles of damaged bricks, some of them almost returned to the earth from whence they came? Or perhaps even more promising, that small hill of scrap metal? Surely the police had already searched through the debris. Come to think of it, she remembered seeing one officer carrying two likely-looking pieces of tin away as soon as Laurette's body had been removed. If Zoe was to find anything, she'd need to look where the police hadn't. As if in answer, the breeze picked up again, rattling a thin sheet of tin that appeared to have blown over from someone's roof.

After a brief inspection, she found the tin innocent of blood. Same with the rest of the heaped-up junk, including a pile of bricks that at first had looked suspicious. If there had been any blood left, the recent rains had washed it away.

Keeping an ear open for any sounds signaling Fabian's return, Zoe entered the Belcoeurs' rickety storage shed. The day was sunny, but the shadows cast inside the small building were so deep she had to wait until her eyes grew accustomed to the dim light. The tiny window at the far end of the shed created more problems than it solved, because the contrast gave a hard edge to the shadows that fell across a small chest in the corner. A humidor? If someone wanted to hide anything, the cabinet might be the perfect place. As she inched her way through the gloom, she bumped into the sharp corner of a table strewn with odd-looking objects. Not certain what they were, she would investigate them next.

But first, the humidor. It was a pretty little thing. Despite the seriousness of Zoe's search, she marveled at the detail work that had gone into creating a nearly airtight storage cabinet for a gentleman's tobacco. Its woodwork reminded her of Belle Epoque design, except for the cabinet door, which displayed a faded painting of an American Indian holding out a sheaf of tobacco leaves to a Pilgrim. The cabinet's legs were carved into four long snakes, their heads reared up, mouths open, fangs at the ready.

An ironic message from its creator to beware the smoky treasures within?

But Zoe wasn't here to appreciate pretty furniture, so she reached down to open the humidor's door, only to find the hinges so rusty it took her more than a few minutes to pry the door open. When she finally managed it, she found its insides empty except for the faint odor of ancient tobacco.

Swallowing her disappointment, she turned away from the little cabinet and shuffled over to the worktable, where she gazed in bemusement at the odd contraptions strewn across its surface. Some were metal; others, a combination of leather, wood, and metal. Whatever they were, they looked to be in terrible shape, half-consumed with rust. Near these mysterious objects sat a large bowl filled with vinegar—her nose identified the liquid immediately. Several rusted screws and bolts lay soaking in it. Next to the bowl were two brushes, one metal, one made of the stiff bristles employed by maids to scrub badly stained floors.

Of course! The table was the Belcoeurs' worktable, where

the sisters cleaned their wares before offering them for sale at inflated prices.

This realization made Zoe study one object more closely. The thing consisted of two boot-shaped pieces of hardwood—ash? oak?—held together by screws. A quick recheck of the vinegar bath showed that the rusting screws in the solution matched the cleaner screws on one side of this strange "boot." Running across the top of the misshapen boot were several strips of gleaming metal, each ending in a four-inch-long metal crank that looked like it had been designed for a child's jack-in-the-box toy. Puzzled, she picked up the boot in her left hand and turned the crank with her right. Instead of yielding a happy surprise, both sides of the boot began to close in slow, jerky increments. Startled, she put the thing back down. Although the leather part of the boot had been cleaned to a fare-thee-well, a darkling series of spots remained across its surface.

Why would anyone want a wooden boot?

Zoe moved on to the next object, a decorative metal "wand" almost a yard long, with a leather-wrapped handle on one end, and on the other end, a metal orb the size of a large apple. Dotted throughout the orb's surface was a series of fingernail-sized openings that reminded her of the censers priests use to spread incense during Mass. At the end of the orb protruded a sharp metal spike, making the object look almost like a weapon.

Next to this "wand" lay several more implements, but their uses were obvious. They were whips, their nail-studded lashings blunted from heavy use.

With a shock, Zoe realized she was looking at the same kinds of medieval torture devices she'd once seen in a Paris museum. The boot-shaped object was called a Malay boot. The wand was a lead sprinkler. They were probably being cleaned before being sold to private parties, because they were too grim for flea markets.

She remembered Etienne Mercier, the cheerful pig farmer, telling her the Belcoeur sisters had been unable to save anything from their burning château, but that wasn't true, was it? It had become obvious to Zoe that some of their flea market wares had once belonged to a fine home—possibly theirs. Nothing Zoe had purchased from the Belcoeurs had been faked, so that dark honesty was probably true of the torture devices, too. Yes, there was a market for such objects, but Zoe hated to imagine the kind of person who collected them. What normal human being wanted the Malay boot, whose sole function had been to slowly crush the bones of some poor wretch? Or the lead sprinkler, its unholy orb designed to sprinkle drops of boiling lead onto its agonized victim until he—or she—begged for death. Compared to those two devices, the whips seemed almost merciful.

As she stood there gazing at the diabolical instruments, the wind outside rose even higher, making plywood rattle and tin panels ruffle like thunder.

Which is why Zoe didn't hear the killer's footsteps behind her until it was almost too late.

"You couldn't leave it alone, could you?"

Chapter Thirty-Nine

Veronique Belcoeur's eyes were narrowed with rage, and she was holding a large brick. For the first time Zoe realized the width of the woman's shoulders, the ropy muscles along her arms developed by hauling around furniture, her scarred face not even a shadow of her sister's beauty. A hand-to-hand struggle with this granite-like woman wouldn't end well.

Then there was that damned brick in her hand, solid enough to crush anyone's skull.

With no place to hide and nowhere to run—even if she *could* run, given her bad leg—Zoe backed up against the work table. There was no traffic noise. No idle chatter from passersby. The birds nesting in the boulevard's chestnut trees seemed shocked into silence. Even the wind had little to say now. It whispered around the scrapyard, murmuring quietly between the bolts of ruined cloth as if trying to evade the madwoman's attention.

"I... I don't know what you mean, Veronique," Zoe stammered. "I was just looking at these things, and...and thinking about buying one. For a joke, you understand. It would be, ah, fun at parties, wouldn't it?"

"Do you think I'm stupid?"

Now that Veronique had moved even closer, Zoe could see how wild her eyes were, and how merciless. Almost as merciless as the woman's ancestors, probably the very people who'd used those torture devices.

"Of course I don't think you're stupid," Zoe blurted, hating the tremor in her voice. "If Laurette had done to *me* what she did to you, I'd have killed her, too!" She wanted to keep the woman talking until she could...

Could what?

"So you are on my side, are you?" Veronique's smile was so cold it almost eclipsed the danger of the brick she held.

"Yes, Veronique, really. Her behavior was terrible, what she did. First, she took Quintrell Sault away from you, then..."

At his name, Veronique spat on the floor. "That pig farmer! I didn't love him, of course. He smelled like his animals. But he wasn't all that bad looking—back then, anyway—and he had a house with a good roof and one hundred and fifty hectares of lush farmland. By the end of the war, that was more than we Belcoeurs were left.

"But men don't live forever, do they? I figured that if I married him, I could easily arrange an accident. Maybe he'd get crushed beneath a tractor. Or eaten by his nasty pigs. I told Laurette what I was planning, but then guess what? Oh, you don't have to guess, do you, Mademoiselle-Too-Smart-for-Her-Own-Good? The minute Laurette pretended to be interested in him, he forgot all about me. Coquette that she was, she teased him along, flirting, getting his hopes up—she was so practiced at that kind of thing! But she had no intention of marrying him. She'd her sights set on someone better looking, someone who didn't have pigs."

Keep her talking, Zoe. Keep her talking.

"Fabian Napier, right?" Zoe said, pleased her voice now

sounded so calm. "But how'd she, I mean *you*, first meet him? Back then you were still living in Amiens, weren't you, and Fabian lived and worked here in Paris, so what am I missing?"

Another cruel laugh, this one muted by a sudden strong wind gust outside.

Zoe's hopes rose with it. *Maybe it would blow this rickety shack down, and then she could run!*

But then, as if the wind merely laughed at Zoe's foolish hopes, it slackened to the point where she could hear Veronique's hiss of rage before she answered. "Ah, but Monsieur Handsome was born near Amiens, and he still had cousins there, some of whom had actually managed to stay alive during the war. Fabian visited them every month and helped them fix whatever machine he could. Cars. Tractors. Plows. One day, a cousin told him that we Belcoeurs had an old tractor he might be able to use for parts, so he drove over..."

Here, Veronique choked, as if the memory still had the power to hurt. "Most of our château was in ruins, and we were living in the stable, surrounded by the pieces I'd managed to save after that German shell hit our château, caved in the ceiling, and set so many fires. But the stable was still standing, wasn't it? The damned Germans had eaten all our horses, hadn't they? Even my precious Flame. I'd raised him from a colt!"

She paused to wipe away a tear before continuing. "Anyway, once Fabian and I had agreed on a price for the old tractor, I saw how amenable he was to a woman's charms—I was better looking then than I am now, you know, although never as pretty as Laurette—and I thought, 'Veronique, you were prepared to marry even worse.'"

At this, Veronique's now-dry eyes drifted down to the brick, as if to remind herself she was still holding it.

To get the madwoman's mind off the ugly thing, Zoe said, "So you romanced him?"

Veronique's smile was chilling, but at least she looked back at Zoe, the brick momentarily forgotten. "I'm not without my own charms. At least I wasn't then. One thing led to another, and Fabian finally proposed. When I agreed to marry him, he helped me move to Paris and situated me in the flat you visited, a place I could stay without gossip until we could marry. He also saw how I'd gathered up some things that would fetch an excellent price here—the fires that consumed our château had moved slowly—so he helped me bring up the pieces I'd managed to save."

Veronique paused for a breath, the old burn scar livid against her sallow cheek.

"But I was the one who came up with the idea of the flea markets, not that I had any intention of selling the finer items there. Those I kept in the flat, awaiting more moneyed buyers." She glanced over at the torture devices. "Did you know that people pay..."

Zoe interrupted her. "Wait a minute. You say Fabian helped *you* move to Paris. Where was Laurette?"

Veronique scowled. "After the debacle with Quintrell, word had gone around Amiens about the Belcoeur family beauty throwing herself at a pig farmer, so our Aunt Selene, whose house had survived the German onslaught, took Laurette in so the girl wouldn't further sully the Belcoeur name. She didn't care if *I* sullied the family name because the Belcoeur family's hopes had always centered on the beautiful Laurette. *I*—the plainer sister—wasn't worth worrying about."

Zoe thought she could hear Veronique's teeth grinding, but that was all right. Veronique's self-justified ravings had given Zoe time to come up with a plan.

Oblivious, Veronique continued, relieved by the chance to unburden herself. "Considering Laurette's behavior with the pig farmer, I should have left her with our aunt. But no, I was too soft for my own good. So when Laurette started sending sorrowful letters about how much she missed me, I borrowed one of Fabian's cars and drove to Amiens to fetch her."

Another tear, another glance down at the brick.

Get her attention away from that thing, Zoe!

"Oh, my, Veronique, you have such a warm heart," Zoe said.

Veronique preened at this praise. More importantly, she stopped looking at her brick.

But Zoe wasn't ready yet, so using the same note of admiration, she asked, "You are wise, too, so I'm sure you did what you could to keep Laurette away from Fabian."

"Of course I did."

"When and how did the two finally meet?"

Veronique's face hardened. "The day before we were to be married he came to the apartment to leave me flowers, but I was out, and..." She swallowed. "Imagine the insult! For all the love he'd professed to me, one look at Laurette, and he was just another faithless man. But then *le bon Dieu* came to my aid. A week later, while Fabian and my whore of a sister were disporting themselves in the back of his garage, I was sitting in the café next to our flat, feeling hopeless, when Gervais walked in."

"The Vicomte du Paget."

"A man worthy of a Belcoeur!" Veronique's abrupt change of mood was made horrific when she caressed the brick in her hand as though it were a beloved pet. A hamster, maybe. Or a kitten. "Gervais and I used to play together when we were children. He had a crush on me at that time. Laurette, well, she was little more than a baby then, so there was no competition from a burping, shitting infant."

Zoe did her best to sound sympathetic, even though her skin felt like fire ants were crawling all over her body. "Then that burping, shitting infant grew up..."

"Yes, she grew up to destroy my dreams, even though I'd saved her life." Seeing the surprised expression on Zoe's face, she said, "You didn't know? Well, I did. I saved her. When the first German shell hit our château, she'd been modeling a new dress for our parents, while as usual, I was sitting unnoticed in the corner. Then came the explosion, and the roof fell in. Somehow, I wasn't hurt, but Laurette and my parents lay under a burning beam. My parents were killed outright, but Laurette was still alive. She was my baby sister, you understand, and like everyone else, I loved her! The flames had begun to catch at the drapes, so there wasn't much time, but I couldn't let her die, could I? So I took a chair leg, and as the flames licked at my hands, I pried that burning beam off her. Although burned myself—you can still see all the scars—I carried her through the fire to safety. Then I laid her on the grass and went back into the house again and again, running through the burning rooms to save what I could before the fire reached them."

Zoe was almost ready. "You are so brave!"

Veronique nodded, accepting the praise as her due. "Yes, yes, but if I could do it all over again, I would have saved more furniture, not a little whore who would turn out to be my worst enemy. Laurette repaid my efforts by taking away every chance I had for happiness!"

Despite herself, Zoe was beginning to feel pity for the woman, not that it mattered. Slowly, so Veronique wouldn't notice, she shifted her balance to her good leg. "Didn't Laurette understand what she was doing to you?"

Veronique vented a cackle. "Oh, Laurette understood, all right. She enjoyed it! She bragged that as soon as she married Gervais, she'd take everything that hadn't been destroyed by the Germans, *everything*, including the furniture, the Rub...ah, even our mother's paintings. She was going to be *Laurette, Vicomtess du Paget*, and she wanted to bring to the marriage riches befitting the Belcoeur name, not come to him like some peasant girl with no dowry."

"You didn't have to allow that." *Slowly now. Slowly.*

Another wild cackle. "You didn't know Laurette! To you, she was merely this beautiful young woman who knew a lot about clocks, when she was so much more—or less—than that. She was a spoiled child who'd always gotten exactly what she wanted, and would continue to get it. When she told me her plan, she was standing right where you stand now, laughing at me while I was busy cleaning some of the objects I'd saved before the entire château went up in flames, telling me to hurry up because it was all going with her, and so I...I..."

"So you killed her."

The cackles stopped, replaced by a mask of grief. "I didn't mean to! I was cleaning that damned Malay boot to sell to a private buyer." Here she motioned to the torture device. "Without thinking, I slammed her in the face with it. That big screw handle... It went into...into her eye... I...I was frantic, and I carried her outside into the light where I could see better, so I could help her, but...but it was too late."

An accident. An impulsive act by an angry woman whose heart had been broken once too often.

Zoe's sympathy rose again. "And you're still grieving for her."

"She was my baby sister!" Veronique wailed.

Softening her voice, Zoe asked a question she already knew the answer to. She just wanted to hear it. "But why kill Katrina? She never did anything to hurt you."

The mask of grief disappeared, replaced by a cold stare. "Because she'd seen me enter the scrapyard just before Laurette was killed. I'd told those stupid men at the Sûreté that I was working at the other flea market on the north side of the river. I had been there earlier in the day, but the girls hadn't marked the time, so they confirmed my alibi, and I thought everything was fine. But then Katrina started avoiding me. Once, when I caught her watching me, I saw *fear*. I knew what that meant, so before she could talk to the police, I put a brick in one of those piecework bags the old bitch next to our table was selling, and went to Katrina's flat, and I...I took care of the problem. What does it matter, anyway? She was just another damned German."

That cold stare frightened Zoe more than Veronique's former rage, and Zoe knew why. The woman was getting ready to use that brick in the same way she'd used one on Katrina.

"I'm so sorry you've had to go through all this," Zoe began, and for a moment, Veronique appeared to relax at this tendered sympathy. But Zoe saw Veronique's fingers tighten on the brick and that the madwoman's arm was slowly stretching back to build the momentum necessary to smash the brick into her face.

Veronique was so intent upon her own deadly plan, she didn't notice Zoe's own fingers curl around the Malay boot.

Zoe rushed her, slamming the metal edge of the boot against Veronique's head with newfound strength. Veronique fell but almost immediately scrambled to get up. "What...?" She reached out a clawed hand.

Zoe hit her again, this time even harder.

Veronique never made it back to her feet.

Chapter Forty

Veronique had left the gate open, so Zoe didn't have to worry about climbing it again. Instead, she bolted through it, ran down the narrow passage and out into the street, screaming for the police.

The first person to come to her aid was Fabian Napier, returned from picking up the headlight lens. He started into the garage to phone the police but stopped halfway there. Proving that chivalry was not yet dead, he changed direction and ran back to the storage shack to render aid to the unconscious Veronique.

So Zoe used his telephone to called the Sûreté herself.

This time Henri picked up the phone.

Chapter Forty-One

August 1, 1924
Paris

Zoe stood at her easel contemplating the state of her almost-finished painting. After a long examination, she decided she'd used too much chrome yellow, a cheerful color that belied the painting's subject.

Yes, that brightness had to go. Taking a rag, she wiped away every splash of cheer, substituting a cool ochre. What had been light was now dark. However, the painting still lacked something, and she'd be damned if she knew what it was. Maybe if she took a break, she'd be able to think it through. After all, she'd been at this since sunup, and the gold-tinged light bleeding through the windows announced that the sun had already begun its passage west.

Deciding that a glass of Merlot might help clear her head, she cleaned her brushes and laid them on the taboret. Sighing, she stepped away from the easel again. There was less than a half bottle of Merlot left in the kitchen—Madeline must have been cooking with it—but it would be enough. She poured the remainder into a large glass, and carried it into the sitting room, where she collapsed onto a chair, from which she could still see the painting.

Unlike the color of the vivid sky outside her window, the painting's sky was a ghost, its pure blue murdered by the smoke from the war's guns.

Speaking of ghosts...

Veronique might soon become a ghost herself. French justice could be swift, and the guillotine still stood on rue Georges Clemenceau. Then again, the French didn't much like executing women. Especially *pregnant* women. There were whispers that in some countries, France among them, condemned women often asked their jailers to impregnate them in order to stave off execution. After all, what decent judge would condemn an innocent baby to death?

Zoe didn't want Veronique to die. Yes, the last of the once-noble Belcoeurs had killed two women—the Court had agreed about that—but there were, as one presiding judge pointed out, extenuating circumstances. The panel had yet to determine what her punishment should be: life or death.

Zoe prayed for mercy. Failing that, for a friendly jailer.

But if Veronique wound up visiting Madame Guillotine, it was Zoe's own actions that had set that grisly process into motion. And she'd have to deal with that guilt.

As for Fabian Napier, she knew the mechanic would grieve Veronique's death. As bizarre at it might seem, it was obvious the man still cared for her. While attending to Veronique's wounds, he'd finally realized that by exchanging Veronique for Laurette's empty charms, he'd exchanged gold for dross.

For all her sins, Veronique was twice the woman Laurette had been. After saving her sister from death in their flaming château, she'd run back into that funeral pyre to retrieve her parents' bodies, then ran back again and again to save as many treasures as possible. As it had turned out, during the Sûreté's search of the sisters' flat, the Belcoeurs', treasures had included a Rubens and two Caravaggios. Veronique had covered up those priceless works with three bad paintings she'd attributed to her dead mother.

Well, the Louvre had them now. At this very moment, some art restorer had to be cursing under his breath as he cleaned away Veronique's purposely crude paintings to reveal the masterworks underneath. Zoe hoped the judges would take their salvation into account when time came to pass down the woman's sentence.

As Zoe pondered Veronique's possible fate, the telephone rang. Three short and one long.

She considered not answering. Henri, after discovering Zoe's role in solving the murders, could barely speak to her, and when he did, it was to scream invectives. Did she really want to hear it all again?

Of course not. But he might think she'd been cowed by his bad temper, so she put her wineglass down, rose from the chair, and walked toward the telephone, determined to match invective with invective.

Steeling herself, she picked up the telephone. *"Allô?"*

"We've decided to do it next Sunday." Isabeau Joubert, former victim, now avenging Valkyrie.

"Isn't that a little fast? Father Arnaud's only been at his new parish for two weeks. Give him time."

"My contacts in Lavoisier tell me that his new cleaning girl was seen crying as she left his house. She's only fourteen, Zoe."

Fourteen!

Their testimony against the licentious priest hadn't worked out the way they'd planned. Instead of defrocking Father Arnaud for his attempted rape of Isabeau, the bishop had merely moved him to a different parish.

Zoe sighed. "He likes them young, doesn't he? Well, in that

case, you can pick me up on the way down to Lavoisier. The more accusations we can hurl before Mass, the better."

Isabeau chuckled in anticipation. "You, me, Yves, and our darling Reynard. Yves is bringing twenty copies of his photographs. We'll hand them out around the village to alert everyone."

"Henri will murder me if he finds out," Zoe said.

"No, he won't. Murder's against the law."

Zoe laughed. "See you on Sunday, then. What time?"

"Seven. Reynard told me Lavoisier is quite a long drive from Paris, and we want to get there before noon Mass."

After hanging up, Zoe returned to her chair and sipped at her Merlot to kill the bitter taste in her mouth. Only partially soothed, she decided to forget Father Arnaud for the moment and focus on something more optimistic—the day the Pinkerton detectives would find Amber.

Did anything else really matter?

The phone rang again. Three shorts, one long.

Zoe was so startled by receiving two calls in one day she almost didn't answer. Once she overcame her shock, she decided it might be Isabeau again, with further information about Sunday's trip to Lavoisier.

But when Zoe finally picked up the phone, Nurse Hélène Arceneau was on the other end.

"She's sitting up!" Hélène said, breathless. "Actually sitting up! She's unsteady of course, and Henri has to help hold her upright, but Zoe, less than an hour ago…"

"Wait! Who…? Who are you talking about?" Zoe's own voice broke, hoping, she would hear the right name, hoping this wasn't a dream.

"It's Gabrielle, Zoe!" Hélène sobbed and laughed at the same time. "She even put her feet on the floor, as if she wanted to walk! And she's *talking*, Zoe! She's slurring her words like she's had too many glasses of wine, and she's smiling a funny lopsided smile, but she's back, she's really back. It's a miracle!"

Zoe's sobs matched Hélène's, but like her friend's, they were mixed with laughter. "Gaby is actually aware? Her mind...?"

"Her mind is clear! And the expression in her eyes proves that she comprehends everything. Oh, Zoe, we're so happy! I just had to share the news because I know how much you love her. I would have called earlier, but..."

"No 'buts,' Hélène. I understand. This is wonderful news, but of course you had to take time to compose yourself. And Henri! How is he?"

"He is in ecstasy!" Laughter overcame the sobs. "Babbling like a baby! It's going to be some time before any of us are composed. You must come and see her, let her know whose voice she's been listening to all this time."

It took Zoe a moment to reply. After clearing her throat, she said, "Perhaps tomorrow. For now, let's leave Gaby and Henri to celebrate together. And you, of course, Hélène. You've been more than a nurse to her; you've been a friend."

"As have you. One of the words she managed to say was '*Zoe.*'"

Zoe closed her eyes. In the background, she heard more laughter. Henri's baritone. And a light, clear note that had to be Gabrielle's.

She straightened her shoulders.

The time had come.

The time to end it.

After taking a steadying breath, she said, "I'll stop by tomorrow, then. And I'll want to talk to Henri, so if you could leave us alone for a few moments...?"

"Yes. Yes. I understand." Hélène's voice was more somber now because she understood. "He'll be sad to lose you."

And I'll be sad to lose him. "He has his wife back, Hélène, and that's all that matters."

Zoe softly replaced the receiver.

For a while, she just stood there allowing waves of relief and happiness and sadness wash over her. Yes, it was time to say goodbye. It should probably have been over months earlier, but Henri'd had his needs, just as she'd had hers.

Now what she and Henri had shared was over.

She took a deep breath and looked toward the future, seeing her beloved Le Petit Bibelot with a *mother's* eye, not an artist's.

Sitting room. Studio. Boudoir. Only three rooms, plus kitchen and toilette. When the Pinkerton Agency found her child, where would she sleep? A young girl needed a room of her own! Zoe knew she couldn't sacrifice her studio because an artist's studio was holy ground. And the mirrored boudoir at the other end of the house from the studio was too small. Granted, the large sitting room could be broken into two rooms, but only by turning beauty into something ugly. The architectural lines of her little trinket of a house would vanish, and for an artist, beauty was as important as love.

Well, *almost.*

The only way she could actually lengthen the house was to build over her garden. The lovely garden that, during the course of her six years in Paris, had given her solace among the bougainvillea, the irises, the roses, the lilies, the narcissi...

She would yank out those fragile flowers by the roots to build a worthy bower for her little girl. Believing with all her being that that day would surely come, she would begin that work tomorrow.

But for now, she had a canvas to finish. Before Hélène's phone call, her mind had been awhirl with everything that was wrong with the unfinished painting, possibly because she'd arrived at the realization she'd seen too much horror. Families destroyed by the war. Husbands grieving stricken wives. A priest ignoring his vows.

She had been blinded by all that unhappiness, tricked into

believing that horror and sorrow were the only powers left in this broken world, a world where if you scratched a saint, you would always find a monster.

But that wasn't true, was it? There *was* good in this world! There *was* self-sacrifice. There *was* love. Strengthened by a new purpose, Zoe walked back into her studio to resume her painting of love among the ruins.

A portrait of Veronique Belcoeur carrying her sister through the flames.

Epilogue

Most people believed that dreams came true in Paris, but Zoe had once questioned that. Life was too hard, and whatever your dreams happened to be, they got left behind during the struggle to stay alive. But the events of the last few months had proved her cynicism wrong, hadn't they? Dreams *did* come true in Paris. Today was proof. Sister reunited with sister. Husbands reunited with wives. Friends reunited with friends. Mothers with...

Avak had insisted upon driving Zoe to Le Havre without charge and to be allowed to stand next to her at the pier. So, too, had her many friends, all of whom were worried about her, if...

To hell with ifs!

Zoe had insisted that her friends—Kiki, Archie, Madeline, Isabeau, Madame Arceneau, one-eyed Dominique Garron, and Reynard, in a yet-again touched-up portrait mask—stay far back because she couldn't endure their chattering. The roar of the ship-welcoming crowd was noise enough.

Zoe needed stillness. Silence. To be ready.

Just in case.

She had arrived at the pier fully two hours early to make certain she would be the first to greet the big ocean liner. So much for her wish for silence, because as the morning wore on, the crowd became increasingly boisterous. As soon as the gangplank rumbled down, some people began singing "La Marseillaise," some, "The Star-Spangled Banner." Still others sang national anthems she hadn't heard since the Olympics. At times, a flirtatious wind merged all their voices.

Zoe's throat was too raw to sing anything.

The late autumn weather was merciful, almost as if it were ashamed of its behavior during the Olympics. So here she stood, damp and sweltering in a too-heavy coat while the noise roared around her.

It roared even louder when the passengers began to disembark.

A sea of faces flowed downward. Some smiling. Some crying. Some apprehensive. Some sang along with the crowd.

Faces.

Faces.

Faces marching down the gangplank toward Zoe, almost all of them White.

More faces.

More faces.

Then...

A tall woman with sepia-colored skin, holding the hand of a blue-eyed little girl the color of amber.

The world fell silent.

Zoe could hear neither the screams of the seagulls nor the conflicting anthems.

Then the playful wind carried the tall woman's voice as she bent down and said to the child, "Say it like we practiced, remember?"

The child looked toward Zoe. Blue eyes met blue eyes.

Without thinking, without a plan, Zoe ducked under the rope holding the crowd back and ran toward the gangplank, slapping away the hands of those who tried to hold her back.

She ran.

Ran.

Ran. Arms outstretched.

When she reached the halfway point of the gangplank, recognition flared in her mother-in-law's eyes. Smiling, Dorothy leaned over the little girl and said again, "Remember?" Or yelled. Zoe couldn't tell which.

Zoe ran upward, falling twice, and not caring.

Almost there.

"*My baby!*" someone screamed.

Then flesh touched flesh. Softness melted into softness.

Suddenly Zoe could hear again, hear her own sobs, could hear her daughter's sweet voice saying...

"*Je t'aime, Maman.*"

Author's Note

Researching a book can lead a writer down a rabbit hole so convoluted that she can get stuck in it for a while.

The oddest thing I learned was that one of Marc Chagall's paintings was used as the roof of a rabbit hutch. He later—perhaps in gratitude to the rabbits that didn't nibble away his painting—created a series of "bunny" paintings (source: *The Love, The Dreams, The Life of Chagall*, by Jean-Paul Crespelle).

But how did Chagall's paintings disappear in the first place?

Just before WWI began, Chagall made a trip to Russia to marry his longtime fiancée. Not realizing that the world would soon explode into war, the artist locked up approximately 150 canvases in his La Ruche studio in Paris. While he was gone, someone cut through the lock, leaving it open, and the space was slowly gutted. Chagall's landlady at La Ruche took several paintings and used one of them to cover her rabbit hutch. Before more paintings were taken to benefit rabbits, Blaise Cendrars, Chagall's best friend, "rescued" what was left and sold them. Cendrars pocketed the money.

The paintings Chagall left at the Der Sturm Gallery in Berlin suffered a similar fate. By the end of the war, Chagall's 40 paintings and 160 gouaches had disappeared, with none of the proceeds falling into their creator's pocket.

But onto a happier subject.

Although not much of a sports fan, I also journeyed down the history rabbit hole to learn about the personal lives of certain sports stars at the 1924 Paris Summer Olympics. The biggest surprise arrived when I was researching two of the more well-known medal winners: Johnny Weissmuller and Duke Kahanamoku, both record-breaking, multi-medaled swimmers.

Sports fans know about Johnny Weissmuller's gold medals in the 1924 Paris Olympics, but film fans know him because of his starring roles in the highly successful Tarzan movies.

What most people don't know is that Johnny was a real-life hero, not just a sports or Hollywood hero. As recounted in David Fury's biography, *Johnny Weissmuller, Twice the Hero*, Johnny actually saved lives.

On July 28, 1927, the Lake Michigan excursion steamer, *Favorite*, sank during a severe squall, carrying seventy-one passengers. Many were saved when Johnny and his brother Peter—they had been on a nearby boat—repeatedly dove into the sunken wreck and brought the still-living to the surface. Early on during the rescue, Peter, who'd been trained as a lifeguard, stayed on their boat and administered CPR, while Johnny, the stronger swimmer, continued to dive into the turbulent waters to weave his way through the sunken cabin. Between them, the brothers saved eleven lives.

But Johnny Weissmuller wasn't the only Olympian to become a real-life hero. On June 14, 1925, Duke Kahanamoku, Johnny's teammate in the 1924 Paris Olympics, saw the sports fishing boat *Thelma* capsize near Newport Beach, California, where Duke was surfing. Using his surfboard and diving skills, he managed to pull eight people from the water and ferried them back to shore on his surfboard.

Read on for an excerpt from Lost in Paris
the first book in the series!

Chapter One

—— Zoe ——

December 1922
Paris

Despite the sudden snowstorm, Poker Friday was going well at the pretty little house on Rue Vavin. Zoeline Eustacia Barlow—"Zoe" to her friends—was almost fourteen hundred francs up. But then the marquis had to go and ruin everything.

"Too bad about Hemingway, is it not?" Fortier said, in that aristocratic nasal twang that always grated on Zoe's nerves. "His poor wife will certainly pay the price." Although well into his forties, Fortier's patrician face was clear of wrinkles, and despite the long scar on his cheek from German shrapnel—he'd fought bravely in the War to End All Wars—he was still handsome.

But handsome is what handsome does.

"What are you talking about, Antoine?" Zoe asked, trying to keep the annoyance out of her voice. She held two pairs, treys and fives, and a lonely jack, but had been counting the cards and knew Fortier held two eights and at least one ace. Her friend Jewel Johnson, lead dancer at the Moulin Rouge, appeared to be hoping for a flush, and the infamous artist's model, Kiki of Montparnasse, didn't have much of anything. Neither did Kiki's escort, Nick Stewart, of the filthy rich Boston Stewarts.

Zoe couldn't decide what to do. Raise? Hold? Draw?

Outside, a cruel gust of December wind rattled the house's tall windows, giving a twinge to her left leg, the one she'd broken as a child, but Zoe had fed enough coals into the ceramic-faced iron stove to keep the sitting room toasty. Even if a finger of chill did manage to creep inside, the excellent Montrachet they were drinking tasted robust enough to fight it off. With good friends, fine wine, and a possibly winning poker hand, all should have been well, but thanks to Fortier, it wasn't. Maybe she should stop inviting the old bore to her Poker Fridays.

Fanning away the cigarette smoke wafting toward her from his stinking De Reszke, she said, "The last I saw of the Hemingways, they were fine."

Fortier lifted one edge of his lip in a sneer, which irritated Zoe even more than his voice did. On one of her many trips to the Louvre, she'd come across a portrait of Fortier's lordly ancestor, the sixth Marquis Antoine Phillippe Fortier de Guise, who'd lost his head in the French Revolution. The current marquis's sneer was the same as his ancestor's.

Zoe tried her best to concentrate on her cards, but Fortier's comment stirred the other players, too. Count Sergei Ivanovic Aronoffsky—who had folded early—said, "You truly haven't heard of your friend Hadley's misfortune, Zoe? Why, all Paris is abuzz!"

Dominique Garron, the war artist who'd lost an eye covering the Battle of the Marne, glared at Fortier with her remaining hazel orb. "Who cares about the Hemingways? Shut up and play your cards, Antoine, so we can get started on another hand." Like the count, Dominique had already folded, recognizing danger when she saw it. Same as sculptor Karen Wegner, with whom

Dominique was finishing off a bottle of Cognac Gélas to drown her poker sorrows.

As the war artist leaned back against her chair, a glowing shred of tobacco from her Gitane drifted down to the chair's maple arm. The expensive fifteen-piece art nouveau dining set had only been delivered last week, and Zoe was quite proud of it. Trying not to think about her new chair's fate, she said to the count, "Since Fortier's so busy smirking, perhaps you could tell me what's going on with the Hemingways. I've been too busy painting to keep up with the latest gossip."

The count gave her a gentle smile. She'd always seen a touch of El Greco in Sergei Ivanovic Aronoffsky's gaunt, hollow-cheeked face. His arms and legs were thin, too, testaments to the hungry months he'd spent on the run from the Bolsheviks. "You announce you've been painting? Ha! As if we couldn't tell, dear Zoe. We can smell the turpentine and linseed oil from here. I don't understand why you can't copy the others of your kind and maintain a separate studio. It's certainly not because you're hurting for money."

At this, Kiki giggled. Zoe didn't.

Your kind?

One aristocrat at the poker table was bad enough, but whenever two of them showed up on the same evening, snobbery ran rife, and Zoe sometimes found herself in sneaking sympathy with the mobs who'd dragged her friends' lordly forebearers to their deaths on the guillotine. True, the count's woes were more recent than Fortier's. Only five years earlier, when the Bolsheviks took over Russia, the poor man lost his wife, his grand estate, and two Rembrandts. In the odd way of the world, his luck had almost immediately turned. Upon reaching the welcoming arms of Paris, he'd met and married a wealthy French widow. Shortly thereafter, he found himself widowed again. Despite the count's travails, he still looked down his nose on the untitled. One would think that Jewel's love would cure him of his snobbery, but it hadn't happened yet.

Zoe sighed, thinking it was no wonder the Bolsheviks had shot *his* kind against their tapestried walls. However, it was rumored Sergei had managed to escape the bloodbath with a small hoard of diamonds, and since he was a laughably bad poker player, she'd grown to appreciate the extra pin money his inclusion at her Poker Fridays earned her. Besides, despite his occasional bouts of arrogance, she'd grown fond of the man. Unlike other aristocrats she could mention, at least the count had a heart.

Feeling the need to defend the acrid aromas in her snug little house, she said, "Now, now, Sergei. I'm a painter, and like most painters, I keep odd hours. Two and three a.m. often find me working, so having my studio here keeps me from walking the streets in the wee hours and being confused with another sort of woman."

At this, everyone laughed, but the mischievous Kiki pretended to find more than humor in Zoe's off-color joke. "Walking the streets? But, Zoe, *chérie*, it would be fun! Perhaps you and I could do that together."

Since the raven-haired model's spat with her lover, photographer Man Ray, she'd been attending Zoe's Poker Fridays with a variety of new suitors, all of whom had loads of money. Zoe didn't mind. The young men were always good for a laugh, and wasn't that what Paris was all about? Laughter and good times? Nick Stewart, Kiki's suitor-of-the-moment, wasn't a half-bad artist himself, despite the color blindness that ran amok through his inbred Boston family. But color blindness had never hampered a Dadaist, what with the urinals, hair clippings, and other nonsense objects they hung on gallery walls and called *Art* with a capital A. Few of them bothered to paint anymore, including Nick, who was currently working on an installation combining shoelaces and chicken bones.

Kiki's outré comment begged an answer. "Walk the streets together, Kiki? Sorry, but I must decline. I don't have what you French ladies call *savoir faire* or your beauty, and I'd wind up with a less-than-top-notch clientele. And who wants to have sex with hobos?" Directing her attention back to the marquis, Zoe asked, "Now, what were you saying about Ernest and Hadley?"

Not that Zoe cared about Ernest Hemingway, having once observed the bully sucker punch an inoffensive young man in La Closerie des Lilas café just for the thrill of seeing him fall. But she did care about Hadley. She'd often wondered how such a sweet-natured woman could put up with the ill-tempered man, who remained far from the success he imagined himself to have attained. Love, probably. Love, that old betrayer. Love, that old destroyer. For the past four years, Zoe had taken pains to avoid it. One broken heart was enough.

Oblivious to his hostess's feelings, Fortier was more than happy to expound on the Hemingway scandal. "The story I hear is that Hadley lost all of Ernest's manuscripts. Every word he ever wrote, even that certain-to-be-terrible novel he was working on."

Zoe frowned. "That makes no sense. How could Hadley lose his manuscripts? She's not his secretary."

"I know the answer to that," the count said, his mournful countenance buoyed by a semi-smile. "It happened aboard a train. One of the porters at the Gare de Lyon, a Russian like myself, gave me chapter and verse of the incident."

"Do tell, since we're all agog," snapped Fortier, jealous that Sergei had stolen his place on the soapbox.

With an indulgent nod, the count cleared his throat. The story he then related was a troubling one, in which poor Hadley did indeed emerge as irresponsible. A few days earlier, while Ernest was in Switzerland reporting on the Lausanne Conference, he'd run into a publisher who asked to see some of his fiction. Thrilled, as any aspiring novelist would be, Ernest immediately telegraphed Hadley, who had stayed behind in Paris, to post him a few stories and his unfinished novel.

Under most circumstances, this would have been a sensible enough request.

But Hadley had fallen ill with the flu, Sergei continued, which is why she hadn't accompanied Ernest to Lausanne in the first place. Anxious to please her husband, she'd staggered around their tiny apartment collecting the manuscripts, and in her delirium, packed up the carbons as well. She stuffed everything into a valise. Hoping to surprise him, she hitched a ride with their landlord to the Gare de Lyon, where she bought a ticket on the Paris-Lausanne Express. Once aboard, Hadley placed the valise under her seat. Still feverish, she went back out on the platform to purchase a bottle of Evian for the long journey.

"The porter told me that when the poor woman returned to her seat, the valise was gone," Sergei finished. "So I ask you, Zoe, an important question, one for which you, as her most trusted friend, should have the most informed answer. Yes, all Paris is aware of Ernest's habit of knocking down unsuspecting men in cafés, but do you know if he is also in the habit of knocking down his wife? Given the enormity of her crime, should we worry about pretty Hadley's safety?"

Zoe was so miffed it took her a moment to answer, and when she did, she discovered she'd lost the poker hand. Kiki, the little sneak, had been holding an inside straight and had been too foxy to let it show. The sly cat was still raking in the francs when Zoe finally found her voice.

"Ernest may be a bullyboy in the cafés, Sergei, but I doubt he hits Hadley. She's the one with the money, remember. Ah, did I hear you say she packed the originals *and* carbons?"

"Everything."

Acknowledgments

Authors do not work alone, so many, many thanks to Barbara Peters, Diane DiBiase, and Beth Deveny for making this book as good as possible. Among the many other sources I used were *Expatriate Paris* by Arlen J. Hansen, *Selected Writings* by poet Blaise Cendrars, *Chagall: A Biography* by Jackie Wullschlager, *Marc Chagall, an Intimate Biography* by Sidney Alexander, *Secrets of the Sûreté* by Commissioner Jean Belin, *When Paris Sizzled* by Mary McAuliffe, *Everybody Behaves Badly* by Lesley M. M. Blume, *Shocking Paris* by Stanley Meisler, *Picasso* by Arianna Huffington, *Paris Without End* by Gioia Diliberto, *Introduction to Botany* by Arthur W. Haupt, *Ernest Hemingway* by Mary V. Dearborn, *French Women and the First World War* by Margaret H. Darrow, *Everybody Who Was Anybody* by Gioia Diliberto, *Harlem's Hellfighters* by Stephen L. Harris, *Swimming at the 1924 Summer Olympics, 1924 Olympic Official Report*, Getty Images, DRJ, Reference Specialist at the Library of Congress. Finally, thanks to Hualan Jiang, of the International Olympic Committee, for clarifying two conflicting reports. Any errors in this book are mine, not theirs.

About the Author

© Paul Howell

Betty Webb is the author of the bestselling Lena Jones mystery series (*Desert Redemption, Desert Wives*, etc.) and the humorous Gunn Zoo mysteries (*The Panda of Death, The Otter of Death*, etc.). *Lost in Paris*, the first book in her new mystery series set in 1922 France, was released in 2023. The second Paris mystery, *The Clock Struck Murder*, followed in spring 2024. Betty has worked as a graphic designer in Los Angeles and New York City but eventually became a journalist. She spent twenty years as a reporter, interviewing everyone from U.S. presidents to astronauts who walked on the moon, Nobel Prize winners, and polygamy runaways. In between her frequent trips to Paris, Betty lives in Scottsdale, Arizona, with her family. You can contact her at bettywebb-mystery.com.